PRAISE FOR R.C. RYAN AND THE MALLOYS OF MONTANA

MATT

"Ryan has created a gripping love story fraught with danger and lust, pain, and sweet, sweet triumph."
—*Library Journal*, **starred review**

"Ryan takes it to the next level in the first book of her new Malloys of Montana series...Fans know that hot Montana men are Ryan/Langan's specialty (the McCords series, anyone?), so get cozy in your favorite reading nook and enjoy!"
—*B&N Reads Blog*

"The beguiling first novel in the Malloys of Montana contemporary series from Ryan (a pen name for Ruth Ryan Langan) depicts the lure of the mountains as a Chicago lawyer falls for a handsome rancher...Touching and romantic, Ryan's portrayal of a city slicker falling for a cowboy delves into the depths of each of their personalities to find common ground in their love for the land. Readers will eagerly anticipate future installments."
—*Publishers Weekly*

"With tough, sexy cowboys set against the beautiful, rural landscape of Montana, [*Matt*] is a must-read."
—*RT Book Review*

LUKE

MONTANA HEARTS

Also by R.C. Ryan

WRANGLERS OF WYOMING
My Kind of Cowboy
This Cowboy of Mine
Meant to Be My Cowboy

MONTANA STRONG
Cowboy on My Mind
The Cowboy Next Door
Born to Be a Cowboy

THE MALLOYS OF MONTANA
A Cowboy's Christmas Eve (available as an e-novella)
Reed

COPPER CREEK COWBOYS
The Maverick of Copper Creek
The Rebel of Copper Creek
The Legacy of Copper Creek

WYOMING SKY
Quinn
Josh
Jake

THE McCORDS
Montana Legacy
Montana Destiny
Montana Glory

MONTANA HEARTS

2-in-1 Edition with *Matt* and *Luke*

R.C. RYAN

FOREVER

NEW YORK BOSTON

Forever
Hachette Book Group
1290 Avenue of the Americas, New York, NY 10104
read-forever.com
twitter.com/readforeverpub

Matt and *Luke* originally published in 2016 by Forever.
First 2-in-1 edition: March 2022

Forever is an imprint of Grand Central Publishing. The Forever name and logo are trademarks of Hachette Book Group, Inc.

The publisher is not responsible for websites (or their content) that are not owned by the publisher.

The Hachette Speakers Bureau provides a wide range of authors for speaking events. To find out more, go to www.hachettespeakersbureau.com or call (866) 376-6591.

Library of Congress Cataloging-in-Publication Data has been applied for.

ISBN: 9781538709443 (mass market 2-in-1)

Printed in the United States of America

CW

10 9 8 7 6 5 4 3 2 1

MATT

For my son, Tom.
Firstborn.
Fiercely protective of his family.

And for my darling Tom.
First love. Though gone,
still watching over us all.

PROLOGUE

Glacier Ridge, Montana—1997

The town of Glacier Ridge dated to the 1860s. A time of Western migration, when millions of buffalo roamed the Montana plains. It had seen plenty of legends in its time. Miners discovering gold at Grasshopper Creek. Gen. George Armstrong Custer and his cavalry. Railroad tycoons and, later, oil barons. But the closest thing to legend now in the sleepy little town was the Malloy family. Rancher Francis Xavier Malloy was married to Grace Anne LaRou, the daughter of legendary Hollywood director Nelson LaRou, who had become famous in her own right by spending a lifetime photographing herds of wild mustangs that roamed the Montana wilderness. Collectors paid a fortune for her original photographs, and researchers and even government bureaucrats sought her advice on how to manage the wild horses. Add to that Frank and Grace's handsome, reckless sons, Patrick and Colin, and the fact that Patrick ran off and married a gorgeous girl named Bernadette when they were just seventeen, leaving the gossips with plenty of things to whisper about. Soon Patrick and Bernie gave birth to three good-looking sons who seemed to be as wild and reckless as their daddy and granddaddy, so folks around Glacier Ridge just naturally figured they'd have plenty to talk about for another generation or two.

It was a given that there was never a dull moment when the Malloys were around.

Twelve-year-old Matthew Malloy, already known as a wild child around the town of Glacier Ridge, was asleep in the top bunk, enjoying a dream. A dream that mirrored the day he'd spent up in the hills with his grandpop Frank, father Patrick, and uncle Colin, who, at twenty-two, was always laughing and teasing and seemed more like a big brother than an uncle. With the first snowstorm of the season rolling in, they'd driven the last of the herd to winter in the south pasture, and had spread a ton of hay from a flatbed truck before heading back to the ranch house for dinner.

Their sprawling Montana ranch was home to four generations of Malloys. Matt and his younger brothers, ten-year-old Luke and nine-year-old Reed, shared a section of the restored house with their parents, Patrick and Bernadette, who still behaved like teenagers, whispering behind their hands, stealing kisses when they thought no one was watching, and laughing over shared secrets. It was obvious to all who knew them that they were still crazy in love.

Frank Malloy, whose Irish ancestors had cleared this raw wilderness, loved sharing the ranch chores with his sons and grandsons, while his Gracie Girl, as he called his wife, often took to the hills for weeks at a time photographing the herds of mustangs that roamed the open range.

Gracie's father, crotchety old Nelson LaRou, was now slowed by age, forcing him to give up his opulent homes in Connecticut and Hollywood and move in with his daughter and her family on this ranch, which he called the middle of nowhere. Though he constantly complained about the rugged lifestyle, it was no secret that he reveled in the company of his only daughter and was adjusting to the slower pace of life on a working ranch. The family loved it when he regaled them with tales of all the famous movie stars of the past. If only he would use a hearing aid, all their lives might be a bit easier. Gracie liked to say her father heard only what he chose to.

In his sleep Matt was smiling at one of Uncle Colin's silly jokes, until the dream dissolved and he was jolted into wakefulness by the sound of a door slamming somewhere below, followed by a chorus of voices. Not that it was anything new. In a family the size of his, voices raised in anger and laughter, as well as the occasional thump of a fist, were as natural as the lowing of cattle.

But this was different somehow. He sat up in bed, completely awake, and heard a woman's voice that sounded too high, too shrill, to be his sweet grandmother Gracie's. And yet he knew it to be hers. And a low, deep growl that could only be that of his sweet-natured grandpop, Frank, sounding more like a wounded bear.

There were other voices. His uncle Colin cursing. The cultured tones of his great-grandfather Nelson, more a moan than a voice. And the low rumble of strangers, all trying to be heard above the din.

Matt ignored the ladder alongside his top bunk and jumped to the floor. He noted idly that his younger brothers were undisturbed by the commotion.

The words drifted up, clearer now as he opened the bedroom door and stepped into the hallway.

"Impossible. They can't be..."

"...I tell you...lost control in the snow."

"I saw more than one set of tire tracks when I went there to document it on film."

"They could have been made by Sheriff Graystoke's police car, Nelson." Deputy Archer Stone's mouth was a taut line of raw emotion. "Or by mine, or even one of the ranch trucks."

Matt was halfway down the stairs when the voices went abruptly silent. He glanced down to see half a dozen faces tilted upward, all eyes focused on him. His grandparents were in parkas tossed hastily over their robes, as were his great-grandfather, still holding a movie camera, and the ranch cook, Yancy Martin, hair in wild disarray. His uncle Colin was still in his torn denims and sheepskin parka, obviously caught finishing chores in the barn. Sheriff Eugene Graystoke and his deputy stood in snow-covered boots that were dripping water on the hardwood floor. And over by the door, still as a statue, was old Burke Cowley, his hair and clothes dusted with snow. He was a cowboy who had been with the family for as long as Matt could remember. He stood, eyes downcast, his agitation apparent only by the way he was twirling his Stetson around and around in his hands.

All of them looked grim.

It was Gracie, her face ghostly pale, her eyes red-rimmed from tears, who rushed toward her grandson.

"Oh, Matthew." She reached her arms as if to clutch him to her, but he shrank back, just out of reach.

He turned to the sheriff. "It's Mom and Dad, isn't it?"

No one spoke.

"Are they in the hospital?" At the sound of ten-year-old Luke's question, everyone looked beyond Matt to see the two younger boys, hair rumpled, eyes wide with a million questions, standing at the top of the stairs.

Matt turned pleading eyes to his grandfather. "What happened, Grandpop? Somebody tell us."

His family was rendered mute.

It was old Burke who lumbered across the room and put a big, wrinkly hand on the boy's shoulder, while he signaled for the two younger ones to come closer. "Your ma and pa were in an accident out on the highway. Their car slid off the road and hit a boulder. They're both gone."

"Gone where, Burke?" Nine-year-old Reed's voice raised to a youthful bellow. "You tell us right now. Where are they?"

Burke's jaw clenched, as if bracing for the blow he was about to deliver. Then the old man cleared his throat twice before he managed to say, "I'm sorry to tell you this, boys. They're dead. I hope you can take some comfort in the fact that your ma and pa died together, just the way they'd want it."

Colin crossed the distance between them, wrapping his three young nephews in a tight, hard embrace while his voice trembled. "I know this is a shock. I know what you're feeling, 'cause I'm feeling it, too. And I know I can't be your dad. Nobody else could ever be my brother

Patrick. But I swear I'll be here for the three of you." He turned to include the others, so locked in shock and grief they had no words. "All of us will be here for you. We're family. And we'll do everything in our power to keep you boys safe and happy."

"Happy?" The very word mocked Matt. He pushed free of his uncle's arms, staring defiantly at all of them.

Time stopped. He heard a buzz of voices, and felt hands reaching for him and his brothers as the family gathered around, determined to offer aid and comfort.

He was aware of only one thing. His sweet, pleasant dream had just become a nightmare. His mother and father, the people he loved more than anything in his young world, were dead. Gone too soon from his life.

And though he and his brothers had all these people willing to surround them with love, Matt knew that nothing, not now, not ever in this life, would be the same again.

CHAPTER ONE

Rome, Italy—Present Day

A limousine glided toward the sleek, private jet parked on the tarmac of Rome's Fiumicino Airport. The uniformed driver hurried around to open the door as two men exited.

Matt Malloy extended a handshake. "Thank you for your hospitality, Vittorio. And please thank your lovely wife for the tour of her family's vineyards. That was a bonus I hadn't expected. Tell Maria I hope I didn't overstay my welcome."

The handsome, white-haired man gave a vigorous shake of his head. "You know how much we enjoy your company, Matthew. The vineyard was all Maria's idea. She said to expect a case of her family's finest wine in time for your summer holidays. You do take a holiday from ranching, don't you?"

Matt chuckled. "Ranchers like to say our only day off is our funeral."

"Do not say that, even in jest." The older man shook his head before closing a big hand over Matt's shoulder. "It is always a pleasure doing business with you, my friend."

"The pleasure is mine." After a final handshake, Matt turned away and greeted the crew at the bottom of the steps before ascending to the plane's interior.

Within minutes the steps had been lifted and the hatch secured, then the pilot announced their departure.

As soon as they reached their required altitude, Matt unbuckled and retreated to the small bedroom in the rear of the aircraft. When he returned to the cabin, he had already shed his suit and tie and replaced them with denims, a comfortable flannel shirt with the sleeves rolled to the elbows, and a pair of well-worn Western boots. Just as easily he shed the attitude of a worldly, successful businessman and became once again a rancher, a man of the soil, eager to return to the life he loved.

Matt leaned over the shoulder of his pilot as the plane cast its shadow on the vast herds darkening the hills below. "Now there's a sight I never grow tired of."

"Can't say I blame you." Rick Fairfield, with his trim build and graying hair cut razor short, could never be mistaken for anything but a former military pilot. He adjusted his mirrored sunglasses. "After nearly three weeks out of the country, it's got to be a good feeling to be home again." He glanced at Stan Novak in the copilot's seat. "Let's bring this baby down."

Matt returned to the cabin and fastened his seat belt for landing. A short time later, after thanking the crew, he deposited his luggage in the bed of a truck that stood idling beside the small runway and climbed into the passenger seat.

Behind the wheel was Burke Cowley. Burke had spent his younger years tending herds on ranches from Montana to Calgary, until he'd settled on the Malloy Ranch, working his way from wrangler to ranch foreman. With his white hair, leathery skin from a lifetime in the weather, and courtly manners, he was a cowboy in the traditional mode. Strong, silent, watchful.

"Welcome home, Matt."

"Thanks, Burke. I see the weather's turning." Matt slipped into a battered parka.

"Springtime in Montana. Shirtsleeves one day, winter gear the next. Was it a good trip?"

Matt shrugged. "Satisfying. Is everyone home?"

"You bet." Burke nodded. "By now they've finished their chores and they're just waiting for you so they can enjoy the special dinner Yancy's been cooking all afternoon."

Matt was smiling as they drove along the wide gravel driveway that circled the barns before leading to the rear of the ranch house.

As Matt stepped down from the truck he turned. "You coming in?"

Burke grinned. "Wouldn't miss it. I'll just park this in the barn and be back in no time."

Matt hauled his luggage up the back-porch steps, experiencing the same little thrill of pleasure he always felt whenever he returned to his family home.

"Matthew." His grandmother was the first to greet him as he stepped inside and dropped his luggage in the mudroom.

Matt simply stared. "Gram Gracie, you never age."

"Go on. Look at all this gray hair."

Despite the strands of gray in her dark hair, she was as trim as a girl. She was wearing her trademark ankle-skimming denim skirt, Western boots, and a cotton shirt the color of a ripe plum, the sleeves rolled to the elbows.

She flew into his arms and hugged him before drawing a little away to look into his eyes. "I missed you."

"No more than I missed you."

Matt kept his arm around her as they made their way into the kitchen. "Hey, Yancy."

At his words the cook and housekeeper, who stood all of five feet two, his salt-and-pepper hair cut in a Dutch-boy bob, set aside a pair of oven mitts before hurrying over to extend his hand. "Welcome home, Matt."

"Thanks. I've missed this. And missed your cooking. Something smells wonderful."

The cook's face softened into a mile-wide smile. "I've fixed your favorite."

"Yancy's Fancy Chicken?" Matt used the term he'd used since childhood to describe the cook's special chicken dish that never failed to bring compliments. "If I'd known, I'd've had the pilot get me here even faster."

They were enjoying a shared laugh when a handsome man with a lion's mane of white hair entered from the dining room. Gracie's father paused for a moment. Standing ramrod straight, his starched white shirt and perfectly tailored gray pants brightened by a cherry-red silk scarf knotted at his throat, Nelson LaRou looked exactly like the director he'd once been, who had commanded an array of Hollywood's rich and famous.

He hurried toward them. "Welcome home, Matthew."

"Thanks, Great One." Matt ignored the outstretched hand and gathered his great-grandfather into his arms for a bear hug.

Though the old man remained straight backed, his stern countenance softened into a smile. It had taken him years here on the ranch to accept such casual signs of affection. In truth, he was still learning. And he liked it more than he would ever admit. Just as he loved the nickname the boys had given him all those years ago. *Great-grandfather* was just too long. They'd shortened it to Great One, but he sensed that it was more than a title. It spoke of the esteem in which they held him, which tickled him no end.

He cleared his throat. "How was Rome?"

"As amazing as ever. I wish you'd have come with me. Vittorio's wife took me on a tour of her family's vineyards. Every time I sampled another wine, I thought of you and all those fancy wines you brought from your places in Connecticut and California."

Nelson crossed to his favorite chair. "I hope you thought enough of me to bring some home with you."

"I'm having it shipped."

"It flipped?" He turned, cupping a hand to his ear. "Can you flip some my way?"

"*Shipped*, Great One. It's being shipped from Italy."

"Good. Good." Nelson settled into a comfortable easy chair in front of a huge stone fireplace just as the rest of the family began arriving.

The family's often-absent son Luke ambled in from the barn and rolled his sleeves, washing up at the big sink in the mudroom. Where Matt was tall and lean, his dark hair cut short for his trip to Rome, Luke was more muscular, honed by his never-ending treks to the mountains that called to him. Thick, long hair streamed over his collar.

He hurried over to welcome his brother back. "Another tough assignment, right Matt?"

"Right. But somebody has to do it. And I manfully accepted the challenge."

The two were still sharing grins when Reed strolled down the stairs and clapped Matt on the shoulder. Tall, wiry, with his long hair tied back in a ponytail and his rough beard in need of a trim, their youngest brother looked as though he'd just come in from months in the wilderness. "You're alone? I was hoping you'd bring a couple of Italian beauties with you."

"Wishful thinking, little brother. You'll have to go to Rome and do your own shopping."

"That works for me. Next time you're heading to Italy, you've got a traveling companion."

"You always say that, until it's time to actually go. Then you realize you'll need to wear a suit and tie and get a real haircut, and you find way too many things that need your attention here on the ranch."

Reed gave a mock sigh. "The trials of a cowboy. Never enough time for the ladies." He looked up. "Speaking of which, here's the ultimate cowboy now." He grinned at the handsome man in faded denims and plaid shirt strolling into the kitchen. "When's the last time you took a pretty lady out to dinner, Colin?"

His uncle was already shaking his head, sending curly dark hair spilling over his forehead. "So many females, so little time." He grabbed Matt in a bear hug. "'Bout time you got your hide back here. I was beginning to think you'd been seduced into moving to Rome permanently."

"I did give it some thought. But then I wondered who'd handle all the family business if I just up and relocated."

Matt's grandfather, Frank, chose that moment to walk in from the hallway. It was easy to see where his son and grandsons got their handsome Irish looks. From his twinkling blue eyes to his towering frame, he was every inch the successful rancher who'd tamed this rough land with sheer sweat and tears. Though his hair was streaked with gray and his stride was a bit slower, he was still able to work alongside his wranglers without missing a beat.

With a wink at his wife, he reached up and ruffled Matt's hair the way he had when his grandsons were little. "Any day you get ready to walk away, don't you worry, sonny boy. I can still negotiate contracts on behalf of the family business."

"Or hire a staff of lawyers to handle it for you."

At Matt's words, Frank pretended to groan. "You think it would take a staff to replace you, sonny boy?"

"At least a staff. Maybe an army." Matt grinned good-naturedly before accepting a longneck from Yancy's tray.

The others followed suit. Nelson accepted a martini, which Yancy had learned to make to the old man's specific directions.

When old Burke walked in, the family was complete. They touched drinks in a salute, and tipped them up to drink.

Matt looked around and felt his heart swell. He never grew tired of this scene. His brothers, his uncle, his grandparents, and his great-grandfather all here, as they'd been since he was a kid, surrounding him with love. Yancy cooking. Burke standing just slightly outside the circle, like a fierce, vigilant guardian angel.

Outside the floor-to-ceiling windows, the tops of the mountains in the distance were gilded with gold and pink and mauve shadows as the sun began to set.

Life, he thought, didn't get much better.

"Dinner's ready."

At Yancy's familiar words, they circled the big, wooden harvest table and took their places. Frank sat at the head, with his Gracie Girl at his right and their son, Colin, to his left. Matt sat beside Colin, with Burke beside him. Luke and Reed faced them on the other side, with Nelson holding court at the other end of the table.

After passing around platters of tender, marinated chicken, potatoes au gratin, and green beans fresh from the garden, Yancy took his place next to Reed.

Matt took a bite of chicken and gave a sigh of pleasure. "Yancy, after all that great Italian food, this is a real treat. I can't tell you how much I've missed this."

The cook's still-boyish face creased into a smile of pleasure at Matt's words.

"Okay." Luke pinned his older brother with a look. "Enough about the food. I want to know what happened with Mazzola International. Are they in?"

Matt put aside his fork before nodding. "They're in."

"They signed a contract?"

"Their lawyers still have some work to do. But Vittorio and I shook on it. And that's good enough for me."

Luke reached over to high-five his brother.

Matt laughed as he looked around the table at the others. "I figured that news would make Luke's day."

Colin shot a meaningful look at his nephew. "Does this mean you intend to give up all those reckless pursuits and settle down to raise cattle?"

"Reckless pursuits?" Luke arched a brow.

His uncle narrowed his gaze. "I caught a glimpse of you on your Harley, heading into the wilderness. You were doing one of your daredevil Evel Knievel imitations, as I recall."

Luke gave one of his famous rogue grins. "The way I see it, jumping a motorcycle off a cliff, or hiking through the mountains with nothing more than a camera, a rifle, and a bedroll"—he turned to his grandmother—"searching for that elusive white mustang stallion you've been tracking for years, is no distraction from work. They help prepare me to be a better cowboy."

"Or an aimless drifter," his great-grandfather muttered.

Luke's grin widened. "There's nothing aimless about it, Great One. It's preparing me for whatever life throws at me." He turned to Matt. "Enough about me. Tell us more about Rome."

Matt paused for dramatic effect before saying, "I brought back a little something for you, too, Reed."

Their younger brother looked up in surprise before narrowing his eyes in suspicion. "Okay. Give."

"I know how you've been hoping to make a mark in the green industry..."

Reed nodded. "Organic. Pure beef with no hormones, no antibiotics."

"Exactly. Leone Industries has agreed to a limited contract, to test the market. If they can see enough profit, they'll sign for the long term." He studied the excitement that had leapt into his brother's eyes. "Just remember. It's only a limited contract until they test the market."

"It's a foot in the door." Reed sat back, too excited to

finish his meal. "And there's an entire generation of buyers out there just waiting for this. If Leone Industries will give it a fair trial, this will become the gold standard for prime beef. And we'll be there first."

"Hah." Nelson sipped his martini and frowned. "Food fanatics. That's what they are. Now in my day—"

"Not now, Dad." Grace kept her tone light, but there was a hint of steel in her words. "Let Reed enjoy the moment. This is something he's been preparing for since he was barely out of his teens."

"You got that right, Gracie Girl." Frank Malloy patted his wife's hand before turning to his grandson. "You realize this means you'll have to work twice as hard to see that you have enough healthy cattle to fulfill this contract with Leone."

"I don't mind the work, Grandpop."

"I know you don't, sonny boy, and you never have. You've been tending your own herd since you were knee-high to a pup."

Reed flushed with pride. "I'll need to get busy segregating one herd and seeing that they meet all the requirements to be truly organic."

"And I'd like to get in one more trip to the mountains and see if I can spot a herd of mustangs for Gram Gracie before I settle down and do my lonesome cowboy routine."

At Luke's deadpan expression, they all burst into laughter.

"Yeah. That'll be the day, sonny boy." Frank squeezed his wife's hand.

All of a sudden, with so much good news springing from Matt's Italian trip, everyone seemed to be talking at once.

Matt sat back, looking around the table, listening to the chorus of voices, and smiling with satisfaction.

He'd missed this. All of it.

He'd grown impatient to get back to his roots.

But now, seeing the animation on their faces, hearing the excitement in their voices, he knew without a doubt it had all been worth waiting for.

CHAPTER TWO

Matt descended the stairs, feeling like a new man. There was nothing like a night spent in his own bed, after so many nights away.

Spying Yancy alone in the kitchen, he helped himself to coffee. "Am I the first one up?"

The cook set crisp bacon on a nest of paper napkins to drain. "The last."

"I am? Where is everyone?"

Yancy looked over. "Colin drove Great One to town. Luke, Reed, and Frank are up on Eagle's Ridge for the next week or so. Ms. Grace is out trailing one of her herds. No telling when she'll be back."

Matt walked to the floor-to-ceiling windows to stare at the mountain peaks in the distance just as Burke stepped into the kitchen from the mudroom.

"Then I guess I have some downtime coming. I think I'll head up to the hills for a week or so."

The ranch foreman's face creased into a smile. "I figured as much. Every time you come back from one of those fancy, high-powered trips, your first order of business is to get back to your roots. You going to drive one of the trucks, or ride old Beau?"

"I'm thinking Beau needs a workout as much as I do." Matt idly drained his coffee before setting the empty cup on the counter. "If anybody asks, I'll be up on North Ridge for a while."

"I'll let them know. You going to take time for breakfast?"

Matt shook his head and turned to Yancy. "Would you mind packing up some of that food?"

"I'll send as much as you can eat."

Matt shrugged. "I guess I'll take enough for a week or so."

"Done." The cook was already opening a pantry door and reaching for an array of zippered bags and pouches in various sizes.

Matt disappeared up the stairs and reappeared a short time later carrying a duffel filled with his gear, along with a rifle and ammunition.

Yancy handed him a parcel containing the food packets, all carefully labeled. "I sent a similar cache along with your grandmother. There's no telling how long Ms. Grace will be gone."

"As long as it takes to get the pictures she's aiming for." Matt tucked the parcel under his arm and started toward the mudroom, where he snatched up his hat before heading for the door.

"I'll see you in a week or so." He walked out the back door and headed toward the barn.

Not long after he was astride a big bay gelding, saddlebags overflowing, riding across a meadow that led to the hills, black with cattle.

Though it was early April, it still felt like winter in the hills surrounding the Malloy Ranch.

Matt stood in ankle-deep snow chopping wood. It was a chore he always found soul satisfying. Especially after weeks away from home.

It wasn't that he didn't enjoy wheeling and dealing with high-powered lawyers and corporate executives all over the world. And he certainly couldn't complain about the front-row seats at sporting events and the expensive dinners and shows. But even in the Eternal City, with its fine wines and fabulous food, after a week or more, it was like eating too much candy. He found himself craving the simple food, familiar chores, and nights with only the lowing of cattle to break the silence.

He slipped into his parka, which he'd tossed over a log, before filling his arms with fresh firewood. Nudging the door to the range shack open, he tracked snow across the floor to the fireplace, where he stacked the logs neatly before heading out for more.

When his cell phone rang, he plucked it from his pocket. "Hey, Gram Gracie. How's that herd of mustangs?"

"As wild as ever. They've added six pretty little fillies to the herd. There's a third mare big as a house and ready to deliver any day now."

"You hoping to capture the birth on film?"

"That I am. I've already been planning where to set up my cameras for the best angles. Now if only she'll cooperate and have that foal nearby. With these feisty mares,

I never know where I'll end up having to track her. I just hope she doesn't wander down one of those ravines. I really want these pictures for my collection."

"My money's on you, Gram Gracie." Matt paused. "Are you calling for my help?"

"In a way. But not with the herd. I just got a text reminding me about a meeting I'd agreed to. Some lawyer who represents a group of wild-animal federations had set it up, hoping for my take on the best way to preserve wild animals, especially those being removed from the government's endangered list. Since I'm away, I was hoping you could take my place at the meeting."

"Sorry. I'm not at the ranch. I'm up on North Ridge, spending some time at the range shack."

Everyone in the family knew about Matt's love of that particular section of land. From the time he'd been very young and missing his parents, he'd always found solace in this special place. He'd already staked it out as the spot he'd like to build his own house one day.

"Oh dear. How about Luke or Reed?"

"Up on Eagle's Ridge with Grandpop."

He heard his grandmother blow out a breath. "I guess this calls for desperate measures. Since the lawyer is traveling all this way, I'd say it isn't too much to ask him to travel just a bit more. Would you mind an intrusion on your privacy for an hour or two?"

Matt gave a dry laugh. "Never mind my privacy. What about the time he'll waste getting up here by horseback and down to the ranch again?"

"Since Burke is picking him up from his plane, maybe Burke could drive him up and wait until the two of you exchange views before he takes him back to town."

Matt shrugged. "I'll call and arrange it. Providing the phone service continues."

Gracie's tone softened. "I know. It's the same here. One minute a clear line, and the next my phone is dead for hours. Thank you, Matt darlin'. I owe you for this."

"I'm happy to help out."

"I know you are. I know, too, how much you value your alone time in the hills, especially after a long business trip. I'll find a way to make it up to you."

When she hung up, Matt dialed a number and spoke in staccato tones. "Burke. I promised my grandmother I'd meet with some animal activist lawyer. Instead of driving him to the ranch, would you mind driving him up here?"

The old man's tone was incredulous. "You're inviting someone to invade your privacy?"

"It's for Gracie. And it's only for an hour or so. I'd really like you to wait and take him back down as soon as we're through with our meeting."

"Sure thing. When should I expect him?"

"I don't have a clue. Gracie said it would be sometime today. I guess he'll call you when his plane gets in. And you may as well pack a bottle of Grandpop's good Irish whiskey while you're at it. A lot of these Eastern lawyers aren't happy with the local wine and longnecks we've got stashed up here. While I answer this guy's questions, maybe you could deliver supplies to the crew up in the pasture, and then drive him back to town when we're finished."

"Sure. I could do that." Burke cleared his throat. "Hell, son, I'll be happy to sit a spell with the wranglers. I haven't been up there for weeks. I'll head out as soon as the lawyer gets here."

Matt disconnected and stowed his phone in his pocket before bending to retrieve another armload of firewood. As he hauled it to the cabin, he thought about Burke. It didn't take much to make the old man happy these days. He'd been positively bubbling over with joy at joining the wranglers, if even for an hour or so.

He glanced out the window. He and Beau had time to ride across the north pasture and back before his precious solitude was interrupted by this unplanned bit of business.

Matt unsaddled his horse and filled the troughs with feed and water before stepping out of the lean-to behind the range shack that served as a storage shed and stall.

He'd had a great time riding across snow-covered pastures, drinking in the sights and sounds that nourished his soul. Using high-powered binoculars, he'd followed the path of a pair of eagles soaring on currents of air, and had paused to watch a pure white mustang stallion leading his herd toward a box canyon that offered shelter and food. He intended to relate the location to Gram Gracie, since she'd been hunting that stallion for a year or more. Every member of the family had spotted it at one time or another, but it always managed to disappear before she could capture it on film.

Hearing the sound of an engine, Matt ran a hand through his scruffy beard and rounded the cabin in time to see Burke just stepping down from the driver's side.

The old man was grinning like a fool as he circled the truck and opened the passenger door.

Matt stopped in midstride at the sight that greeted him.

The passenger was tall, blond, and gorgeous. She was wearing a charcoal suit jacket over a skinny little skirt that barely skimmed her thighs. When she stepped into the snow, her high-heeled shoes sank ankle-deep, causing her to hiss out a breath before she gamely forged ahead, extending her hand.

"Matthew Malloy? Vanessa Kettering." Her smile might have been forced, but the handshake was firm. It was obvious that she was a woman who didn't get easily flustered.

"Vanessa." Matt's hand closed around hers while he looked beyond her to old Burke, who was clearly enjoying this little turn of events as he retrieved a laptop case. "Do you prefer Vanessa or Miss Kettering?"

"My friends call me Nessa."

"Okay." He glanced down. "Sorry about the snow. This is springtime in Montana."

"It isn't something you can control." She managed a smile as she removed her sunglasses and looked around. "Though if I'd known our meeting would be in the hills, I'd have dressed more...appropriately."

"I'm sorry about that, as well. I agreed at the last minute to stand in for my grandmother." Matt led the way to the door and held it while she entered.

He shot the old cowboy a killing look before following her inside.

Burke set the leather bag on the table before walking to the door. "I'll just get those supplies you asked for, boss, and I'll be on my way up to the herd."

"Make yourself comfortable, Nessa." Matt turned. "I'll give you a hand with those supplies."

He trailed Burke out to the truck.

"Very funny. You could have called and told me to expect a woman."

"Yeah. I could have." Burke chuckled. "I even packed some of your grandpa's whiskey, just in case she drinks like all those other Eastern lawyers."

"You're enjoying this, aren't you, old man?"

Burke chuckled. "More than I should. I wish you could've seen your face. It was priceless."

Matt burst into laughter. "Okay. You got me. But you have to know I'll find a way to get even for this."

"Oh, don't I know it." Burke was whistling as he hauled a box of supplies to the cabin. He was still whistling as he walked back to the truck and drove away.

Matt glanced at the young woman, who bent to remove first one shoe, then the other, all the while wiping away the snow with a tissue. As she did, Matt found himself admiring her backside in the trim skirt that fit her like a second skin.

When she turned and caught him staring, he tried to cover himself by indicating a rocker in front of the fireplace. "Why don't you sit here and I'll crank up the heat?" Not that he wasn't already feeling more heat than he cared to admit.

While Vanessa settled into the rocker, he added a fresh log and kindling to the embers and soon had a fire blazing.

She gave a sigh of appreciation. "Oh, that feels good." She glanced around the tiny cabin. "Is there someplace I can freshen up?"

"Bathroom's over there." Matt pointed and she slipped into her shoes before crossing the room.

Matt remained where he was, clearly enjoying the view. She had a way of walking that he found fascinating. He figured she'd honed that power walk while competing with her male counterparts. Along with the trim skirt and softly flowing hair, it was a potent mix.

Minutes later she emerged and took her time looking around the room. "This is a lot more comfortable than it looks from the outside. When we first got here, I really thought Burke was having fun with me. Especially since he was grinning from ear to ear."

"Yeah. That's Burke." Matt clenched his jaw, wishing he could have a do-over for the day. If he'd known he would be stuck entertaining some female, he'd have sent her packing without the benefit of a meeting. After dealing with lawyers for the past three weeks, he was weary of the nitpicking that was a part of every negotiation. But having to deal with a female lawyer, and one with a killer body that already had him off stride, was more than he wanted to handle so soon after returning. "That old cowboy's always the joker."

Matt nodded toward the kitchen counter, where he'd unpacked the supplies he'd requested. "Would you like to warm up with coffee, beer, wine, or whiskey?"

She laughed. "I think I'd better keep a clear head while we have our discussion. I'll settle for coffee."

Matt filled a coffeemaker with water and freshly ground coffee. Soon the little cabin was perfumed with the fragrance.

He poured two cups and turned. Vanessa had already laid out several documents on either side of the wooden table in the center of the room, and her laptop was humming.

"Efficient. I like that." Determined to make the best of this, he set a cup in front of her and rounded to the other side. "The sooner we talk, the sooner you can get back to civilization." And the sooner he could get back to his privacy.

She nodded. "My thoughts exactly. Especially since the company jet will be returning from Helena to fly me back to Chicago as soon as I'm ready."

"Your wild-animal federations can afford a jet?"

"I'm afraid not. They're a loosely bound group of animal activists who pay me to represent them in Washington. But one of the board members, Clayton Anderson, made his company jet available, since he was heading on to Helena for business, and he'll be back to pick me up in a couple of hours."

"All right then." Eager to finish the meeting and get rid of this intrusion on his privacy, Matt took a seat and picked up the first page of the mound of documents. "Let's get to it. My grandmother said you want the Malloy take on wild-animal preservation, especially those being removed from the government's endangered species list."

"Exactly. The Malloy Ranch is successful enough to pack some clout with the officials who set the rules. We're hoping the Malloy name will make a difference."

Matt compressed his lips and decided to keep his thoughts to himself until he'd had more time to see just where this was leading.

CHAPTER THREE

I hate to nitpick, but I'd like to clarify this third paragraph." Matt indicated the words on the page, and Vanessa located them on hers before carefully reading.

Her head came up. "You agree with the government regarding the number of animals that have been removed from the endangered species list?"

"I haven't even heard of half these animals, Miss Kettering. I can only speak about those animals located in this part of the country."

She sat back, her arms crossed. "Now I'm 'Miss Kettering.' What happened to 'Nessa'?"

He grinned. "I guess I wanted to make my point."

"Point taken." Her own smile returned. "Please disregard the exotic animals on this list. We'll just concentrate on those located, as you said, in this part of the country. How do you feel about the government's annual roundup of mustangs?"

He sat a little straighter. "Now you've touched a nerve. You have to know that my grandmother is devoted to her mustangs."

"I know that. That's why I was so eager to meet with her and hear her views on the subject."

"I assure you that my views will reflect hers. I've grown up hearing her lament the mistreatment of those wild horses. She's spent a lifetime trailing them, capturing them on film, and seeing to it that our ranch hands deliver precious feed whenever she locates a stranded, starving herd."

Vanessa nodded. "But is she willing to lend her name to a complaint we hope to present to Congress? We're asking that they rescind the law allowing the annual capture and adoption of mustangs, along with the slaughter of those considered too old or ill to be adopted by ranchers."

"I'm afraid, in that particular matter, I cannot speak for my grandmother. In order to use her name, you'll need her complete and unequivocal approval."

"Spoken like a lawyer." Vanessa set aside the documents and sat back, forcing a tired smile. "Is there any coffee left?"

"Sure." Matt walked to the kitchen.

Vanessa took the moment to slowly exhale before glancing at the time on her cell phone. They'd been going over the documents for more than an hour, and she was no closer to having the Malloy stamp of approval on their wish list. At this rate, she wouldn't be out of here until after dark.

This day wasn't going at all as she'd planned. When she'd been given the task of flying to Montana, she'd envisioned a quick meeting at a cozy ranch, and a long, leisurely dinner aboard the company jet while returning to Chicago. She'd actually set up a lunch meeting tomorrow with another client at one of her favorite restaurants on Lake Shore Drive.

She was most comfortable sticking to a busy schedule. As an only child, and the daughter of a high-profile workaholic, she was well suited to this lifestyle she'd carved out for herself. Whether enjoying a power lunch in the hallowed halls of Congress in Washington, DC, or grabbing a midnight drink with her coworkers in her cramped office in Chicago to discuss her next project, she was invigorated by the challenge of the next job, the next client. Now her entire agenda would have to be amended. Matt filled her cup, and then his own.

"Thanks." She looked over as he settled across from her and picked up the next page of the document.

Seeing him look so comfortable in faded denims had her resenting the fact that she'd felt compelled to dress like a proper lawyer for this meeting.

"If you'd like . . ." Her words trailed off at the sound of thunder rumbling across the hills. "Are you expecting a storm?"

He shrugged. "Sorry. I haven't been paying attention. But I wouldn't be surprised. This is Montana. We have a saying: If you don't like the weather today, stick around. It's bound to change by tomorrow."

She tried for a smile, but it was more like an anxious grimace.

"You afraid of storms?"

"No." She picked up a page of the document and tried to nonchalantly stare down, but the words were a blur.

Liar, she thought. She was absolutely terrified of thunderstorms, and had been since she was a girl. But it didn't seem prudent to admit that to a client. Especially one who looked as though nothing in the world would frighten him.

This bearded cowboy, with his shaggy hair in need of a trim, and those shrewd, laser-like eyes, wasn't like the men she knew. There was something unsettling about the way he seemed to anticipate what she would say even before she said it. He seemed much more knowledgeable about the law, and the world beyond these hills, than she'd expected. And yet he never tried to show off that knowledge the way most of the men around her would have. He seemed so comfortable with himself. With his life. With this isolation.

Isolation. Here she was, drinking way too much coffee and wishing she could be anywhere except here, in this cabin in the hills, with thunder rumbling across the sky like the devil himself was throwing a temper tantrum.

She drew in a deep breath, reminding herself that she'd come here hoping to snag a big name for their crusade. He hadn't exactly said no. He'd simply pointed out that he would not give his grandmother's name without her approval.

"All right. I'll hold off filling in your grandmother's name until I have a chance to speak with her." She drew a line through the words before glancing over. "But I'll continue to hope that once we meet, your grandmother will be as outraged as our conservancy is about the inhumane treatment of wild animals. Shall we move on to the next point?"

Matt nodded.

"How does your family feel about shooting wolves?"

He sat back, stretching out his long legs. "I'd say that depends on why the wolf is being shot. Was he attacking a herd? A wounded calf? For that matter, a wounded wrangler?"

"We'll take the wrangler off the table. Obviously, we all agree that a man has the right to defend himself. But to kill a wolf for going after a calf or a herd? Isn't that what wild creatures do instinctively?"

"True. But if, as you say, a man has the right to defend himself, what about his right to defend his property? Should he allow a wolf pack to decimate his herd?"

"I hardly think a few wolves could decimate an entire herd. Or is this really all about profit? And if so, just how many cattle can a pack of wolves eat?"

His lazy smile disappeared, though his tone remained without inflection. "Where is your home, Miss Kettering?"

"We're back to 'Miss Kettering.' I guess this is serious now. My home is Chicago, though I'm often in DC advocating for wild animals. But what's that got to do—?"

"I assume you've never spent any time on a working ranch."

"No, but—"

Matt stood and faced her, leaning both palms on the table so that they were eye to eye. "Ask any rancher what his day is like, and he'll tell you that no two are ever alike. Whether he's dealing with a blizzard rolling over his pasture in the middle of May, just as the cows are calving, or watching mudslides in September washing out an entire road, he has only himself and his wranglers to depend on. The government doesn't send out troops to lend a hand. Organizations dedicated to the preservation of wildlife don't offer to come in and help him relocate his herds to higher ground, or round up the predators that might use that opportunity to kill even more helpless cattle."

Though she flinched inwardly, Vanessa fought to keep her features neutral. It was a habit she'd mastered watching her father, a well-known prosecuting attorney in Chicago. "I'm sorry. I didn't realize you expected help from the government or from our conservancy to lend a hand"—she adopted her most authoritative lawyer's tone—"during your disasters."

"I don't. No sensible rancher would. I'm just pointing out the obvious. When the good people of Chicago experience a force of nature, they know the city, the state, and the federal government will all come to their aid. When ranchers here in Montana experience the wild forces of nature, we have only ourselves to count on. Do you understand what I mean by that?"

"Perfectly. But I don't see what that has to do with wild animals."

"They're cunning. They use such disasters to their advantage, running down exhausted cattle, dragging helpless newborns into the woods for a feast. A ravenous pack could kill dozens of cattle in a matter of days. I hope you understand that a responsible rancher will hunt them down and remove the danger from his herd."

"I...I'm sure I would do the same."

"Good." Matt visibly relaxed, just as another rumble of thunder shook the cabin. Seconds later, a streak of lightning turned the evening sky outside the window to neon before going dark.

Vanessa gripped the edge of the table and turned startled eyes to his. "Is it safe to be here?"

Matt shrugged. "I guess one place is as good as another in a storm." He crossed to the window to see the trees dipping and swaying in a wild dance. "Looks like the wind is picking up."

"Maybe I should go." Vanessa picked up her phone and realized that she had no service. "Oh dear. My phone is dead."

"That happens a lot up here in the hills." He noted that she'd gone pale. "Look, why don't we forget about our discussion for now and stop for dinner."

"Dinner?" She put a hand on her stomach. "I don't think I could eat a thing. Besides, we have to finish soon so I can return to town."

"We need a break. How about a drink?" He walked to the small kitchen counter. "Would you care for some wine?" Without waiting for her answer, he asked, "Do you prefer red or white?"

"Whatever you have."

"I have both."

"Red, then."

He picked up a bottle of cabernet and uncorked it before pouring it into two wineglasses.

When he handed her one, she managed a smile. "I wasn't expecting wine in a rustic cabin."

He returned her smile. "Don't let the looks of the place fool you. This may be my escape from the world, but when I'm up here, I prefer all the comforts of home." He sipped, nodded. "At least all the comforts that matter."

"And what matters to you?"

He led the way to the fireplace, where he stoked the fire.

Vanessa settled herself in one of the chairs, hoping the fire would take her mind off the storm raging outside.

"My family matters. This ranch matters. The herds up here in the hills matter. But what matters most is the Malloy name. We've built a reputation for integrity." He turned and smiled over the rim of his glass. "I'm sure you've noticed that I'm willing to fight tooth and nail to see that our good name doesn't get used indiscriminately by people with well-intentioned causes."

"So, it's not just about business with you?"

"It's good business to protect the family's reputation."

She lifted her glass in a salute. "Well said."

He gave a slight nod of his head. "Thanks." He chose the chair beside her and nudged an ottoman between them. "Put your feet up. And if you'd like to shed those shoes, be my guest." As he said it, he lifted his own feet to the ottoman, crossing one booted foot over the other.

Vanessa followed suit, and though she was tempted to remove her shoes and wiggle her toes, she decided to remain as professional as possible.

As the thunder and lightning increased in intensity, the skies opened up in a torrent of rain that pounded the roof.

When Vanessa tensed, Matt made his way to the kitchen, returning with the bottle of wine. He topped off her glass, and then his own, before settling back in the chair.

She glanced around nervously. "Do you think Burke will be back soon to pick me up?"

Matt shrugged. "He will if the roads are passable."

Her head came up sharply. "You think the storm will wash them away?"

"It happens."

"But how will we know?"

Again that careless shrug of his shoulder. "If Burke can make it here, he will. If he can't, we'll have our answer. Without phone service, there's no way for us to communicate."

"But we're…safe here." Though she said it as firmly as she could manage, the hesitation in her voice gave her away.

Matt reached over and patted her hand. "Yeah. We're safe here."

Vanessa sat very still, trying to show absolutely no emotion. She was sure this cowboy was just trying to be reassuring. But his touch had had the opposite effect. In fact, she was practically vibrating from it. Tiny darts of pleasure prickled along her spine.

Nerves, she told herself. A simple case of nerves. She'd always been this way in a storm. And this one was even more frightening, because she was feeling so far out of her element. Here she was in a remote cabin in the hills of Montana, spending way too much time on business that should have been cleared up during a simple meeting. And would have, if the woman she'd hoped to meet with hadn't been unavailable.

She shot a sideways glance at the man seated beside her. She'd expected to meet with some backwoods cowboy. Despite his wild, mountain-man look, Matthew Malloy just didn't fit the image at all. From the give-and-take so far, she saw he was smart, savvy, and tough enough to take care of himself and his family.

"You seem to have quite a bit of knowledge of law. Was that your college major?"

Her question brought a smile. "College, when I could manage the time, was spent on business as much as law.

Though I do admit to loving the challenge law school presented. I never finished, though."

"Why?"

He chuckled. "Life got in the way. And I told myself that if I could make the ranch successful enough, I could hire a big-city law firm."

"And did you?"

"Yeah. But I still like to read every line of a contract, especially since my signature seals the deal."

Vanessa grew thoughtful. No wonder his grandmother had recommended this particular grandson to handle the interview in her absence.

Matt got to his feet and walked to the small kitchen. "I think I'd better get some dinner started. If Burke comes, no harm done. But if he can't get through, you won't starve to death."

Vanessa looked up with a quick, nervous smile. "What can I do?"

He paused. "For now, why don't you just relax in front of the fire?"

As another rumble of thunder, closer now, shook the cabin, she nodded her agreement. Setting the glass of wine aside, she leaned her head back, fighting the tension that knotted her insides. Breathing deeply, she struggled to find a calm place in her mind. Not an easy thing to do, with so many appointments that would have to be juggled if she happened to be delayed here. She prided herself on always being on time. It was part and parcel of who she was. What she was. A disciplined, organized, efficient workaholic. And here she was, being asked to relax and roll with this fickle weather.

Within minutes, exhausted by the long flight, lulled

by the warmth of the fire and the wonderful aroma of onions in a skillet wafting on the air, she was able to blot out the thought of the storm raging outside, and the appointments she would miss, and was soon drifting on a cloud of contentment.

CHAPTER FOUR

Vanessa's head came up sharply as she jolted awake. She'd been asleep only a few minutes, but it was enough that she felt a quick rush of embarrassment at her lapse.

She turned her head to see Matt stirring something on the stove. She breathed deeply, feeling suddenly ravenous. She picked up her wineglass and strolled to the counter, where she perched on a wooden bar stool and watched Matt work.

He looked over. "Hungry?"

She nodded. "I didn't realize how much until now. Something smells wonderful."

"Yancy's chili. And I have some bread warming in the oven."

A giant rumble of thunder had him looking at her. "Sounds like the storm's directly overhead now. This should be the worst of it before it blows past."

She tried to take comfort in the thought that it would soon be over, but the sound of rain lashing the windows had her shivering.

Seeing it, Matt nodded toward a plaid afghan tossed over the end of a bunk. "Wrap that around you. It'll keep the cold at bay."

"Thanks. I think I will." She crossed the room and draped the warm plaid around her shoulders before returning to the counter.

Matt rummaged through some containers in the supplies he'd brought and gave a murmur of pleasure. "Here it is." He uncovered a plastic bowl filled with greens, before uncorking a bottle of liquid. "Yancy makes the best salad dressing in the world." He glanced at Vanessa. "I dare you to find one better in Chicago."

"That's a pretty bold bet." She shot him a knowing grin. "We have hundreds of fine restaurants in the Windy City."

"I've sampled a lot of them. But none could compare with Yancy's dressing."

She thought about arguing, but instead glanced around. "Will we eat at the table, or here at the counter?"

"Let's use the table." He nodded toward a cupboard beside him. "Dishes in there. You'll find silverware in that drawer."

While she set the table, he filled two salad bowls with greens and set the container of dressing beside them.

Vanessa carried them to the table.

Matt dropped the oven-warmed bread into a basket and snagged the bottle of wine before crossing to the table.

After tasting Yancy's dressing, Vanessa gave a sound of approval. "Oh, that's wonderful."

"I thought you'd like it." Matt broke off a piece of crusty bread. "This is home baked, too."

"Your cook could work in any fine restaurant in the country. What keeps him at your ranch?"

Matt grinned. "You'll have to ask him. He's got quite a tale to tell. But I suspect Yancy wouldn't be tempted to leave Montana for twice the salary."

He pushed away from the table and returned minutes later with two steaming bowls of chili. On a tray between them were dishes containing shredded cheese, red pepper flakes, snippets of green onion, and crispy crackers.

"Before you start eating, I'll bring you a glass of water."

When he set the glass in front of her, she shot him a look. "Do you think this is my first taste of chili?"

"It's your first taste of Yancy's chili." He dug in and was finishing his second spoonful when he heard the quick gasp of breath across the table.

He looked up in time to watch Vanessa down the water in one long swallow.

"That was"—she reached for a word to describe the eye-watering heat—"really spicy."

"The wranglers refer to it as Yancy Martin's gut-burning masterpiece."

"An apt description." She laughed as she attempted a second bite. This time, prepared for the quick burn, she merely smiled before adding a little cheese, onion, and cracker to the bowl. "But I have to say, this may be the best chili I've ever tasted."

Matt looked at her with new respect. "Any woman who can dig into Yancy's chili has to be a lot tougher than she looks."

"Thanks."

While Matt polished off a second bowl, Vanessa finished her first before sitting back and sipping her wine. "That was incredible. From the salad dressing to the chili. A really unexpected treat."

"I'm glad you liked it. I hope you won't take offense at the fact that the chili was a gift from the wild."

At her blank look, he smiled. "The meat was venison. A deer I tracked on the South Ridge a few months ago. Yancy managed to turn it into steaks, hamburger, and stew meat."

"Are you hoping to shock me?" She resisted touching a hand to her stomach, though the impulse was strong.

"Maybe. A little. But in truth, I think you ought to realize that there's another valid reason for killing animals in the wild. Though it may not be necessary in Chicago, here in Montana we not only care for the land, but we live off it. Deer are plentiful, and though some ranchers hunt them for sport, my family only kills enough to eat."

"Now that you've brought up the fact of sport hunting, I have to ask: Shouldn't it be regulated, for the sake of preserving wild species?"

He stared into his glass. "That sounds noble. But what about the rancher who can barely make ends meet by ranching? Is he to be denied the chance to open his land to hunters who pay very generously for the privilege of sleeping under the stars and stalking their prey on a range in Montana?"

"Again, you make it all about profit."

He glanced over. His eyes narrowed slightly. "And you make *profit* sound like a dirty word. For every successful rancher here in Montana, there are a dozen barely hanging on. There are ranches, many of them in the same family for generations, being auctioned off every month. Do you know what that does to a man whose only dream was to carry on the work of his father and grandfather? I've seen proud men reduced to tears because they've lost everything. So, if opening their land to hunters, or turning their places into dude ranches so city folk can experience life on a working ranch, helps pay the bills, I say more power to them."

Vanessa bit her lip. "You're very persuasive. You'd probably make a very good trial lawyer."

"Just hoping to give you another point of view."

"You have. And I intend to take it under advisement." She shoved away from the table. "Since you cooked, I insist on cleaning up."

As she filled the sink with hot water and began washing the dishes, Matt surprised her by walking up beside her and picking up a towel.

"I said I'd wash them."

"I appreciate that. And I'll dry." He reached over her head and returned a bowl to the cupboard.

Vanessa went very still, feeling a tingle along her spine.

When he returned a second bowl, the back of his hand brushed her hair and she experienced little pinpricks all along her skin.

It had to be fatigue. And the fact that she was jumpy because of the storm. Still, it had her holding herself stiffly until he'd put away all the dishes.

"How about a fresh pot of coffee?"

She merely nodded.

A short time later she carried two cups of coffee to the footstool positioned between the two rockers in front of the fire.

Matt followed with a plate of brownies.

As the storm blew itself out, they sat by the fire, nibbling Yancy's homemade brownies, sipping coffee, and taking opposing sides in the discussion about wild animals.

At least, Vanessa thought with a sigh of relief, they were no longer arguing. Rather, they both seemed to be enjoying the give-and-take, and the satisfaction each time one of them made a valid point in their favor.

As the fire burned low, Vanessa stifled a yawn.

Matt pointed to the bunk bed in the corner. "Let's face it. Burke isn't getting here tonight. If he could get through, he'd have been here hours ago. You can bunk there."

"Where will you sleep?"

He pointed to the pullout sofa bed.

She needed no coaxing. She barely had the energy to slip out of her shoes and suit jacket before draping the plaid afghan around herself and dropping onto the bunk.

She'd expected the bunk to be hard, and it was. But she was too tired to care. She was asleep almost as soon as her head touched the pillow.

Matt added another log to the fire and filled his cup with coffee before adding a splash of his grandfather's fine Irish whiskey. Easing off his boots, he settled himself into the rocker and nudged the footstool to a more comfortable position.

The rain gentled to a steady patter on the roof.

He leaned his head back, enjoying the sounds of the night and the hiss and snap of the logs on the grate.

He'd expected to resent this intrusion on his privacy.

Always before, he'd treated this alone time in the hills as his sacred right, especially after a long overseas trip. And this cabin was much more to him than a simple range shack. It was his very private domain. His haven. And had been, since the loss of his parents. But he had to admit that he'd enjoyed the spirited debate between himself and this woman. Vanessa Kettering. Nessa.

His lips curved into a smile. Nessa. The nickname suited her.

She was bright. Sharp. Quick with a response to every question he'd thrown at her.

And gorgeous.

He turned to glance at the woman asleep across the room. She'd drawn the plaid afghan up to her chin. Even with her eyes closed, he could see them. A rich maple-sugar brown that could sharpen with anger or go wide with fear. And when she smiled, they crinkled at the corners. That smile did something to his heart.

His first impression of her had been all wrong. With those long, long legs, the city suit, the designer shoes, and that mane of blond hair dancing in the breeze, she'd looked as out of place stepping out of Burke's truck in the wilderness as a prom queen at a mud-wrestling match. But once they got down to the business that had brought her here, she'd been an able opponent.

He had to admit that he'd actually enjoyed their little tug-of-war. And wouldn't mind going another round or two in the morning.

That admission had him smiling.

He drained his cup and got to his feet. Across the room he set the empty cup in the sink before turning to the pull-out sofa bed.

He preferred to sleep naked. But out of deference to his guest, he simply stripped off his shirt and peeled away his socks.

Climbing beneath the covers, he lay listening to the soft patter of raindrops on the roof.

It took him longer than usual to fall asleep. He tossed and turned, trying in vain to get comfortable. But an hour later he was still wide awake and crossing to the window to stare out into the darkness.

He absently reached for one of Nelson's fine cigars and held a flame to the tip. Smoke curled above his head as he studied his beloved hills, which were shrouded in darkness, looking like silent sentinels keeping watch over the herds they nurtured.

As a boy, he'd dreamed of traveling to exotic places to escape the tedious work that he and his brothers were expected to share. It had seemed, to a boy of twelve, that there were too many adults directing his life, taking away any chance of making his own choices. And yet the older he got, the more he learned, and the stronger his bond with this land and his family became. He'd traveled the world and hadn't once found a place that compared with this.

It was his roots. His anchor. His passion.

He stubbed out the last of his cigar and made his way back to bed, lying as still as possible, listening to the soft, steady sound of breathing from the figure across the room.

He was intrigued by her. Fascinated with her quick mind.

Who was he kidding? It wasn't her mind he'd coveted.

Not only was she absolutely beautiful, but the entire

time they'd been debating, he'd had to fight an overpowering desire to kiss her. That admission made him feel like a teenager with a crush on some hot movie star. And the fact that her mere presence in his space had him thinking things better left alone just added to his discomfort.

Sometime in the small hours of the night he finally fell into a deep, exhausted sleep. But only after assuring himself that he would find a way to send Vanessa Kettering back to Chicago first thing in the morning, even if it meant slogging through waist-high mud to do it.

And then he could return to the business of enjoying his wilderness.

He could savor the solitude that he'd always craved. The solitude that had always managed to soothe his lonely, restless soul. A soul that yearned for something…something indefinable triggered by the loss of his parents that no other relationship had since been able to fill.

CHAPTER FIVE

Vanessa awoke and lay very still, fighting through the last cobwebs of sleep. After a few moments of confusion, she remembered where she was. A cabin in the hills of Montana. And then a second thought. Matthew Malloy.

Keeping the blanket hugging her like a shield, she peered around in the dim light of the fire's embers. Spotting the figure on the sofa bed across the room, she tossed aside the blanket and made her way to the tiny bathroom.

She couldn't recall the last time she'd slept in her work clothes. She felt rumpled and thoroughly uncomfortable as she undressed and stepped under the shower's spray. Though the water was only lukewarm, it wasn't cold enough to have her shivering. Minutes later she dried herself and wrapped a towel around her hair before dressing in the same wrinkled clothes she'd slept in. Then she tossed her head and finger-combed her hair, letting it fall in soft waves about her shoulders.

She made her way to the kitchen and put on a pot of coffee. While it perked, she crossed to the fireplace and struggled to add a log to the embers. When she'd finished, she watched as a thin flame began to lick across the dry bark. Satisfied, she stepped back with a smile.

"Not bad for a city slicker."

Matt's voice had her swiveling her head to give him a startled look.

"Sorry," she said. "I didn't mean to wake you."

"Don't apologize. I'm usually awake at dawn. I'd have helped you with that log, but I didn't want to scare you and have you drop it on your foot."

"I probably would have. So thanks, I think. At least I managed by myself." She gave a self-conscious laugh, knowing he'd been watching her struggles. "Well, barely."

"You did just fine. You wrangled a log half your body weight into the fireplace. That takes some doing."

At his words of praise, she felt an unexpected glow.

When he stood up, she found herself gaping before she managed to look away. He was barefoot and naked to the waist, his denims unsnapped and low on his hips.

"I heard the shower. I hope you gave the water time to heat up."

"I didn't know it would get warmer."

A smile teased his lips. "You took a cold shower?"

"Not cold, exactly. But not really warm."

"I apologize. I should have warned you. The water tank is heated by the fireplace."

"Gee. Thanks for not telling me sooner."

"You're welcome." He crossed the room and paused outside the door to the bathroom. "But thanks to your efforts, I get to enjoy a really hot shower."

"Just remember. For that, you owe me big-time."

"I'll figure a way to pay you back." He shot her a wicked grin.

When he closed the door, Vanessa let out a long, slow breath. She could think of one way he could pay her back. What a gorgeous body. All sculpted muscle and sinew. A body so toned, he could be a poster boy for a major weight-training company. If this was any indication of what Montana cowboys were like, she wanted more.

How had she not noticed last night? She must have been a lot more travel weary than she'd realized.

A short time later she looked up from her coffee to see him wearing a flannel shirt with the sleeves rolled to the elbows and a pair of faded denims. As he bent to pull on his boots, his hair and heavily bearded chin sparkled in the light of the fire with little droplets of water from the shower.

He looked over with a grin. "I've got to say, the smell of that coffee has me starving."

"Me, too." She felt a quick rush of guilt, knowing it wasn't food she'd been thinking about.

"Since you made the coffee, I'll rustle up breakfast." He moved around the stove and grabbed a skillet, then went to work frying sausages and eggs with the ease of someone who knew his way around a kitchen.

"Something tells me this isn't your first time cooking for yourself."

He shrugged. "When you grow up on a ranch, you'd better know how to take care of yourself. There's nobody trailing behind to cater to your needs."

"How about your mother? Is she a good cook?"

He paused for just a fraction before flipping the eggs

onto two plates. "My parents died when I was twelve. An accident on a snow-covered road."

"I'm sorry." Vanessa accepted the plate from his hand and led the way to the table. As he sat across from her, she added, "I lost my mother when I was fifteen. Cancer."

He met her look across the table. "It never goes away, does it? There's always a shadow lingering somewhere in our mind."

She nodded.

For a few minutes they ate in silence, feeling an odd sense of shared pain.

Matt shoved back his chair and retrieved the coffeepot, topping off her cup and then his own.

When he sat down he leaned back. "Do you live at home, or do you have your own place?"

"I live with my father. I toy with the idea of getting my own place. But so far I've resisted, since I travel between Chicago and DC so often. We really enjoy each other's company. Often my dad works so late, I may as well live alone. But when he does manage to get home for supper, it's nice to have the time to visit and catch up on life."

Matt smiled. "What does your father do?"

"He's the district attorney for Cook County."

Matt's raised brow said more than words. "No wonder he often doesn't make it home for supper."

"Yeah." She shook her head. "And on top of that, he's a workaholic. He can't leave it at the office. Most nights he brings home stacks of documents to read late into the night."

"Those must be some pretty high-profile cases he's dealing with."

Vanessa nodded. "He often jokes that there must be

something in Chicago's air to bring so many criminals to his district."

Matt regarded her. "So that's why you went into law?"

She shrugged. "In the beginning. I've always wanted to be like my dad. Especially since losing my mother. He used to say the two of us were joined at the hip. If I get hurt, he bleeds. If I have a problem, he won't sleep until it's resolved. So it was a given that I'd study law. But midway through my courses, I realized that I didn't want to pursue criminal law. I found myself wanting to get involved in social justice."

"And that led to animal activism."

"Exactly. It's something I'm passionate about. And I think I can make a difference."

"Is your father disappointed that you didn't follow him into criminal law?"

She chuckled. "I'm sure he's had some twinges. He made it clear that there would always be a place for me on his staff. But I think he's proud of the fact that I want to make my own way."

Matt nodded. "He should be proud."

She eyed him over the rim of her cup. "Even though my choice has brought me to your doorstep to meddle with your privacy?"

He threw back his head and laughed. "Yeah. Lucky me. Now I get to spar with an animal activist who's passionate about saving every wolf, deer, and bear in these hills."

"Bear?" She raised a brow. "Have you seen bears in this area?"

He gave a negligent shrug. "Sure. And right about now they're waking from hibernation and feeling mean and hungry. Want to go on a mission to feed them?"

"That depends. Would I be the food?"

He wiggled his brows like a mock villain. "You'd be a tasty morsel, little lady."

That had her laughing aloud. "Gee, thanks."

He started to gather up the dishes, and once again, as she had the previous night, she stopped him. "You made breakfast. I can clean these."

"Okay." He got to his feet and removed his parka from a hook by the door. "I'll chop some logs. It'll give me a chance to see what damage that storm did."

When he was gone, Vanessa finished her coffee before picking up the dishes and heading toward the sink.

Yesterday she'd thought being stuck in this godfor-saken wilderness was the worst possible situation. Today, after a good night's sleep and a satisfying breakfast, it was feeling more like an adventure.

Of course, having had a good look at the sexy cowboy sharing this adventure put a whole new spin on things.

As she washed the dishes and stowed them away, she found herself smiling. If she hurried, she might catch him chopping wood.

Visions of silly cowboy movies played through her mind. A gorgeous hunk, shirtless of course, working up a sweat while whittling away on a downed tree. A helpless maiden being scooped up in his arms, clinging breath-lessly to her hero.

She shook her head to clear her thoughts. First of all, he may be gorgeous and hunky, but she was no helpless female in need of strong arms. And second, she was quite certain the cowboy who brought her here would be driv-ing up very soon to return her to civilization.

And though she would miss the spirited give-and-take

of last night with Matthew Malloy, it was time she got back to reality. If she spent too much time up here, she might just lose touch altogether.

Matt gathered up an armload of logs and made his way to the cabin just as Vanessa pulled open the door.

While she held it, he stepped inside and deposited the wood alongside the fireplace.

"That was quick."

He wiped his hands on his pants before turning. "I can't take credit for chopping all of this today. Some of it was left over from yesterday."

"Is there much damage from the storm?"

He nodded toward the doorway. "See for yourself."

She stepped outside and he followed.

"There's no snow." She looked down. The ground, which yesterday had been snow covered, was now a sea of mud.

"Yeah. Better watch where you step. Some of that could be ankle deep."

She paused to study a giant evergreen leaning at a precarious angle. "Isn't that dangerous?"

Matt nodded. "I'll have the crew take it down as soon as they can get up here with some chainsaws."

"What's holding it up?"

He shrugged. "Probably some roots buried deep enough to keep it from falling all the way."

"Could it have crushed the cabin last night?"

He smiled. "From the angle it's leaning, I'd say it was in a better position to take out a couple more trees." He pointed. "It would have taken Noah's flood to carry it this far."

She gave a sigh of relief.

Matt pointed to a rock ledge not far from the cabin. "If you stand up there, you can see for miles."

As she started forward he moved along beside her until they reached the ledge. He closed strong fingers around her wrist. "This is as far as you want to go." He pointed. "That ravine may not look too deep, because it's covered over with a wild tangle of brush. But it's actually a drop-off that falls hundreds of yards down. It would be like dropping from the top of one of your Chicago skyscrapers."

With a hand to her throat she stepped back from the edge, feeling a quick, jittery rush of panic.

"Are you afraid of heights?"

She shook her head. "I didn't think so. But that left me a little...shaky."

Or was it the nearness of this man as he surveyed his land? His kingdom? Or maybe it was the strength in those fingers as they'd closed around her wrist. The mere thought of him had her sweating. Whatever the reason, she was feeling breathless. And more than a little shaken.

At the sound of ringing, Matt retrieved his cell phone from his pocket. "Hey, Burke. I'm surprised we can get a signal up here." He listened, then added, "Okay. I'll tell her."

As he tucked his phone away he turned. "Burke thinks the trail is passable. He's leaving camp now. By the time he gets here, he'll have a pretty good idea of the damage done and whether or not he can make it back to the ranch."

Vanessa swallowed back a twinge of unexpected disappointment. Her little adventure had just come to an end.

"Well." She reached for the cell phone in the pocket of her skirt. "I guess I can phone home now."

She pressed the button for her father's number and was surprised when his message came on without a single ring.

"Hi, Dad. It's me. Sorry I couldn't get through to you until now. I'm hoping to be home before too late tonight."

Feeling oddly deflated at not being able to speak with her father, she turned toward the door. "I guess I'll just gather up my papers and be ready to leave. I wouldn't want to hold Burke up."

Before Matt could follow her inside, his phone rang again. He remained outside, listening in silence.

When he finally stepped into the cabin, he crossed to the kitchen and began filling a box with food containers.

She watched him. "Won't you need that?"

He shook his head. "Looks like I'm leaving, too. I'll have Burke haul this down the mountain while I ride behind on my horse."

"Is anything wrong?"

He looked over, his face devoid of emotion. "Just some storm damage at the ranch."

"I hope it's nothing serious."

He gave a shrug. "Nothing new in these parts." He set the box on the floor near the door. "I'm sure we'll handle it."

Hearing the sound of a truck's engine, she started past him. As her body brushed against his, she felt a sudden, shocking sexual jolt.

She paused for a mere moment, tipping her face up to his, her eyes wide, her breath catching in her throat.

Matt reached for the door, but instead of opening it, he

kept his voice low. "I'm sorry again you had to spend the night."

"I'm not." The words slipped out before she had time to think. Then, trying to cover her lapse, she bit her lower lip. "I'm not sorry, Matt. Whenever I look back on this, I'll think of it as my excellent Montana adventure."

He was staring at her mouth in a way that had her throat going dry. There was a hint of a smile on his lips. "I hope I won't be a villain in your memory."

"Far from it."

Something in the way she said it had him looking from her mouth to her eyes.

Alarmed that he could read her thoughts, she blindly reached a hand to the door, only to have her hand come in contact with his.

She pulled it away as though burned, but it was too late. The rush of heat had her cheeks going bright pink.

"Nessa…"

She looked up to see him watching her in that quiet, closed way.

Before she had a chance to think about what she was doing she stood on tiptoe and touched his mouth with a soft butterfly kiss as light as a snowflake.

His eyes narrowed. His hands gripped her shoulders and for a moment he hesitated, as though considering. Then he lowered his head, staring into her eyes before covering her lips with his.

He kissed her with a thoroughness that had all the breath backing up in her throat. His lips, warm and firm, moved over hers with an intensity that had her heart pounding in her temples. There was such controlled strength in him. In the way he held her. The way he touched her. The way he kissed her. It was the most purely sensual feeling she'd ever experienced. She had a sudden urgent desire to see all that cool composure slip away.

Caught by complete surprise, her papers slipped from her hands, spilling onto the floor as she leaned into him, craving more.

He lingered a moment longer, as though unable or unwilling to break contact.

Breathing hard, his fingers closed around her upper arms, and he held her a little away while his eyes narrowed on hers. "Sorry. My fault."

"No. Mine. I . . ." She stared at the documents on the floor, as though unaware of how they got there.

They both dropped to their knees, gathering the papers, studiously avoiding touching.

When they stood, they both heard the sound of a truck door being slammed.

As the cabin door opened, they stepped apart, neither of them willing to look at the other.

CHAPTER SIX

Burke stood in the open doorway. "I hope you're ready, Miss Kettering. We've got a long drive ahead of us through a sea of mud."

"I'm...ready." Completely flustered, she held her laptop and folders to her chest as she stepped outside.

Burke trailed her, carrying the box of supplies that had been sitting by the door.

Matt strode to the kitchen counter and filled the other boxes.

While Vanessa settled into the passenger side, Matt and Burke made several trips back and forth from the cabin to the truck, storing boxes in the rear of the vehicle.

Then, as the old cowboy climbed into the driver's side and started along a muddy trail, Vanessa turned in time to see Matt leading a horse from the lean-to behind the cabin.

She glanced at Burke, who merely grinned. "I warned Matt it would be a messy slog, but he wasn't about to leave old Beau behind."

"Do you think they'll make it?"

At the worried look in her eyes he merely chuckled. "No matter the condition of the trail, my money's always on Matt Malloy. That man could make it through a blizzard, a nor'easter, or the storm of the century."

"You make him sound like Superman."

"Better than that, Miss Kettering. Superman's fiction. Matt's a real flesh-and-blood cowboy. I don't think there's a crisis in these parts that Matt couldn't overcome."

Vanessa sat back, pondering the old man's words.

What was it about Matt Malloy that had her behaving like someone she didn't even know? Take that kiss. She'd actually initiated it. And why? At the moment she wasn't sure. But at the time, she'd been incapable of resisting the urge. And once started, she felt as though she'd unleashed a hurricane.

That mouth. Those clever lips. Those strong arms holding her as gently as if she were delicate crystal.

Instead of pushing away, she'd become completely caught up in the moment. She couldn't recall the last time a man's kiss had had such an effect on her. She'd been absolutely drowning in feelings, and all in the space of a couple of seconds.

Though she tried to keep from looking back, every once in a while she would swivel her head to see Matt on his horse, navigating the trail some distance behind their truck.

Before they were even halfway to the ranch, the truck was covered in mud, as were the horse and rider behind them. But despite the conditions of the trail, the horse never stumbled or slowed its pace. And the man astride his horse sat tall in the saddle, looking as regal as a king surveying his kingdom.

Old Burke glanced in the rearview mirror before turning his gaze on her. "How'd you like to be riding with him?"

She'd been thinking the same thing. Despite the terrible conditions of the trail, there was something so raw and primitive about Matt Malloy, she'd been daydreaming about riding behind him, her arms wrapped around his waist, her face pressed to his neck. The mere thought had her shivering.

"I guess I should be glad I wasn't dressed for riding."

He joined in her laughter. "My thoughts exactly. Though I do love my horse, I'll take the comfort of this truck anytime, especially after a storm like the one we had last night."

Her own laughter rang hollow in her ears. In truth, she would take the sea of mud anytime over the comfort of this truck, if only she could have her hands on Matt Malloy.

To keep from thinking about him, she plucked her cell phone from her pocket and dialed her father's cell. She left another message before calling his office, where she left a similar message.

Puzzled, she made a mental note to try him again on the plane ride home.

Matt had to keep forcing his attention back to the treacherous trail. The thought of Vanessa Kettering kept blurring his focus.

He prided himself on always being in control. Ever since the tragic death of his parents, he'd assumed the role of leader to his two younger brothers, though he was still as wild and free as he'd always been. He worked hard at leaving the spontaneous, juvenile behavior to Luke and Reed. He'd trained himself to be disciplined and deliberate, steering the family business in a safe direction, always weighing both sides of an issue before making a decision that he knew would affect his entire family.

And back there in the range shack he'd thrown caution to the wind to do something just for the hell of it.

He would like to blame it on the situation. A small, cramped cabin. A gorgeous, unexpected woman interrupting all his carefully laid plans of solitude. The fact that he'd been forced to watch her sleep just a few feet away. But the truth was that those were all flimsy excuses for his out-of-character behavior. He'd kissed her simply because he'd wanted to.

It was only a kiss, he told himself. But again, truth won out, and he was forced to admit that, despite the fact that he'd kept it as light as possible, that simple touch of her lips had been an assault on all his senses. An explosion of light in his brain, followed by a rush of heat before the floor beneath his feet began to go all crazy and actually tilt until he'd nearly lost his balance. And all the while, thoughts of taking her right there on the cold, hard floor of the cabin had played through his mind.

What in hell had happened to his logic? His common sense?

He didn't know what intrigued him more. The fact that he was actually sorry that Vanessa Kettering was leaving, or the fact that he'd behaved like some kind of lonely mountain man bidding a final farewell.

A mountain man. He ran a hand through his rough beard and swore. Wasn't that how she saw him? As some kind of Neanderthal?

Still, she hadn't slapped his face, though he'd deserved it. And he could tell himself that he read an invitation in her eyes, especially after that sweet little kiss she'd given him first, but that didn't give him the right to take advantage. She was a guest. Here to interview his grandmother. And the fact that she'd been forced to spend the night didn't give him any rights.

He swore. It had been just a quick kiss. And yet, even now, slogging through mud that required his full attention, he couldn't stop thinking about it. And about the woman who'd felt so damned good in his arms.

It was a lucky thing she was leaving. He wasn't going to see her again. Because if he did, he'd be tempted to share much more than a kiss.

Vanessa Kettering had been a lovely distraction, but now he needed to get his mind back on the family business.

Matt hosed down his mud-spattered horse and toweled him dry before turning him loose in a pasture. Though old Beau had stood perfectly still during the entire process, Matt could have sworn that sly animal was smiling and enjoying being pampered. And once in the pasture, the old horse kicked up its heels and broke into a gallop.

It was exactly how Matt felt. Some time in the hills, one unplanned kiss, and he felt like a stallion just turned loose in a field full of sleek mares.

He looked around at the portion of roof ripped from

one of the outbuildings. A section of fence was missing, obviously blown away in the wind. And a corral gate stood at an odd angle, having been nearly ripped off its hinges during the storm.

How much more, he wondered, had been damaged by last night's storm?

He trudged up to the house, where he kicked off his boots before bending to a sink in the mudroom to wash.

In the kitchen, a chorus of voices told him that most of the family had gathered around to meet their unexpected guest.

Yancy was pouring coffee while his grandfather and great-grandfather were chatting up Vanessa. Across the table, Luke and Reed, fresh off the range and looking like wild mountain men, were staring at the newcomer with obvious, wide-eyed approval, while Colin was leaning against the kitchen counter and, like the lone cowboy he was, watching from a discreet distance.

" . . . wind so strong last night it blew a section of fence onto the roof of the barn." Frank chuckled. "I'm just glad I wasn't out during the worst of it. I'd probably be up there, too."

He glanced over as Matt paused in the doorway. "Hey, sonny boy. You look like you've been out playing with the hogs."

"Yeah." Matt grinned. "Making mudpies. Since I assume you've all introduced yourselves to Miss Kettering, I'll leave you to visit. I'll be downstairs in a while."

When he was gone, the cook set out a plate of chocolate chip cookies still warm from the oven.

"My favorites." Nelson jokingly snatched up the entire plate and held it to one side. "Glad you made these for me, Yancy, but you should have made enough to go around."

"Talk about hogs..." Luke reached over his great-grandfather's shoulder and grabbed the plate from his hand. "You could at least give our houseguest the first choice."

With a laugh, Vanessa accepted one from the plate before Luke passed it around to the others.

"I'm getting mine while the getting's good." Burke helped himself to two, as did Colin.

Vanessa bit into one and gave a sigh of pleasure. "I can't remember the last time I tasted homemade cookies."

"Then you're traveling in the wrong circles, little lady." Yancy transferred another batch from the baking tin to a plate and handed it to Frank. "I bake something fresh every day."

She looked over. "You're kidding."

The cook shrugged. "On a ranch this size, with a family like the Malloys, it's as natural as breathing. I think every one of them has a sweet tooth."

She gave a shake of her head. "You bake every day? I feel like I fell into a parallel universe. What happened to my world of coffee shops on every corner, and baked goods that were fresh last week and filled with preservatives?"

Burke and Yancy shared a smile as Yancy poured himself a cup of coffee. "I recall feeling that way when I first arrived here. I looked around at this big house, and this loud, crazy family—"

"Hey. Who're you calling crazy?" Reed reached out and helped himself to a warm cookie.

Yancy continued as though he hadn't been interrupted.

"—and I realized that, no matter how isolated this place was from the rest of the world, I never wanted to leave."

"How long ago was that?" Vanessa asked.

"Thirty-five years ago."

"That long?" Vanessa helped herself to another cookie. "Have you ever regretted staying?"

"Just about every day," Luke answered for him.

That had the others laughing.

Yancy merely grinned. "Oh, I may have thought once or twice about exchanging kitchen duties for some time spent up in the hills with the herds, especially in the middle of summer." He looked down at himself—all five feet two inches—and rolled his eyes. "But then I see how hard those wranglers work, and I remind myself that I've got the best life of all."

"Just remember, Yancy." Nelson helped himself to another cookie. "This family's got dozens of guys who can babysit cattle. But there's only one guy on this ranch that could put Hollywood's gourmet cooks to shame. So don't even think about giving it up to ride herd on some ornery cows."

They were still laughing when Matt descended the stairs. He'd shaved off his rough beard and was dressed in a clean pair of denims, a crisp shirt, and shiny boots.

"I see we've got almost the entire family here. All that's missing—" He looked over as the back door burst open on a gust of wind and his grandmother kicked off mud-caked boots before hanging her parka on a hook. "I take that back. Now the entire gang is under one roof."

Gracie rolled her sleeves and washed before stepping into the kitchen.

As she did, Matt said, "Vanessa Kettering, this is the

woman you came here hoping to interview. Gracie, this is—"

"—the lawyer from the wildlife federation?" Gracie's face creased into a wide smile. "I'll be darned. Just when I was feeling bad about having a lawyer invade my grandson's privacy, it turns out to be a beautiful young woman."

"Yeah." Reed exchanged a knowing look with Luke and their uncle Colin. "What're the odds? If I'd been up in the hills, I'd probably have to share my range shack with a bobcat."

"Or a toothless old wrangler looking for work," Luke added.

While the others laughed, Gracie offered a handshake, giving Vanessa a long, considering appraisal. "Aren't you kind of young to be worrying about the fate of wild things?"

Vanessa clasped Gracie's hand. "I didn't realize there was an age requirement for this sort of work."

Gracie merely smiled. "You're right, of course. But most of the requests I get about the mustangs come from folks my age, who have the time to worry about such things. Most young people are too busy trying to jump-start a career to give a thought to the plight of wild animals."

"Here, Gracie Girl." Frank held a chair. As she sat, he put his arms around her and brushed the back of her neck with a kiss. "I was worried about you up in those hills in that storm."

She turned and touched a hand to his cheek. "I found shelter in a little cave beneath some rocky outcroppings. I'd have stayed in the truck, but the way it was rocking in that wind, I was afraid it might topple clean on its side. And by the time the storm blew over, the herd I'd been trailing was long gone. I was cold, wet, and I figured I'd better head home while the trails were still passable."

"I'm glad you did, my girl." Frank kissed her lips and kept his arms around her when she picked up the cup of coffee offered by Yancy.

His concern, and their obvious devotion to each other, wasn't lost on the others.

Matt turned to Burke. "I guess we'd better get Vanessa to town. She has a plane to catch."

Yancy offered his hand. "It was nice meeting you, Miss Kettering. If you're ever in Montana again, I hope you'll come back for a visit."

"I'd love to, Yancy. And call me Nessa. Thanks for the coffee and cookies. These were the best ever."

"My pleasure, Nessa." The cook was beaming.

Vanessa turned to the others, but before she could say her good-byes, there was a loud knock on the door.

Burke opened it to admit the sheriff and his deputy, who hung their hats on a hook and cleaned their boots on a rough boot-scrubbing mat before stepping into the kitchen.

Eugene Graystoke was a plainspoken, take-charge man who came from a long line of ranchers. Smart, dependable, and tough, he'd been sheriff for over twenty-five years. From the beginning, he'd quickly earned the trust of the folks in Glacier Ridge, who called on him for everything from a drunken ranch hand driving on the wrong side of the road to a family squabble that ended up in a brawl. He even aided in trailing an errant bull or two, when they managed to break through a section of fence.

His deputy, Archer Stone, had grown up in Glacier Ridge with Patrick and Bernadette. Ruggedly handsome, he walked with a swagger that was always more pronounced when he was in uniform.

After greeting the family, Eugene turned to Vanessa. "You'd be Miss Kettering?"

She seemed surprised. "I am. And you are...?"

"Sheriff Eugene Graystoke, ma'am. My deputy, Archer Stone." The sheriff cleared his throat. "I was contacted by a Captain Dan McBride of the Cook County PD. You know him?"

She nodded. "I know of him."

The two men accepted coffee from Yancy before Eugene took a seat at the table and his deputy remained standing behind him.

The sheriff fixed Vanessa with a piercing look. "As I understand it, you accepted a flight on a corporate jet headed to Helena."

"That's right. But—"

He held up a hand. "I'll talk, ma'am. You'll just do me the courtesy of listening."

Seeing the grins on the faces of those around her, Vanessa felt heat stain her cheeks and fought to compose her features. It was obvious to her that this man was accustomed to taking charge.

"The jet made a quick stop at Glacier Ridge, then immediately after depositing a lone passenger"—he peered over the rims of his glasses—"it continued on to Helena. Anyone tracking that flight figured all its passengers were going directly to Helena."

"Tracking the flight...?" At his upturned palm she compressed her lips together and made a quick nod of her head.

"Good." He looked around at the others, aware that he had their complete attention. "Now, ma'am, this is where it gets tricky."

CHAPTER SEVEN

The family stared at Sheriff Graystoke with matching looks of puzzlement.

At their frowns, he held up a cell phone. "This was delivered to me by the Montana State Police. I'm told it's untraceable. Like they use on those spy thrillers on TV. When we're ready for a conference call, I'm to dial the number of Elliott Kettering."

"My father...?"

Without a word the sheriff entered the number in the speed dial, then turned on the speaker.

Seconds later an image came into focus on the phone's screen.

"Nessa?"

"Dad..." Vanessa reached for the phone, but the sheriff shook his head and continued holding it facing her as the others gathered around to watch and listen.

"Vanessa, this is Captain McBride."

Vanessa could make out the police officer's face next to her father's.

"Sorry, Elliott," he said to the man beside him. "I think it best if I set the scene, so to speak."

"I don't understa—"

McBride cut off Vanessa's protest. "As you know, your father's office has been involved in a very high-profile case."

Vanessa nodded. "DePietro."

"Exactly. In the past few days, the accused saw his air-tight alibi fall apart on the witness stand. If convicted, Diomedes DePietro will be going away for a very long time. At his age, he'll likely die in prison. A very well-connected man like that, about to see his empire crumble, will often resort to anything to remain free. In this case, immediately after the trial ended yesterday, your father received a threat stating that if his office continued its prosecution of this case, he would lose his most precious possession."

Vanessa looked at the image of her father in the phone.

"Nessa, he was telling me very plainly that his people would go after you."

"But I—"

"These people don't make idle threats. I have no doubt your life is in danger. The exact words were, 'Unless a mistrial is declared, Kettering will pay with the life of the one he holds most dear.' That can only be you, Nessa."

"And then," Captain McBride added, "when we got word that the plane parked in Helena, the same plane that would be bringing you home, had been damaged, we feared the worst."

"Damaged? It was a storm—"

"And how do you know that?" the police captain asked. "The fact that it happened during a storm just makes the local authorities reluctant to consider that it might have been a criminal act. But taken with this threat, it's far more likely that the damage to the landing gear was man-made and not the result of any storm. That's why we have federal agents going over every inch of that plane right now."

Her father ran a hand through his hair. "I've been trying to reach you ever since I got that threat. Then, when I heard about the damage to the plane, I was desperate to hear from you. But when you never answered—"

"What about Clayton Anderson and the crew? Were they injured? "

"No serious injuries," Captain McBride's voice rang out. "The hospital in Helena reported that all are doing fine. But they had no report of a female passenger."

"Oh, Dad. I didn't know. The storm made it impossible to communicate. And then when I tried to call you, I couldn't get through. Not even at your office." She studied his haggard appearance. "I can only imagine what you've been going through."

He gave a weary shake of his head.

Captain McBride cleared his throat. "The fact that you couldn't get through was no coincidence."

Vanessa's brow shot up.

"We insisted on taking all the phones that had any messages from DePietro to our lab to be tested for evidence. That included both your father's cell phone and his office phones."

Vanessa swallowed. "Then you think there's a very

real possibility that this man intends to make good on his threat."

The police captain's voice deepened with authority. "Until all the tests on the plane are completed, we will continue to believe that it was a first attempt. We aren't foolish enough to believe it will be the last. DePietro's network is vast. That's why we've suggested that you be taken to a safe house until this trial is over."

"A safe house?" Her voice rose with anger. "You must be kidding."

Her father's tone was abrupt. "This is serious, deadly business, Nessa. Until this trial ends, I need to know you're safe from DePietro's threats, if I'm to be free to do my job."

"What about *my* job, Dad? What am I supposed to do for the weeks, maybe months, that this trial goes on?"

Captain McBride interrupted. "Are you saying your job is as critical as your father's?"

Elliott Kettering held up a hand before Vanessa could say a word. "The captain doesn't mean to insinuate that my job is more important than yours, honey. Right now, we're all feeling a little shell-shocked, and we may be careless with our words." He took a breath. "Nessa, when I couldn't reach you, I went through hell and back."

His daughter fought back a sudden sting of tears. "I can't even imagine what you were thinking. I'm sorry, Dad. The Malloy Ranch is huge, and much of it is wilderness. Matthew Malloy explained that they often can't get phone service in such remote areas. So I didn't really think much about the fact that I couldn't reach you."

"Which was fortunate for all of us," the captain remarked. "If we couldn't track you, neither could

DePietro's people. That's why I've asked Sheriff Graystoke to take your cell phone and replace it with one from our lab that can't be tracked."

"But all my contacts—"

"—will be transferred to your new phone. But I'll ask you to keep your calls to a minimum while you are at a safe house."

Though Matt had remained silent during this exchange, he looked at his family.

As if reading his mind, his grandmother gave a quick nod of her head.

He broke his silence, in an aside to Vanessa. "If you don't like the idea of staying at a safe house, what would you think about spending time here?"

"And hide?" She looked horrified. "I have a job to do."

Matt nodded. "And you were doing it in Montana. You could continue doing it." Before she could protest, he added, "My family's ranch is the perfect place to be able to see and study wild animals in their natural habitat, and nobody around here will even question your presence."

"But you forget. Somebody knew I'd gone to Montana, if the captain's theory about the damage to the plane is correct."

The police captain shook his head. "Montana is a big place. The plane was damaged in Helena. That suggests that DePietro's people assume you're there. And now, since the place is crawling with feds, they've lost their only lead."

"But the pilot had to file a flight plan." Sheriff Graystoke spoke in staccato tones. "If these people look into it, they'll know the plane made a brief stop in Glacier Ridge."

Elliott Kettering's voice sounded as weary as he looked. "Nessa, taking you to a safe house will put my mind at ease. I'm not comfortable allowing a family I've never met to take my daughter into their home and see to her safety—"

"I can see to my own safety"—her voice lowered with repressed annoyance—"thank you."

At her outburst, Elliott gave his daughter a gentle smile. "Yes, you can. And always have. Don't you see? I need to be assured of your safety if I'm to do my job. There hasn't been time to investigate the Malloy family, as well as all its employees."

She took in a deep breath, wishing she'd been given time to consider.

Sheriff Graystoke used the silence to speak his mind. "I know you'll have to do a thorough investigation of anyone charged with the safety of your daughter. But until your authorities can do that, you have my word that the Malloy family gets high marks around here for honesty and integrity. I can't think of a safer place for your daughter to stay, as long as they're willing."

Elliott's weary voice held a note of optimism. "Nessa, maybe this Montana ranch could be a short-term solution. I'm told it's vast and sparsely populated. If you don't object, and the Malloys and Captain McBride agree, I suppose it could be your refuge, but only until the trial ends. And the way the trial is going, that could be within another week or so."

"Or months."

At his daughter's words he nodded. "Or months. But I believe it'll be more like weeks. Could you handle another week or two in the Montana wilderness?"

Hearing the plea in Elliott Kettering's tone, Matt lifted a hand to halt Vanessa's protest. "Since my grandmother was the one you've come to Montana to interview, it could be the perfect excuse to spend some time with her." He winked at Gracie, who was listening as intently as the rest of the family. "If you're lucky, you might even get invited along on one of her photo treks into the hills tracking her precious herds of mustangs."

At that, Vanessa's eyes widened.

They could all see the wheels turning in her mind.

Her father leaned closer to the camera. "What do you say, Nessa? Are you willing to stay in Montana until the trial is over?"

"I guess I have no choice. I can stay here and do what I love, or be stuck in a safe house somewhere, pacing the floor."

Elliott gave a long, deep sigh. "Thank you, my sweet Nessa."

"Will we be able to talk again?"

The police captain shook his head. "The less contact your father has with you, the safer you are."

His next words were directed at the Malloy family. "I hope you understand that it's my duty to have all of you thoroughly investigated. If there are any skeletons, this would be the time to reveal them before my investigators uncover them."

Matt spoke for all of them. "You're welcome to do your job, Captain."

Elliott Kettering continued drinking in the image of his daughter on the phone's FaceTime, as though memorizing every feature. "I can't tell you what this means to me, Mr. Malloy."

"It's Matt. And I'm happy to be of service, Mr. Kettering."

"It's Elliott. I know I'm asking a great deal. This will be an intrusion on your family's privacy. But all of you will have a worried father's eternal gratitude."

The police captain's face filled the screen. "Sheriff Graystoke, your number has been programmed into the cell phone for Miss Kettering. Vanessa, I can't stress enough just how serious this threat is. If you sense any danger, or even something that doesn't seem quite right, just turn on that phone and your location will be instantly relayed to your father and to our police headquarters. Even if you don't have time to call, we'll see this as a message from you. I'm going to disengage now. Say your good-byes quickly."

Elliott's voice was deep with passion. "I love you, Nessa."

Vanessa gave a long, deep sigh before saying the thing she'd said to her father since she was a teen. "I love you more, Dad."

As the two lawmen quietly took their leave of the family, the image disappeared, and the line went dead.

While Nessa sat with her chin in her hands, trying to digest all that she'd just heard, the Malloy family moved to the far side of the room, gathering around a fireplace surrounded by comfortable sofas and chairs, talking in low tones, giving her the privacy she deserved.

Grace sat by the fire, allowing the men to carry on a muted conversation while she studied the young woman alone at the table. Vanessa Kettering was obviously distraught by the news she'd just received, and struggling to make sense of it. But to her credit, she hadn't dissolved in tears or allowed herself to be overcome by fear. Instead she was sitting as still as a statue, her only movement a finger going around and around the rim of her empty cup. Probably mimicking a quick mind mulling every little nuance of the words so recently spoken.

Grace turned to her father. "Do you remember that movie you directed with that British actress? The one who showed up late every morning, keeping an entire cast and crew waiting?"

Nelson frowned. "Hillary Burnside. Nasty diva. Though nobody alive could equal her talent."

Grace smiled. "That's the one. Do you recall the plot?"

Nelson's eyes lit with the memory. "Of course. She had to seek shelter from a foreign agent bent on..." He stopped and shot her a look. "Her character felt completely out of place in that small New England town. But once she realized the danger was imminent, she became as clever and devious as the man who was tracking her."

Frank laced his fingers with hers. "This isn't a movie, Gracie Girl. This is real life."

"All too real," she whispered. "But all the same, we need to circle the wagons around this young woman. She may be caught by complete surprise, and very much aware of the danger she's been placed in, but I sense a smart woman who would rather die than show an ounce of fear."

She turned to Matt. "You spent some time with her in the cabin. What do you think?"

"That you have a pretty good sense of her. At least the woman I met. When she realized she was trapped in the hills, she adjusted. And though I sensed a deep-seated fear of storms, and the one that rolled over our heads was worse than most, she never gave in to the fear."

Grace glanced around at her family. "We'll need to remain alert."

Matt's eyes narrowed slightly, the only sign of his inner turmoil. "This is my responsibility. I was the one to suggest she stay here instead of go to a safe house."

"And I was the one she initially came here to interview. Her safety is on all of us." Grace sighed and stood. "And now, if you don't mind, I really need a shower and a change of clothes."

She crossed the room and touched a hand to Vanessa's shoulder. "Come with me and I'll show you to our guest suite."

Vanessa pushed back her chair.

Before they could walk away, Matt was beside them. "You go ahead, Gram Gracie. I'll show Vanessa to her room."

His grandmother shot him a grateful smile before heading up the stairs.

Matt retrieved Vanessa's briefcase and computer from the mudroom before leading the way up the stairs and along a hallway, where he opened a door and stood back, allowing her to precede him.

She looked around with interest.

The room was filled with light from a pair of floor-to-ceiling windows. Along with a king-sized bed, there was a wall of shelves holding an assortment of leather-bound books. A flat-screen TV was positioned atop a desk. A pair of chairs and a round table stood in a little alcove, inviting reading or just a comfortable place to enjoy the breathtaking scenery.

Matt opened a door leading to a spa-sized bathroom, with a glass-enclosed shower, jet tub, and marble counter with double sinks.

Vanessa managed a smile. "Am I sharing this with your entire family?"

"Afraid not. This is just for you."

She shook her head in wonder. "I wasn't expecting all this luxury."

"You mean way out here in the wilderness?" He affected a perfect drawl. "Well, you see, ma'am, the family's outhouse is out of commission this week, so you'll have to make do with this old thing."

She laughed and looked at him. "Thanks. I needed that."

His voice lowered. "I know you've just been handed a lot to deal with. But I hope you realize you're not alone. Just let us know what you need, and we'll see to it. My family and I are here for you."

She took in a breath. "I feel so guilty about bringing this to your doorstep."

"You didn't do anything to feel guilty about. This wasn't your choice. But now that we're aware of the threat, we can take precautions."

When she didn't say anything, he moved close enough to touch a hand to her cheek. Just a touch, but they both stepped back as though burned.

He was the first to look away.

As he headed toward the door he called over his shoulder, "Make yourself at home. And when you're ready, you'll find us either downstairs or out in one of the barns."

She looked down at her wrinkled suit. "I'm not dressed for a barn tour."

He turned back. "Yeah. What was I thinking? Meet me downstairs when you're ready to drive to town for some suitable clothes."

"Is it safe for me to show my face in town?"

He thought a moment. "I'll run it by the family. I'm sure we can come up with a plausible reason for you to be here."

CHAPTER EIGHT

Matt held the truck's door. "Climb in, Cousin Van."

"Cousin Van?" Vanessa couldn't help laughing. "Who came up with the name?"

"My great-grandfather." Matt rounded the cab and climbed into the driver's side, fastening his seat belt before starting along the curving ribbon of driveway that led to the interstate. "He was always good at revising scripts. As of now, you're Burke's niece, Van Cowley, on your first-ever visit to our ranch. I think Burke is enjoying this as much as the rest of us, since he's never had a relative before. Real or fictional." He held up a hand. "No. Don't bother thanking me. You can thank the Great One for this."

"The Great One?"

"That's what we call our great-grandfather. He loves it, since he considers himself one of the greatest directors of all time. And, in fact, he was."

"Director of what?"

"Movies. He was a pretty famous Hollywood director back in the fifties. Nelson LaRou."

"Nelson LaRou." She looked over, eyes wide. "Oh my gosh. I've heard of him. But I never dreamed I was talking to a famous Hollywood director. Did he know all the movie stars?"

Matt nodded. "Not only knew them, but directed most of them in their biggest movies. He was a pretty big deal."

"So your grandmother grew up in Hollywood?"

"And in Connecticut, where they kept a second home. As you can imagine, old Nelson wasn't too happy about his daughter marrying a rancher and moving to Montana."

"But he's living here now. He must have had a change of heart."

"What he had was a change of health. And he realized that if he wanted to see his only child and his grandchildren, he'd have to swallow his pride and move to the middle of nowhere."

"Has he adjusted?"

"I'd say so. Or we've adjusted to him and his demands. Yancy has learned to make a mean martini, just the way old Nelson likes it. And every once in a while Yancy surprises us with some exotic dish that Nelson once had at the Hollywood Grill, one of his favorite places."

"You have such a fascinating family. A famous director. A revered grandmother who photographs herds of wild mustangs in the wilderness. And your grandfather, Frank, who's absolutely bedazzled by her every time he looks at her."

That had Matt smiling. "Yeah. You can see the love

and devotion whenever they're together. I can't picture one without the other."

"How about your hunky, rugged uncle Colin? Is he married?" When Matt shook his head, she asked, "Engaged?"

"Not a chance. There isn't even a serious romance going on. He's too busy riding herd on us, and on the ranch."

"One of these days the right woman will come along, and he'll find himself in over his head."

Matt shot her a sideways glance. "Are you speaking from experience?"

She flushed. "I only know what I've seen with my friends. Even the most dedicated singles among them cave when the love bug bites."

"Looks like they need better bug spray." They both laughed as they rolled along the highway.

Vanessa found herself fascinated by the view of rolling green hills in the distance, black with cattle. "When do we leave your land?"

"Not for another couple of miles."

"Miles?" She turned to Matt. "Do you sometimes have to pinch yourself when you see all this land and realize it belongs to your family?"

Matt smiled, trying to see it through a stranger's eyes. "I guess it looks impressive, but it's what I grew up with. Are you ever in awe when you look around your city?"

She laughed. "I don't own it. Besides, it's not exactly as awe inspiring as this."

"It would be to a kid who never saw a big city like Chicago before."

That had her nodding. "I guess you're right. Maybe we all take what we have for granted."

"Well, drink in your fill of Glacier Ridge, Montana, since it's the only view of a city you'll have for a few weeks."

Seeing the way she gripped her hands together in her lap, Matt felt a tug of annoyance at himself. She'd had barely a minute to herself to process all that had happened. "Sorry. Do you feel like talking?"

She fell silent and gathered her thoughts before saying, "I guess I'm still reeling. Part of me feels terrible that I can't be home to comfort my father. I can't even imagine what he's going through. I know he wants this conviction more than he's wanted anything in his career. But any threat against me has to be a huge distraction. I don't know how he'll be able to continue to focus through the rest of the trial."

"Exactly what the bad guys are hoping. If the DA drops the ball, they win." He cleared his throat. "Your dad's a pro. He'll figure out a way to use his anger and frustration against his opponent."

She turned her head to stare out the side window. Her voice sounded weary. "I hope you're right."

"What about you? How are you going to deal with the threat to your safety?"

"When I saw my mom growing sicker and weaker, I went into a real panic. What would we do? How could we live without her? And my dad told me something I'll never forget." She took a breath. "He said we all have times when we're so scared, we want to run and hide. And that's the time when we have to stand our ground and face down our fears." She took a deep breath. "I've already been through the worst. After losing my mother, I guess I can face anything life throws at me."

In a gesture of comfort he reached a hand to hers.

Her head came up sharply, and he abruptly returned his hand to the wheel.

For the next hour, as they drove toward town, Matt kept up a running commentary on the various points of interest.

Vanessa clutched her hands together and wondered about her reaction to this man. Her hands were still overly warm, and all he'd done was touch them.

A short time later, he tapped her shoulder and pointed to a lone cowboy on a hill. "There's my Montana."

She struggled to ignore a quick little thrill. She'd felt this same awareness when he'd been setting dishes in the cupboard over her head the previous night. She'd absorbed the same pinpricks of pleasure.

"And this is the famous town of Glacier Ridge."

She forced her attention to the place that she'd barely noticed on her arrival. It had been merely a tiny town on her way to an important interview.

"On this side of Main Street is D and B's Diner. It's owned and operated by Dot and Barb Parker, twin sisters who've been fixtures in this town for more than fifty years."

Vanessa studied the tidy little white building with a door and shutters painted with black-and-white polka dots. "Is that in honor of their namesake?"

Matt nodded. "You got it. Old Dot loves polka dots. That's all she wears, too. And since she claims to be older than Barb by four minutes, she insists on being in charge. But maybe that's a good thing, because she draws in families, and especially cowboys from all over the area with her dandy cowboy-sized burger, and chili almost as good as Yancy's."

He pointed. "And over there is Snips. It started out as a barbershop and beauty shop owned by Gert and Teddy Gleason. Now they've added a spa to the building next door. They haven't named it yet, but folks around here are calling it Dips."

At her puzzled look he explained, "They dip their hands and feet, and sometimes their entire body in all kinds of fancy mud and green tea baths and stuff. So... Dips."

"Snips and Dips. You've actually got a spa in Glacier Ridge." That had Vanessa shaking her head.

"So they tell me." Matt grinned. "Though I haven't been in there to see it for myself."

"Where do you get your hair cut?"

He shrugged. "Usually Yancy cuts our hair whenever we come in from the range looking too shaggy."

She gave him an admiring glance. "Give Yancy my compliments. He does a nice job."

Matt's smile turned into laughter. "I'll be sure to let him know you approve. He's been itching to get his hands on Reed's ponytail. But my brother's having none of it. So, if you'd like a trim while you're staying with us, just let Yancy know."

He pointed. "Over there is the police chief's office, and beside it, the jail."

"Does the town ever get any criminals?"

"A few, now and then. Mostly cowboys who come to town to spend their paychecks and drink too much at the Pig Sty."

Vanessa shot him a look. "You're kidding, aren't you? There's actually a bar called the Pig Sty?"

Matt pointed to the faded sign. "The real name is

Clay's Saloon. It's just across from the jail. Back in Grandpop Frankie's day, old Clay Olmsted used to own a pig farm until he decided there had to be an easier way to earn a living. So he sold his farm and moved to town. He bought an old, boarded-up store, called it Clay's Saloon, and never looked back. But folks around here mostly refer to it as Clay's Pig Sty."

Matt added with a laugh, "One of our early sheriffs, Vinny Thurgood, figured he ought to build his jail as close to the potential drunks as he could, so he built his office and jail right across the street from Clay's place. Of course, it was a dirt road when they both started out. But now it's a proper paved street, suitable for an important town like Glacier Ridge."

They laughed, then Matt pointed to the end of the street. "There's the courthouse, and up on the hill is the high school and church."

It was, Vanessa noted, the perfect picture of a small-town church, surrounded on three sides by a cemetery.

"And just beyond the city limits," Matt added, "is the fairgrounds. When the ranchers around here finish roundup, they always gather there for the annual rodeo. A mile or so beyond is the local airport, where you landed."

He turned the ranch truck, parking in front of a tidy little shop sporting a red-and-white-striped awning with the name Anything Goes.

Matt stepped out of the truck and circled around to the passenger side, holding the door for Vanessa. "Like the name says, you can find anything and everything right here."

He led her inside and winked at the pretty woman

heading toward them. "Hey, Trudy. I'd like you to meet Burke's cousin, Van Cowley."

"Nice to meet you, Van. What's that short for?"

"Van...Vanilla. My parents love the smell of it, the taste of it. So..." Vanessa shrugged, her cheeks turning a becoming shade of pink as she found herself getting caught up in the charade. "They named me Vanilla."

Matt covered his laughter with a cough, hoping nobody noticed.

"Well, Van, I'm Trudy Evans. This is my shop. What are you looking for?"

"She needs some ranch gear. Jeans. Boots. Shirts and...stuff." Matt was trying to choke back his laughter and not embarrass her further by mentioning underwear.

"Packed the wrong things for your visit, did you?"

At the woman's long, steady look, Vanessa found her cheeks growing warmer. "Yes, I...misjudged."

Matt backed away. "Yancy gave me a list of supplies to pick up. When I'm done with his shopping, I'll pick you up here and settle your account."

The woman nodded. "I'll take care of everything, Matthew."

Vanessa was already shaking her head. "I have my own credit card."

Matt smiled at her. "I'll settle with Burke when we get back to the ranch, since your card's no good here, Van."

At his emphasis of her phony name, Vanessa realized that she'd almost made a serious mistake. "Thanks."

She could see his shoulders shaking as he walked away, and knew he was getting a kick out of this. Not only that, but leaving her here alone to deal with this messy lie.

At that she gritted her teeth.

Vanilla Cowley.

She felt like a total idiot.

"Ready to shop, Van?"

"Sure thing, Trudy." She stood a little taller and decided she would let go of her embarrassment and try to enjoy the next hour or so by spending Matt Malloy's money. In fact, lots of his money.

It was the least she could do to even the score.

Trudy led Vanessa to the back room of the shop. It was equipped as a fitting room, with a three-way mirror and hooks along the walls for hanging clothes.

Vanessa set the underthings she'd chosen on a wooden bench in the corner.

"Now these are my best slimming jeans." Trudy held up a pair in Vanessa's size. "They've got a built-in tummy trimmer. Not that you need it," she added with an admiring glance. "But since you're just visiting, you probably don't want to bother with regular working jeans. Most of the ranchers around here just want something serviceable for mucking stalls and ranch chores."

"Why don't you leave both kinds?" Vanessa took them from Trudy's hands and set them aside. "I may as well give everything a try."

Trudy beamed. "You'll need some shirts and a sweater or sweatshirt. It can get pretty cold most mornings and evenings around here until later in the summer."

"And a pair of sturdy boots," Vanessa added.

"I'll be right back."

Vanessa could see Trudy rubbing her hands together. She was already counting her profits.

It took almost two hours trying on jeans, tops, boots,

and a parka, as well as a denim jacket. She even found a baseball cap that she figured would come in handy.

Trudy paused in the doorway and took in the bench, now holding an array of clothing.

Vanessa was dressed in slim denims, Western boots, and a pretty pale blue turtleneck, topped off with the denim jacket. "I think I'll wear these and you can bag the rest."

"You made good choices. Will there be anything else?"

Vanessa shook her head. But minutes later, as she was looking around, she caught sight of a Western hat in the softest brown suede. Pausing in front of a mirror she tried it on, expecting to feel silly. Instead, she was pleasantly surprised. Not only did it look right, with her hair falling long and loose, but it felt perfect with her new outfit.

"You can add this to the bill."

Trudy walked over to cut off the tag. Glancing at the clock on the wall she smiled. "You made good time. I see Matthew has just finished with his order, too."

She motioned toward the street, where the ranch truck was just pulling up, its back loaded with sacks of supplies.

Matt stepped out and paused in the doorway for a moment, staring intently at Vanessa, as though unwilling to believe what he was seeing.

"Well." The smile came slowly, spreading across his handsome features. "Now you look like Burke's niece. That old cowboy's going to be mighty proud of you, Van..."

He took some time reaching into his pocket and withdrawing a credit card. When Trudy handed him a pen, he seemed distracted as he signed it and returned the card and receipt to his pocket.

He turned to Vanessa. "I think maybe we'll stop at Clay's Pig Sty for a beer and a sandwich before we head home."

"Okay." Vanessa offered a handshake to the shop's owner. "Thanks again for all your help, Trudy."

Before she could pick up the packages, Matt was there, grabbing a dozen handled bags.

Outside he stowed them in the truck before catching Vanessa's hand and leading her across the street. Once there he released her hand.

It took her a few moments before her breathing returned to normal. She didn't know if it was the way he was looking at her, or the fact that he'd held her hand as they crossed the street. It was such a sweet and unexpectedly courtly gesture. But for now, there was no time to figure it out as she stepped into the saloon.

Inside, they were assaulted by the smell of onions on a grill, and the sizzle of burgers.

Hank Williams was wailing about being so lonesome he could cry, and men's voices were punctuated by occasional curses and laughter.

A white-haired man in jeans and suspenders, his rolled sleeves revealing Popeye muscles, waved to them from behind the grill. "Matt Malloy. They let you off the ranch in the middle of the day? You got a broken arm or something?"

"Just had to pick up some supplies for Yancy." He cupped a hand to his mouth. "What's the special, Clay?"

"Pork sausage. Pulled pork sandwiches. And for the hungry—"

"And the brave," one of the cowboys at the bar shouted, to a chorus of raucous laughter.

"—there's stuffed pork chops."

"What's in the stuffing, Clay?" another customer shouted.

"I call it my mystery stuffing."

"That's why you've got to be brave to order it," the first cowboy added, to another round of laughter.

Matt joined in the laughter before turning to Vanessa. "Want to be brave, or do you want the pulled pork sandwich?"

"Pulled pork."

"And to drink?"

She shrugged. "Whatever you're having."

He had to shout their order to be heard above the noise. "Two longnecks, and two pulled pork sandwiches, Clay."

"Got it. Grab a table. I'll be right there." The old man bent to his grill.

Matt led the way through the haze of smoke to a table in the rear of the room where the music wasn't as loud.

A short time later the owner hurried over with their order.

"Clay Olmsted, I'd like you to meet Burke's niece, Van Cowley."

"Nice to meet you, Van." He set down two beers and two plates loaded with sandwiches and curly fries, as well as a big bowl of coleslaw. "Didn't know Burke had any kin. Never heard him talk about family in all the years I've known him."

"Well, I guess he never figured I'd come all this way to visit."

Clay straightened. "Where you from, Van?"

"Chica—"

Matt's voice drowned her out. "Saint Louis."

The old man looked from one to the other. "Never been there. To either place." As he ambled away, Vanessa lowered her head and stared hard at the table. "Sorry. This just isn't working."

Matt lay a hand over hers. "Hey. At least you know how to think on your feet. But"—he paused to bite back his grin"Vanilla?"

She was shaking her head. "See? I'm no good at lying." She tried to pull her hand away.

He tightened his grasp. This time his laugh broke free. "Well, I have to say Vanilla Cowley is a stretch. But since you dug that hole, you're just going to have to stand in it."

She grinned. "Such a stupid name. But it was the first thing that came to mind."

"It works. You're doing just fine." His voice deepened even while his smile grew. "And you're looking just fine, too."

"You don't think it's too much. I mean the boots, the jacket, the . . . hat?"

"It's perfect. You're perfect."

"I wasn't sure about the hat. But once I put it on, it just felt right."

He picked up his beer and took a long pull, to keep himself from gushing. The truth was, that first glimpse of her back in the shop had all the breath backing up in his throat. In the course of a couple of hours she'd gone from cool, polished city lawyer to the most gorgeous country girl he'd ever seen. She wasn't just perfect. She was breathtaking.

She slanted him a catlike look. "I enjoyed spending your money."

He laughed out loud. "I just bet you did."

"I actually bought more than I needed. To get you back for laughing at me."

She bit into her sandwich, then shot him a look of amazement. "This is good."

"Why wouldn't it be?"

"I thought, the way those men were teasing, that the food would be horrible."

"Clay's a good cook. Maybe not as good as Yancy, but he knows his way around pork."

"Of course. The Pig Sty. I guess I forgot about that." She looked around at the gleaming floor and tables and chairs. "I guess with a name like that, I expected it to be filthy, and the food to be barely tolerable."

"Don't let a name fool you."

"This from the man who just gave me a new identity."

He looked around, relieved that nobody was near enough to overhear them. "You might want to keep that to yourself."

"Right." She sipped her beer and polished off the rest of her sandwich. "Vanilla Cowley knows how to keep secrets."

CHAPTER NINE

Matt walked to the counter to pay their bill.

Clay Olmsted rang it up and handed Matt his change before saying to the young woman beside him, "Bye, Van. Be sure and say hello to your uncle."

"My...?" She caught herself. "Yes. Uncle Burke. I'll do that. The pulled pork sandwich was the best."

The old man brightened. "Next time you're here, try the stuffed pork chops."

One of the regulars at the bar called out, "That's why we call him Colonel Clay. His secret ingredient is in the stuffing."

To a chorus of laughter, Matt and Vanessa walked outside.

Before crossing the street Matt caught her hand. At the truck he held the passenger door while she settled inside before circling around to climb up to the driver's side.

As they pulled away, a car fell into line some distance

behind them, leisurely trailing along Main Street until they left town and turned onto the interstate.

Vanessa swiveled her head, trying to take in all the things she'd missed on their way here.

"Oh, look at those hills in the distance."

Matt followed her direction, trying to see everything through her eyes.

"There's so much space here. I bet there are more cattle than people."

He nodded. "You'd be right about that."

"And it's all so clean and fresh and pretty. No streetlights. No throngs of pedestrians. No office buildings, or smoke from buses, or horns honking."

"Just remember you said all that when you complain about no fast food places, or easy transportation when you need a prescription for pain, or directions to the nearest hospital when a friend is about to deliver a baby."

She laughed. "Okay. Point taken. I'm sure there are plenty of drawbacks to living so far from civilization. But just allow me my fantasies for a little while longer, will you? It's called trying to make the best of a situation."

"And you are." He laid a hand over hers. "I know this isn't easy for you."

When she clasped her hands in her lap, he glanced in the rearview mirror. Though the car remained far behind them, he had an uneasy feeling. "How would you like to make a detour on the way back?"

She shrugged. "You're the driver."

"Okay." He slowed the truck before turning the wheel.

Though there were no exits, he merely left the highway and started across a bumpy stretch of field toward a distant hill.

The vehicle that had been trailing them stopped, but didn't follow.

"What's up here?" Vanessa was straining to see beyond the high ground.

Matt drove up and over the incline, cutting off their view of the highway. He continued on until they came to a swollen stream that was overflowing its banks.

He parked and stepped out before speaking to the sheriff on his cell phone. Scant minutes later he took Vanessa's hand and led her to a small promontory overlooking the water.

"This is Malloy Creek."

She turned to him. "You actually have a creek named for your family?"

He nodded. "My great-great-grandfather, the original Francis Xavier Malloy, came here from Ireland and cleared this land. When the state was charting its landmarks and asked the name of this creek, he decided to name it for himself."

Matt pointed to the hills beyond. "In the middle of summer, this will be nothing more than a small stream. But right now, with all the snow melting high in the hills, it's a gusher. Old Francis X. realized there was enough runoff to irrigate these fields. This was where his first herd of cattle grazed, and later, when he moved them to higher ground, this was where he planted enough crops to see him through the winter. According to legend, the minute he saw this place, he thought of the green fields of Ireland, and knew his future lay right here."

"That's nice." She shielded the sun from her eyes as she peered around. "I guess to someone far from home, it would be comforting to feel something familiar."

"Yeah." Matt held his silence and allowed her to drink in the view, knowing she was seeking her own comfort in a strange place.

Nearly an hour later they returned to the truck and headed for the ranch.

Matt noted that the car that had been trailing them was nowhere to be seen.

He'd reported its presence to Sheriff Graystoke, who had assured him it would be checked out immediately.

It could turn out to be a real threat, or it could mean that he was seeing danger where none existed. The sheriff had suggested another possible explanation for that car. It could be someone sent by the Chicago police to investigate the Malloy family.

Whatever the reason, he recognized a duty to report anything that seemed out of place. He had no intention of ignoring something that could prove to be a real danger.

He felt responsible for the woman entrusted to his family's care. Though neither of them had asked for this, he felt it was his job to keep Vanessa Kettering safe until she was able to return to the life she'd left.

After putting away all the things she'd bought in town, Vanessa stepped into the kitchen to find Yancy and Nelson sharing coffee at the big wooden table, their heads bent close in quiet conversation.

The both looked up as she entered.

"Sorry." She hesitated. "I didn't mean to interrupt anything."

"You didn't." Nelson waved her close. "We're talking about an unsolved Hollywood mystery from the fifties."

Yancy produced a thick hardcover book with a lurid

cover depicting a bloody female draped over the arm of a blood-soaked sofa. "Natasha Leonid. She was a legend in the thirties and forties." Yancy flushed. "I'm afraid Hollywood scandals are my passion. I love reading about them. I especially love the unsolved murders. And since Nelson lived through a lot of them, he knew the people involved."

Vanessa turned to Nelson. "Matt told me who you are. The minute I heard your name, I knew of you. What an exciting life you've led."

The old man puffed up his chest, obviously enjoying the moment.

Yancy motioned toward the coffeepot. "Would you like some?"

Vanessa shook her head. "Matt and I had lunch in town. I promised him I'd join him when I put my things away."

"He and the others are out in the barn." Yancy pointed toward the back door. "The first barn is for equipment. The second is where some of the horses or farm animals in need of attention are stabled." He glanced at her new clothes. "You look pretty, Nessa. You shouldn't go out there. You wouldn't want to get your new duds all dirty."

"These are work clothes, Yancy." She couldn't help grinning. "Though I can't imagine what kind of work I'll be doing."

Nelson set aside his cup. "You might want to stay here and join us for coffee. I'm not sure a big-city lawyer like yourself is ready to join the Malloy ranchers in their favorite pastime."

"I promised myself I'd earn my keep here."

"Then at least find a pair of rubber boots that fit you before you walk into the barn."

"If you say so." She turned toward the mudroom and exchanged her new leather boots for a pair of cracked rubber ones. As she opened the door she called over her shoulder, "What can be so hard about caring for a couple of farm animals? I think this could be fun."

The two men exchanged a look. And as the door closed behind her, they burst into peals of laughter.

Taking a last deep breath, Vanessa stepped from sunshine into the cavernous interior and paused to allow her eyes to adjust to the gloom. The first thing that assaulted her was the smell. It was an outhouse, only magnified a thousand times. And then there were the sounds of men's voices raised in laughter, bouncing off the walls.

Seeing her in the doorway, the voices stilled.

Luke called, "Hey. You're late."

"Late?"

"Yeah. Matt said you were putting away your gear. So we decided to work a little slower than usual so you wouldn't miss out on all the fun."

Getting into the spirit of teasing, Reed pointed to a wall of ranch implements hanging on hooks. "Grab some gloves and join us."

"Okay." Vanessa crossed to where Matt was standing. "Where do I find gloves?"

"Here." He reached into his back pocket and handed her a pair of well-worn leather gloves. "You'll need these."

She slipped them on and followed him to a stall, where Reed was knee-deep in wet, smelly straw.

"This is what the horses leave behind. It's part of a rancher's daily routine. We have to fork up the old straw and spread clean. Since you need to start slowly, we'll do the forking and leave the spreading to you."

"I thought..." She stopped to look around the empty stalls. "Where are the horses and sick animals?"

"No sick animals at the moment. But we turned the horses into the corral so we can get our work done in here." Matt led her toward a stall that had recently been cleaned and showed her how to spread fresh straw.

While she bent to her task, the three brothers cleaned the rest of the stalls, keeping up a steady stream of conversation and jokes, often at their own expense.

"So." Reed paused to rest his hands atop his pitchfork while he eyed Luke. "I heard your phone ringing around midnight. Who called?"

His brother shrugged. "Nobody."

"Is this the same nobody who said she never wanted to see you again?"

Instead of a reply, Luke gripped the handles of the wagon. "This is pretty full. I'll be right back."

Vanessa couldn't help staring at he shoved the overloaded wagon through the doors as if it weighed nothing. She'd expected his brothers to lend a hand.

He returned a short time later with the empty wagon, only to pick up his pitchfork and continue on as before without a word.

Matt joined in where his younger brother had left off. "You're not going to evade our questions, bro. So why did this nobody phone you if she never wanted to see you again?"

Luke never missed a beat as he lifted a heavy load and

deposited it in the wagon. "She didn't say anything about never 'speaking' to me again."

Matt and Reed exchanged a look before Matt deadpanned, "So when are you and nobody getting together again?"

"She wants me to join her and some friends at Clay's Pig Sty Friday night. And she said to bring Reed along."

Reed paused. "So she can look at me instead of you? Not that I don't understand," he added, "since I'm a whole lot better looking."

"She's invited some friends. One of them is Carrie."

Reed snorted. "If Carrie Riddle was standing in the doorway of our barn right this minute, wearing nothing but her birthday suit, I wouldn't bother to turn and give her a look."

Luke gave a laugh. "Oh, you'd look, bro. You may try to pass yourself off as a saint in front of our guest, but I know you better'n that. You'd look."

Matt and Vanessa stood back, enjoying the banter.

"Okay. So I'd look. Hell, I'm a guy. But that's as far as it goes. I'm not interested."

"You feeling sick?" Luke touched a hand to his brother's forehead. "Carrie Riddle's had the hots for you since she was fifteen. I'm not asking you to marry her. But you could at least go to town with me Friday night."

Matt shook his head. "I hate to be the bearer of bad news, but Burke is expecting both of you to spend this weekend up on the South Ridge helping him and Colin with the herd."

Luke turned to stare at his brother. "Then I guess you'll get your wish."

Reed looked puzzled.

"I think Carrie was planning on showing you her birthday suit. Now you won't have to worry about ignoring her."

Reed turned to Luke. "Well, that will solve your problem about your 'nobody.' She won't have to worry about seeing you again."

"There's always next week."

Matt glanced at Vanessa in time to see her convulsed in laughter. He was laughing as he ambled over. She kept her voice low. "Do they go on like this all the time?"

"Endlessly."

She shook her head. "And I thought nothing exciting ever happens in a small town."

Overhearing her, Reed called, "There should probably be a billboard just outside of town. Horny cowboys. Women in birthday suits. You just never know what you'll discover in Glacier Ridge, Montana."

Still laughing, Matt nodded toward the last cleaned stall. "Come on. I'll give you a hand and we can let these two get on with their fantasies."

"You mean Nobody and Birthday Suit don't really exist?"

"Oh, they're real." Luke hung his pitchfork on a hook before peeling off his work gloves. "But Friday night is big business in Clay's Pig Sty for every wrangler who gets a paycheck. And that means that every female old enough to drink, and some who ought to be home doing schoolwork, will be helping them spend it. Frankly, I'd rather muck stalls on a Friday night than have to head to town. So"—he turned to Matt—"herding cattle on the South Ridge sounds about perfect to me."

Matt watched Reed follow suit, hanging up his pitchfork before heading toward the open doorway of the barn. "You okay with the weekend plans?"

Reed shot him a quick grin. "Nobody's gonna miss me."

"I'll just bet she will."

They were still chuckling as they ambled out.

CHAPTER TEN

Matt led the way to the corral, where the horses were grazing. Leaning on the fence, he turned to Vanessa. "Do you ride?"

She nodded. "From the age of eight until I was twelve, I was horse crazy. I pestered my parents until they allowed me to take jumping lessons at a suburban hunt club. I know they were terrified that I'd be hurt, and they couldn't understand why I was so in love with horses, but they couldn't stand to see me pout, so they gave in."

"I bet you were great at pouting."

She chuckled. "It's an art form that most girls learn. Boys"—she shrugged—"not so much. It just isn't attractive on a boy. But I was a champion pouter. I wore down my poor parents until they would have rather taken a sharp stick to the eye than see me pout another day."

They laughed. Matt glanced skyward. "I think it's too

late to ride today, but if you want, we could take a couple of horses into the hills tomorrow."

She nodded. "I'd like that."

"It's a deal, as long as the weather cooperates." He turned toward the house. "We'd better clean up before supper."

Vanessa looked down at her dung-covered boots, grateful that Yancy and Nelson had urged her to leave her new ones behind. And then she realized that those two had known exactly what kind of work she'd be doing in the barn.

Those two sly old men. And they hadn't given her a word of warning. She laughed at herself as she walked beside Matt.

He glanced over. "What so funny?"

"Me. I really didn't have a clue what ranching was like. I guess I still don't."

"Don't beat yourself up over it. How could a Chicago lawyer know what the typical day is like on a ranch in Montana? Besides, there really is no typical day. Ranching is like bungee jumping. Every morning you take a leap of faith and expect that wherever you manage to land, at least you'll land on your feet."

"And if you land on your head? Then what?"

He held the back door and allowed her to precede him. "You get through your day while nursing a headache."

"Great. I'll try to land on my feet."

"I'd put money on that. You strike me as a woman who always lands on her feet." He eased off his boots and headed toward the oversized sink.

Vanessa did the same and watched as he lathered up to his elbows, then placed his hands under the faucet. The water poured out in a steady stream.

"A hands-free sink. I'm impressed."

He winked. "Maybe we knew a city lawyer was coming, and we didn't want to look like yokels."

She washed and reached for a thick white towel from a stack on the shelf above them. "Or maybe the city lawyer needs to alter her mental image of Montana ranchers."

He smiled. "Actually you can thank Reed for this, and for dozens of other New Age gadgets. He's our tech nerd. Reed's favorite hobby is browsing through catalogs of all the latest equipment. He just informed us that he's thinking of ordering a drone."

She turned to him. "A drone? What for?"

He shrugged. "To keep track of things. With a spread this size, we usually do flyovers with one of our planes to check on the herds every week or so."

Vanessa shook her head. "A drone. Who'd have thought?"

As they stepped into the kitchen, Yancy looked up from the oven. "Well, did you get a chance to do a little work, Nessa?"

She nodded. "I'm grateful that you suggested those rubber boots."

"Got a taste of mucking stalls, did you?"

"I did. And I got to step in a lot of yucky straw and other things too disgusting to mention."

The old cook grinned. "Consider that your ranch baptism."

"Are you saying it will get easier after that?"

"Not at all. But next time you volunteer, you'll be prepared for the worst." He stirred something on the stove. "Dinner in an hour."

"Just enough time for a long, hot shower," Matt muttered.

"That sounds heavenly." She trailed Matt to the stairway.

Once in her room she stripped off her filthy clothes, which had been brand-new just hours earlier, and stood beneath a hot spray, sighing with pure pleasure.

An hour later, dressed in clean denims and a simple cotton shirt the color of raspberries, her hair flowing long and loose below her shoulders, she made her way downstairs and followed the sound of voices and laughter to the kitchen.

While Yancy put the finishing touches on the meal, the rest of the family was gathered around a big, open fireplace on the far side of the kitchen. Their comfortable chairs had been arranged in a semicircle to take advantage of both the fire and the amazing view of the sun setting on the peaks of the hills in the distance.

"...comes with an instruction book as thick as a Bible." Reed was gesturing with his longneck. "I can't wait to get my hands on it."

"The instruction book or the drone?" Luke shot a grin at the others, who were enjoying Reed's obvious excitement.

"Both."

Matt beckoned Vanessa over. He pointed to a tray on the counter, holding an array of bottles and glasses. "What would you like to drink before we eat?"

She noted the opened bottle of pinot grigio, and the glass in Gracie's hand. "I think I'll try that."

Matt handed her a stem glass of pale, chilled wine.

"So when do we get to see this glorious new toy?" Frank asked.

"It might take a while. First I have to look into any rules and regulations that might bar its use in Montana."

Nelson frowned. "Rules and regulations. In my day..."

Grace shot him a look that had him pausing.

"The company guaranteed delivery by the end of the month." Reed turned to his brothers. "But don't even think about using it until I get a chance to read through the manual. I don't want anyone messing with it and screwing up the controls."

Matt winked at Vanessa and said in an aside, "Our technonerd is at it again."

Overhearing, Luke added, "I know a couple of women at Clay's Pig Sty who wish Reed could get as excited about seeing them on Friday night as he does about his gadgets."

"It doesn't matter what they think." Colin looked at his nephews. "You're both spending the weekend up in the hills with the herd."

Reed finished his beer. "Actually, I prefer the company of cattle to anything I'd find at Clay's."

"There's something twisted in that mind of yours, bro." Luke tipped up his longneck just as Yancy set a salad bowl and a cruet of his homemade dressing in the center of the table.

"Dinner's ready." Yancy sliced roast beef on a platter before setting it aside.

Nelson finished his martini and nibbled the olive before pushing out of the big, overstuffed chair he'd claimed by the fire. He strolled to his usual spot at one end of the table. "I hope you made your au gratin potatoes to go with that fine beef, Yancy."

"I did, Great One." Yancy set a casserole dish on the table.

Vanessa found herself smiling at his use of the old gentleman's nickname. As Matt had said, "Great One" suited Nelson LaRou perfectly. From his tailored pants and shirt to the apricot silk ascot that would look over the top on any other man, he could only be called great. The Great One.

Her smile grew when Frank and Grace held hands as they crossed the room. Frank held her chair as she took her seat. Then he settled himself at the head of the table.

Matt put a hand beneath Vanessa's elbow, leading her toward the table as the rest of them took their places.

Burke sat beside Colin, while Yancy moved back and forth from the stove to the table, handing out platters of roast beef, a dish of steamed vegetables, and a basket of crusty bread still warm from the oven.

As they helped themselves before passing the dishes around, Vanessa couldn't believe the amount of food. But then, they had all engaged in hard, physical labor the entire day.

"Your roast beef is done to perfection, Yancy." Nelson reached for the casserole. "And your au gratin potatoes"— he touched thumb and finger to his lips—"sublime."

"And this bread." Grace looked over at the cook. "You've added something."

"Asiago. And just a bit of herbs."

"It's wonderful."

Yancy beamed. He turned to Colin. "That rainstorm may have done us a favor. Most of the snow disappeared just in time for calving."

Colin nodded. "But now we have the mud to contend with. I just hope we get a few mild weeks and lots of sunshine to dry up the ground before they drop their calves."

Vanessa was listening with interest. "The cows don't give birth in the barns?"

Matt shook his head. "That might work on a small spread. Our herds number in the thousands. We've got teams of wranglers with each herd, assisting with difficult births. And for a first-time mother, there are plenty of those. But for those days immediately following the birth, the cow and her calf are vulnerable to everything nature can throw at them. Snowstorms. Predators."

"Are they in enclosures?"

"They're on open range."

"How can you possibly keep them all safe?"

"We can't. But we do our best. We post wranglers to ride the perimeter of the herds through the night. That helps to discourage predators. But a few always manage to slip past and snatch a newborn. Don't forget. Hunger makes them bold."

She tried not to shiver at the image that came to mind. A hungry wolf dragging a bleeding newborn into the brush, where others waited for a feast. And then a cow, heavy with milk, waiting for a calf that would never return.

This wasn't what she wanted to think about over such a wonderful meal.

Later, as the conversation swirled around her, Vanessa looked at her empty plate. Even though her appetite had been curbed by her thoughts, she'd managed to eat more in one sitting than she would usually consume in two or three days.

Grace smiled at her family around the table. "How about dessert in the family room?"

"Sounds perfect." Frank pushed back his chair and offered his arm to his wife.

The others followed them past a formal dining room and into a large room dominated on one wall by a huge stone fireplace. Across the room were floor-to-ceiling windows looking out at rolling hills that only days ago were covered in snow. Now, after that storm, they were already showing hints of spring green.

As they settled into comfortable chairs and sofas, Yancy passed around cups of steaming coffee before cutting into a chocolate cake layered with cherry filling and topped with cherry-vanilla ice cream.

When Vanessa bit into it, she couldn't help sighing. "Oh, Yancy, I don't think I've ever tasted anything better."

"Thank you, Nessa." He was beaming as he took a seat by the fire and helped himself to dessert.

"I can't remember the last time I ate this much at one time," she said with a laugh.

"Nothing like a good meal after a day of ranch chores." Luke helped himself to a second slice topped with more ice cream.

"Well, Vanessa." Grace sipped her coffee. "Now that you've seen our town, what do you think?"

"It's a pretty little town. I enjoyed myself. Just as Matt promised, I found everything I needed at Anything Goes. And we had a great lunch at Clay's ... saloon."

"Go ahead," Reed teased. "You can say Pig Sty."

Everyone laughed.

"All right. Lunch at Clay's Pig Sty was surprisingly good."

"But not as good as dinner, right?" Yancy winked at Reed.

"Of course not. After a meal like this, Clay would have to become a gourmet chef to top it."

Again, the cook beamed at her praise.

Luke shot a knowing smile at Reed. "And now that you've become…intimately involved with our barns, how would you rate them?"

Amid much laughter she kept a perfectly straight face. "Really big. Really stinky. And the hardest work I've done in years. But I will admit that when I was young, I took jumping lessons, and after every class I was required to groom my horse and hose down her stall, as well. I would rate hosing as a much easier manner of hygiene than shoveling."

"So hosing has your vote?" Reed looked around at the others.

"Definitely."

Luke slapped a hand to his forehead. "Why didn't you think about putting drains in every stall when you built that barn, Grandpop? Think of all the work you could have saved us."

Frank nodded. "In fact, I'm thinking that very thing. Technonerd, is there a solution to our problem of no drains?"

Reed pretended to think before saying solemnly, "Just think of all the manure we'd waste, putting it down the drain. I vote that we get more willing workers."

"And where do we get these workers?"

Reed looked pointedly at Colin. "I do believe it's your duty to find a wife and begin producing your share of workers, Uncle."

Colin nearly choked on his coffee while the others laughed.

Luke joined in the fun. "I think you should skip the hills this weekend and spend your time at the Pig Sty. I've heard any number of women say they'd like to have Colin Malloy's baby."

Colin said with a straight face, "I just may take you up on this and go wife hunting at the Pig Sty. I'm sure that would make my family proud."

The teasing continued until the fire had burned to embers.

With a yawn, Grace set aside her empty cup. "I don't know about the rest of you, but I need my sleep. And tonight, it's in a real bed. I love trailing my mustangs in the wilderness, but after a while, I start missing my bed."

"And the husband who keeps your feet warm," Frank added.

One by one the others got to their feet and called good night before taking to the stairs.

Grace paused. "Vanessa, if there's anything at all that you want or need, please let us know. I hope you'll be comfortable while you're here."

"Thank you, Mrs. . . ."

"Gracie," the older woman prompted.

"Thank you, Gracie. I really appreciate all that you're doing for me."

Vanessa stood and thanked Yancy again for the lovely dinner before calling good night to the others.

Matt put a hand under her elbow as they walked up the stairs. At her door he paused, and she saw the same look in his eyes that she'd seen in the cabin, just before he'd so shockingly kissed her.

She couldn't control the sudden pounding of her heart.

"Good night . . ." His hand was on her shoulder. Just the lightest touch, but she could feel it clear to her toes.

His head was lowering, and she knew with absolute certainty that he was going to kiss her.

She stood perfectly still, waiting. Wanting. Yearning.

Matt's phone rang.

With a muttered oath he retrieved his cell phone from his pocket and looked at the ID before saying, "Sorry. Bad timing. But I have to take this."

"Of course." Stung by the way the mood had been shattered, her tone was sharper than she'd intended. "I wouldn't want to intrude on your personal life."

Vanessa turned away and opened her bedroom door.

Just then she heard Matt say, "Yes, Sheriff."

She paused and saw the frown that furrowed his brow.

Putting a hand on his arm she whispered, "If that's about me, I'd like to hear."

He touched the Speaker button, and together they both heard the sheriff say, "Our state boys are trying to get a verification from the Chicago PD on that vehicle you saw tailing you today."

Vanessa's head came up sharply and she stared pointedly at Matt.

"Captain McBride suggested that it was probably sent by the Chicago PD to keep an eye on your family until they've had a chance to check you out."

Matt's tone was low with anger. "First of all, if this is a sample of Chicago's finest, they get a failing grade. If I could spot their car following my truck, they're amateurs. And second, the Chicago PD has had hours to get back to you on this, Eugene. I don't like this one bit."

The sheriff's tone was rough. "I'm with you on this, Matt. I'm really sorry. You did everything right, but they're letting it slide on their end."

"Or they think we're a bunch of hicks and they don't need to be invisible."

"That could be." A hint of weariness crept into the sheriff's voice. "As soon as we get a response from Chicago, I'll pass it along to you. In the meantime, stay alert to anything."

"Yeah. 'Night."

As Matt slid his cell phone into his pocket, he heard a hiss of anger from the woman beside him.

Looking into Vanessa's eyes, which were dark with fury, he braced himself for the storm he could see coming.

CHAPTER ELEVEN

So that was the reason for the sudden romantic side trip this afternoon?"

"Romantic side trip?" Matt was thrown off stride.

"When you showed me that amazing creek named after your ancestor. At the time, I couldn't decide if you wanted to get me alone, or if you were trying to impress me. And now I realize you just wanted to play hide-and-seek with the car behind us. And you never bothered to mention it to me?"

"I didn't want you to be alarmed until I knew whether or not it was a threat."

"So you just decided to pat me on the head. 'Don't you worry your itty-bitty mind, little lady. I'm here to protect you.'"

"It wasn't like that—"

"It *was* like that. This is my life. My safety we're talking about. I don't want to be kept in the dark while my big, fierce protector takes charge."

"Look, I was wrong. I made a mistake in judgment—"

"You bet you did." She jammed a finger in his chest. "I won't be treated like some helpless female who's going to fall apart at the first hint of danger. We're talking about someone who's made serious threats against me. I have the right to know everything that's going on, if I'm going to make the choices that help me stay alive."

"You're right—"

"And furthermore, if you ever dare to keep such a thing from me again—"

He caught her finger and deliberately lowered it from his chest. "I get it."

"I hope you mean that."

The slight tremble in her voice sounded a warning. Realizing that she was close to tears, Matt went from angry to frustrated and then to sudden alarm that she would cry in front of him. "Look. I told you I get it."

"You'd better, because..." She blinked, then blinked again, furiously. "I can take care of mys—"

Matt froze. No. Not tears. He'd rather face an angry drunk in the saloon, or a blizzard up in the hills, without any shelter or gear, than face a single tear from a woman's eyes. Especially this woman, who was fighting so desperately to be strong.

But it was too late. Moisture slid from beneath her tightly closed lids and rolled down her cheeks.

She lifted a fist to her face and angrily swiped at them, but they just fell harder, faster.

She started to turn away. "I'm so furious right now..."

Oh hell. Though the last thing he wanted to do was

touch her, he had no choice. "Wait. Listen." He turned her into his arms and could feel the front of his shirt growing damp. "It's all right to cry..."

She tried to push away. "I am not crying—"

"Of course not. I get it." He pressed his lips to the hair at her temple. "But sometimes it's okay to just let it all out."

"I'm just so angry. You had no right—"

"I didn't. And you have every right to be mad."

He waited until the waterworks stopped before reaching into his pocket and handing her his handkerchief.

She wouldn't look at him as she blew her nose and wiped the last of the tears from her cheeks. When she finally stepped back he closed his hands over her upper arms, holding her when she tried to turn away. "Nessa, I'm really sorry. I overstepped my bounds. Blame it on my genes. All the Malloys inherited them. We're really vain enough or stupid enough to believe we have the power and the muscle and the will to rule the world. I guess we're legends in our own minds."

She was silent for so long, he worried that he'd only made things worse by trying to make a joke.

She lifted her head. Though her eyes were still red and puffy, there was a glint of something in them. Amusement? Understanding?

"Okay. I guess I overreacted. And that's something in my genes."

He tried for a smile. "Am I forgiven?"

She took in a deep breath. "As long as you promise you'll never do it again."

"Cross my heart."

She started to turn away, then turned back, a hint of

a smile touching her lips. "Sorry about the tears. I really hate crying."

"I get it. I'm not too fond of seeing them."

She stepped into her room. "Good night, Matt."

"Good night, Nessa."

He waited until she closed her door before moving on to his own room. Once there he crossed to the wall of windows to stare at the darkened hills in the distance.

Damned independent female.

And wasn't she damned gorgeous, even when she was mad?

Especially when she was mad.

If ever he'd wanted to kiss her, it was then. But with that temper, she'd have cut out his heart and fed it to the wolves.

He was grinning as he undressed. Not a bad way to die.

Vanessa showered and dressed in her new denims and a lemon-yellow T-shirt. Tucking her pant legs into leather boots, she grabbed up her denim jacket and headed down the stairs.

In the kitchen, Frank and Gracie were sipping coffee in front of the fireplace, while Yancy was busy at the stove.

She glanced around. "Are we the first ones up?"

Yancy shook his head. "The last. Luke, Reed, and Colin left at dawn to head to the South Ridge."

"The Great One?" Just saying that name had her smiling.

"Heading to town with Burke. His annual physical at the clinic. He'll be there most of the day."

"And Matt?" It galled her to have to ask, but she felt connected somehow to him, and found herself hoping he hadn't gone along with the others.

"In the barn. Tackling morning chores. He'll be in soon."

She turned away. "Maybe I'll give him a hand."

Yancy indicated a tray of mugs and glasses, along with a carafe and a tall pitcher on the counter. "Suit yourself. But you might want to help yourself to coffee and juice first."

"Thank you." She poured herself a glass of orange juice and tasted before looking over at him. "Did you make this fresh?"

He shrugged. "Is there any other way?"

"I buy mine by the half gallon at the store."

He gave a mock shudder.

Gracie beckoned her over. "How did you sleep, Nessa?"

"Very well, thanks." A lie. She'd tossed and turned for hours after that little scene with Matt. It still irritated her that he'd kept secret the fact that he'd thought they were being followed. And then, after wrestling with the lingering anger, she'd had to deal with the sinking feeling that DePietro's people could already know where she was staying. Not a good night. But she would never admit it to these good people.

"I want to thank you again for making me feel so welcome. It can't be easy to have a stranger in your house."

Frank linked his fingers with Gracie's and shot her a blazing smile. "We love having you, Nessa. Don't we, Gracie Girl?"

"Indeed. I told Frankie last night that it's rather nice for me to have another woman around. I've been living with all these men for so long now, it's really pleasant to hear a woman's voice in the mix."

They looked over as the back door opened and Matt trudged into the mudroom, kicking off his boots, tossing his gloves on a shelf, and hanging his hat on a hook on the wall.

They could hear the water flowing before he finally stepped into the kitchen. He greeted his grandparents, while his gaze remained steady on Vanessa.

"'Morning." He stayed where he was.

"Good morning. I'm sorry I'm too late to lend a hand with the mucking."

He smiled then, as he realized this was her way of saying that all was forgiven. "You were going to help?"

"That was the plan. But then I got sidetracked with Frank and Gracie."

"There'll be other mornings." He turned toward the stairs. "I'll be down in half an hour."

"Make it fifteen minutes," Yancy called. "Breakfast is almost ready."

Vanessa watched until Matt disappeared up the stairs. When she turned, both Frank and Gracie were staring at her.

She busied herself at the counter, pouring a cup of coffee. Then she turned to them. "Would you like more?"

Frank held out his cup and she crossed to him, topping off his cup and then Gracie's. And still the two were looking at her so steadily, she was grateful to turn away and replace the carafe on the counter. She was even more grateful that the two of them began carrying on a conversation, allowing her to relax.

Matt was as good as his word, strolling into the kitchen just as Yancy was setting a stack of pancakes in the center of the table.

He took a seat beside Vanessa and held a platter of ham and eggs toward her while she filled her plate. "I heard the caravan leaving around five. They'll be up on Eagle's Ridge by now."

Frank nodded. "A good day for it, too. I was afraid we might get another storm, but it blew over around midnight, and that sunshine is just what we need."

He held the plate of pancakes while Gracie helped herself.

She ladled warm maple syrup with walnuts and blueberries over the stack. After her first bite she smiled at the cook. "Yancy, you always know just what I'm craving after a trip to the hills."

"You're just like your daddy. The Great One loves his cookies. You love your walnut-and-blueberry pancakes."

Frank closed a hand over hers. "If you'd like the moon to go with it, just say the word, Gracie Girl."

Her smile bloomed. "And you'd fetch it, wouldn't you?"

"You know I would."

Vanessa felt a trickle of warmth around her heart. These two sweet people were so in love it felt like an invasion of privacy to be allowed to watch and listen.

When they'd finished breakfast, Frank held Gracie's chair. "Ready to head into town, Gracie Girl?"

"I am." Hand-in-hand they turned to Matt and Vanessa. "We're off to Glacier Ridge," Gracie announced.

Matt set down his cup. "Any reason in particular?"

"Just a date with my girl." Frank winked at his wife before turning to Yancy. "We'll probably be home by supper time, but if we're late, don't wait for us."

They left, still holding hands.

Matt glanced at Vanessa. "Ready to take the horses for a run?"

"Maybe not a run. But I wouldn't mind a nice, slow canter across the field."

"Let's do it." He stood. "Great breakfast, Yancy. If anyone asks, we'll be up in the pasture."

"You've got a good day for it." Yancy was already clearing the table as Matt and Vanessa made their way toward the corral.

Matt left Vanessa standing in the sunlight, watching the horses play in a fenced pasture. Minutes later he led two saddled horses from the barn.

"This is Ginger." He held the reins while Vanessa pulled herself into the saddle of a palomino mare with a flaxen mane and tail.

She accepted the reins while he mounted old Beau. Then she leaned over her horse's head to run a hand along her silken mane. "Ginger is beautiful."

Matt nodded. "She's one of Gracie's favorites. You'll need to keep control. She likes to have her head."

"A female with an attitude." Vanessa laughed. "No wonder I already like her."

As they started across the back field, Matt pointed toward a windswept parcel of land surrounded by a wrought-iron fence. "That's our family plot."

Nessa's eyes widened. "Your own private cemetery?"

He laughed at her tone. "Yeah. It's not so unusual. This is where they lived. This is where they should be allowed to spend eternity."

They dismounted, and Matt opened a pretty gate before leading her inside the enclosure. The grave markers were simple stones bearing the names of family members, their birth and death dates clearly etched.

Matt paused beside a double marker. "These are my parents."

Reading their names, and the same date of death, sent a tiny shiver along her spine. "They were so young."

Matt nodded. "The Great One will never be persuaded it was an accident. He's convinced there was a second set of tracks in the snow when he first went to record the scene on film. It's the director in him," Matt explained as she arched her brow. "But with so many other vehicles arriving so quickly, it couldn't be proven. And we were all so stunned, we couldn't focus on anything except the fact that they were gone."

She touched his shoulder. "I'm sorry."

"Thanks." He took a moment to run his hand along the top of the stone before turning away.

Still feeling the warmth of her touch, he helped her into the saddle before pulling himself up on Beau. As they started out, Matt trailed behind for a moment, watching the way Vanessa handled her horse, until he was satisfied that they were a good fit.

What a pretty picture they made. Two blondes out for a morning ride. Nessa's hair streamed out behind her, and Ginger's mane and tail drifted on the breeze.

There were a million chores he ought to be seeing to. But he was happily ignoring all of them to show Vanessa Kettering around the ranch.

A female with an attitude. No wonder I already like her.

Her words played through his mind.

It occurred to him that he was enjoying the time spent with this woman way more than he'd expected to.

He would sort out the why of it another time. For now, he intended to simply enjoy the day, and the pleasant company.

He urged old Beau into a trot until they caught up with Ginger. Slowing his horse, they moved along at an easy gait until they reached the top of the hill.

They paused to look out over the undulating hills and valleys spread out around and below.

"Oh, Matt." Vanessa sighed. "This is like something in a movie. It's so vast and so breathtaking. How can your family ever possibly see to all of it?"

"It takes a lot of work."

"And to think that your ancestors did this on their own."

"Yeah." He took a moment to drink it in, and realized that it was only through the eyes of others that he truly understood just what his family had accomplished. "With so much acreage, it's a good thing we have planes."

"You mentioned them before. How many?"

"Just two small prop planes."

"Who pilots them?"

"We take turns."

She shook her head. "I guess I shouldn't be surprised. After all, this is Montana, and you're living and working on land the size of a city. But do all of you fly?"

He nodded. "All but Great One. Even Gram Gracie has her pilot's license, though she rarely needs it, since she usually flies with Grandpop."

She chuckled. "Is there anything you don't do?"

"I haven't parachuted out of a plane yet, but there's always tomorrow to try a new challenge. And don't mention it to Luke or Reed. Those two are always up for a dare."

"Are they as reckless as they appear?"

"Even more. I can't think of a single thing they haven't tried. If it's dangerous, they're first in line to go for it."

"And you?"

He shrugged and decided to change the subject. "See that creek down there?"

She nodded.

"I'll race you."

He saw the light that came into her eyes.

"You're on." She nudged Ginger into a run and set off at a furious pace.

Matt watched for a moment, enjoying the sight of her, leaning low over her mount, pale hair streaming behind her back.

He'd known instinctively she couldn't resist a challenge, which was why he'd issued this one.

He gave Beau his head, knowing the big horse was itching to run.

It was thrilling to feel all that unleashed power as the gelding stretched out its long legs and ate up the distance, easily passing the smaller, lighter mare.

As they raced past, he heard her rich, ripe oath.

"Same to you, ma'am," he drawled. "I'll see you at the finish line." He lifted his hat in a salute as he flashed by.

CHAPTER TWELVE

Ready for a break?"

Without waiting for her reply, Matt slid from his horse. Vanessa did the same. They'd been in the saddle for more than an hour.

She pressed a hand to the small of her back. "How far have we gone?"

Matt shrugged. "A couple of miles. Sorry, I forgot that it's been years since you rode a horse."

"I'm a bit rusty, but I'll be fine."

They walked along the ridge of a hill, and paused to drink in the view of hills carpeted with pale spring grass that had cropped up overnight, thanks to the rain. For as far as they could see, the higher elevations were darkened with cattle.

She stared out at the panoramic view. "Are your grandparents really on a date?"

"You bet." He chuckled at the look on her face. "Poor

Grandpop dies a little every time his Gracie goes off on one of her camera safaris."

"Then why does he let her go?"

"Let her go?" He turned to her with a look of surprise. "Did you just hear yourself? Those two have been a team for almost fifty years. But I've never known either of them to monitor the activities of the other. They're completely free, which is why their bond is so tight."

Her smile was slow in coming as his words sank in. "Oh, Matt. That's just beautiful. They seem so old-fashioned. But their attitude is really fresh and modern."

"Yeah. They're quite a pair." His smile said much more than his simple words.

"Where will they go on their date?"

He shrugged. "I know they'll make a stop at Anything Goes and stock up on whatever they need. Then probably some old-time movie at Flicks. That's the only theater in town. Half the movies they show were directed by the Great One. He's become Glacier Ridge's famous adopted son. And then Grandpop will want to stop for some apple pie along with all the gossip fit to repeat at D and B's Diner. Dot and Barb know everything that's happening almost before it happens. And they're only too happy to share everything they know with all their customers."

That had Vanessa laughing. "It must be such fun to be part of a small town where everybody knows everybody else."

"Not to mention everybody else's business."

"I guess that's the downside of a small town."

Matt held Ginger's reins. "Ready to get back in the saddle?"

"I am if you are." Vanessa pulled herself up before taking the reins.

When Matt was astride Beau, they moved out at a relaxed pace, while Matt took the time to point out places of interest.

"That creek is where I learned to swim."

"Did your father teach you?"

He shook his head. "It was an unintended consequence. I got tossed by a mustang and landed in the water. I probably swallowed half the creek, bobbing up and down like a cork, hollering for help, until I realized I was all alone, and if I wanted to live, I'd better swim to shore."

"Just like that?" She looked horrified. "You could have drowned and nobody would have ever known."

He laughed. "Yeah. That thought crossed my mind. And that's a really strong motivation to learn to swim. There's no better teacher than necessity."

She could only shake her head as she considered what a tragedy it could have been for his family. Still, this family seemed to thrive on adventure and danger.

What had Burke said? He'd put his money on Matt. Better than a fictional Superman. He was a real-life cowboy. One who'd apparently learned his lessons the hard way.

They meandered along the banks of the stream and paused to allow the horses to drink.

Vanessa slid from the saddle and perched on a fallen log. Matt did the same.

She looked over at him. "I love your private family cemetery. It must be nice to have all your ancestors so close, including your parents."

"Yeah. It feels right knowing they're here on the land

they all loved." He looked over. "How about you? Visit your mother's grave?"

She shook her head. "In the first year or two my dad and I went nearly every week. We'd sit there and cry and hold each other. I know it forged a bond between us that we hadn't had before."

"And now? Still visit her grave?"

"Not often. We both came to the realization that it was painful. Like pulling a scab off a wound that had just begun to heal. So we found new ways to honor Mom. My dad hosts an annual golf outing in her memory, and I serve as hostess at the awards dinner. All the profits go to finding a cure for breast cancer."

"That's nice. It had to be hard, though, losing your mother just when you were about to have so many firsts."

"Firsts?"

He shrugged. "I'm assuming first date, first high school dance. First kiss?"

She arched a brow. "Are you asking, or merely speculating?"

He laughed. "Sorry. I thought I was being subtle about getting into your personal life."

She joined in the laughter. "Actually it was all of the above. Not to mention first love. His name was Todd Brody, he played football, and all the girls had a crush on him. He asked me to senior prom, and I forced my poor dad to go shopping with me for a pink, sparkly gown, and Cinderella shoes that looked like they were made of glass. I even talked Dad into letting me wear my mother's necklace. Then, halfway through the dance, I found Todd in the girls' bathroom in a really hot liplock with Heidi, head cheerleader and prom queen."

"Wow. How'd you react to that?"

"It was pretty predictable. First I started to back out. All I wanted to do was hide somewhere. Then my temper took over and I confronted them, telling them both exactly how I really felt. And then I called my dad, crying hysterically, and begged him to come and get me." She shook her head, remembering. "Poor Dad thought I'd been attacked or something. He arrived with fire in his eyes, ready to defend his baby's honor. But by then I'd taken another look around and decided I wasn't going to run away. Instead, I'd make everyone know that I didn't care that much"—she snapped her fingers—"about Todd Brody and Heidi-boyfriend-stealer. So while my dad was watching, I found Heidi's date standing around looking lost, and I asked him to dance. About that same time Heidi had discovered that Todd had two left feet, but when she came looking for her date, he was too busy dancing with me to bother. And we were both having the time of our lives."

Vanessa started laughing as she remembered. "At the end of the dance, my dad drove me home and I told him what had happened. He said he was proud of me for not hiding or running away from the pain of embarrassment." She shook her head. "That's when he gave me what I will always think of as 'the lecture.' He reminded me that life is never fair. But no matter what it throws at us, or how often we get knocked to the ground, we have to be strong enough to get up and try again. And then he said, 'Remember that Garth Brooks song you love? Honey, you could have missed the pain, but then you'd have also had to miss the dance.'"

Matt studied her with interest. "A really cool lesson."

She nodded. "And a really cool song with a message. I'm sure you've been told pretty much the same."

He grew thoughtful. "After the accident that took our parents, Grandpop used to remind me that every hurdle we're forced to jump makes us stronger. I figured he was the strongest one of all. But one day I caught him in the barn, mucking stalls, and when I walked over to help, I realized he was silently weeping."

"Oh." Vanessa touched a hand to Matt's arm.

Matt went very still. "That was the first time I saw my grandfather cry. I vowed, if I had anything to say about things, it would be the last. I decided that I'd never do anything to break his heart."

"So you've become the fierce protector. Big brother to your reckless younger siblings, Luke and Reed. Caretaker of your uncle, your grandparents, even Burke and Yancy…"

He was shaking his head. "It's not like that."

"Then you're not hearing what I'm hearing."

He fell silent.

She touched a hand to his. "I remember one of my college courses. We had to map out every classmate's birth order, to see if they fit the prevailing statistics. Those who didn't were then asked to provide additional information. Some were changed by the death of a sibling. Others by a traumatic incident in the family. I'd call yours a double whammy."

He looked at her.

"Firstborn and also loss of parents. Both guaranteed to make you want to take charge."

"Bingo." He smiled. "What about you?"

"Same thing. An only child is most often anxious to

please the parents. The loss of my mother made me even more determined to please the survivor. So I'll never know if I'm a lawyer because it was my heart's desire, or because I know how much it means to my dad."

He turned his hand palm up and linked his fingers with hers. "Do we have no choice in these matters?"

She looked down at their joined hands and fought to dismiss the sudden rush of warmth. "I think there's no point in fighting it. We're doomed."

"Maybe that's a good thing." His smile added to her warmth. "So you're saying we may as well just go with our feelings?"

"Why not?"

"I was hoping you'd say that. I hope you won't mind if I start now." He leaned close and nibbled the corner of her mouth.

"Wait." She put a hand to his chest, pushing away. "I wasn't suggesting..." She stood, breaking contact.

"I was." In one quick motion he stood up beside her, gathering her close. "That kiss back at the cabin left me curious."

"It was just a quick good-bye when I thought I was leaving."

"A very nice good-bye. And now...hello again."

He covered her mouth in a kiss that wiped her mind blank of every thought but one. The man had moves. Really good moves. This felt so good, so right, she never wanted it to end.

She wrapped her arms around his waist and held on as the world seemed to ever so slowly spin and dip, leaving her lightheaded, while a burst of heat poured through her, leaving her limbs weak.

For the space of a heartbeat he held her a little away, as though trying to assess what had just happened. And then, with great care, he framed her face with his hands and kissed her with a thoroughness that had them both sighing.

His hands were gentle as they slowly slid from her face to her neck and across the slope of her shoulders. He held her as though she were fragile glass. Cautious. Careful, lest she break.

When at last they drew apart, his eyes were narrowed on her with a look she couldn't fathom.

She struggled to cover the tremors that were still rocketing through her system. "Satisfied?" Her voice was husky with feeling.

His smile came then. A dark, dangerous smile that had her wondering at the way her heart contracted.

"Not nearly. But I guess that will have to do. For now."

Why did his words sound like another challenge?

He caught the reins of her mare and handed them to her.

She could feel the shocking tremors along her arm at the mere touch of his hand on hers.

She pulled herself into the saddle and waited for him to mount Beau.

As they rode across a meadow, she struggled to focus on the amazing scenery. It was impossible. All she could think of was that kiss and the way it messed with her mind.

This man was unlike any she'd ever known. There was danger here, she thought. But not the kind she wanted to run from. What was so mind-blowing was the fact that she knew she was walking into the eye of the storm, and she wanted to run headlong into it.

As the two horses and riders came up over a rise, they slowed to a walk.

Vanessa was laughing as she turned to Matt. "Now that Ginger and I are comfortable with each other, I challenge you to another race. I think we're ready to give you and Beau a run for your money."

"Just can't get enough of losing, can y—?" His words cut off as he caught sight of a black SUV barely visible in a stand of evergreens about a hundred yards away.

"Stay here." His staccato words stung the air as he turned Beau in the direction of the vehicle.

It took Vanessa several seconds before she made out the car and realized what had him so upset.

Ignoring his order, she turned Ginger and followed.

Before Matt was halfway there the car's engine revved and it took off, spitting dirt from its wheels as it gained speed and disappeared into a stretch of woods.

Matt memorized as much of the license plate as he could before it was gone. Knowing he couldn't catch up with the retreating vehicle, he dropped to his knees in the dirt, searching for anything that might have been left behind. Finding the remains of a half-smoked cigar, he wrapped it in his handkerchief and tucked it into his pocket.

"Who were they?" Vanessa remained in the saddle.

"I couldn't see. The windows were darkened. It was a Montana license plate, but it could have been a rental."

He pulled out his cell phone and pressed the sheriff's number.

Vanessa dismounted and walked close enough to hear the bark of the familiar voice.

"Sheriff Eugene Graystoke here. What's up, Matt?"

After describing what he'd seen, and as much of the license plate number as he could recall, the sheriff's voice grew louder with excitement. "Would anyone at the house have spotted them?"

"Not likely. My grandparents are in town. The rest are up in the hills with the herds. Yancy is the only one at home, and if he's busy in the kitchen, he may not have seen or heard a thing. But we'll head home now and ask."

"I'll have the state boys check the car rental places. There aren't that many in this area, but they could have driven from Helena or even any small airport in Montana."

"One of them smokes a cigar. I have what's left of it."

"Good. I'll want that and anything else you find. And Matt, it goes without saying that you're not to let Miss Kettering out of your sight."

Matt saw the way her eyes narrowed slightly. "I understand."

When he disconnected, he took his time returning his phone to his shirt pocket.

When he turned, he decided to keep things light. He touched a finger to her mouth. "Is that a pout?"

She slapped his hand away. "First you once again rush off without letting me in on what you spotted. And now your sheriff tells you not to let me out of your sight? Does your sheriff really believe you can just snap your fingers and I'll be safe?"

Matt sobered instantly, all hint of humor wiped from his eyes. "That's what he'd like. But he's been in this business long enough to know that he can't always get what he wants. That's why we all have to work together until your father's trial is over." He lowered his voice. "I know you resent feeling helpless. You're used to seeing to your own safety, and this has you rattled. But look at it from the sheriff's point of view. He's been given the job of keeping a big-city district attorney's daughter safe on his watch. Knowing Eugene the way I do, he'd much rather have you locked in a cell than roaming free on our ranch. But as long as he's stuck with this deal, he'll do everything in his power to deliver you safely. Even at the cost of his own life."

Those words took all the wind out of her sails.

She lowered her head for a moment, to hide the emotions that flitted through her mind.

When she lifted her head in that proud, almost haughty manner he'd come to recognize, Matt knew that she'd come to terms with the reality of her situation.

"I'm sorry. I must sound like a spoiled, entitled brat. And I want you to know that I appreciate all that you and your family, as well as Sheriff Graystoke and the Montana State Police, are doing on my behalf. I really resent having so many people working so hard just to keep me safe from some monster."

"I know. But as soon as the trial ends, so will the threat to you."

"Well, that's our hope." She met his look with a clear eye. "Unless, of course, DePietro has ordered revenge regardless of the outcome."

Matt clasped her hand. "In that case, we'll keep on working until all of his men are caught and rendered useless."

She glanced at their hands. "Thanks, Matt. You're a good influence on me. I'm almost ready to believe you."

"Believe me." He held her hand a moment longer, closing it between both of his and giving her a long, lingering look before catching the reins and holding them while she mounted.

When he was in the saddle, he kept Beau alongside Ginger as they crossed the meadow in silence and made their way to the barn.

Once inside, as Matt turned their horses into stalls and added feed and water to their troughs, Vanessa sank down on a bale of hay and thought about what had just happened.

She thought she would be safe here because of the isolation of this vast ranch. But even here, someone had managed to find her, and had been watching for a chance to do her harm. Unless, of course, the sheriff could find another plausible explanation.

And if she wasn't safe here, then where?

She shivered.

She wanted to believe that Matt and his family could offer her a refuge. But somewhere in the dark recesses of her mind was the thread of fear that an evil man, on trial in Chicago, had already found a way to carry out his threat.

CHAPTER THIRTEEN

As they stepped from the barn, Matt could see the sheriff's car parked near the back door. A ranch truck came into view. Behind the wheel was Frank, with Gracie beside him in the passenger seat.

Matt took Vanessa's hand and strolled leisurely toward the house, hoping to give the sheriff time to speak privately to his grandparents, without fear of Vanessa overhearing.

The three were standing on the back porch, heads bent in quiet conversation.

As he drew near, Matt called out, "Sheriff? Any news?"

The lawman shook his head.

Matt's eyes narrowed slightly on his grandfather. "You cut your date short?"

Frank shrugged. "When Eugene called us with the news, we decided we'd rather enjoy Yancy's dinner than whatever Dot and Barb were offering at the diner."

Matt held the door while the others trooped inside, where Yancy was frosting a four-layer torte.

The cook looked up in surprise. "You're back early." He looked beyond Frank and Gracie to add, "Hello, Sheriff."

"Yancy." Eugene Graystoke removed his Stetson. "You see any vehicles around here today?"

Yancy glanced from the sheriff to Matt, who stood slightly behind his grandparents. "Has something happened?"

"Nessa and I spotted a car up in the hills. It had darkened windows, so we couldn't see inside."

Vanessa was worrying the cuff of her shirt. The only sign of agitation.

Yancy shook his head. "I didn't see a thing. Didn't hear anything, either. Could they have driven in from the Interstate?"

"Not likely." Matt frowned. "But they could have taken a back road, if they knew the area well enough."

Eugene sighed. "I knew it was a long shot. If they're checking out the ranch, they wouldn't be careless enough to be seen from the house. But the fact that you spotted them, Matt, tells me they may not know a whole lot about just how sprawling your ranch is. They may have thought they could conceal themselves in the woods and watch all the comings and goings from a safe distance. I'd bet money they weren't expecting you to come riding in practically on top of them."

He turned to Frank. "If you don't mind, I'd like to talk to Burke and the boys up in the hills. They may have seen something unusual."

Frank nodded. "You want to call them or head on up there?"

Eugene thought a minute. "No sense riding all that way when a call can let them know what I'm after, as long as they happen to be in an area that has phone service. I'd like everyone here, including your wranglers guarding the herds in hill country, to report anything out of the ordinary."

Frank clapped a hand on the sheriff's shoulder. "Consider it done."

Eugene headed for the door. "I'll make that call outside." He paused and looked at Vanessa. "I'm sorry this adds to your distress, Miss Kettering. I hope you know I'm doing everything in my power to keep you safe."

"I know that, Sheriff." She managed a smile. "And I appreciate all your help."

When the sheriff stepped outside, she turned to Matt's grandparents. "I'm so sorry this caused you to cut your date short."

Gracie squeezed her hand. "Frankie and I have had more dates than we can count." She shot a quick glance at her husband before adding, "On the way home, we talked about my next trek to the hills."

Matt raised an eyebrow. "You just got back."

"But I came back early because of the weather. Just look at all that sunshine. With new foals arriving, the mustangs will be forced to stay in one place for a while, until the mares and their newborns are able to travel. This is the perfect time for me to set up my gear and chronicle the new life cycle."

His grandmother exchanged a glance with her husband before turning to Vanessa. "I'd say it's the perfect opportunity for you, too. Now that you're not on any sort of timetable, how would you like to accompany me into the hills and immerse yourself in the life of wild horses?"

Vanessa's eyes widened with excitement. "You wouldn't mind having me along?"

"I'd welcome the company. But I need to warn you about a few things. I travel light, and it's pretty primitive up there. I can't count on the herd stopping near one of our cabins or shelters at night. I cook over a campfire and sleep under the stars, unless the weather turns. Then I sleep in my truck."

"But I'd get to see the mustangs up close?"

"As close as they'll allow. You may get to witness a birth or two. And sometimes a death. Just remember, this is nature, raw and natural. It won't be pretty and airbrushed. It can be wonderful, but it can also be heart-breakingly brutal."

"I understand. When do we leave?"

Gracie gave a laugh of delight. "Oh, what fun to have a traveling companion who's young and eager. Let's shoot for tomorrow morning. Unless Mother Nature decides otherwise."

"I'll go up and pack now."

"Remember. We travel light. I prefer to dress in layers. You'll need a parka and boots for chilly or rainy mornings and nights, and something for warm afternoons. We sleep in our clothes, and we have to be prepared to head out whenever the herd starts moving."

As Vanessa started up the stairs, Matt remained in the kitchen. His voice was low. "You think it's wise to do this now?"

"I can't think of a better time." Gracie linked hands with her husband. "Frankie and I discussed it on the way home. If someone is targeting our houseguest, it's too late to keep her presence here a secret. But it would be almost impossible for them to find her in those hills."

"They found her today, while riding across the meadow."

"That could have been an accident. As Eugene pointed out, they may have thought they could hide out in the woods and watch the ranch. They may have been caught completely by surprise when you and Vanessa spotted them."

"Maybe." His eyes narrowed. "But I don't like the idea of you and Nessa alone in the hills."

She touched a hand to his arm. "I feel quite certain that you and Frankie will see to it that we're never completely alone."

He smiled then and felt his tense shoulders relax. "You're a sly one, Gracie Malloy."

"I just happen to know my men." She turned away. "Yancy, I'm really looking forward to tasting that torte after dinner."

The old man smiled. "I'll see there's enough left over to send along with you on your trek tomorrow."

"That would be grand."

As she and Frank walked away, Matt let himself out of the house and made his way to the barn.

There he did what he always did when his mind was troubled. He chose a pitchfork from a hook along the wall and began mucking stalls.

There was nothing like hard, physical work to free him to turn a problem over and over until he'd looked at it from every possible angle.

He and his family, along with all the wranglers, would

have to form a protective ring around the two women while keeping just out of sight. Not an easy thing anywhere, but especially in the wilderness. With mustangs, there was no set pattern. No trail or path. They moved at the whim of nature and their stallion leader.

Still, it had to be done. If a vehicle could breach the safety of their isolated ranch, it made sense to take Vanessa high in the hills, and hope it was enough to discourage anyone bent on evil from following.

He paused to clench a fist. He would move heaven and earth to keep Gracie and Vanessa safe, while still leaving them free to savor their journey into the wild.

Vanessa studied the meager clothes in her closet. It wouldn't be difficult making a decision about what to take along on her trek to the wilderness.

The wilderness.

Grinning wildly, she did a quick little turn. Oh, how she wanted to share this news with her father. She'd actually fished out her cell phone before it dawned on her that she could no longer indulge in that lovely ritual. Always, she'd enjoyed sharing every bit of good news with him, before calling her friends, especially her best friend, Lauren. Lauren McCotter, who'd been her BFF since kindergarten.

Though she and Lauren had followed very different careers paths, they managed to meet at least once a week or so, either for morning coffee or a drink after work, to catch up on each other's life. They had a shared history that was a tighter bond than that of sisters. Lauren was the sister she'd never had.

She sat down on the edge of the bed, fighting a sudden

ache around her heart. The reality of her situation hit her with all the force of a physical blow. She'd been cut off from everything that was familiar and comfortable. Her father. Her friends. The people she worked with. And all because some madman, who thought himself above the law, was willing to do whatever it took to stay out of prison.

She felt a rush of love for her father, knowing how he must be torn between his duty to the people who trusted him to prosecute such men and his fierce need to protect his only child. How he must be suffering as he went about his daily routine, keeping his feelings carefully hidden beneath a façade of cool reserve.

Through the years she'd watched him handle the media after a sensational criminal case. He'd earned a reputation for being low-key and thoroughly professional. One investigative reporter, eager to earn his stripes by breaking through that wall of reserve, had, after a particularly grueling interview, given Elliott Kettering the nickname Iceman.

It pained Nessa to see the man she adored misunderstood and ridiculed. But, as he'd reminded her often, it came with the territory. The district attorney of any large city was fair game for criticism. As her father said, he was damned if he won a high-profile trial and damned if he lost. And always, he was suspected of hoping to use his position to move on to higher office, even when that wasn't the case at all.

And now this threat to her safety was just another price to be paid.

As Elliott Kettering's daughter, she needed to be as strong as he'd always been.

She stood and paced to the window. She would put

aside her fears and get through this. And what better way to spend her time than with Grace Malloy, one of the most respected researchers in the field of wild horses?

Spotting movement outside the barn, she watched as Matt led a horse toward a corral. She couldn't take her eyes off him. Everything about the man exuded strength and confidence and purpose. The way he walked, those long strides matching that of the horse. The slow, easy lift of his hand as he removed the lead rope and ran an open palm over the horse's muzzle.

She gave an involuntary shiver, and thought about his hands holding her, touching her.

He was the epitome of a Western hero. All muscle and strength and easy charm. And ever since their uncomfortable introduction, she couldn't stop thinking about him.

She'd thought, earlier today, that he had chosen that isolated area near the stream for his own advantage. And when he'd kissed her, she'd been certain of it. But then he'd been the one to step back from that ever-so-tempting edge and suggest they return to the ranch. She'd actually had a moment of keen disappointment before coming to her senses.

He'd been right, of course. They needed to keep this on a purely professional level.

Maybe she was just a little annoyed that he'd been the first to do the sensible thing, when in the past she'd always assumed that role. Or maybe she was suffering some regret that they couldn't have let the passion they were feeling play out to its logical conclusion. If so, she didn't want to probe this too deeply.

She huffed out a breath. And hadn't she once again spent way too much time thinking about Matt Malloy?

She crossed her arms over her chest, turned away, and walked to the closet.

Time to make a decision about what to pack for tomorrow's grand adventure. She was traveling to the wilderness to see, up close and personal, a herd of wild horses. While she and Gracie were alone together, she would have plenty of time to interview the foremost authority on how mustangs lived and how they survived.

And when she returned to Chicago, and later to DC, she could report back to the wildlife organizations she represented how to make the lives of these beautiful creatures safer and better.

This was a rare opportunity, one she'd never dreamed possible, and she planned on making the most of it.

CHAPTER FOURTEEN

By the time Vanessa descended the stairs for dinner, she could hear muted voices in the kitchen. She walked in to find everybody gathered around the fireplace, enjoying drinks and appetizers. Even Colin, Luke, and Reed, as well as Burke, were there, fresh from their duties with the herds. It was obvious from the look of them that they'd barely had time to shower and change. Their faces were heavily bearded, their hair in need of a trim.

Yancy held a tray of drinks for her inspection.

"Thank you." She accepted a glass of wine and turned to the others.

Reed, heavily bearded, shaggy hair tied back in a ponytail, his well-worn denims faded and torn, had the look of an Old West gunslinger as he turned to her. "I hear you're about to go on one of Gram Gracie's famous wilderness treks."

Vanessa's smile widened. "I can't wait."

"It shows. You look like a kid at Christmas."

"Is it that obvious?"

Nelson, enjoying his martini, eyed her over the rim of his glass. "I can't imagine a fashionable, big-city lawyer like you climbing over mountains and slopping through muddy fields just to get close to a bunch of smelly creatures."

"Where's your romance, Dad?" Grace touched a hand to his arm. "If you were directing Vanessa in a film, you'd have soft music playing in the background while she danced through a field of wildflowers."

Something about her words had Matt lifting his head to stare at Vanessa through narrowed eyes.

Nelson nodded. "I would indeed. Beautiful women in fields of wildflowers sell movies. But I was never fooled by what I was doing. Movies are pretend. You're taking her into the harshness of the real world, Gracie Anne." He turned to Frank. "Of course, there was a time when I couldn't imagine a daughter of mine living on a ranch, let alone climbing all over Hell's Half Acre chasing wild animals."

"And now, you're living on a ranch yourself, Great One." Luke tipped up his longneck and drank, while the others shared smiles.

"True enough." Nelson set aside his empty glass. "It took some getting used to. But I have to say, Yancy's fine food and excellent martini skills have made the transition smooth enough." He looked around at his daughter and son-in-law, his grandson Colin, and then at his three great-grandsons, all of them rugged and handsome enough to have been leading men in his films. He gave one of those lazy, satisfied smiles. "Not that being with all of you hasn't been enough reward. But there's something to be said for fine food and liquor."

"Spoken like a true Hollywood icon," Luke drawled.

Burke accepted a longneck and, as was his custom, stood just outside the circle of family, like a guardian angel watching and listening in silence.

When Yancy announced that dinner was ready, they moved across the room, settling comfortably at the big harvest table.

Luke held a huge platter while his great-grandfather helped himself to a chicken breast. The others at the table easily passed around a Caesar salad, tiny new garden peas, and a basket of sourdough rolls fresh from the oven.

Nelson took a first bite and turned to the cook with a look of absolute delight. "Chicken cordon bleu?"

Yancy grinned. "You've been talking about it for weeks now. I figured it was time I took the hint."

"But this is"—the old man took a second bite and closed his eyes for a moment—"exactly the way they served it at the Brasseri."

Yancy couldn't hide his pleasure. "Glad to hear I nailed it."

"More than. Oh, this takes me back . . ."

Around the table the family shared knowing looks. They had no doubt they were about to be entertained by the Great One's memories of a bygone Hollywood.

"Anthony would pick me up in the limousine at exactly six o'clock. We would drive to the Brasseri, and Marcel, my favorite waiter, would set a martini in front of me the moment I was seated in a booth."

"Always a booth, and never a table," Luke explained to Vanessa.

"Exactly right. Tables were for the tourists who came in to stare at celebrities. Or for the gossip columnists," he added with a trace of contempt, "who spent a fortune tipping the waiters for any hint of scandal they could reveal in their rags."

"Even Marcel?" Frank nudged Gracie, knowing that would raise his father-in-law's hackles.

"Marcel was above such things. Totally incorruptible. He knew more secrets than anyone in Hollywood, but took them all to his grave. That's why, while the others came and went, he remained as head waiter at the Brasseri for over twenty years."

Vanessa turned to Grace. "Did you ever go along with your father?"

Grace shook her head. "Rarely. Over Dad's objections, Mother insisted that I attend a private girls' school in Connecticut, as she had."

"Which meant that I was forced to fly across the country regularly, just to spend time with my wife and daughter." Nelson chuckled. "It was the price I paid to love the most beautiful woman in Connecticut. That is until Grace Anne chose to attend college at UCLA over the elite Eastern university that had been her mother's alma mater. Madeline was horrified, of course, because it meant that she would have to return to the glitter of Hollywood if she wanted to see her own daughter."

"And then," Frank interjected, "just when Nelson thought he'd won the upper hand in their marital tug-of-war, my Gracie Girl made a fateful trip to Montana to photograph some scenery for her final year in filmmaking at UCLA, and ended up leaving both Connecticut and California behind."

Vanessa, caught up in the story, looked over with surprise. "You never went home?"

Grace linked her fingers with Frank's. "I never even went back to graduate. Nothing was going to make me leave this handsome cowboy for even a week."

Colin leaned back in his chair and regarded his parents. "And I've been thankful ever since."

Luke slapped his uncle on the back. "Not as thankful as all the pretty ladies in Glacier Ridge. Who would they drool over if you weren't around to make their hearts flutter?"

Colin gave a dry laugh. "In case you haven't noticed, you and your brothers have replaced me as hunk of the day."

"You might want to look around the next time you're in town." Reed exchanged a grin with his brothers. "Word is, every rancher in Glacier Ridge keeps his wife and daughters locked indoors until Colin Malloy leaves town."

"Trust me." Colin huffed a breath. "They're all safe. I'm not even looking."

"But they are. And drooling," Luke added as the others laughed.

"Speaking of drooling..." Grace turned to Yancy. "I think we'll take our dessert in the great room. And as soon as possible. I've been thinking about that torte for hours."

"Yes, ma'am." Yancy began setting plates and cups on a trolley, along with a carafe of coffee and a bottle of fine whiskey.

As they made their way to the great room, Frank huddled with Burke, who reported on the herds, the wranglers, and the weather in the hills, before being apprised of Gracie's latest plans to journey there.

"So, Nessa." Reed waited until his great-grandfather was comfortably settled into a big, overstuffed chair by the fire before sitting nearby and stretching out his long legs to the warmth. "Have you decided what you'll take along on your first visit to the wilderness?"

"I thought some jeans, a hoodie, maybe a parka, and boots."

"Well, that takes care of tomorrow morning." Reed grinned at his brothers across the room. "What about the days after?"

She shot a puzzled look at Grace. "Didn't you say we'd be traveling light?"

"I did. Just ignore the teasing. But Reed's right. You may want to add a few things. You'll need a couple of tees or a tank. Shorts. Sunblock. And I'd advise you to bring along some sturdy work gloves."

"And if you don't have room for the work gloves, at least make room for the shorts." Reed's smile went up a notch.

Yancy moved among them, serving his torte with dollops of chocolate chip ice cream, along with cups of coffee.

Nelson looked up after his first taste. "Is that hazelnut I detect, Yancy?"

"You've got a refined palate, Great One. It is hazelnut."

The old man brought his fingers to his lips in an exaggerated display of delight. "You've outdone yourself again, my man. I do believe this torte is better than any I ever tasted at the Brasseri."

Yancy made a formal bow. "The highest compliment ever."

"And well deserved."

Around the room the others were too busy enjoying their dessert to bother with words.

Yancy set a trolley along one wall, in case anyone wanted seconds. Then he settled into his favorite, well-worn chair by the fire and sipped his coffee.

Seeing him, Vanessa looked surprised. "You're not having any of this fabulous torte, Yancy?"

He gave her a pleased smile. "I'm glad you think it's fabulous. My real dessert is watching everyone enjoying the things I made. Truth is, I never had a sweet tooth. Now, if this were chili, I'd have seconds and thirds."

"Then I'll just have yours, too." Luke ambled across the room and cut another huge slice before mounding it with ice cream.

"Careful," Colin called. "All those pretty young things in town like their cowboys lean."

"You sure about that?" Luke winked at his brother Reed. "Now that our old uncle is past looking at women..."

"Who're you calling old?" Colin sipped his coffee.

Reed couldn't resist jumping in. "Luke's right. You said you're not even looking at women anymore. I'd say that makes you old."

"I'm only ten years older than Matt." Colin turned to his nephew. "Why aren't you defending me?"

Matt grinned. "You're on your own, old man."

Colin nodded toward his father. "You going to let these upstarts talk to your son this way?"

Frank dropped an arm around Gracie's shoulders. "Son, I've learned that there's only one thing that ever stops a man from looking at beautiful women. That's when he's snagged the most beautiful woman of all. And since I've already got her, and I'm too content after such a fine meal to do more than listen, I'll just let the four of you carry on." He turned to Vanessa. "See what we have to put up with? They're constantly ragging on one another, and we'd probably send them all packing and tell them to find their own ranches if they weren't so helpful around this big ol' ranch."

"Helpful?" Reed shot a knowing look at his brothers. "Grandpop, if you sent the four of us packing, you'd have to hire an entire army of wranglers to replace all these muscles and brains."

"You forgot to mention egos." The older man's eyes danced with laughter as he turned to Burke. "And I mean giant egos."

That had Burke roaring with laughter.

Reed crossed the room and held out a bottle of whiskey. "I think your brain just short-circuited, Grandpop. How about a splash to give it a jump-start?"

Still laughing, Frank held out his cup.

Reed turned to the others. "Any takers?"

Nelson lifted his cup. "I wouldn't mind a bit."

"I'll have some, too, son," Burke's eyes were crinkled in glee.

The rest declined, and Reed replaced the bottle on the trolley.

Vanessa had a sudden thought. "My cell phone didn't work up in the hills." She turned to Grace.

Frank answered for Gracie. "That's true, darlin'. They're pretty unreliable. Way up there, you're pretty much on your own."

"So, if there's . . . trouble . . ." She flushed. "Not that I'm expecting any but . . ."

Frank gave her a reassuring smile. "My Gracie Girl knows how to get the word out if she has any trouble."

Beside him, his wife nodded. "I have my rifle, Nessa. If I fire it, they'll hear it clear across the hills and come running from all directions."

"Have you ever had to fire it?"

The older woman gave her a gentle smile. "A time or two. Just to see if my men were paying attention."

They all laughed as Burke explained. "When Miss Gracie calls, this entire ranch drops everything to get to her."

Frank kissed his wife's cheek. "That's because she's the heart and soul of this place."

"And don't you ever forget that." She tried to sound stern, but everyone in the room could hear the warmth in her voice.

A short time later, as the fire burned low, Grace was the first to get to her feet. "Time I turned in. You might want to think about it, too, Nessa. We have a long day ahead of us tomorrow."

As she and Frank made their way upstairs, the others began drifting off to their rooms, calling good night as they did.

When Vanessa set aside her cup and got to her feet, Matt stood. "I'll see you to your room."

"That's not necessary. If you'd like to stay and chat with Burke . . ."

The old cowboy shook his head. "I'm heading to the bunkhouse. We'll be leaving for the herd before dawn." He crossed to her and took her hand in a courtly gesture.

"You'll have a grand time with Miss Grace. I hope you soak it all up."

"Thank you, Burke. I can't wait. Good night."

As she climbed the stairs, Matt followed. When they came to her room, he reached around her and opened the door. Once she was inside, he surprised her by stepping in behind her before leaning against the closed door.

She turned. "Is there something you want to say?"

"Something I need to do." His voice was low. Quiet.

His eyes were so clearly focused on her, she felt the magnetic pull of them. "If you're here to warn me..."

Without a word he dragged her against him. Her hands automatically lifted to his chest, as though to brace herself, but there was no time.

And when his mouth covered hers, there were no thoughts but one. Oh how she'd wanted this. Only this.

When he wrapped her in those strong arms, she felt the quiet strength of him and thrilled to it.

The more he drew out the kiss, the more her body softened, melted into him, until she could feel him in every part of her.

He lifted his head just enough to nuzzle her cheek, her eye, her forehead.

She gave a long, deep sigh. "You were so quiet tonight, I was afraid you were angry that I was going with Gracie." She lifted a hand to his jaw. "I know I shouldn't be taking any chances, but..."

"You've got a right to be concerned." His words, spoken against her temple, sent shivers along her spine. "But try to put everything aside and just enjoy this time with my grandmother. It's a once-in-a-lifetime experience."

"It is." She looked into his eyes. "But if you're not angry, why were you so quiet?"

"I'm not a patient man. And all evening, while my family was having such a good time teasing you, I just wanted you alone. For this." He lowered his head and took her mouth again.

Curls of pleasure had her insides quivering.

He changed the angle of the kiss and gathered her against him.

She returned his kisses with a hunger that caught them both by surprise.

When at last he lifted his head, he framed her face with his big hands and stared at her with a look that burned clear through to her soul. "I'm leaving now."

"You could...stay."

"Not tonight. You need your sleep." He studied her a minute longer before turning toward the door.

As he opened it he muttered huskily, "When you come back, I'll want a whole lot more than a few stolen kisses."

He stepped away and pulled the door shut behind him.

She studied the closed door before crossing the room to stand at the window and stare at the night sky.

Matt's words had her touching a hand to her heart, which was pounding inside her chest.

When you come back, I'll want a whole lot more than a few stolen kisses.

Not just words.

It had been a promise. A promise that left her absolutely breathless.

CHAPTER FIFTEEN

It wasn't yet light outside when Vanessa descended the stairs and dropped her backpack in a corner of the kitchen.

Gracie and Frank were huddled in front of the fireplace, heads bent in quiet conversation.

Yancy was draining bacon on a bed of paper towels.

Matt and Burke stomped in from the barn, pausing to remove their boots and hang their hats on pegs along the wall before washing at the big sink in the mudroom.

Spotting Vanessa, Grace hurried over. "I figured you'd be up early. How'd you sleep?"

"Badly. Too excited, I guess."

"You'll sleep tonight."

Frank chuckled. "That's a fact. After climbing around these mountains, trying to keep up with my Gracie Girl, I guarantee you'll sleep like a baby."

Vanessa was working overtime to keep from staring at

Matt, but when she turned his way, he winked, and she could feel her face getting all warm.

"'Morning, Nessa."

"Good morning." She ducked her head, wishing she could control the blush spreading up her throat and across her cheeks. She hadn't reacted to a guy this way since she was sixteen. But it was impossible to act all cool and composed after last night, and the promise he'd made. Just the thought of it made her body tingle.

He nodded toward the backpack. "That's it?"

"Yeah." She turned to Grace. "I added a tee and tank and some shorts, but I don't have any work gloves."

"We've got a shelf full of them in the barn. Remember to pick up a pair before we head out."

"Okay." Vanessa chose a glass of orange juice from a tray on the counter.

Matt snagged a mug of coffee and handed it to Burke before taking a second one for himself.

"Breakfast is ready," Yancy called. "Actually, this is a second breakfast. I served Luke and Reed and Colin theirs more than an hour ago. They're halfway to Eagle's Ridge by now."

Matt held a chair for Vanessa before sitting beside her. He held a platter of scrambled eggs while she served herself. "You'd better take more than that," he said, grinning at the small portion on her plate.

"I don't think I can eat a thing. Nerves, I guess."

"That's all right." Frank dug into his bacon and eggs. "I saw all the food Yancy packed up for you and Gracie. You could survive up in the hills for a month or more and still not run out of things to eat."

"Yancy understands the way an appetite sharpens when

you're living in the hills." Grace slathered wild strawberry preserves on her toast. "You did send along some of that torte, I hope?"

Yancy nodded. "I made sure that was the first thing I packed, Miss Grace."

"Good. The rest is lovely, of course. But that torte..." She let her smile speak for itself as she finished eating.

Half an hour later she and Frank shoved away from the table and led the way toward the mudroom, with Vanessa trailing behind.

She turned. "Thank you for that great breakfast, Yancy. And for all the food you're sending along with us."

"You're welcome, Nessa. Now relax and enjoy your trek into the wilderness. With Miss Grace along as tour guide, I'm sure you'll have a grand adventure."

Before she could pick up her backpack, Matt snatched it up and moved along beside her as they made their way to the barn.

He handed her a pair of work gloves. "See if these fit."

After trying them, she nodded and he tucked them in with her things before stowing the backpack in the truck and holding open the passenger door.

Before she could climb up, Matt laid a hand on her arm. Just a touch, but she felt the quick curl of heat as she turned to him.

"Yancy's right. With Gram Gracie along, you'll have the time of your life."

"I hope so. I'm so eager to see a herd of wild horses, I'm twitching."

"Yeah. I can feel it." He leaned in and touched his mouth to hers.

It was the merest touch of his lips to hers, but it affected her so deeply she couldn't feel her hands or feet as she turned and climbed into the truck and fumbled with the seat belt.

Matt closed the door and reached in the open window, tugging on a lock of her hair. "Go make some memories."

Grace set a rifle on a rack behind the driver's seat. Vanessa lifted a brow in question, but she merely grinned. "I don't suppose you shoot?"

At Vanessa's quick shake of her head, Grace touched her hand. "Not a problem, Nessa. I shoot well enough for both of us. And I'd never go into the wilderness without my rifle."

She turned the key in the ignition, and the truck rolled out of the barn. Instead of heading along the gravel driveway, she drove the truck across a flat stretch of ground.

As the older woman waved and called something to Frank, Vanessa stared at the reflection in the side-view mirror of Matt standing straight and tall, his eyes now hidden behind sunglasses.

As eager as she was for this adventure, she had the sudden, almost overpowering desire to run back and fall into his arms and beg him to kiss her one more time.

Go make some memories.

With a sweet smile she sat back and looked around as they drove across a pasture before veering up and up to a high, grassy meadow. Fields so green they seemed like a Hollywood set. The green gradually gave way to a background of colorful bitterroot. And still the truck continued, following no particular trail as it climbed and climbed until they came to the edge of the wooded area. Once there, all Vanessa's senses sharpened. The bright sun became dappled, and the air was heavy with the fragrance of evergreen and wildflowers. Colorful birds darted from tree to tree. And as her eyes adjusted to the dim light, she could make out movement. A herd of deer. An eagle lifting from the forest ground with something dangling from its beak.

As the eagle soared, so did her heart. She felt wild joy and a sense of quiet peace. The teeming streets of her city faded away, as did the danger that hovered like a dark shadow. She was actually in the wilderness of Montana, with Grace Anne LaRou as her tour guide. And waiting for her back at the ranch was a handsome cowboy whose kisses promised paradise.

Hours later the truck came up over a rise, and Vanessa gave an audible gasp at the panorama spread out before them. To one side were bleak, barren mountains rising up like a vertical wall from a half-moon-shaped lake, glistening in the sun. On the other side was a series of grassy ranges, each one folding into the next, for as far as the eye could see. And all of them ringed by towering mountain peaks in the distance.

"Oh, this looks like some sort of lost world."

At Vanessa's words, Grace nodded. "That's exactly how I think of it. My very own uncharted, untouched piece of heaven."

She put the truck in gear, and they drove slowly along a high ridge until Grace parked the vehicle under a rock ledge.

"I've used this spot before. It's a good place to make

base camp. There's a stream over there"—she pointed to a rock-strewn bank and sunlit water meandering just beyond a stand of trees—"and a cave here, once we make certain there aren't any bears calling it their home."

"Bears?"

"Just a precaution," Grace said with a reassuring smile. "Afterward, we'll walk a bit, see if we can find any trace of the herd. But we'll return and sleep here tonight. If the weather holds, we can sleep under the stars." Her tone lowered. "There's nothing quite like sleeping under the stars. Ever tried it?"

Vanessa shook her head. "Not even when I was a kid at camp. We always slept in cabins."

"Then you're in for a treat. But if it rains, we'll have shelter under that shelf of rock." She turned to Vanessa. "First we'll check out this cave."

The two women exited the truck and Grace led the way, carrying a battery-operated lantern. She switched it on before stepping into the cave. Vanessa, trailing behind, looked around nervously, praying she didn't see feral eyes looking back at her.

When they'd checked out the cave and found it empty and, though small, high enough for them to stand in, they walked back out into the brilliant sunlight.

Grace turned off the lantern and set it in the back of the truck, which was littered with her photographic equipment. She looked at Vanessa. "You ready to hike these hills?"

"I can't wait."

Grace smiled. "Let's do it."

* * *

They hiked for nearly an hour, with Grace pausing every so often to kneel in the grass and examine the ground for signs of horses.

Each time she stopped, Vanessa used the time to stare around with a feeling of awe. This amazing place was even more than she'd hoped for. Sweeping vistas of lush rangeland and breathtaking views of mountains towering in the distance, looking exactly like the pictures she'd carried in her mind.

Here there were no highways. Not even rough roads or the tracks from farm implements. No man-made buildings. No people. The Old West. Raw and untamed. Looking as it had for centuries. A land untouched by human hands.

"Ah." Hearing the exclamation from Grace, Vanessa hurried over.

"Look." Grace pointed to something in the grass. "Fresh droppings. A lot of them."

"But how do you know it's from horses and not some other animals?"

Grace stood. "Each animal has its own distinct markings. In this area there are pronghorns, elk, even higher up there"—she pointed to the mountain peaks—"Rocky Mountain goats. But this tells me the horses are near. And since it's fresh, they'll be close by, giving the mares time to deliver their foals and grow sleek and fat on all this grass."

Vanessa's heart was beating overtime. "Will we keep on climbing?"

Grace shook her head. "This sunlight will fade quickly once the sun drifts behind that ridge. We'll head back to camp now and settle in for the night. It's time to figure out what we'll have for dinner."

Vanessa touched a hand to her stomach. "I'd forgotten about food. But now that you mention it, I know I'll be ready to eat after we get back."

"Nerves beginning to fade?" Grace asked with a grin.

"Yeah." Vanessa took a moment to look around before turning to follow Grace's lead. "Now that I'm here, and it's even better than I'd hoped, I'm feeling... relieved."

"You're going to feel even better when we see what special things Yancy sent along."

"Oh, I hope he sent along some of that chicken."

"You can have my share. I'm just hoping he packed a big slice of that chocolate-hazelnut torte," Grace said, laughing.

"How did you find this place?"

Vanessa sat with her back against a boulder, which was still warm from the fading sun, enjoying Yancy's chicken cordon bleu and a roll heated over a firepit Grace had fashioned of some rocks and tree branches.

"I was twenty years old, a college senior, using my spring break to do a film study of the Montana wilderness." Grace paused to eat the last bite of Yancy's torte before setting aside the plastic plate and filling a cup with coffee. "While up here, I saw my first herd of wild horses. There was this wonderful black stallion standing perfectly still on a rock ledge, keeping watch over his herd grazing in a meadow below. I turned my long-range lens on him and began filming. He was magnificent. I lost my heart in an instant." Her voice lowered. "Sadly, he spotted me, leapt down from the ledge, and began herding his mares and their young in the opposite direction. I wasn't just disappointed. I was determined to see him again, and to film him with his herd. It became my obsession."

"Did you ever find him?"

Grace smiled. "Not that year. Before I could pack up and try to track the herd, the most handsome man I'd ever seen rode up out of the wilderness, and I lost my heart for the second time in a single day. Francis Xavier Malloy was simply magnificent. So much better than any of the Hollywood actors I knew who pretended to be cowboys. This man was the real thing. And when I learned that I was on his land, and that he didn't have a wife and children, and he looked at me in the same wild, almost primitive way that stallion had looked, I knew that I never wanted to leave."

"It must have been a terrible shock to your parents."

"*Shock* is much too mild a word." Grace chuckled. "You heard what Dad said last night. It was bad enough that I'd gone off to Montana without a chaperone. But to learn that I intended to stay and marry a rancher I barely knew—he was ready to have me committed."

"How did your mother react?"

Grace smiled. "Mother was the one who really surprised me. I'd expected her to be too embarrassed to even admit to her society friends what I'd done. Instead, she called me to say that she wasn't at all surprised that I was marrying my first love. She said she would expect no less of her daughter, and that she wished me and my rancher all happiness. She offered to come to the wedding without Dad, since he was sulking, but I told her we intended to marry quickly and without any fuss, and that she could come to Montana and meet him whenever she could persuade Dad to join her."

"Wow." Vanessa poured herself a cup of coffee and wrapped her hands around it in the chill of evening. "What did she think of your Frank?"

Grace's voice softened. "Mother died that year, before she had the chance to meet him. But it was enough to know I'd had her blessing." She brightened. "I've always felt that even after her passing, she was pressing Dad to soften his heart and get to know his only child's husband. And, of course, you can see how successful she was."

She and Vanessa shared a smile.

"That's really sweet."

"Yes, it is. I'm a lucky woman." Grace stifled a yawn. "And now, we'd better get our bedrolls ready. I have a feeling I'll be asleep in no time."

After banking the fire, she and Vanessa set their bedrolls close enough to enjoy the warmth of the hot embers through the night.

As Vanessa snuggled in, she stared at the canopy of stars overhead. Grace was right. This wasn't like anything she'd ever experienced. She'd never before seen stars so big and bright, it felt as though she could reach up and touch them. And the night air, though chilly, whispered over her face, leaving her feeling fresh and clean.

Make some memories, Matt had whispered. And oh, wasn't she just?

Oh Dad, she thought. *If only you could be here, safe and sound, away from danger, away from the all-consuming work that takes up so much of your time, to share this with me.*

And then she thought about Matt Malloy. How would

she describe him to her father? A cowboy. A rancher. A businessman. A man she would trust with her life, though she'd known him a scant few days.

With a feeling of deep contentment, she drifted into sleep.

CHAPTER SIXTEEN

Vanessa turned toward the warmth at her back before opening her eyes to see that Grace had added a fresh log to their fire.

She yawned, stretched, then sat up with a start. "Did I oversleep? How long have you been up?"

"Relax, Nessa. I just woke a few minutes ago, and thought I'd stoke the fire before breakfast."

Vanessa slipped out of her bedroll and pulled on her hiking boots before stowing her bedding in the back of the truck. "Tell me what I can do."

Grace was busy uncovering a metal storage bin and removing several packets. She handed over a blackened coffeepot that looked as though it had seen years of wilderness treks. "If you'll take this to that creek over there and fill it, we'll have coffee."

Vanessa returned and spooned ground coffee into the basket before placing the pot on a grate over the fire. Soon the air was perfumed with the wonderful fragrance of coffee, along with the mouthwatering aroma of onion-laced skillet potatoes, as well as ham and eggs.

"All the comforts of home," Grace proclaimed as she filled two plates.

As the two women dug into their breakfast, Grace couldn't help grinning at her young friend. "No loss of appetite this morning, I gather?"

Vanessa laughed. "I'm starving."

"That's what hiking these hills does to a body. I'm always hungry up here."

"I can understand why. We must have walked miles yesterday."

"We'll walk even more today. But I promise you, we won't even notice."

"I'd walk through fire just to see a herd of mustangs."

"I remember those same feelings of utter excitement. It's always been the same for me. The magnetic pull of wild horses. Just knowing they're close by has my heart beating faster. Now, tell me how you felt sleeping under the stars."

"It was just as you said. But I really never expected it to be so grand."

"You don't mind the lack of modern facilities?"

"What lack?" Vanessa lifted her hands to encompass the green hills, the blue sky with its puffy clouds, the stream gurgling behind them. "It seems to me we have all the comforts of home, and none of the annoyances. No phones ringing. No schedules or deadlines." She sighed, searching for words. "Honestly? Though I would have never believed I could be saying this, I think I could learn to love this way of life."

"Now you're in trouble," Grace said with a laugh. At Vanessa's expression she added, "That's exactly how I got hooked. A night under the stars. A herd of mustangs. A handsome cowboy..."

Vanessa felt her face grow warm.

"Speaking of which...What do you think of my grandson?"

Trying to be coy, Vanessa shrugged. "Which one?"

Grace threw back her head and laughed. "Try that on someone else. I've seen the way you and Matthew look at each other. You're not even aware he has two brothers."

Vanessa couldn't help joining in the laughter. "Am I so transparent?"

"To anyone who bothers to look at you, Nessa." Grace turned. "Let's get this campsite put to rights so we can get on the trail."

The two women worked together, banking the fire, cleaning their dishes in the stream, and stowing them inside the metal container stored in the back of the truck.

After checking their supplies in their backpacks, and adding Grace's rifle and the photographic supplies, which they divided between them, they set off across the high meadow in search of the herd, with Grace leading the way.

As they crested a hill, they paused to enjoy the view. The hills around them, each one folding into the next, were green and gold, with a sky so blue it hurt to look at it. The sun shot the distant peaks with shimmering gold and mauve while a mist drifted over the lake far below.

"I think you're my good luck charm, Nessa." Grace slipped on a pair of sunglasses. "I don't think I've ever seen a prettier day."

As they walked, they chatted amiably.

"Matt said he was twelve when his parents died."

"Yes." Grace paused to lower her backpack to the grass before sitting on a smooth, sun-warmed rock. "Sudden death changes the lives of everyone involved. Until then, Frankie and I had more happiness than anyone deserves in this life. Two sons who loved this ranch as much as we did. A beautiful daughter-in-law who loved us as much as we loved her. And three grandsons who delighted all of us, just by being."

She looked toward the brooding mountains. "We were all so carefree. Our biggest concern was doubling our herds and topping the previous year's profits. And then, suddenly, none of that mattered. All of us were changed forever."

She met Vanessa's look. "Matthew and his brothers were as carefree as boys can be, especially boys growing up on a vast ranch, being best friends, doing all the rough-and-tumble things boys do. But from the moment they were given the news of their loss, Matthew was no longer just a twelve-year-old boy. He became, in an instant, guardian and protector to two younger ones. My wild, fearless, dangerous grandson became"—she shrugged—"responsible."

She lifted her head, as though speaking to the air around her. "That singular event changed our entire family. Our son Colin had been the kid brother who had adored his older brother. All he'd ever wanted was to be like Patrick. And now he had to step up and become not only father to three lost boys, but also the only son to Frankie and me. And we were in such grief, we were nearly blinded by it. So was my father, who'd come to live with us so he could watch his family grow, and suddenly he had to bury a grandson and watch his great-grandsons struggle with their loss. And then there were Burke and Yancy, whose losses were as great as ours. They may not be blood, but they're family just the same."

Vanessa caught Grace's hand. Squeezed. "I'm sure you all struggled."

Grace nodded. "Of course you understand. Matthew told me you lost your mother as a teen. Once death touches you, you feel vulnerable. You—"

Vanessa finished for her. "—You realize it can happen to you and to all those you love. You can never again take anything for granted. In the blink of an eye, it can all be taken away."

Grace stood and wrapped her arms around Vanessa, and the two women embraced, letting the tears flow as they shared a strange and painful bond.

For Vanessa, it was an epiphany. She had never before shared her grief with a woman who had likewise suffered such loss.

They'd hiked for several hours before Grace suddenly held up a hand and pointed.

Vanessa was stopped in her tracks by the sight of a herd of horses just ahead. Their leader, a ghostly gray stallion, stood a little apart from the others, head lifted in the air, alert to any danger.

Grace pointed again, and Vanessa smiled at the black-and-white spotted mare calmly grazing while her foal nursed.

Vanessa stood perfectly still, savoring her first view of wild horses. Though she remained quiet, she was doing somersaults inside. In her mind she was wildly dancing and singing and clapping her hands in sheer delight.

She was really here. In the Montana wilderness, just a hundred yards away from a herd of mustangs.

She wasn't even aware that she was crying until Grace drew an arm around her waist and offered her a handkerchief.

Surprised, she dabbed at the moisture running down her cheeks.

"I understand," Grace whispered. "I've had that same reaction so many times."

Hearing her, Vanessa got past her embarrassment over being all weepy, and simply savored the moment.

She was here. The horses were here. And her heart was nearly bursting with a feeling of wild joy.

They spent the rest of the day watching the herd.

Vanessa had assumed Grace would move closer and maybe even walk among them. But all the older woman did was sit on the boulder, aiming her camera at the various mares, and often at the stallion, snapping off picture after picture.

By the time the sun had made its arc over the distant mountains, Grace beckoned Vanessa to follow, and they made their way back to camp.

Once they were out of sight of the herd, Vanessa was free to give voice to her enthusiasm.

"Oh Gracie, I can't believe I'm here, doing something I've always dreamed of doing. I admitted to Matt that I was horse crazy as a young girl. I wouldn't let up until my parents allowed me to take jumping lessons at a nearby stable. And then I grew up and life and work got in the way. But now...these wild horses..." She gave a dreamy sigh. "It's my dream come true. They're so beautiful. And those foals. Just so precious." She danced around, unable to contain herself any longer.

Then she paused as a thought struck. "Did you see the way the stallion watched us?"

"I saw."

"Was he thinking of charging us if we moved too close?"

Grace chuckled. "If we were predators, he would. But with people, whenever he feels threatened, he simply leads his herd to safety."

"So he knows the difference between people and other animals?"

Grace smiled. "Indeed. And because this herd is so isolated, he may not even feel threatened if we moved among them. But for today, I wanted to let him get used to seeing us."

"Did you see how many mares had foals?"

"Six. I counted them."

"I did, too. They're so cute. I could hardly keep from dashing into their midst and hugging them."

"I wouldn't advise it, Nessa." Grace gave a dry laugh. "Did you see the roan mare? The red one? She looks like she'll foal any day now."

"Do you think you'll get to capture it on film?"

"Oh, I hope so." After walking around their campsite, quietly studying the truck and their gear, Grace went to her camera equipment, sorting through lenses and cameras. "I hope you don't mind if I delay fixing something to eat until after I've assembled everything I'll need to take along tomorrow."

"You do that, and let me handle fixing our supper."

"You don't mind, Nessa?"

"I'd love to. After all, Yancy did all the hard work. All I have to do is choose what to heat up." Vanessa opened the metal container and began rummaging through the labeled packages of prepared food. "Do you have anything in particular you'd like to eat, or would you like to be surprised?"

"Surprise me."

Later as they sat around the fire, contentedly enjoying Yancy's thinly shaved roast beef sandwiches with thick potato wedges and creamy coleslaw, Grace looked over. "Excellent choices, Nessa."

"Thanks. Not that it matters. I don't think Yancy is capable of fixing anything except the best." She bit into her last potato wedge. "How long has he been your ranch cook?"

"I guess it's over thirty years now."

"How did you find him? Did you advertise for a cook?"

"Advertise? I'm afraid not. It didn't happen that way." Grace sat back, sipping coffee. "It was late October or early November, as I recall. My son Patrick heard a knock on the door long after dark. He opened it and we heard him let out a furious oath." She shook her head. "Frankie hurried over to see who was there. Burke was carrying a boy, who looked to be about ten or twelve, who had blood dripping from a gash on his forehead, and he was barefoot. I don't know which was more shocking—the blood or the bare feet on such a cold night. Burke said he found the boy collapsed in our barn, trying to hide under the straw. The boy could barely walk, he was so exhausted and wounded, so Burke carried him inside and set him in front of the fire, while I ran around looking for a blanket

to wrap him in. Just about that time there was a pounding on the door, and Frankie opened it to a man with a
rifle in his arms and fire in his eyes. He said he was Rhys
Martin, looking for his no-good son Yancy. Frankie told
him he had to leave the rifle outside if he wanted to come
in. So he dropped the rifle, and when he spotted the boy
he was across the room in a flash and hauling him up
so he could pound his fist in his face. Burke and Patrick
pulled them apart, and when they got the man to settle
down enough to say his piece, they learned that this boy
was actually eighteen, even though he was no bigger than
a ten-year-old. Rhys Martin blamed his own son for all
the setbacks in his life. Because of 'this scrawny kid,' as
he called him, his wife had died while giving birth to him.
And ever since, all manner of bad things had happened.
Cows were dying. Crops were failing. He was losing his
ranch."

Vanessa couldn't hide her shock. "He thought it was
all his son's fault?"

Grace nodded. "His whole life, according to Rhys
Martin, was ruined because of this boy. And he was going
to beat some manliness into him, if it was the last thing
he ever did."

Vanessa was wringing her hands, clearly caught up in
what she was hearing. "What happened then?"

Grace gave a soft smile. "We all listened in silence,
and then Frank asked Yancy if what his pa said was true.
Yancy said it was. Nothing had ever gone right since he'd
been born. And his father held him accountable for every bad thing that had ever happened. Then Frankie asked
the father if he loved his boy. Rhys Martin asked how
anyone could love a misfit like that. He said not only

did he not love Yancy, but he wished he'd never been born." Grace's voice lowered. Softened. "For my Frankie, that was the last straw. He told Burke to call the sheriff. Rhys Martin ran out the door, knowing he'd be arrested for abuse. Frankie raced to the door to let him know that Rhys would never be allowed to come close to his boy again. And if the sheriff found him, we would all testify against him."

"Did the sheriff find Rhys Martin?"

"There was no sign of him. He left his failing ranch behind, without a trace."

"Did Yancy ever see his father again?"

Grace shook her head. "And never wanted to. He once confided in Frankie that he believes he was born on that fateful night. Living with us, taking such joy in cooking, he found the life he'd always wanted, and he was never going back."

Vanessa poured herself another cup of coffee. "My dad likes to say that everyone has a story to tell."

"I'm sure, as a district attorney, your father hears more stories than most."

Vanessa nodded, deep in thought. "You realize you saved Yancy's life."

"We did. But he has more than repaid us in his loyalty and generosity to our family."

"I can understand why. What a hellish childhood he must have had."

"And what a good man he's become."

A short time later, as the two of them cleaned up the remains of their supper and slid into their bedrolls, Vanessa thought about the sweet cook who always had a big smile and an even bigger heart.

However painful his childhood had been, he'd risen above it.

And it was no surprise to her that the Malloy family had been Yancy's guardian angels. From everything she'd seen of them, they had the most open, loving, welcoming hearts for anyone fortunate enough to enter into and be touched by their lives.

CHAPTER SEVENTEEN

Grace was up before dawn, and the sounds of her movements had Vanessa sitting up and shoving hair from her eyes.

Grace set a coffeepot over the fire before looking up. "Good morning. How did you sleep?"

"I don't think I moved all night."

"Are you sore from all that hiking?"

"A little." Vanessa rolled her shoulders. "Nothing I can't manage. I just feel...eager to get back to the herd."

Grace laughed. "Spoken like a true adventurer. Let's eat and get started."

Within minutes Vanessa was dressed and had stored her bedding in the back of the truck.

"We'll need to bring along enough food and water to get us through the day and night."

Vanessa's eyes went wide. "We're staying with the herd?"

"Possibly." Grace gave a mysterious smile. "It will all depend on our mare. She may have already given birth. If so, we'll be there and back in no time. But if I get a chance to photograph the entire delivery, we'll stay until it's over, regardless of the time it takes."

Vanessa put a hand to her heart. "Oh, Grace, I hope we get there in time."

They ate quickly, then filled their backpacks with what they would need for the day and night, choosing to leave their bedrolls at camp and take only warm parkas for the night.

They were on the trail within the hour. And by the time they reached the herd, the sun was just climbing above the peaks of the nearby mountains.

They quickly scanned the horses, holding their breath as they counted the mares and their foals.

"The same number as yesterday," Grace whispered.

"That's good. Right?"

Grace nodded and pointed. Not far away was the mare they'd spotted the previous day, so swollen it looked as though she might explode if she didn't soon give birth.

Grace began assembling her equipment.

Vanessa watched with interest as the older woman set up a tripod, chose from an array of lenses, and then fixed one to a camera that she then mounted on the tripod. She kept a second camera dangling around her neck. In a bag at her feet were several more cameras and dozens of lenses.

The two sat down beside a boulder and watched the herd in silence.

Following Grace's lead, Vanessa learned to remove her water bottle, or a packet of food, with as little sound and movement as necessary, so as to not draw attention. Though the stallion, whom Vanessa had secretly named Ghost, continued to stand watch, he had also begun moving among the mares, even turning his back on the women to graze.

"You see," Grace said in a low tone. "He's beginning to accept our presence here."

"That's good?"

"That's very good."

In the hours that followed, the two women shared food and several long, impassioned discussions about the wild horses, and what role animal groups and the government ought to play in their lives.

It was clear, from the fervor in Grace's tone, that she believed the mustangs should be left alone as much as possible, to roam free and live as they always had.

"What about the freezing cold? What about starvation when snow covers their source of food?" Vanessa pressed the issues that were uppermost in the minds of the members of her various animal associations.

"These are wild creatures. Nature equips them to survive the cold. Unlike domestic animals, they grow a thicker, coarser coat that can see them through the coldest temperatures. They've learned to adapt. Whether it's a blizzard or a raging summer storm, they figure things out."

"Are you saying you've never fed them?"

Grace gave a mysterious half smile. "Frankie and I have hauled tons of hay up here on a flatbed truck when Mother Nature turned on us and delivered a killing winter. But if we didn't help out, most of these horses would survive, just as they have all these centuries."

Vanessa pressed her. "But some would die."

The older woman leaned close. "Here's the difference between hauling some feed and meddling. Some years back, someone concerned about the herds of wild horses decided that they ought to set up some feeding stations and put birth control in the food. It stands to reason that would be the humane method of curbing the size of the herds. Right?"

Vanessa nodded. "Sounds sensible to me."

"Consider this." Grace's tone took on that of a lecturer. "Nature dictates a time for everything. That's why, in the wild, creatures give birth in spring, when there's an abundance of food for the mothers who nurse, and a gentle climate in which to raise up the young so they're strong enough to face winter's wrath."

"Well, yes, that makes sense."

"Except to the agency who messed with nature. Within a year or two, after the herds wandered hundreds of miles from the feeding stations, the birth control wore off, and many of the animals began conceiving at the wrong time of year. I came across mares that had foaled in the dead of winter, long before their natural cycle would have dictated. With little food, the mares' milk dried up. With several feet of snow on the ground, the foals couldn't move. Since a mother couldn't leave her foal behind, often both mare and foal froze to death in a blizzard. Those poor, vulnerable animals never had a chance."

Vanessa put a hand to her mouth, her eyes wide with shock. "Didn't those in charge research all of this before they started the project?"

"Apparently the clever committee that dreamed up the plan never gave it a thought. Often, within large agencies, compassion for the very ones they're supposed to be taking care of isn't high on the list." Grace paused. "I sent some of the photos to Washington to let them see the damage that had been caused. I never got a response."

"Oh, Grace." Vanessa was clearly moved. "I'm so sorry."

The older woman touched a hand to her arm. "Actions have consequences. So often we want to do the right thing, but if we don't think things through, we pay a high price for our well-meaning decisions."

Seeing the herd moving closer, the two women fell silent. But it was clear that the things Grace had told her left Vanessa deep in thought.

Grace lifted a hand in a silent signal.

Vanessa glanced across the field to where the heavily pregnant mare was standing. At first there was nothing to set her apart from the other mares nearby, except her size. Though Vanessa would expect the mare to be agitated, or breathing heavily, all she could see was a calm, quiet horse circling a patch of grass, but not eating.

Circling. Circling.

As though seeking a soft spot to recline.

Within the hour the mare folded her forelegs, kneeling, before dropping down in the grass. She remained very still, lying on her side, though her breathing had increased considerably.

Vanessa glanced at Grace. Between the camera mounted on the tripod and the wide-angle lens on the camera around her neck, Grace was busy catching each amazing moment on film.

A short time later Vanessa realized that the foal was coming quickly now. A gush of water, a tiny hoof visible through the opaque film of fluid, and suddenly, the foal slipped free of its mother and lay in the grass, while the mare licked it clean.

"It's so tiny and helpless."

"Only for a short time." Grace kept her focus on the mare and foal. "You won't believe how quickly that little one will be on its feet and trailing after its mother."

"Oh, Grace." Vanessa clutched the older woman's arm, so caught up in the beauty of the birth she could hardly speak.

"I know." Grace's smile was radiant. "Isn't it the most amazing sight? Every time I have the good fortune to witness such a miracle, I'm humbled and grateful."

As Grace went back to snapping off photos, Vanessa's attention was riveted on the mare and her foal.

As a girl she'd loved horses. So much so, she'd used every argument she could think of to persuade her parents to allow her to ride jumpers. And despite her mother's great fear that her only child might be seriously injured partaking in such a dangerous activity, she had reluctantly given her permission. But only, she insisted, because she could see the passion that burned in her daughter for the horses.

That passion had never died, but it had faded in her teen years. She'd thought her efforts on behalf of the animal foundations had been enough to feed that passion. Now, suddenly, in this amazing moment, it was back, and stronger than ever. Now, finally, she understood why she'd forsaken criminal law to become an advocate for the protection of wild animals. And why she'd been drawn to interview Grace Anne LaRou Malloy, the foremost expert on the West's wild horses.

She needed to be here. Right here in the Montana

wilderness, watching the birth of a foal, and thrilling to the very fact that a wild stallion, feeling edgy and protective of his herd, was allowing her to be this close to them.

Because of her father, and her government association, she'd met many famous dignitaries, even world leaders. But none could even come close to this singular experience.

Her heart was beating overtime just knowing she was, right this moment, living her childhood dream.

"Oh, Grace. I'll never be able to thank you for this experience. For this day."

"I believe this is the hundredth time you've thanked me, Nessa." Grace hefted her backpack, relieved to see their campsite up ahead. It had been a long, emotional day, and now that the adrenaline was wearing off, she could feel her energy flagging. She would be grateful for the chance to relax and unwind.

Vanessa's laughter trilled on the air. "I know. I just can't stop thanking you. This has been the most amazing day of my life." Seeing the older woman's concentration, Vanessa stopped her. "Here. Give me your pack."

"I can manage. I always—"

Vanessa took it from her and draped it across one shoulder. As she started to bolt ahead, Grace put a hand to her shoulder. "Wait. I'd like to . . ."

Vanessa paused. "What?"

Grace's smile stayed in place. "Nothing. I just like to check out my surroundings before I go stumbling into camp."

"Did you do this the other times we returned?"

"Of course. I arranged certain things in certain ways,

knowing if they were altered, it would mean we'd had visitors."

Because she was wearing sunglasses, Vanessa couldn't see the older woman's eyes. But she could see her swivel her head slightly, taking in the lay of the land.

Vanessa felt a prickling at the back of her neck. "Do you see something?"

"It could be nothing." Laying a hand on her arm, Grace signaled her to remain behind as she paused to pick up a zipper pull that must have fallen from a parka. "Did you lose this?"

Vanessa shook her head.

"I don't believe it was here this morning." Holding it in her hand, Grace walked to the truck and tested the driver's side door.

Though it was locked, she dropped to her knees and retrieved a piece of thread from the grass. When she stood, she plucked her phone from her pocket. Seeing that it had no signal, she lifted her rifle in the air and fired a shot.

The sound of it echoed and reechoed across the hills.

Vanessa flinched at the sound of the thunder of the gunshot matching the thundering of her heart. She hurried to stand beside Grace. "What's wrong? Are we in trouble? Has somebody been here?"

Grace nodded. "I need to see if anything's missing."

While the two worked side by side checking their supplies, a horse and rider appeared over a ridge.

Vanessa stared in stunned surprise to see Matt dismount and hurry over.

"Your grandmother only fired her rifle a minute ago. How could you possibly get here so quickly?"

"I was...nearby."

He turned to his grandmother, who pointed to the truck. "I did what you told me, Matthew. I tied a thread to the door handle." She held out the piece of thread. "I found this in the grass. Torn in two. Have you seen anything out of order?"

"Not a thing." He walked a short distance away, studying the ground. "The grass isn't flattened by tires or hooves. No tracks. If anyone tried to jimmy the lock, they came here on foot."

"In the middle of the wilderness?"

He nodded. "I know it sounds crazy. But we've been guarding the perimeter since you arrived. No vehicles in or out. That doesn't mean they couldn't have come in by horseback. If there were only one or two of them, they may have managed to sneak past us."

Vanessa knew her jaw dropped. "You've been guarding us?"

Ignoring her question, Grace looked skyward. "A plane? A helicopter?"

"We'd have seen and heard them."

"Then someone went to a lot of trouble to come all this way without taking anything. When they found the doors of the truck locked, they could have broken the windows, or jimmied the locks, and helped themselves to anything they wanted."

Matt's eyes narrowed. "You had your rifle with you?"

She nodded.

"They may have come to steal it, hoping to leave you helpless. But I agree that they could have forced their way inside the truck and helped themselves to the rest of your supplies, unless..."

"Unless what?"

"My first thought is the thread could have simply snapped in the breeze." He shrugged. "Or, if someone was here, maybe they saw the thread after they tried the door, and realized they'd been detected. There was no way to tie it back together and hope you wouldn't notice. So they decided to leave it in the grass just to let you to know they know you're on to them. Even if they couldn't accomplish much, they've managed to add another layer of fear and intimidation."

Grace mulled that for a moment before nodding. "All right. So now we know that they know where we are. But they have to know we'll redouble our efforts to evade them."

"Maybe they spotted our wranglers in the area, and realized they would be caught if they didn't run immediately."

"Maybe." Grace saw the way Vanessa was staring at the two of them, and realized that an explanation was in order. She turned to the young woman and extended a hand. "I'm sorry, Nessa. It isn't right to keep secrets, but I didn't want anything to spoil your first trip to the wilderness, so I thought I'd just keep to myself the fact that our men would be looking out for us."

"I shouldn't be surprised. But now that I know, I feel terrible that my being here has caused so many people to work overtime to keep me safe."

"They're keeping both of us safe. And they don't mind." Grace turned to her grandson. "Do you?"

He kept his gaze firmly on Vanessa. "It's what family does."

Grace glanced at the cold ashes in the firepit. "As long

as you're here, Matthew, why don't you get a fire going and stay for supper?"

"Thanks. I'd love to." He winked at her. "I was hoping you'd ask."

He added a couple of logs and some kindling, and soon had a fire blazing.

Grace started toward the stream to fill the coffeepot, leaving Vanessa alone with Matt.

As soon as Grace was gone, Vanessa crossed her arms over her chest, her tone lowered with righteous accusation. "I had the right to know what this trip was costing you and your family."

"All it cost was manpower, and we have plenty of that."

"Manpower that's needed with the herds. You said yourself it takes every wrangler you have just to keep a ranch of this size working efficiently. And here I am, living out my fantasy at the expense of so many others."

Matt's voice was as calm as hers was harsh. "You're our guest, Nessa." When she opened her mouth to protest, he held up a hand. "Maybe not by your choice, but our guest all the same. And there's no way in hell my family would allow you to be in any more danger than necessary."

She lowered her arms to her sides and turned away. The only indication of her agitation was her booted foot tapping a nervous tattoo. "No more secrets, Matt. I can handle danger better than I can handle being treated like some poor helpless female."

"I can't argue with that. There's nothing helpless about you." He touched a hand to her arm. "Am I forgiven?"

She kept her face averted. "Of course. As long as you

give me your word you won't shut me out of any decisions being made about my safety."

"You have it."

"Good." She huffed out a breath before turning toward the truck.

She rummaged through the supplies in the metal container, noting Yancy's careful labeling of each packet.

Matt stepped up beside her. "Need some help?"

She held up two packets. "I'll let you decide. Turkey and stuffing, or roast beef and gravy?"

"Turkey." He held out his hand. "I'll set it on the grate."

She found a packet of mashed potatoes and walked up behind him. "You can heat these, too. And I'll find that container of salad I spotted yesterday."

They worked companionably together, assembling plates and utensils.

When at last Vanessa dropped down on a sun-warmed rock, Matt sat beside her. "So. Has your wilderness experience been all you'd hoped for?"

"Oh, Matt." She looked up at him, eyes shining with excitement. "It's been amazing. We found a herd. The stallion didn't challenge us, and today we got even closer and watched a foal being born." She shook her head, as though unable to take it all in. "Your grandmother caught it all on film. And it was…" She took in a deep breath. "I know you'll think I'm being melodramatic, but it was magical. I was afraid to move. Afraid even to breathe. I was sure at any moment our presence would spook the herd and they'd scatter. Or worse, I'd wake up and discover it was all just a dream."

He was staring at her in a way that had her going still and silent.

"What's wrong?" she asked.

"Nothing. Just wondering who you are and what you've done with that cool, unemotional workaholic lawyer named Vanessa Kettering."

She started to laugh, but she was cut off as he kissed her. She absorbed little sparks all through her over-charged system.

When he lifted his head she leaned in. "Do that again. Please."

"My pleasure, ma'am." With a wolfish smile he dragged her close and kissed her until they were both breathless. "Want more?"

She put a hand on his chest. "Anything more and I'd have to crawl inside you, which could prove embarrassing when your grandmother returns."

At the mention of Grace, she shot him a puzzled look. "Where is Grace? She was just going to the stream for water."

With the thought of danger uppermost in their minds, they were both up and running, fearing the worst.

Before they were halfway to the stream Grace came strolling toward them, hair dripping, carrying her hiking boots.

"I thought I'd give you two a few minutes alone. And then, once I got there, the cool water looked so inviting, I had to wash." She shot a girlish glance at her grandson. "If you hadn't been here, Matthew, I'd have probably walked back to camp as naked as the day I was born to slip into something clean and warm. But I was feeling charitable, and I decided that wasn't a memory a grandson of mine ought to bear for the rest of his life."

"Thanks for that." He managed a smile, though his

heart was still pounding. "But next time you decide to give us some time alone, don't wander so far away from camp."

Grace turned to Vanessa. "You see? Let a man into your adventure, or your life, and he just has to start giving orders."

CHAPTER EIGHTEEN

Nessa tells me you found a herd." Matt sat in the grass, his back resting against a rock, feet stretched out to the warmth of the fire, enjoying dinner and the pleasant company.

"We did. Not the one I've been looking for this past year, led by that magnificent white stallion." Grace glanced at Vanessa. "This one had a gray leader."

"I named him Ghost," Vanessa admitted.

"You named him?" Matt gave her a bemused look. "Next thing you know, you'll want to take him home with you and make him your pet."

She blushed like a schoolgirl. "I don't know why I admitted that to you. Now I'll probably never hear the end of it."

"You've got that right."

Watching the two of them, Grace couldn't help smiling. "I hope at least a few of the photos I took of a mare delivering her foal are good enough to put up for sale."

"Gram Grace, I've never known any of your pictures to be less than exceptional."

Grace winked at Vanessa. "He's just a little bit prejudiced."

"As he should be." Vanessa set aside her empty plate. "There aren't too many men who can brag about their famous and talented grandmothers."

"Now you sound like my Frankie." Grace sighed. "That man just purely dotes on me."

"I noticed. And I can see why." Vanessa shared a smile with Matt. "Does he ever come with you on these wilderness treks?"

"When he can spare the time. I love having him along. He does all the grunt work and allows me to concentrate on my photography."

Matt chuckled. "Is this an invitation for me to stay and shoulder Grandpop's load?"

"I was hoping you'd take the hint." Grace looked at him over the rim of her cup. "Especially now that we've had proof of a visitor."

"Then it's settled." He put his hands under his head and glanced skyward. "Looks like a perfect night for sleeping under the stars. Especially since I texted the others to let them know I was here."

Grace crossed to him and kissed his cheek. "Bless you, Matthew."

As she walked toward the truck to retrieve her bedroll, Vanessa turned to him. "Your grandfather's not the only one who feels the love. She dotes on you, too."

He merely grinned. "It's my charm."

When she tossed her pillow at his head, he caught it one-handed before dropping it. "Careful, woman," he drawled. "That's an invitation to a duel."

"Pistols at dawn? Will I be branded a troublemaker?"

"I might have something else in mind. But be warned. You'd be branded all the same."

His words, spoken lightly, sent a thrill along her spine.

Grace returned and set out her bedroll near the fire. She snuggled into its warmth and drew up her knees, wrapping her arms around them. "Nessa, tell me how a smart big-city lawyer took up the cause of wild animals. Has this always been your passion?"

Vanessa smiled. "I think so. I wasn't always aware of it, but my dad says he recognized it way back in my earliest days. He tells me I was always the champion of the underdog, including Jeepers, our third-grade mascot."

Grace smiled indulgently. "A dog?"

"A hamster."

Grace exchanged an amused look with Matt before asking, "What made Jeepers an underdog?"

"Over our midwinter break, we came back to discover that the student who had volunteered to take him home for the holiday had forgotten and left him behind in the classroom. The poor little thing was hiding under his empty food dish and shaking so badly when he saw us, our teacher thought he was having a seizure. I insisted on holding him until the tremors subsided. After class I told my teacher I was taking him home so he wouldn't have to be alone overnight."

"So a hamster changed your life." Matt winked at his grandmother.

"Jeepers may have been the start, but it was a coyote while I was in high school that sealed the deal."

"A coyote in Chicago?" Grace was laughing. "This should prove to be quite a story."

"Yes. Poor thing made the headlines. A lost, terrified coyote was spotted dodging cars along Division Street, and before an animal control officer could catch it, a woman screamed that she was afraid for her life and a police officer was forced to shoot it, even though the poor, frightened thing was running away from her, and not toward her. That's when I realized that wild animals needed an advocate."

Grace glanced at her grandson, who was staring at Vanessa with a look that was both fierce and tender.

She'd seen that look before. In her son's eyes when he'd looked at his bride at the age of seventeen. In her husband's eyes the first time Grace had seen him, riding into her camp, demanding to know who she was and why she was on his land. She'd lost her heart to him in an instant, just as he'd lost his heart to her.

She pretended to yawn behind her hand as she slid deeper into her bedroll. "I hope you two don't mind, but after the day I put in, I really need to sleep."

Matt blew her a kiss, while Vanessa called, "Good night, Gracie. Thanks again for this amazing day."

Though Grace could have stayed awake another hour or more, the sound of their muted voices, and the gurgle of the stream nearby, soon lulled her into sleep.

Matt filled two mugs with coffee and held up a bottle of whiskey. At Vanessa's nod of approval, he splashed some into each cup before passing one to her.

He sat beside her, and they leaned against his saddle while stretching their legs toward the fire.

"How do you like sleeping under the stars?"

Her smile was radiant. "I'm loving it."

"Really?" He turned to study her. "You're not missing all the comforts of home?"

"I'm not. And that surprises me. I expected to feel out of my element here. I mean, no showers, no shampoo, no change of clothes. And the bedroll isn't much of a cushion against the hard, cold ground. But"—she sighed—"instead of feeling like a homesick kid at camp, I feel like I was meant to be here."

"I'm glad. I know it can't be easy, finding yourself far from everything familiar."

"That's just it. Though I've never been here before, I feel as though somehow this place has been waiting for me to discover it." She turned to him. "I hope this doesn't sound crazy, but this whole day has been like a dream come true for me. The herd. The mare giving birth. Watching the stallion not only accepting our presence but turning away, ignoring us, as though he'd already figured out that we weren't there to do harm. It was"—she exuded barely controlled excitement and energy—"too amazing for words. And I've embarrassed myself by thanking your grandmother so many times, she's probably sick of hearing my voice."

"I can't imagine anyone who wouldn't enjoy hearing that voice." He lifted a hand to the lock of hair that had drifted across her cheek. He tucked the hair behind her ear, then kept his hand there, his fingers stroking the side of her neck. "You voice is mesmerizing. And so are you, Nessa."

He leaned close and brushed a soft kiss on her lips. She kept her eyes open, seeing herself reflected in his dark gaze.

As he started to pull back she lifted a hand to his cheek. "Could you...? Could you just hold me a little longer?"

"It would be my pleasure, ma'am." He gathered her close.

It started off as a mere touch of mouth to mouth, but it quickly turned into a sizzle of heat that had them sighing as they took it deeper, lingering over the kiss until they were struggling for breath.

Matt glanced toward his grandmother's bedroll. "We'd better think about getting some sleep."

"I should be tired." Vanessa sighed. "But the truth is, I'm so keyed up, I'm not sure I'll be able to sleep at all." As he started to move away she put a hand on his arm. "If I haven't told you, Matt, I'm so relieved to have you here."

"Even though I've intruded on your privacy?"

She bit her lip. "I know I reacted badly, and I'm sorry for that."

"I'm sorry, too. I never wanted anything to spoil your grand adventure."

"I thought it couldn't get any better than today, seeing the herd of mustangs, and the bonus of seeing a foal born. And Grace is so comfortable here in the wilderness that I trust her to know exactly what to do. But in truth, I feel safer having you here with us."

"Careful. I could be your biggest threat of all." He swept another quick kiss over her mouth before getting to his feet. He walked to the far side of the fire and tossed down his saddle before lying beside it. Wrapping a parka around himself, he winked before closing his eyes.

Vanessa smiled and turned to stare into the flames.

She'd been so surprised when Matt had turned up at their camp, just minutes after Grace fired off a shot. And she'd been stunned and horrified to think their entire family and their ranch hands had been forced to forgo their own chores in order to keep her safe. Still, the more she thought about it, the more she realized that it gave her great comfort to know Matt had been around the entire time, watching out for their safety.

Watching out for their safety.

It was Matt's way. Seeing to his younger brothers, his uncle, his grandparents. Whether he'd chosen this path, or it had been chosen for him by the Fates, he was singularly qualified to take responsibility for everyone he cared about. The land. The ranch and wranglers. And now, a woman who had come unbidden into his life and couldn't leave until the threat of danger was eliminated. And though she was secretly terrified, not only for herself but for her father, she felt somehow safer knowing Matt was here. His strength, not only physical, but that inner core of steel as well, made her believe that no harm could come to her as long as Matt Malloy was beside her.

It was, she realized, one very compelling reason to love him.

Love?

She rolled to her side, watching the flames flare up, sending sparks into the darkness.

It didn't seem possible that she could have such feelings for a man she hardly knew.

She was attracted to him. She trusted him. And she was

enchanted by his family. Plus, because of him, she was living her dream. But that didn't add up to love. Did it?

Hadn't her father once joked that every young woman he knew fell in love with the idea of love at least once in her life before finding the real thing?

There had been boyfriends, dates, flings, and one rather serious relationship that had ended badly, though in truth she couldn't believe she'd ever shed a tear over such a shallow man. And though she'd had varying degrees of joy and sorrow, over-the-top happiness and moments of sheer bliss, she'd never felt like this. Out of her depth, and floundering, and doing her best to stay one step ahead of a man like Matt.

A man like Matt.

He wasn't like the boys she'd grown up with, the young lawyers she'd competed against, or the men with whom she now worked. There was a toughness to him, a rough-around-the-edges attitude that let you know he meant what he said and did what he thought right, no matter the consequences. He had a shrewd mind. A head for business. Could hold his own in a debate. A true cowboy.

He was a man's man. And yet, he treated her with almost old-fashioned courtliness. He was such a contradiction.

How would she know if what she was feeling was real or some glorified idea of the old fairy tale every child had been fed? Handsome prince discovering the princess of his dreams. Superman and Lois Lane.

But was it love?

She should call it what it was. Lust. Oh yes, now that was something she could admit to. She wanted Matt. Couldn't get him out of her mind. With every day that passed, she found herself more and more tempted by the idea of making love with him. But making love wasn't the same as loving someone completely, unselfishly.

They lived in two very different worlds. When the trial was over, and the threat removed, she would return to her life, and all of this would just be a pleasant memory.

She closed her eyes, weary of the debate she was waging with herself. This need to examine every side of an issue had always been both her blessing and her curse.

For now, for this night, she needed to turn off her logical lawyer's brain and just let it be. It was enough to know that Matt was here, just a few feet away, ready to slay any dragons that threatened.

Not that she needed any help with dragons. She'd been fighting them alone for years now, thank you very much.

But having a partner nearby, someone watching her back, was a real comfort.

It was her last conscious thought before drifting off to sleep.

CHAPTER NINETEEN

The morning was cool and damp. The mountain peaks were cloaked in mist. After a quick breakfast, they packed up the gear they would need for the day and started out across the high meadow.

Matt held his horse's reins loosely, choosing to walk with the women and lead his horse. They had tied their supplies behind the saddle, freeing their hands.

Grace's eyes were crinkled with happiness. "Matthew, I must admit, having you and Beau has lightened our load considerably." She turned to Vanessa, who was walking beside Matt. "Don't you agree, Nessa?"

"Absolutely. Those backpacks were getting heavier each day."

"That's because I kept adding more camera equipment each day, or didn't you notice?"

Vanessa chuckled. "Oh, I noticed." She glanced at Grace's rifle, which Matt had shoved into a boot of the saddle. "I didn't want to admit this, but the last time I carried your rifle, I almost knocked myself out when I turned too quickly."

"That's quite a visual. The next time you're in DC, presenting your thoughts to your wildlife commissions, that ought to keep you grounded."

Matt's dry remark had the three of them laughing.

"I'll leave that part out of it while I brag about my adventures in the Montana wilderness. And I guarantee that I will brag about it."

Matt shot her an admiring glance. "I'll just bet you will."

"You can't blame a girl for doing whatever it takes to impress the bureaucrats in Washington."

Grace nodded in approval. "Oh, I'm sure you've already impressed them, my dear. How many of their young attorneys would bother coming all this way just to see for themselves how their rules and regulations affect the very creatures they're hoping to protect?"

Vanessa's cheeks flamed. "You make me sound noble. The truth is, I'm having the time of my life. I wouldn't trade this for all the personal meetings with congressmen and -women, or those boring cocktail parties I'm forced to attend just to make the proper connections."

Grace looped her arm through Vanessa's. "I'm sure there are a lot of ambitious young lawyers who would be thrilled to have your job."

"Oh, don't get me wrong. I love my job. But these last few days are so far outside my realm of experience. I'd always hoped to have times like this, but I never really believed it was possible." She squeezed Grace's hand. "Thanks to you, I'm living my dream."

* * *

By the time they reached the herd of mustangs, the sun broke from behind the clouds. Soon after, the day quickly heated up. Each time they removed a layer of clothing, Matt stored it in his saddlebags.

Grace set up her cameras, then snapped off shots of the various mares and their precious foals, and often took aim at the majestic stallion, alone and aloof, standing on a sloping meadow, keeping watch over his herd.

Vanessa appointed herself keeper of the equipment. Whenever Grace wanted to move the tripod, or requested a change of lens, or another camera, Vanessa was there to assist. She had soon stripped down to her shorts and a tank top, and was still too warm.

For his part, Matt hauled the supplies, set up a campfire far enough from the herd that they wouldn't be spooked, and prepared a lunch that had both women sighing with pleasure when they finally took a break.

"Matthew, have you been taking lessons from Yancy?" Grace sat in the grass, polishing off the last of her skillet potatoes and roast beef.

He chuckled. "All I did was warm up whatever he sent along."

"It tastes amazing." Vanessa took a long drink from her water bottle.

"Hiking for miles in all this fresh air makes everything taste better." Matt studied the way she looked in denim shorts and a white tank, revealing that willowy body and long, shapely legs. He couldn't keep his eyes off her. It was all he could do to keep from drooling.

At the end of their meal Matt passed around chocolate

chip cookies. "I'll concede that Yancy's cookies could win any baking contest hands down."

"They could indeed." Grace savored every crumb.

A short time later she stood. "Time to get back to the horses. I want to take advantage of all the sunlight I can."

Vanessa held up her water bottle. "I'm heading to the creek to fill this. Anybody else need water?"

Grace shook her head. "I have enough. I'll see you back at the herd."

Vanessa ambled to the stream and knelt on the banks. When she stood, Matt came up behind her and dropped his hands to her waist, pulling her firmly to him.

"I've been thinking about this all morning." He spoke the words against her ear, sending shivers along her spine.

"So have I." She turned into his arms and offered her mouth.

He took it with a hunger that had them both sighing.

Vanessa wrapped her arms around his waist and slid her palms up his back. "I didn't think anything could ever distract me from wild horses, but right now I'm not even tempted to watch the herd. I just want to stay here in your arms."

"Talk about a distraction." He looked her up and down with a smile of pure pleasure. "I don't believe I've ever seen a woman look as sexy in shorts as you look in these."

"Then I'll have to remember to thank Trudy Evans for recommending them."

"I'll just thank heaven for the way you look in them." He nibbled a trail of kisses from her throat to her ear. "You feel so good here, I'd gladly stay for hours. But I'm afraid if you don't go, and soon, my grandmother might stumble across a shocking scene."

She couldn't help batting her lashes at him. "Now that's mighty tempting, cowboy." She gave him one last kiss before pushing free of his arms. "But I really do have an obligation to save Grace from shock."

He turned her into his arms. Against her temple he growled, "It's gotten so bad, I actually found myself praying for rain this morning, just so our fearless leader might be persuaded to head back to the ranch. I figured somewhere between here and there I could get you alone."

She touched a hand to his cheek. "There's always to-morrow."

"Another day?" He groaned. "Woman, you've got a very mean streak in you."

Her smile was quick and dangerous. "So I'm told."

As she started away he bent to pick up the bottle that had slid from her hands. "Don't forget this."

She glanced back, then burst into laughter. "I guess that kiss had my mind a little more muddled than I thought."

"Care to try again?"

She caught the fierce look in his eyes and shook her head. "One more and I'd never be able to leave." She took the bottle from his hands and sprinted up the hill, leaving him staring after her with a look of naked hunger.

Late in the afternoon the clouds returned, completely obliterating the sun.

Grace lowered her camera and glanced at Matt and Vanessa. "Why didn't one of you mention that storm coming in?"

"I didn't want to bother you." Matt was busy loading

her discarded equipment into his saddlebags. "That brooding sky should make for some impressive pictures."

"Until it opens up," Grace remarked drily. She snapped off a few shots of the angry sky before removing the camera from around her neck and placing it in a waterproof case.

Vanessa hurried over to help her pack up the rest of her cameras and lenses.

When they had everything stowed in their backpacks, Matt secured them behind the saddle, and the three of them turned toward their base camp, while keeping an eye on the storm clouds.

They paused at the top of a meadow and caught sight of Frank's truck parked alongside Grace's.

"Oh, Frankie's come to join us." The radiant smile on Grace's face said more than her words. She quickened her pace, and Matt was left to lead his mount more slowly, with Vanessa by his side.

He turned to Vanessa with a smug smile. "My prayers have been answered."

"You wanted another storm?"

He shrugged. "I just wanted anything that would give us an excuse to leave here and slip away by ourselves. Are you game?"

She smiled, and it was answer enough.

By the time they reached the trucks, Grace and Frank were locked in a tender embrace.

Grace stepped back a little, to touch a hand to her husband's cheek. "Is something wrong back at the ranch, or did you just miss me?"

He gave her a smile that banished all the dark clouds.

"I always miss you, Gracie Girl. And there's nothing wrong. I just wanted you here in my arms."

Then he glanced over at Matt holding his horse's reins, as a jagged sliver of lightning streaked the sky, followed by a rumble of thunder. "Storm's rolling in fast."

"I noticed." Matt crossed the distance between them to hug his grandfather.

Frank tugged on a lock of his wife's hair. "You find a herd?"

"I did. Not the big one, but this one had a mare ready to foal, and I caught it all on film."

"I'm glad, my girl. Does that mean you're ready to head home, or do you need more time up here?"

She shook her head. "I have all the pictures I need for now. And with that storm, your timing couldn't be better."

He nodded. "If we play our cards right, we ought to get back to the ranch in time for supper." He turned to Matt. "How about I drive Gracie in my truck, and you and Nessa can ride in Gracie's?"

"That'll work." Matt tied his horse behind Frank's truck. "You mind hauling Beau?"

"Not at all. But why don't you take him?" Before Matt could answer, Frank got busy stashing his wife's camera equipment in the backseat of his truck. "Let's get out of here, before we get blown away. We'll celebrate a successful trip with one of Yancy's fancy chicken dinners."

Matt's tone was deliberately bland. "You might want to eat without us."

Frank sent him an assessing look. "You're staying here?"

Matt gave a negligent shrug of his shoulders. "I

thought I'd check on that old range shack along the way. But you don't have to worry about us. If the storm gets too rough, at least we'll have shelter."

"Sure thing." Frank looked at Matt's horse. "I'll see old Beau gets an extra portion of feed tonight."

"Thanks, Grandpop."

Frank glanced beyond his grandson to the young woman standing quietly to one side. "I guess this is good-bye then. We'll see you back at the ranch, Nessa."

She merely nodded.

Grace hurried over to hug her. "I'm so glad you came with me, Nessa. I've never had a better companion."

"Thank you so much. I've fallen in love with your mustangs. You'll never know what this time in the hills has meant to me."

"I think I do." Grace gave the young woman a final hug before turning away and climbing into the passenger side of the truck.

Frank put the vehicle in gear and, with Beau trotting along behind, they started across the meadow. He watched the young couple in his rearview mirror before turning to his wife. "Did you know that was coming?"

Grace's voice was warm with laughter. "The story about needing to check on the range shack?"

He chuckled. "Then you're not buying it either?"

"Not a word of it." She laced her fingers with his. "I'm not sure they're even aware of how much their eyes reveal. But Frankie, those two are head over heels. And tumbling faster every minute."

He squeezed her hand and put a foot on the brake. "Want to go back and rain on their parade?"

"Don't even think about it." She patted his shoulder.

"Though it would be great fun to see their faces if we showed up to spoil all their plans."

He paused for a moment more before leaning over to kiss her mouth. "Okay. I'll go along with whatever you say. But only because if I turned back now, I'd ruin my carefully planned night alone with you, Gracie Girl. I have to say, that bed's been awfully empty without you."

He turned on the radio, and the two of them began humming along with Barbara Mandrell and the old country-and-western tune about sleeping single in a double bed. That had them both laughing out loud as Frank carefully navigated the rolling hills and meadows that spread out before them, leading them home.

CHAPTER TWENTY

Matt watched his grandfather's truck until it dipped below a ridge.

When he turned, Vanessa was staring at him with a puzzled look. "You need to check out a range shack?"

"Yeah." He circled the truck and opened the passenger door, helping Vanessa inside before walking to the driver's side, climbing in, and putting the vehicle in gear.

"Is it nearby?"

He seemed to be deep in thought. "What?"

"The range shack."

"Oh." The corners of his lips curved slightly. "It's a fair distance, but it was the best I could come up with on such short notice."

She removed her wide-brimmed hat and shook her hair. "You're not making any sense."

"I know. That's what you do to me."

She was grinning. "Now this is all my fault?"

"You bet. If you weren't wearing those sexy shorts and that second skin you call a tank top, I'd have probably had enough self-control to head home. But now, having been forced to spend the day looking at you, I'm barely holding it together."

"Ah." She said the word on a sigh as the truth dawned. "This is all just an excuse to get me alone."

"Now you're thinking." He shot her a dangerous smile. "Alone and naked."

"Couldn't you have come up with something a bit more believable than checking out a range shack?"

"Do you object?"

"Not at all, cowboy. Although I do object to having to drive a fair distance."

"We could always stop right here."

She glanced at the black, swirling clouds overhead. "Not on your life. I want shelter from this soon-to-hit storm, and I want it as fast as possible."

"Yes, ma'am." He floored the accelerator and the two of them were laughing like children as they flew up ridges and down gullies until, at last, they caught sight of a cabin looming in the distance.

She turned to him with a look of surprise. "Isn't this the same cabin where we first met?"

"It is."

"Well, aren't you the clever one."

"Yes, ma'am. I am. Or at least I try to be, as I said, on short notice."

He pulled up beside the cabin and helped her from the truck. Before they could take a single step his arms were around her, dragging her close in a fierce embrace. "I know we should get inside, but this can't wait."

His hungry mouth found hers and nearly devoured her.

She responded with equal hunger, her arms around his neck, holding on to him like a lifeline as a wicked wind blew up and buffeted them with such force it nearly blew them apart.

They were so caught up in the kiss, they were startled when the sky opened up and they were hit with a drenching rain.

Matt lifted his head, struggling to get his bearings. "Sorry. Looks like we didn't beat the storm after all. My key . . ." He fumbled in his pocket before turning toward the door, all the while keeping his arm firmly around Vanessa to shield her.

As he struggled to unlock the cabin door, she put a hand over his. "Let me help."

"Or we could just stand out here and try that kiss again."

"Not until you get me out of this rain."

Laughing, they turned the lock and stumbled inside.

"Oh yeah. This is better." He backed her against the closed door before pressing his body to hers and taking her mouth in a kiss so filled with desperate need it had her head spinning.

She kissed him back, pouring herself into it, impatient for more, until they were both struggling for breath.

"I need to . . ." He stripped away her tank, revealing a tiny nude silk bra that had his eyes narrowing. "Oh, lady, you do know how to get my blood hot."

"You're welcome." Her lips curved as she reached for the buttons of his shirt.

As it dropped to the floor she ran her hands up his arms, across his shoulders, and down his chest, making little humming sounds as she did. "You have the most amazing body."

"Why, thank you for noticing, ma'am. It's all yours. Do with me what you want."

She gave a tortured laugh. "That's really generous of you."

"Anything for my lady." He shucked his boots and jeans and dragged her close, pressing hot, wet kisses to the sensitive hollow between her neck and shoulder.

She arched her neck, loving the feel of his clever mouth on her flesh. But when he moved lower, down her throat, then lower still, to take one erect nipple into his mouth, all she could do was sigh and clutch blindly at his waist.

As he moved from one breast to the other, the pleasure continued building until it became so intense, she whispered, "Matt. Please. I don't think I can wait."

"Now I'm 'Matt' instead of 'cowboy.'"

"I thought that would get your attention faster."

"You have my complete attention, Nessa." He tugged away her shorts and the tiny nude bikini beneath.

For the space of a heartbeat, all he could do was stare. "God, you're incredible. I can't wait to get my hands on you."

And he did. Touching her everywhere. With teeth and tongue and fingertips he took her on a wild, dizzying roller-coaster ride that had her writhing with frantic need and trembling for more.

"Matt . . ." When she touched him as he was touching her, she could feel the raw passion blazing through him.

The moment her hands came in contact with him, he

pressed her back against the rough door and kissed her until they were both struggling for breath.

His eyes were fixed on hers. "I thought I could be civilized, and show you all kinds of clever, seductive moves, but I can't wait. I need you now, Nessa. This minute."

With her back to the rough door he lifted her off her feet.

"Yes." The single word was torn from her dry throat. She could barely speak over the feelings that had completely taken over. "I need you, too. Now." She wrapped herself around him and let her head drop back as he thrust into her.

Her body had become a mass of nerve endings. Raw. Sensitive. She could feel him in every pore. His hands, those wonderful, calloused, rough hands, moving over her. His mouth burning a trail of heat down her throat.

He began to move with agonizing, deliberate slowness, and with each thrust she was moving with him, desperate to find release.

His thundering heartbeat kept time with hers.

As his movements increased, she moved with him, climbing frantically upward, higher, then higher still.

She could feel him pulsing with that same need, and rockets began going off in her head.

Her heart racing, her breath hitching, she climbed up and up, moving with him until behind her closed lids, brilliant fireworks exploded.

At his shuddering response she opened her eyes to see herself reflected in his blue depths, and could feel her body, her mind, her heart exploding in a shattering climax.

She shattered into fiery pieces before drifting slowly to earth.

"Sorry." Matt's face was buried in the hollow of her throat.

"Umm. For what?"

He knew he could die happy now. Or maybe he had. Maybe this was heaven. "I was rough." He struggled to lift his head. He looked into Vanessa's eyes. "I really intended to get us to the bed."

"There's always next time."

His smile bloomed. "So you'll go for seconds?"

"Or thirds." She managed to move enough to bring a hand to his cheek. "As long as you promise you'll do all that again."

"Deal. In fact, I really wanted to do more. Lots more. But then I lost control."

"Did you ever."

"And it's all your fault. You and that sexy smile."

"I thought it was my sexy shorts and tank."

"Those, too." He caught her by the shoulders. "You okay?"

"A little weak in the knees. Hold on to me."

"Happy to. I'll never let you fall."

"I know. That's one of the many things I lov—" She caught herself in time and said simply "Like about you."

He lowered his head and took her mouth. "That was pretty amazing."

"Yeah." She heard the torrent of rain on the roof. "Did I imagine fireworks?"

"I thought I heard some. Saw bright lights, too."

She nodded. "Exactly. That was some trick, cowboy."

"Wait till you see what else I can do."

"You going to show me?"

"You bet." He scooped her up and carried her across the room to the bed. "This is a tight space, but then I don't think either of us will complain."

"Not on your life. Now"—she wrapped her arms around his neck—"about those things you're going to show me..."

"Did anybody ever tell you you're a glutton, lady?"

"Hey. I've been on a starvation diet."

"Me, too." He nibbled her shoulder. "And now, if you don't mind, I'd like to feast"—he moved lower, and heard her little hum of pleasure—"on you."

Vanessa stirred and felt the mattress sag seconds before she looked up to see Matt beside her, holding out a glass of red wine.

She shoved hair from her eyes and sat up. "I can't believe I dozed in the middle of the day."

"Only for a few minutes. And only because you had some great exercise." He handed her the wine and settled himself beside her in the narrow bunk. "It gave me time to haul in the supplies."

Thunder boomed overhead, shaking the cabin. "It's still storming."

"From the looks of things, it may rain all night."

"Gee." She shot him a sideways glance. "How original. A storm holding us captive in this cabin, far from civilization. Whatever will we do?"

He laughed and reached for a second glass of wine on the small night table beside the bed. "Don't you worry your head, little lady. We'll think of something. Especially since you're already naked and in my bed."

"I figure I played hard to get long enough, cowboy."

"Yes, you did. And nearly drove me around the bend, woman."

"Now I'll make it easier. I'm all yours."

He drew an arm around her. "I feel like I won the lottery."

"Yeah. I'm feeling like a winner, myself." She turned to him. "This wine is really good."

"From a friend's vineyard."

"They have vineyards in Montana?"

He smiled. "Italy. Last time I was there I toured his wife's family vineyard and they shipped me a couple of cases. I told Burke to haul some up here whenever they arrived at the ranch."

"Italy. You do get around, don't you?"

"I do." His tone lowered, deepened as he kissed the tip of her nose. "But right now, there's nowhere I'd rather be than here. With you."

"I'm glad." She set aside her wine and wrapped herself around him. "I hope you don't mind if I snuggle."

He set his glass beside hers and gathered her firmly against him. "I think, Miss Kettering . . ." He felt the need rising again, and wondered how in the world he'd managed to wait so long for this woman. "I think snuggling is the perfect thing to do during a Montana thunderstorm. In fact, we should have tried this that first time we were up here."

She was smiling, a lazy cat's smile. "It wouldn't have been at all professional of me to snuggle with a man I'd only just met."

"I guess not. But it would have been a hell of lot more fun than discussing government regulations regarding wildlife."

And then there were no words as they shut out the thunder, the lightning, the whole universe, and lost themselves in their newly discovered world of lovemaking.

CHAPTER TWENTY-ONE

V anessa stirred as Matt slid from the bed. "Where are you going?"

The cabin was dark, except for the glowing embers on the grate. The sky outside the window was midnight black. Though the thunder and lightning had ceased, a steady rain beat a tattoo on the roof.

"I'm going to feed you."

"Now? In the middle of the night?"

"I don't know about you, but I'm ravenous. And after all that exercise, I need to restore my energy"—he bent and kissed her mouth—"for the next round."

"You make it sound like a prizefight."

"More like a marathon. And we're both winning the race."

She chuckled. "All right. Now that I'm a winner, and awake, I'll give you a hand with our midnight supper."

She reached for his shirt, still on the floor where they'd left it, to cover her nakedness.

Matt was barefoot and stripped to the waist, wearing only his jeans, which were unsnapped.

She followed him to the little galley kitchen. "I'm glad you thought to bring along the last of our supplies. Was that by design or accident?"

He shot her a grin. "It was no accident. The minute I knew we were leaving that mountain retreat and I was going to be driving Gram Gracie's truck, I decided to confiscate whatever was left."

"Aren't you the sly one." She opened the metal container and removed several packets. "Chicken or steak?"

"Definitely steak." At her look he added, "It goes with red wine."

"Of course." She held up another packet. "Rice or potatoes?"

"I'll let you choose the rest."

"A mystery feast then." She set aside several packets and arranged the food on a cooking tin, which she then set over the hot coals.

While their food heated, Matt tossed a salad and divided it into two bowls, which he carried to the low table set in front of the fire, along with the bottle of wine.

A short time later, with a log blazing on the fire, and their meal ready, they sat, sipping wine and enjoying sizzling steak and twice-baked potatoes loaded with chives and cheese and sour cream, as well as a salad dressed with Yancy's balsamic-vinegar-and-oil.

With a plaid afghan around her shoulders, Vanessa gave a sigh of contentment as she finished every bite. "I wouldn't trade this moment for the fanciest meal anywhere in the world."

"Have you traveled the world?"

"Some. England, Scotland, Ireland." She thought a moment. "Spain. And the Greek islands."

"Italy?"

She shook her head. "That's on my to-do list. How about you? Besides Italy, of course."

He topped off her glass. "All the places you mentioned. Plus Iceland."

"Really?" She turned to him. "Why?"

"They import everything. And one of the things they import is Malloy beef."

"That's pretty impressive."

He smiled and reached over to play with a tangle of her hair that had slipped forward. "I was hoping to impress you."

She absorbed the little tingle of pleasure at his touch. "You don't need to. I'm already impressed by everything I've seen here."

"And I'm impressed by what I'm seeing." He took the glass from her hand and set it on the table beside his before leaning close to kiss her. "I could look at you all day every day for the rest of my life and never get tired of what I'm seeing."

With a sigh she wrapped her arms around his neck. "Same goes for me, cowboy. Who would have believed a hardworking rancher could be such eye candy?"

"You're just trying to flatter me so you can have your way with me."

"Maybe." She looked up at him and batted her lashes. "Is it working?"

"You bet."

They came together in a slow, languid dance of love.

Matt set a fresh log on the fire before joining Vanessa in bed. They sat side by side, listening to the soft patter of rain, sipping fresh coffee, and talking.

"That day we took a ride across the hills, you told me your grandmother is a pilot. I haven't been able to put that out of my mind. I'm so impressed by her. How did that happen?"

"When she married Grandpop, there wasn't much civilization around these parts except for a few dirt roads. The quickest way to anywhere was to fly, and at first she relied on her Frankie to take her. But then, after she found herself alone on a ranch with two sons, and Grandpop often a hundred miles away with a herd on one of the mountains, she figured she'd better learn to take care of herself. It was just a natural progression that my dad and uncle got their pilot's licenses as soon as they were old enough. And just as natural that my brothers and I would do the same."

"Do you remember the night your parents died?"

Matt's eyes narrowed slightly. "It's seared into my memory. The family in shock. The sheriff and Archer Stone, his deputy, trying to make sense of it. And the Great One, really agitated after returning from the crash scene."

"He went there?"

"With his movie camera. He recorded everything he could. It's just second nature to him. The snow-covered highway. The mangled car. The two blanket-covered bodies by the side of the road."

Vanessa shook her head. "I don't know how he could bear to even look at something so painful and brutal. Something so close to his heart."

"He felt responsible."

Her eyes widened. "Why?"

"He'd loaned his fancy car, the one he'd brought with him from Hollywood, to my folks for a night in town. Mom and Dad were so excited. Nobody ever drove that Rolls. It was parked in the barn, and probably would still be sitting there, unused, but the Great One urged them to take it as a special treat."

"Oh, that poor old dear. No wonder he felt responsible."

"The Great One believes this was no accident. He believes it was something sinister, and that there was a second pair of tire marks in the snow that night. We've all looked at the film, and we all agree there are other marks, but the authorities insist they were made by all the people who intruded on the scene. Besides the sheriff's squad car and his deputy's, there was a rancher passing by who saw the fireball, and a couple of wranglers tending a herd who heard the crash. And then my uncle and grandfather, who drove the Great One to the site. And there's no disputing that there were way too many tire marks littering the crash site. According to the official report, it was just a terrible case of speed, a driver handling an unfamiliar vehicle during a snowstorm, and a layer of ice that made the roads dangerously slick."

"Does your great-grandfather ever talk about it?"

"Not to us. He knows how painful it is. But I've come upon him discussing it with Yancy. Both of them are obsessed with long-ago Hollywood crimes, and I think they're always trying to find a similarity between them and our family tragedy. But the minute any of us walk in, he changes the subject. Still, I doubt he'll ever let go of his belief that a crime was committed. And it may have been avoided if my father had been driving one of the ranch trucks instead of a fancy Rolls Royce."

Vanessa brushed a kiss to Matt's shoulder. "How awful that he carries that guilt."

"Yeah." Matt stepped out of bed to retrieve the coffeepot from the fire and topped off their cups before climbing beneath the blankets.

He drew an arm around her shoulders, determined to change the subject. Even after all these years, he found it too painful to think about. "It has to be tough not hearing from your father the last few days, especially with everything that's been going on. I know you two are close."

"That's the hardest part of all this. We've always talked every day. And now, with this blackout, I don't even know how he's doing. Not personally, and not with the trial."

"I'm sure he's missing you every bit as much as you miss him. But from what I've read about him, he's tough as nails."

"That's the reputation the press gave him. The Iceman. But they don't know the man I know."

"No one ever knows family except those intimately involved." He linked his fingers with hers. "Tell me about him."

It was the best thing he could have said. It was like opening a dam.

"When I was little, he was busy working every case he could. My mom and I did everything together. And then, when I was thirteen, and my mother got sick, I remember him being home for days at a time. I kept pestering with questions, but he was really good at evading. And then one day he just sat me down to explain that my mom wasn't getting better. That all the treatments weren't helping. And then he told me that she had cancer, and I was so scared, and so angry at him for keeping that secret from me when I could have been"—she paused—"nicer to her. Kinder. I could have tuned into her needs instead of selfishly worrying about school and tests and friends." She took in a breath. "I told him I felt cheated. He understood my anger. And he promised me that he would never again keep anything from me."

"And then I did the same thing as your father. I thought I'd spare you by handling things myself."

"Exactly. I hate being afraid. But even more, I can't stand being kept in the dark. I have a right to know what's going on, so I can find a way to deal with it."

The lines of worry in her face relaxed. Her voice lowered, softened. "As for my dad, once we got past the secrets, we formed a pact. And now, he's just the best father. He really cares about everything I do. After my mother passed away, he did double duty, being both father and mother to me. He never missed a school event. He even took off work whenever there was a parent-teacher meeting or an after-school activity. He was just always there for me." She sighed. "And now I can't even imagine how hard it must be for him to pour himself into all the details of this trial while being forced to trust his daughter's safety to others."

"I'm sure he has plenty of eyes and ears. Not just the Chicago PD but any private investigators they've brought onto the case. You're the daughter of an elected official. They're all feeling responsible for your safety. They're charged with reporting to him or to his office on a daily basis. I'm betting he knows more about you and your daily activities than you do about him at this point."

She sighed. "I hope you're right, Matt. And I hope it isn't distracting him from the trial. He really needs to feel free to do his job, no matter the outcome. This man he's prosecuting is a vicious criminal disguised as an important city official."

Matt squeezed her shoulder. "You heard what he told you by phone. In a matter of days or weeks, this will be resolved once and for all."

And then, seeing the tension returning to her eyes, he drew her close for a kiss. And another.

As they came together, all the troubles of the past and present slipped away.

Later, while he watched her sleep, Matt thought about all they'd shared. Now, finally, he understood her need for complete honesty. Even though her father's intentions had been admirable, hoping to spare her the pain of her mother's illness, his secrecy was hurtful.

As for Matt, he'd revealed more personal history with her in this one night than he'd ever told another living soul. Not even his own family. He and his brothers never talked about the loss of their parents. And because of the pain he could sense in his family, he'd refrained from bringing up the subject. But with Vanessa, all that changed. She was so easy to talk to. She listened. Really listened to all he had to say. But it was deeper than that. She was smart. She was sensitive. And she really cared about him, his family, his life.

He liked the fact that she was crazy about her father. Coming from a close, loving family himself, it mattered to him. *She* mattered to him, though he didn't want to probe the why of it too deeply.

She was getting to him.

Who was he kidding?

She'd gotten to him the minute they met.

Then she was just a sharp mind in a pretty face wrapped up in a gorgeous body.

Now she was so much more.

He wasn't ready to admit just how much more. But the fact was, he wasn't looking forward to the day she would be free to leave.

Free to leave.

The thought rankled.

He didn't want her to leave.

Not now. Not ever.

And that fact was so alien to a man like him. He'd spent a lifetime caring for his entire family and had never once given a thought to his own future, other than how it would be linked to this ranch.

He'd always kept outsiders at arm's length. And now, though it was far too soon, he found himself thinking about how Nessa fit into the picture. She was no longer an outsider. She mattered to him. Perhaps more than she ought to.

And that fact scared the hell out of him.

CHAPTER TWENTY-TWO

Vanessa lay very still, listening to the sound of birds outside the cabin. After a day and night of storms punctuated by thunder and lightning, and of rain drumming the roof, it was a soothing, relaxing sound.

She looked over at Matt, who was gloriously naked, one leg resting over hers, an arm wrapped protectively around her.

She felt safe with this man. Safe in all ways. Not just safe from the outside world, but safe to be herself. No pretense. No airs.

She could tell him anything, and knew instinctively that he would listen and not judge. Except for her father, she couldn't think of another man who bore that distinction.

But why? What was it that set Matthew Malloy apart from others? He was handsome, but then, so were dozens of other men. He was smart, but she'd attended law school with plenty of smart men who had never affected her like this. He was serious and funny. Shrewd and charming. All business, until he decided to play. His playful side, such a contradiction from the man she'd first met, delighted her more than she cared to admit. In truth, she loved everything about Matthew Malloy.

Loved?

Though the word teased the edges of her mind, she didn't want to probe this too deeply. It was too soon. Her life was too complicated. She didn't want or need another complication. Wasn't it enough that she was the object of death threats? Even though she felt safely removed from them, they were there in the background, real, deadly, taunting her. And there was the absence of her father. She missed his presence in her life. Theirs was such a comfortable, loving relationship. She hated that he was dealing with not only a career-changing trial but also a dangerous foe who had threatened to stop at nothing to walk free. And he was doing it alone, as he'd been forced to deal with everything alone since the death of her mother. On the one hand she wanted to be there with him, to offer aid and comfort. On the other she knew that he was grateful to have her here, safe and protected, so that he could give his full attention to the trial.

She struggled to put aside such thoughts. There was nothing she could do to help her father, except to stay here and to stay safe. But she felt a measure of guilt that, while her father was forced to slay his dragons alone, she was here having a grand time with Matt.

Matt. His hand moved along her side and she felt the now familiar sizzle of anticipation at his touch. His hands were work worn. A working cowboy's hands. Strong. Steady.

She loved his hands. Loved having them on her.

His breath was warm as it tickled her cheek. She delighted in kissing him. His face. His body. His mouth.

She leaned in, hoping to touch her lips to his.

It was then she realized that he was awake and watching her.

She paused. "I was planning on kissing you awake."

"Be my guest."

She laughed. "It won't work now. You're already awake."

"Part of me is. But one kiss, and you'll wake the rest of me."

"Oh." Such a small word for the rush of feelings that surfaced as an image came to mind. An image of their glorious night of lovemaking.

She leaned even closer. With her eyes on his she nibbled a chaste kiss to his mouth. His arms came around her, pinning her to the length of him. And then she was lost. Lost in the wonder of the pleasure only he could give.

"I need coffee." Matt slipped from bed and stepped into his jeans.

"I saw some sort of biscuit dough in the supplies. Maybe I'll try my hand at pancakes."

He looked at her. "Pancakes?"

She flushed. "Or not. But I'll try."

"Pancakes are good." He rummaged through the metal container and lifted a package. "But even better with crisp bacon." He set out strips of bacon on the cooking tin.

Vanessa pulled on a pair of denims and a T-shirt and joined him in the kitchen area, looking through the supplies until she found the biscuit dough.

After reading the directions, she turned with a smile.
"I can do this."

"Great. I didn't know you cooked." He stood watching
as she mixed it with milk and poured several large circles
of thin pancake batter beside the bacon.

He placed the tin over the hot coals. A short time later,
when their breakfast was ready, he set a log on the grate,
and they settled in front of a roaring fire to enjoy their meal.

"Perfect pancakes. Yancy had better watch his back."
Matt sat back, smiling over at her. "You're just full of hidden talents, aren't you, ma'am?"

"I've barely scratched the surface."

He shot her a look. "Now you tell me. What else am I
missing?"

Her voice was a soft purr. "You'll just have to wait and
see."

His grin was quick and dangerous. "I'll show you mine
if you show me yours."

She slapped his hand. "You're such a guy."

He shrugged. "Can't blame a guy for trying."

They shared a laugh.

He sat back and finished his coffee. "We'll have to
pack up soon and head back to the ranch."

"I know." She laid her hand over his. "This time alone
with you has been special."

"For me, too."

She could feel him studying her. As he'd been studying
her ever since she'd first arrived here in Montana. It
warmed her. It thrilled her. It frightened her. Not Matt, she
realized, but the feelings he aroused in her. She'd never
felt like this about any other man, and it was delicious and
oddly uncomfortable, all at the same time.

"There are things I want to tell you."

"Things?"

"Feelings. They're . . ." He paused. "They're still pretty new, but since we're sharing secrets . . ."

"I don't know if you're ready to hear this, but I need to say it anyway. In all these years, I've never before known a woman who's ever made me think about love, commitment, and happily-ever-after."

Seeing her look of stunned surprise, he squeezed her hand before getting up and crossing the room to pull on his shirt, parka, and boots.

"Wait, Matt. You tell me something this important, this earth-shattering, and then you just calmly turn away?"

"I realize this came out of the blue. Sorry. I'll give you some time. If I had my way, we'd never leave. So, if we hope to get out of here"—he kept his back to her—"I'm going out to chop some wood."

Then he turned and gave her a blinding smile. "We have a rule up here. A cowboy never leaves one of the range shacks until he's replaced whatever was used while he was here. That way, the next one who has need of shelter will find it ready."

"Sounds like a good rule."

"Yeah." He returned to bend close and give her a long, slow kiss.

"Another rule?"

"That one was just for me. Never leave your woman without first kissing her." He straightened and walked outside.

Your woman.

His woman.

Warmed by his words, thrilled by them, she stared at the closed door and sat back as a slow smile spread across her lips.

Matt loved her.

And she'd said not a word. Though her heart was in her throat, and in her mind she was dancing on clouds, she'd remained still and mute.

Maybe because she was afraid to admit just how she was feeling. It was too new. Too delicious.

She couldn't recall another time when she'd done so little and had so much pleasure doing it. No alarm clocks. No fast-paced schedule to adhere to. No airports from Chicago to DC and back. No small talk with people she barely knew. No fighting to change rules set in stone by some bureaucrat years before she'd been born.

Here in this simple place, she'd found peace and contentment.

And love.

She drained her coffee and carried their dishes to the small sink.

To the steady sound of an ax splitting logs, she made up the bed, tidied up the space, and looked around with a nod of appreciation. This little cabin had been her sanctuary and her heaven. It was primitive by any standards. Just a rough bed, a fireplace for heat, and cold water. But she wouldn't trade it for the finest spa or resort.

Because of Matt.

Just the thought of him warmed her. He loved her.

Love.

She touched her hands to her hot cheeks and couldn't help grinning.

She looked up as a rumble, like thunder, seemed to echo

across the hills. Another storm blowing through? Would Matt try to drive through it, or remain here until it blew over? She hoped they could remain. It would be such fun to extend their time here.

Fun? It would be heavenly. Another day and night in Matt's arms, with no distractions. No ranch chores. No loud, teasing brothers or family members to intrude.

She blinked. In truth, she was already missing his rowdy brothers and raucous family. After a lifetime alone, she loved the crazy laughter, the wild teasing, the loving interaction of the entire Malloy clan.

One thing was certain. Despite the threat of danger hanging over her head, she'd never had a better time anywhere than she had here, with Matt and his large, loving family.

She grabbed a battered denim jacket from a hook by the door when she realized that the chopping had stilled. She would help Matt haul the logs inside and see what their plans would be going forward.

She ran to the door. Before she could reach it, it was yanked open, and a burly figure seemed to fill the entire space.

The stranger was tall, bearded, and menacing. And in his hand was a terrifying looking automatic weapon aimed directly at her.

"Matt...?" She couldn't seem to make her mouth work over the constriction in her throat.

"Your cowboy's dead."

The roar. Not thunder. Gunfire.

Matt dead?

"No! Matt—" She tried to push past the man, but he

swung the weapon in a wide arc, hitting her in the head so hard it knocked her to the floor.

Pain, hot and swift, crashed through her brain. She struggled to clear the black spots dancing in front of her eyes. She touched a hand to her head and felt the wet, sticky mass of blood oozing through the hair at her temple.

Ignoring her obvious pain, the stranger grabbed her arm, hauling her roughly to her feet and dragging her through the open doorway.

In the clearing she saw a second man standing beside Grace's truck. Through the open doorway of the vehicle she saw Matt slumped behind the wheel. The front of his parka was stained with his blood.

The man cupped his hands to shout, "Got him inside, though it was like lifting an elephant. This cowboy's all muscle."

"Quit complaining and get that truck going. We need to move now."

The second stranger started the engine before slamming the truck's door closed. Reaching inside the open window, he engaged the gear. The truck lurched forward.

The vehicle moved slowly toward a rock ledge. The same ledge Matt had once pointed out to her. At the end of it lay a sheer drop-off that fell thousands of feet to a heavily wooded canyon below.

Vanessa watched in horror as she realized what they intended.

Tears of pain and rage blinded her as the truth dawned.

The truck, with Matt inside, could rot in that primitive forest for years without ever being spotted from above.

No one would know what had happened here. She and

Matt would both be dead, and the killers would be free to return to Chicago, to report to the vicious thug who had ordered all this, without fear of reprisal.

Without Matt's body, without hers, the crime would go unpunished.

Her father would know, and the knowledge would eat at him for a lifetime. And there was nothing he could do to stop this madness. Worse, nothing she could do.

Still holding her firmly by the arm, the bearded stranger shoved her into the passenger side of an SUV, its windows tinted so that the occupants couldn't be seen. Her wrists and ankles were bound by plastic restraints. Her cell phone was taken away and pocketed by her captor before he climbed behind the wheel and waited.

Minutes later there was a terrible explosion sending flames high in the air.

The sound of it, and the heat it generated, were so overwhelming, the very earth beneath them trembled. The vehicle gave a great shudder. Vanessa realized that Matt's fate had been sealed. At the knowledge that he was lost to her, she was overcome with such grief, all she could do was sob helplessly.

While the flames turned black, whirling and dancing on the breeze, the second man settled into the backseat.

"Okay, Homer. That's done. Let's roll."

As they started away Vanessa turned for a last look. The once peaceful cabin was cloaked in a thick cloud of black, choking smoke curling up from the ravine far below.

Could anyone survive such an explosion? The thought had her going as still as death.

"Oh Matt," she whispered, though she wasn't even aware that she was doing so. She tried to envision him rising up from the smoke and ashes. "Please. Please." Was it a prayer or a plea? Whatever it was, she couldn't put the rest of her thoughts into words. It was all too painful. Too deep. Too real. Too ... impossible.

Unable to wipe at her eyes, she blinked several times, and fell into a deep, dark well of utter despair.

CHAPTER TWENTY-THREE

The SUV kept to the high meadow, moving steadily through a wooded area that shielded them from view of anyone who might pass that way. Since it appeared to be the same vehicle that Vanessa and Matt had come upon the day of their ride, its occupants had apparently learned their lesson. On a ranch of this size, they might encounter employees or family members anywhere, so they kept to secluded places where they were less likely to be seen.

Occasionally Vanessa caught glimpses of herds in the higher elevations, and the thought of wranglers just out of reach had her throat clogged with unshed tears. While the crew went about the business of running a ranch, they were unaware that killers were hiding among them.

"Where are you taking me?"

"To Disneyland," the driver said with a sneer.

The man in the rear seat laughed at his partner's joke.

"My father will hunt you down and find you if it takes him the rest of his life."

"If Mr. D. has his way, that ought to be real soon. When we're done with you, we have orders to get rid of him next. But not until he's done as he's told."

Another burst of laughter from the backseat, and the two men exchanged knowing smiles in the mirror.

The driver's tone was smug. "We figure, once your daddy gets our little video, he'll have to walk away from his day job to search for his little girl."

Video.

They weren't going to kill her yet. They needed her alive if they were planning on sending her father a video.

She knew how this sort of thing worked. A tearful kidnapping victim. Something that would prove the date, so that they could point to the fact that, at least for now, she was still alive. And probably a time limit, which, if not met, would end with the threat of her execution.

"My father would never leave in the middle of a trial."

"Oh, I'm betting he can't refuse to take the bait we offer."

Vanessa fell silent, her heart pounding. How far along was the trial? Had the prosecution concluded its testimony yet? Was that why these men had acted now? Had DePietro concluded that he was going down in defeat?

Mr. D. Of course. Running scared and taking desperate measures.

Beware desperate men, her father often said. When backed to the wall, they become more vicious than feral animals.

As the SUV passed through a thick wall of trees and came up over a rise, the land that was spread out below them appeared as wild and desolate as a moonscape. Here there were no herds. No wranglers. No buildings. Only wilderness for as far as the eye could see.

Vanessa's heart froze. The perfect spot to make their video and send it to her father, as instructed.

As the vehicle slowed to a halt, Vanessa steeled herself. She needed, more than ever, to look calm and composed. She would rather die here and now than give them what they wanted. She would not break down and weep like a frightened victim while they recorded every tear, every quivering moan or sob. She was determined to swallow her terror and show her father a defiant, uncompromising woman who would make the district attorney of Cook County proud.

The driver unlocked the car doors, and the man in the backseat stepped out and cut her ankle restraints before hauling her out roughly by the arm.

"Where do you want her?"

The driver pointed to a large, flat rock. "There."

She was pressed down, arms behind her back, facing a cell phone camera. While the driver recorded, the other man held a Chicago newspaper up to the camera, showing the masthead, the date, and the headline, which read: DePietro Jury to Begin Deliberations.

The driver snarled, "Tell Daddy you've been a bad girl and got yourself caught by the big, bad wolves."

Vanessa kept her silence and lifted her chin defiantly.

His big hand slashed out, slapping her so hard her head snapped to one side, and she saw stars. She was infuriated when tears pooled in her eyes and she bit down hard on the cry that almost burst from her lips.

He swore. "This may be your last chance to say anything

to your daddy. You wouldn't want to leave this world without telling him how much you love him. Right?"

She clenched her jaw.

His voice grew shrill with agitation. "Suit yourself. As for you, Mr. Big Shot DA, take a good look at your smart-ass daughter. She may be a good actress, pretending she's too good to cry, but the blood you see is just a sample of what you'll see in the next video if you don't do exactly as you're told."

Vanessa had forgotten the blood. The sight of it would horrify her father.

The stranger had already turned away, electronically sending the video that would shake her father's world to its very foundation.

The second man yanked her to her feet and hauled her back to the car. Once inside, he affixed fresh restraints around her ankles before slamming her door and climbing into the back.

Minutes later they were once more on their way, keeping always to the wooded areas, away from civilization.

Burke, standing with his wranglers as a herd of nervous cattle milled about, saw the plume of black smoke and whipped out his phone.

"Something's wrong. Get the crew up here now."

He rang off and drove his truck toward the range shack.

By the time he got there, Luke was just parking his Harley, and Reed and Colin were stepping away from their all-terrain vehicles. The three were racing toward the ridge, where the smoke was so thick it burned their eyes.

Because they couldn't see through the black cloud to

the bottom, they began the treacherous descent into the gorge.

Burke hurried toward the cabin, where the door was standing open. An ominous sign. Inside, he stared around, noting the half-burned log in the fireplace, proof that its occupants had been gone only a short time. As for the rest of the cabin, it was spotless. As though Matt and Vanessa had been preparing to leave.

Outside, half a dozen logs were neatly stacked, with one log uncut, the ax lying on the ground nearby.

Burke knelt and touched a hand to the dark moisture in the grass.

Blood. Quite a lot of it.

With a heavy heart he turned away and followed Luke, Reed, and Colin down the circuitous route to the bottom of the gorge.

Darkness came early in the hills. Once the sun had set behind the mountain peaks, the land became cloaked in shadows.

The driver seemed sure of himself as he guided the car across shallow streams and around rocky outcroppings before coming to a halt inside a cave.

Of course, Vanessa thought. These two men had planned this carefully. If anybody happened to be searching by air, this hiding place would never be spotted.

The driver opened the door and stretched his arms over his head, leaving Vanessa to his partner.

As before, her ankle restraints were cut away before she was hauled from the car and shoved roughly to the cold ground inside the cave. Once there her ankles were re-strained tightly, and a rope was tied from her feet to her neck, making movement of any kind painful. Making escape impossible.

The driver retrieved a backpack from the rear of the vehicle and set it inside the cave before announcing, "Honey, I'm home."

Again the two men shared a laugh at his little joke. They were, Vanessa noted, in high spirits since sending the video.

She watched as the driver zipped open the backpack and began removing bottled water and wrapped food.

She asked, "How long will we be here?"

The driver answered for both. "We're here until we're told to leave."

Her throat burned with fury. "I know it was that monster, Diomedes DePietro, who sent you."

The driver's head turned, his eyes hot with anger. "Shut your mouth. You're not fit to speak his name."

"You make him sound like some sort of holy man."

"Compared to your old man, he's a saint." The driver sat down, his back against a boulder, and began devouring a sandwich.

The other man followed suit.

When they'd each eaten several sandwiches, the driver produced a bottle of whiskey. He took a long pull before passing it to his partner, who did the same.

After several minutes he drank again before looking over at her, more relaxed now. "After my father died and my mother was sick, Mr. D. saw to it that she got the finest medical care in the world."

Vanessa wanted him to talk, to keep her from thinking about Matt. And about what was going to happen to her when this ended. "How did your father die?"

"In a shoot-out with a cop who'd caught him during a stakeout, passing money to a Chicago alderman."

Vanessa thought back to the many charges against DePietro. Bribes, money laundering, supplying drugs and prostitutes to politicians in exchange for favors. But none as critical as the murder of a witness set to testify against him.

"Your father died for DePietro?"

"Any one of us would have done the same."

"How does a man like that earn your loyalty?"

He took another long pull of whiskey before passing it to his partner. He crossed his arms over his chest and stretched out his legs, trying to get comfortable on the cold, hard ground. "You tell her, Jasper."

The taller of the two men, whose hawk-like face bore a jagged scar from his eyebrow to his chin, nodded. "Mr. D. rewards loyalty. The pay's good, but the benefits are even better."

"Benefits?"

He and his partner chuckled.

"What sort of benefits?"

"If we're in trouble with the law, he provides us with lawyers. If we do time, he takes care of our families until we get out."

"And why shouldn't he? He's the reason you're in trouble with the law. It's the least he can do for the people he hires to do his dirty work. Wouldn't it be better if he found you honest work to do, instead of sitting back and allowing men like you to get caught up in criminal activities?"

The driver's tone grew sulky. "Shut up and get some sleep. You're going to need it for the morning, Daddy's Girl."

She felt a shiver of apprehension, wondering what could be worse than what she'd already gone through.

As the two men drifted into sleep, she lay awake and troubled.

Each time she closed her eyes, she could see Matt slumped behind the wheel of the truck, blood smearing the front of his parka, and then the terrible sound of an explosion as a plume of black smoke rose up, covering the area with its acrid smell.

She fought tears of pain and rage at the helplessness of the situation.

She was trying to put up a brave front for the sake of her father. But inside she was waging a losing battle, knowing that Matt had paid the ultimate price because of her.

Because of her, the man she loved was dead.

The man she loved.

Now there was no need to dissect those strange, troubling feelings she'd been trying to deny. It was love, plain and simple. And now, he was lost to her forever, and oh, the pain of that knowledge was almost more than she could bear.

All this heartache and loss, brought to the very doorstep of the Malloy Ranch. All these good, sweet people, who didn't even know her father or his opponent in the trial, were now forced to risk their lives for having welcomed her into the circle of their safe retreat, believing the trial would end quickly and they would be relieved of any responsibility.

Frank and Grace had lost a beloved son and daughter-in-law all those years ago, and had helped raise three grandsons. And now, they would be faced with the horrible news of yet another loss.

Matt was a pillar of strength to them. Their firstborn grandson. The strong, steady one among them who, after the loss of his parents, had appointed himself leader of his siblings. He'd worked and studied to become the shrewd business leader of their vast enterprise.

Picturing the grief the entire Malloy family would suffer when they learned of their loss had Vanessa's heart breaking into millions of pieces. And knowing she couldn't be with them, to grieve, to comfort and to take comfort from them, just added to her misery.

While the two killers snored, deep in sleep, she gave in to the feelings of despair and wept bitter, scalding tears.

CHAPTER TWENTY-FOUR

Elliott Kettering sat in his office, surrounded by Chief McBride and his men, forced to watch the video yet again. They'd played it dozens of times now, each man in the special crimes unit looking carefully for anything that would tell them where DePietro's men were holding Vanessa.

While they dissected it frame by frame, Elliott shoved away from his desk to pace. Though he'd remained silent for the most part, a voice in his head was swearing, screaming obscenities at the vicious killer who thought he was above the law.

And for now, he was. That's what had Elliott almost mad with fear. At a thug's command, his precious only child could be brutalized, tortured, murdered. All the power of the Chicago PD, all the wealth of knowledge at the district attorney's service, were helpless to keep Vanessa safe.

A phone call to the Malloy Ranch had only added to Elliott's frustration. The family insisted that Vanessa was with the oldest son, Matthew, in some secluded cabin, and being guarded by a team of wranglers. But when pressed, they had admitted that they had neither seen nor spoken to Vanessa nor Matthew since the previous day. And the wranglers couldn't be reached to confirm their safety.

He should have ordered her to a safe house as soon as this threat had surfaced. And now he was paying the price for his tenderhearted gesture in permitting her to stay at a remote ranch in Montana. To Elliott, it was like sending her to the dark side of the moon. He didn't know these people, or their ranch hands, or their intentions. Despite assurances from his investigators, for all he knew, they could be on the payroll of Diomedes DePietro.

"You know the spot?" Chief McBride's words penetrated Elliott's dark thoughts.

He turned and stood behind the chief, who was seated at Elliott's desk, using a speaker phone.

Sheriff Eugene Graystoke's gravel voice on the other end was loud in the silence of the office. "After viewing the video, Frank Malloy tells me he knows it well. It's on the North Ridge, in a high meadow that isn't used for the herds. Too many dangerous ravines in that area."

"What does he hear from Matt?"

"No word yet. But Burke Cowley, his foreman, should be checking in soon. There's limited cell phone service in the area, and we often don't hear from the wranglers for days at a time."

Elliott's voice cut like a whip. "I don't give a damn about cell service. Get somebody up to that cabin and find the son of a bitch who allowed these bastards to kidnap and video my daughter, bloodied and helpless."

The sheriff's tone was incredulous. "Have you positively identified her as your daughter?"

"You think I don't know my own daughter, you—?"

Captain McBride lifted the receiver, effectively cutting him off. "Sheriff, my entire team has seen the video. It's Vanessa Kettering. Now I know the Malloy Ranch is big, but you need to get somebody up to that cabin right away."

"We're on it."

"Good. I expect to hear from you within the hour."

He disconnected while the sheriff was still responding, and turned to the DA. "I know how you feel, Elliott."

"Do you?" Kettering's face was as dark as thunder.

"Your job is to keep this under wraps until the jury reaches a verdict. Our job is to find your daughter. And we *will* find her, Elliott."

"Don't insult me with platitudes." Angry, frustrated, helpless, Elliott Kettering turned away, too agitated to sit, too furious to meet the eyes of the men scattered around his office. He wanted to put a fist through the wall. He wanted to lash out at someone, anyone. He wanted...

...to hold his daughter in his arms. Just to hold her, and know that she was safe from all harm. Instead, he was forced to pretend to the world outside this room that everything was fine, and that his only concern was awaiting the jury's verdict. A verdict that he prayed would put away for a lifetime the spineless, heartless thug who had ordered this vicious crime against his Vanessa.

His baby girl. His sweet, beautiful Vanessa.

The words played like a litany through his tortured, troubled mind.

Burke thrashed through the brush, cursing his age and arthritis, desperate to get to the bottom of the ravine. The dampened handkerchief tied around his nose and mouth did little to protect him from the smoke that burned his eyes and had him coughing with every intake of breath.

Ahead of him, scrambling over rocks and fallen tree branches, was Luke, who had tossed aside his Harley like a toy on the rock ledge above before jumping into the search. Reed was swearing at the brambles that tore at his flesh with every step, and Colin, always the stoic, silent uncle who kept his thoughts and words to himself, moved doggedly forward.

None of them knew what to expect. All they knew was that something had caused an explosion and a fire, and Matt and Vanessa were missing from their cabin, along with Grace's truck.

It wasn't possible for Matt to lose his way and drive off that rock shelf into such forbidding terrain. He knew this land better than anyone. There wasn't a careless bone in his body.

Burke heard Luke's shout, and followed Reed toward the sound of it. The two arrived at the bottom of the ravine to a scene of such devastation, they were speechless.

"It's a truck," Luke shouted. "I can't tell if it's Gram Gracie's. Too much damage."

He peered through the smoke and flames before shaking his head. "I don't see anyone. Maybe they..."

At a moan, Burke turned. A body, bloody and wreathed in smoke, lay in a snowbank beneath a cluster of evergreens. Because of the dense underbrush, the rain had yet to melt the snow.

"Here!" Burke shouted. "Over here! It's Matt!"

Luke and Reed gathered around while Burke and Colin knelt beside Matt, checking for a pulse.

The old cowboy looked up. "He's alive." To Matt he muttered, "You're one lucky guy. If it weren't for this snowbank, the fall from that burning truck would have clean killed you, son."

He looked over at the others. "Let's get him out of these wet things."

They quickly removed Matt's still-smoldering parka, all the while checking for wounds.

"So much blood." Reed, accustomed to treating animal injuries, probed Matt's chest and shoulder until he located the source of the blood. Leaning close he whispered, "Can you hear me, Matt?"

His brother's eyes flickered, then opened. " . . . hear you."

"You're bleeding from the shoulder. Did it happen during the accident? Broken glass, maybe? Or did something stab you?"

" . . . shot."

"You're saying you took a bullet? Who would shoot you?"

"Thugs. Got Vanessa."

The four men looked at one another in stunned surprise.

Luke's voice was suddenly filled with anger. "She's been kidnapped?"

Matt nodded. "All my fault. Get me up."

Colin put a hand on his chest. "You shouldn't be moved until we're sure nothing's broken."

"Get me the hell up. Now."

His two brothers put their arms around his shoulders and gingerly lifted him to a sitting position. Moments later they helped him to stand, but kept their arms around him to steady him.

Matt's voice was raspy from the smoke. "They got a head start. We need to find her. Now."

Burke shook his head. "It's a long climb up, Matt. You'll never make it."

Through gritted teeth Matt said, "I don't care what it takes. Just get me up there."

"I'll take care of this." While the others watched, Colin sprinted up the ravine and out of sight.

Minutes later he shouted to watch for a rope, which was soon seen snaking down.

"Wrap it around your waist, Matt," he ordered. "I'll use Burke's horse to slowly pull you up."

With Luke on one side, and Reed on the other, and Burke close behind to catch him if he fell, Matt made his way slowly, torturously, up the steep climb until he was on level ground.

For long moments he lay on the ground, breathing labored, eyes closed, as he fought his way through waves of pain. Then, forcing himself to his knees, he looked at the others.

"I counted two men. The SUV with the tinted windows. Sheriff Graystoke has a partial license number, unless they've stolen new plates. They have an automatic weapon, and they have Vanessa. Now get me to the ranch so I can report what I know. Then we're heading out to find her."

Burke glanced from Luke to Reed. "As soon as you get

your brother to the ranch, call for a medevac. He needs to be flown to a hospital."

"Not until I get Vanessa away from those thugs. This is all my fault, Burke. If I hadn't asked you to have your wranglers back off and give me some time alone with her, this never would have happened. I gave those monsters the perfect opportunity to do their dirty work. Now I have to make it right." He turned to Luke. "Your Harley is faster than Reed's ATV."

Colin lay a hand on his nephew's arm. "Luke's may be faster, but Reed's is safer."

"Safe doesn't count right now. You heard me. I have no one to blame but myself." Matt turned to Luke. "Let's go."

With Luke driving, and Matt holding tightly behind him, they left in a roar of engines.

Burke gave a shake of his head. "I know he's hurting. I know he needs a doctor. But with the load of guilt he's carrying, I'd say Matt won't even be able to think about anything until he finds Vanessa, or dies trying. And God help him if anything bad happens to her. I doubt he'd ever recover."

Reed and his uncle nodded their agreement.

They all knew Matt well enough to realize the truth of the old man's words.

CHAPTER TWENTY-FIVE

Oh, Matthew." Grace hugged her grandson fiercely the minute Luke's motorcycle arrived at the back door of the ranch.

Within minutes the rest of the family pulled up in their various vehicles and gathered around. It was clear that all were stunned by the look of him. Between the blood that smeared his clothing, and the smoke and soot from the explosion, he looked more dead than alive. But the fire burning in his eyes left no doubt that he was very much alive and ready to go to war with his attackers.

He brushed off all their questions. "How much do you know?"

It was Frank who answered. "Eugene Graystoke sent us a video uploaded to Vanessa's father by her kidnappers. We feared they had killed you to get to her."

"They think they did. What's this about a video? I want

to see it." Matt strode inside, and the others trailed behind.

Frank put an arm around his wife and bent to whisper, "Courage, Gracie Girl."

Her eyes reflected the pain she felt. "Did you see the blood? Frankie, he needs a doctor."

"You saw the look on his face. He's still standing. That will have to do for now."

Colin, who had remained behind, nodded to his parents. "I've never seen him like this before. And it isn't just his injuries. Our Matt is carrying a heavy load of guilt."

"What does he have to be guilty of?" Grace demanded.

"He asked Burke to keep the wranglers away from the range shack so he and Vanessa could have some privacy."

"I see." Now that she knew, the old woman saw much more. Her grandson had found that one special woman, who had driven him to throw caution to the wind in order to be alone with her. And now he was riddled with guilt for having risked her safety.

Grace sighed and allowed herself to be led indoors.

In the kitchen they gathered around the table and watched Matt's reaction as he viewed the video. At the first sighting of Vanessa, he flinched as though struck by a whip before his eyes narrowed in fierce concentration.

He waited until the short video was over before muttering, "They hurt her. She's bleeding." His hands clenched at his sides in impotent fury. "They hurt her."

Nobody said a word.

He sucked in a breath. "I need to call her father."

Nelson started to say, "I don't think that's a good—"

Grace shot her father a look, and his words of disapproval died.

They watched and listened as Matt called Elliott Kettering at the number Captain McBride had promised would be a direct line to both Kettering and the Chicago PD.

The phone was answered on the first ring.

"Mr. Kettering, Matt Malloy."

Elliott's voice was both angry and weary. "Tell me what happened. And tell me how they managed to take my daughter without taking you."

As briefly as he could Matt described being shot and put into a truck, which was sent crashing into a deep ravine, where it exploded into flame, before he was rescued.

While he spoke, his family looked stunned and horrified to hear him speak so calmly about all that he'd gone through.

"I'm grateful you survived. And now?" Elliott asked.

"I'm back at the ranch and was just shown the video Nessa's kidnappers sent."

Elliott's voice mirrored his fury. "They dared to hurt my daughter."

"Yes, sir. I saw the blood. I want you to know that I hold myself personally responsible."

"I don't see how you can make such a claim when you were shot and nearly burned to death."

"All because of my own carelessness. None of that matters now. But your daughter's safety does. And I give you my word that I'll get her back to you or die trying."

"There's no need. Our state police are working with your authorities there. Let the professionals do their job."

"You don't understand." Matt's voice was pure ice. "Nessa's safety is on me. I allowed this to happen. I won't rest until I find her."

He disconnected then, leaving Elliott Kettering no time to voice any further argument.

He turned to his family. "Play the video again. I want to be certain of the location."

While Yancy complied, Frank said softly, "They'll be long gone from there by now, son."

"I know that." Matt studied the video again before saying, "But I'll start there. They may have left something, some tracks or even something at the scene that I can follow."

Grace looked alarmed. "First, Matthew, you have to see a doctor."

"Not now. There's no time." He turned away. "I need a rifle."

Luke raced from the room and returned with an armload of weapons and ammunition from a locked cabinet in the office.

As he passed them around, Matt said, "I'm taking a truck. Grandpop, I'd like you and Gram Gracie to go up in the plane. Maybe you'll spot something from the air. And Great One, you and Yancy man the phones here, in case the authorities report something. You can relay the information to all of us."

Luke closed a hand over his brother's arm. "I'm going with you."

"No." Matt shook off his hand. "Take your Harley." He turned to Reed. "Your ATV can go places other vehicles can't. Colin, Burke, you and the wranglers take trucks and fan out."

His uncle Colin paused. "Sheriff Graystoke may have something to say about this."

"He and his men will do what they're trained to do. But

I'm not waiting around for anyone. This is on me, and I'm going to do what feels right."

Grace pressed an emergency medical kit into his hand.

He shot her a look.

"There's something for pain and an antibiotic to hold back any infection from that bullet."

"Thanks." His tone was dismissive. "I'll take the antibiotic, but I'm not going to risk getting muddled with pain meds."

As Matt walked away, old Burke paused to say to the others, "I know he's been wounded, and he's going on pure adrenaline. I know you're all worried about him. I am, too. But even so, I'd rather have Matt, injured and angry, than just about any damned army in the world. So if those kidnappers are still anywhere in Montana, my money's on Matt finding them."

Frank squeezed his wife's arm before starting for the door. "You heard the man, Gracie Girl. Let's trust his word and follow our leader."

Sheriff Eugene Graystoke and Deputy Archer Stone arrived at the Malloy Ranch with a swarm of police vehicles. A team of state police sharpshooters had been brought in by helicopter.

The sheriff entered the ranch house and found only Yancy and Nelson in the kitchen. He looked around with a puzzled expression. "I was expecting everybody to be here by now. Where are they?"

"Here and gone." Nelson pointed to the sky. "Frank and Grace are airborne. The rest have scattered, searching for the bad guys."

The sheriff's eyes narrowed with anger. "This isn't

some cops-and-robbers movie, Nelson. This is real life, and an innocent young woman's safety hangs in the balance. Captain McBride wants this played by the book."

"I guess we didn't get that memo." The old man shot the lawman a wry grin.

Archer's voice was low with sarcasm. "How did Matt let this kidnapping happen? I thought he'd appointed himself Miss Kettering's personal bodyguard, and the rest of you his backup army."

As quickly as possible Nelson described what Matt had endured at the hands of the kidnappers.

The sheriff blanched. "How in hell is Matt still standing?"

"He's a Malloy," the old man said simply.

With a muttered oath the sheriff and his deputy turned their backs and strode outside to join their men.

After a lengthy meeting to outline their strategy, they separated and went in various directions, the sheriff still muttering about how he hoped to hell the Malloy family didn't get in his way. Just to make certain, he pulled out his phone and called Matt.

"Yeah, Sheriff." Matt's tone was abrupt.

"I'm at your ranch, where the Great One informed me that you and your family are already out searching for Miss Kettering."

"That's right."

"Just so you know, her safety is our main concern. I don't want any would-be heroes barging in and causing her any more harm than has already been done to her."

At the ominous silence on the line, the sheriff cleared his throat. "Look. I heard what they did to you. I know that this isn't something you asked for, Matt. But now that it's happened, I want you to remain in contact with me and my men every step of the way. The state police have men trained for this very thing. There are more of them than there are of you and your family. But if you happen to find where they've taken her, I want your word that you'll step back and allow us to do our job."

At the continued silence, his voice took on a low note of authority. "Do I have your word, Matt?"

"I've already given my word to her father. I'll see her returned safely to him, or die trying."

"My men and I are here to prevent anyone's death. Yours and Miss Kettering's. So see that you rein in that famous temper, and ask the rest of your family to do the same. You got that?"

In reply, the phone went dead.

Sheriff Eugene Graystoke uttered every rich, ripe swear word he knew as he made his way to his squad car.

Captain Daniel McBride stood before a giant map of the town of Glacier Ridge, Montana, and the thousands of acres of land that made up the Malloy Ranch.

It was one thing to imagine a sprawling ranch, and quite another to see thousands of acres mapped out in three dimensions, with every hill, mountain, ravine, and lake dotting the landscape. The sheer size of the place was mind-boggling. What was even more amazing to a man born and bred on the south side of Chicago was the isolation of the place. He figured there were more cattle per square mile than humans. Thousands of acres of uninhabited land where a couple of thugs could hide without ever encountering another human being.

And in the middle of all that was Elliott Kettering's

daughter. A helpless young woman at the mercy of men hired by a man who, if convicted by a jury, had nothing to lose by ordering another murder. And all that stood in the way of that death sentence was a small-town sheriff and a handful of Montana State Police.

Captain McBride pulled out his cell phone. If he couldn't be there to handle things, he could at least direct the operation and give them the benefit of his years of experience with Chicago thugs.

As soon as he heard Sheriff Eugene Graystoke's voice he took charge, barking orders. "I want all roads leading into and out of the Malloy Ranch to be sealed at once."

The sheriff's tone was gruff. "These men don't need roads. They're so deep in the wilderness, they could drive for days without seeing another human being."

"Then you need aircraft and an army of sharpshooters."

"Already got 'em. They've targeted the area where the video was shot."

"How about trackers?"

"One of the best is already on it."

"One?" McBride's tone was incredulous. "Shouldn't you have dozens?"

"This one knows the land better than anyone. It's Matt Malloy."

"The stupid cowboy who allowed her to be captured? I don't want that clown anywhere near this investigation."

The sheriff's eyes narrowed. It was one thing to have his feathers ruffled when the Malloy family stepped on his toes. It was another entirely to hear a city cop demean the family that had offered shelter to a stranger. "You might want to check that attitude, Captain. We may be small town, but we know how to fight for what's right. Matthew Malloy is one tough cowboy. In a fight, I'd rather have him on my side than a dozen of your finest."

Captain McBride stared at the phone in his hand before letting loose with a string of curses. And though he would never say it out loud, he didn't give Elliott Kettering or his daughter much hope for a happy ending to this mess.

CHAPTER TWENTY-SIX

While Frank piloted the Cessna, Grace sat beside him, her binoculars trained on the land below.

She pointed. "There's Matt's truck."

They circled the area, and could see their grandson kneeling in the grass.

Grace dialed his cell phone number and turned on the speaker so both she and Frank could hear.

"Yeah." Matt's voice showed signs of frustration. Or perhaps pain. It was clear that he hadn't bothered to look at the caller ID. "This is Matt."

"We're above you, darlin'."

"Sorry, Gram Gracie." He looked up and saluted. "Any sign of them?"

"Nothing so far." Grace paused a moment. "Are there any tracks you can follow?"

"Enough to know they're heading west. Straight into the wilderness."

"That could work to our advantage," Frank said. "We know this land. They don't."

"But they've been here long enough to study a map of it." Matt sighed. "If so, they've figured out that just over these hills is a cattle trail that leads to an old, abandoned road that will eventually connect with the interstate. Once on that, it's clear sailing."

"So we need to patrol this area until they decide to make a run for it?"

At his grandmother's question, he hesitated before saying, "Once that happens, it will be too late for Nessa. If this thug directing the operation is found guilty, I don't believe they have any intention of taking her with them."

There was total silence as his grim words sank in.

Grace put a hand to her mouth to cover the little gasp that escaped. "Oh, dear heaven." She looked over at her husband, who gave a slight nod of his head.

Matt's voice sounded a long way off, as though thinking aloud. "These men are hiding somewhere until they get the word from their boss."

Frank cleared his throat. "Then we'll keep searching until we find out where those rats are hiding."

"That's the plan." Matt paused before adding, "How are you at praying, Gram Gracie?"

"I've had a lot of practice over the years."

"Good. I think we could all use some now."

As dusk stole over the land, Vanessa listened to the drone of a plane's engines. Earlier, it had been directly overhead, as though circling, and her heart had nearly burst out of her chest at the thought that someone was searching for her. But now it could be heard growing more and more distant. As the sound faded, and the night grew quiet, all she heard was the snoring of the two men. After they'd polished off several sandwiches and an entire bottle of whiskey, she wasn't surprised that they'd offered her nothing. Why bother to feed someone they considered as good as dead? They'd made it clear to her that their loyalty to DePietro was absolute. Whatever he ordered, they would do without question.

Did her life or death depend on the jury's verdict? Or had this vicious criminal known all along that once she was taken, there would be but one ending?

She shivered as she faced the very real possibility that her fate had already been decided. These two couldn't let her live to identify them. And if, as her father believed, the case against DePietro ended in a guilty verdict, her death would be a criminal's final show of power against the lone man who had stood up to him and his empire.

It was clear that these two were simply awaiting the final word from their leader.

Matt glanced skyward, where the far-off drone of the Cessna told him that his grandparents were heading back to the ranch to refuel and wait until morning to resume their search.

He ought to do the same, but the slim chance that the kidnappers might risk a fire had him still driving slowly across the barren hillside, hoping against hope for any sign of them.

He'd hoped the view from the air would reveal a glint of vehicle somewhere in this vast area. Apparently the kidnappers had given this a lot of thought. There were so many heavily wooded areas, as well as rock ledges and caves, where they could take refuge.

He parked at the top of a hill and stepped out of the truck, staring around at the darkened outline of rocks, trees, and distant mountain peaks. Somewhere in this vast wilderness, Vanessa was cold and frightened. And hurt. The very thought of the blood he'd seen in the video had fury bubbling to the surface. It was that fury, that knowledge that she was hurt, that kept him going.

He'd long ago stopped feeling his shoulder, where a bullet was lodged, radiating an all-consuming pain from the top of his head, down his spine to his toes. His body was now simply numb. But he couldn't stop the thoughts that drove him nearly insane. Vanessa in the clutches of madmen. Men awaiting orders to kill her. Men who didn't care about the pain they inflicted. Men who may have been given license to do whatever they wanted with her before disposing of her body.

His hands clenched into fists at his sides and he closed his eyes against the thoughts and images torturing him. Because of his carelessness, he was reduced to this—chasing after shadows while the woman he loved was suffering.

The woman he loved.

Why hadn't he said more when he'd had the chance? He'd begun to declare his love, and then, seeing Vanessa's wide-eyed reaction, he'd backed off and left the cabin to chop wood and work off some of his restlessness. He'd believed it was too soon to shock her with so many personal feelings. And now he would live with that regret for a lifetime.

He'd known. Maybe not at first. It had been perfectly

normal to confuse lust with love. Vanessa Kettering was gorgeous, smart, funny. What man in his right mind wouldn't be attracted? But long before he'd given in to his passion, he'd known it was so much more. And still he'd worked overtime to keep those feelings low-key.

It was that damnable Malloy pride. Look at his uncle. Colin was forty, and still determined to remain a bachelor. He loved to boast that the woman wasn't born who could tie him down. That same mantra had been adopted by all of them. But they'd all known it was a joke, used to cover up any deep feelings they had. They were all very good at repressing feelings. Of loss. Of pain. But love? Frank and Grace were perfect examples of the way love ought to be. And hadn't his own parents been wildly in love?

It was what he wanted. What they all wanted.

Maybe that was why he'd wanted to soft-pedal his declaration of love. It was the most important emotion in the world, and it could be snatched away in an instant.

What he wouldn't give to be able to declare his undying love to his beautiful Nessa this very minute.

Sweet Nessa. How she must be suffering.

He'd asked his grandmother to pray.

It would take a miracle to find where those monsters were hiding her in this vast tract of wilderness.

Vanessa had put in the worst night of her life. Afraid. Alone. And plagued with horrible images of Matt, dead at the bottom of a ravine.

She needed to get free. But she couldn't imagine a scenario that would persuade these two to release her for even a few minutes. When she'd begged for a bathroom break before dark, the beefy, coarse one, Homer—whom she'd mentally nicknamed Bulk—had told her to soil herself, except he hadn't used such proper terms. And once again the two men had enjoyed his little joke, laughing themselves silly.

So what would persuade them to untie her?

Throughout this endless night, she'd played with a dozen different ideas. Feigning sickness. Pretending to be unconscious. Nothing seemed compelling enough to work to her advantage. They didn't care about her state of health. They had no reason to revive her if she fainted. She was already dead to them.

Dead.

It was so hard to concentrate when her mind always circled back to Matt. The thought of him, lying dead at the bottom of a ravine, his sweet, loving family grieving their loss, brought tears spilling down her face.

Had the wranglers in the distant hills seen the pall of smoke? Had someone come to investigate? Had they made the descent into the fiery hell that had enveloped his body? Would they even be able to identify the truck or the burned body?

Matt, her strong, fierce cowboy, his life cut short because of her. He didn't deserve this. All he'd done was offer his ranch as a sanctuary until the threat of danger was gone. And now she would never see him again. Would never hear that deep, sexy voice. Would never feel those strong arms holding her as gently as though she were some delicate, fragile flower. Would never again know the fierce wonder of his love.

The tears flowed until her throat was raw. She lay on the cold, hard ground of the cave and allowed herself to give in to a feeling of complete, absolute despair that settled over her like a dark cloud.

Hawkface, as Vanessa thought of Jasper, the tall, muscled man who always rode in the backseat, woke from a drunken sleep and got to his feet, swaying wildly.

His movements woke Homer, the driver, who aimed a fist into his middle, dropping him to his knees. "What're you doing?"

"Going out for a pizza." Jasper wheezed out a pained breath before getting to his feet. "Whadda ya think I'm doing? I'm going out to pee."

"Watch out for rattlers."

That made Jasper stop in his tracks. "Do snakes come out before daylight?"

"Who the hell knows? Just saying, there could be wolves or bears or all kinds of wild things in this place."

"It gives me the creeps. This whole wilderness thing creeps me out." Jasper stopped just short of the cave entrance. "Maybe I'll just take a whiz in here."

The driver swore. "Take it outside. I don't want to have to smell it in here."

When Jasper hesitated, Vanessa's mind went into overdrive. "Homer has my phone. If you turn it on, it'll give you enough light to see what's close by."

He reached out a hand to the driver. "Give it to me. I'm not taking any chances on stepping on a rattler."

A scant minute later he turned on the phone before stepping away from the cave.

Watching, Vanessa sucked in a quick breath. Would her little trick work? She strained to peer in the predawn darkness, but could see little more than a thin, tiny circle of light, no bigger than the flare of a match.

Minutes later the hawkfaced man returned and handed over her phone to the driver. "I saw something move in the bushes and it had me so spooked I pissed on my shoes. But at least there weren't any bears or wolves."

"Good. Now shut up and let me get back to sleep."

Vanessa lay in the dark and wondered if anyone in Chicago had time to note that brief instant her phone had been engaged. Had it been on long enough to alert them of her location? Not likely. But it had been worth the effort, if only to lift her spirits.

Now her mind was even more alert than ever. She knew she ought to grab some sleep while these two slept, but it was impossible. Her thoughts kept circling back to Matt. The sudden shocking sound of a gunshot, and then the sight of him, bloody and unconscious, behind the wheel of the truck as it went over the ravine.

My fault, she thought fiercely. *All my fault.*

If she hadn't whined and complained about going to a safe house, he and his family would have never become involved in any of this. And right now he would be home with that big, rowdy family, ready to face another glorious day in his Montana paradise.

Instead, because of her, he would never again work or play or laugh.

Or love.

The pain was sharp and swift.

Like his parents, he was in the prime of life, and far too young to die. Unlike his parents, he left no children to carry on his legacy.

Because she'd lost her mother at such a tender age, she

knew only too well that death claimed the young as well as the old.

There was no denying the fact that death was a harsh reality in her life. One that had left her and her father deeply affected.

Her father.

He would be inconsolable. Whatever the outcome of this trial, he would lose. And would pay the price for as long as he continued to live.

She refused to let that happen. She struggled with the restraints at her wrists and ankles until her flesh was raw and bloody. Though she knew it was an impossible task, she had to try. There would be no superhero flying in to save her. She would have to save herself.

CHAPTER TWENTY-SEVEN

Luke parked his Harley on a flat plateau and walked to the edge, to stare at the surrounding hillsides below. All around him the land lay in darkness.

He slipped his cell phone from his pocket and touched the number that connected him with the others.

"I'm on Glacier Plateau. All's quiet here."

Reed's voice answered immediately. "Eagle's Ridge here. Nothing moving."

Their uncle's words were hushed. "Burke and I are at North Ridge, and we haven't seen anything out of the ordinary. Matt? You there?"

Matt's voice was low, though whether in pain or anger, the others couldn't tell. "I'm at the mouth of Glacier Creek. Plenty of caves and cliffs around here big enough to hide a vehicle or people, but no trace of any, so far. It's still too dark to see what's out here."

"You should head to town, Matt." Colin chose his

words carefully, knowing his nephew didn't want to hear what he had to say. "Check into the clinic and have that bullet removed before the wound becomes infected."

Burke added, "Colin's right, son. The doctor could pump you full of painkillers and antibiotics before you pick up the trail again in a couple of hours."

"I can't leave. No time." Matt's words were clipped. "I have to—"

At the sudden silence, the others held off the questions they were burning to ask.

For what seemed an eternity, they waited.

Finally Matt's voice came back over the line. "I think I saw something."

"What?" Luke demanded.

"I'm not sure. It looked like a small flicker of light in the darkness. Just a quick little flash, and then gone. If I would have blinked, I'd have missed it."

"A cigarette?" It was Reed's voice.

"Maybe. Maybe a lighter or match." He breathed in the cold air. "So far I don't smell smoke, but it's too soon for the odor of cigarette smoke to drift this far."

"What direction did the light come from, son?" Burke's voice had gone soft as a whisper.

"North of here. Maybe a thousand yards. A quarter of a mile or so. I know it's a long shot, but I have to check it out. Since it didn't seem natural, it had to be man-made. I'll go on foot. If it's our kidnappers, they'd hear my truck's engine."

The sheriff, plugged into their line, swore. "Matt, you need to wait—"

Before anyone could say more, the line went dead.

* * *

Matt tucked away his cell phone and snatched up his rifle before starting out in the direction he'd seen the light.

Had it been a light? He was already beginning to question himself. His eyes and his mind could be playing tricks on him, because he wanted it so desperately. If DePietro's thugs were nearby, they would naturally take every precaution to slip away undetected. Still, as eager as they would be to get back to their own comfort zone in the city, the thought that they were alone in this vast tract of wilderness may have caused them to become careless. He sincerely hoped so. He could feel his strength flagging with every hour that passed. In order to overpower two armed men, he would need both the element of surprise and an almost superhuman strength to take them both down without causing harm to Vanessa.

Dear God. Vanessa.

Just the thought of her at the mercy of those animals had his heart rate speeding up.

Fear was an alien feeling for Matt. In his entire life, he'd always been fearless. But now there was a knot of it in the pit of his stomach. Not for himself. His life didn't matter at this point. The fear was that he wouldn't find Nessa in time. A terrible dread that he would fail her when she needed him most.

As soon as Matt disconnected, the others held a hasty phone conference, deciding on the best course of action.

Luke voiced his concern. "If Matt's right, we need to be there as backup. I'm worried about how long he can hang on before he collapses."

"Exactly." Reed said what the others were thinking.

"There are two armed thugs, and only one wounded man standing between them and their goal to harm Vanessa."

"If they haven't already killed her and disposed of the body," Colin muttered.

"They might need her alive for now," Luke reminded them. "I'm thinking that if DePietro is found guilty, his ultimate revenge against the DA will be another video showing her pleading for her life before being killed."

"And what if Matt's wrong?" Old Burke's voice had them paying attention. "Right now we're spread out across some miles, and there's a good chance that one of us might spot them trying to get away, if not now, then as soon as it grows light." He paused before adding, "If we miscalculate, boys, we could all be backing up Matt on a false alarm, while the bad guys make a clean getaway."

Eugene Graystoke's gruff voice cut in. "Burke's exactly right, boys. You need to stay where you are. I've just heard from the Chicago PD. Miss Kettering's phone was engaged for a minute. They're tracking the location now."

Luke was the first to respond. "I hear what you're saying, Sheriff. But I trust Matt's instincts. I'm not waiting for word from Chicago. I'm heading that way now."

Reed could be heard climbing aboard his ATV. "I agree with Luke. I'm on it."

Colin slapped Burke on the arm. "I agree with everything you said. But my gut tells me to go with Matt."

The old man gave a grim smile. "All right then. We're all in. We win, or we lose everything."

They climbed into the ranch truck and turned toward the hills at the mouth of Glacier Creek.

* * *

Before dawn the phone rang in the kitchen of the ranch house. Nelson, who had fallen asleep in his favorite chair, barely stirred. But Yancy, who had paced the floor between cups of coffee, snatched up the phone before it had a chance to ring again.

"Yes?" His single word sounded like a growl in the silence of the room. He listened, then replaced the receiver.

Nelson lifted his head. "Who called?"

Frank and Grace, already dressed after a few hours of restless sleep, hurried into the kitchen in time to hear Yancy say, "Captain McBride in Chicago. There was a report of Nessa's cell phone being engaged, but only for a minute. They waited for her to speak, but it went silent again."

Grace shared a look with her husband. "Is this good news or bad?"

Frank shrugged. "It could mean she tried to make a call and couldn't finish before her abductors stopped her. Or it could be nothing more than someone stepping or sitting on her phone for a moment before they realized what they'd done and moved it."

Grace touched a hand to Frank's shoulder. "I'm going to hope it means that Nessa was reaching out to let her father and all of us know that she's still alive."

"Hold on to that thought, Gracie Girl." Frank turned to Yancy. "Load us up with some food and coffee, Yancy. By the time we finish eating, it will be light enough for us to get back in the air."

Streaks of dawn light painted the hills with pink and mauve ribbons. The air was still, and scented with the earthy fragrance of tiny shoots spearing up through the spring soil.

Matt moved cautiously through clusters of trees, around boulders, his eye on the spot where he thought he'd seen that tiny spark of light. Had he simply imagined it, wanting so desperately to see something, anything, that might give him hope?

It was too late to second-guess himself. Now that he was committed, he would move forward and check out the area.

As he rounded a huge outcropping of rock, he stopped dead in his tracks.

He spotted a cave that was almost completely hidden by a wild tangle of brush. If he'd been driving, he would have gone past it without even seeing it.

Yet here it was. Big enough, from what he could judge, to park a vehicle inside. Tall enough for a man to stand in. Secluded enough for stashing a body that might never be found.

He paused to listen. A sound. Low, rumbling, rhythmic. At first he struggled to identify the kind of machine that would make such a sound. But then, as he pressed closer to the opening of the cave, it dawned on him.

Snoring.

He moved tentatively, one small step at a time, squinting to peer into the darkness of the cave.

It was easy to spot the hulking shadows of the two men, chests rising and falling with each nasal sound.

It took an agony of seconds before he spotted a smaller figure some distance from them.

It had to be Vanessa.

It took all Matt's discipline to keep from rushing to her side. He ached to free her. To save her from her tormentors.

He ached to hold her. Just to hold her.

Instead he circled around the outside of the rock formation, careful to make no sound, until he was on the side of the entrance nearest Vanessa. With his ear pressed to the rock he heard the slight shuffling that told him she was alive.

Alive.

He looked around the entrance and saw her working on her restraints. Blood streamed from her wrists and ankles, where the plastic had cut through her flesh. The rope tied from her feet and wrapped around her neck had her neatly hog-tied, and probably blind with pain, yet here she was, still fighting.

He dug out his knife and stepped inside the entrance, intent on freeing her.

Her head came up and her eyes went wide before flooding with silent tears.

He knelt in front of her, pressing a finger to her lips to keep her from crying out.

In the hazy light of the cave he cut through her restraints and gathered her close.

In that same instant he felt the muzzle of a gun pressed to the back of his head, freezing his hand in midmotion, as a voice broke through the silence.

"Move a muscle, cowboy, and you're dead."

CHAPTER TWENTY-EIGHT

Y ou're alive." The words were wrenched from Vanessa's heart as she reached for him.

There was no time to respond. To reassure her.

Matt turned, keeping himself between the beefy gunman and Vanessa.

In one smooth motion his hand swept out, knocking the gun from the man's hand. Matt was on him in the blink of an eye, wrestling him to the floor of the cave and pounding his fist into the man's face.

He caught the burly man by the front of his jacket and hauled him to his feet, before shoving his head as hard as he could against a boulder. With a moan of pain the man slumped to the ground and lay there, his breathing labored, his broken nose streaming blood.

Matt spun around, determined to get Vanessa away from here, but when he turned, the second, taller man had a choke hold on her, and was pressing a knife to her throat.

"On your knees, cowboy."

Matt dropped to his knees and lifted his hands in a signal of surrender.

Vanessa tried to cry out, but the blade of the knife, sharp as a razor as it pierced her skin, made it impossible.

The man holding the knife to her throat shouted, "Get up, Homer. Hurry. I need your help."

With a scream of fury the hefty kidnapper lumbered to his feet and knocked Matt to the floor of the cave, before kicking him viciously. Then he grabbed up Matt's rifle and used it to batter him about the head until Matt was unconscious.

When his rage was spent, Homer looked at his partner. "I thought we killed this cowboy back at that cabin."

"Maybe he's like a cat, with nine lives."

Jasper chuckled at his own joke, but Homer's eyes were fastened on Matt with a look of pure hatred. "I don't care how many lives he has, he's about to lose all of them."

He swung the rifle one more time against Matt's head with all his strength, determined to beat him to death, but the sound of a text on his cell phone distracted him, and he dropped the rifle.

After reading the text he shot a look at his partner. "The verdict is in. Guilty."

Jasper tightened the knife against Vanessa's throat. "So. Now do we get to kill her?"

Homer nodded. "But first, we send one more video, guaranteed to make her daddy understand the price he has to pay for what he did to Mr. D."

Ignoring Matt's unconscious body, the two men dragged Vanessa roughly out of the cave.

She blinked furiously against the stab of morning light, her eyes gritty from all the tears she'd shed while she was forced to watch helplessly as Matt was being beaten.

Matt. She'd thought him already dead. But now, seeing him alive, and then being forced to watch that horrible attack, she absorbed a heart-wrenching sense of despair.

He'd come back from a gunshot and a fiery explosion, only to endure even more pain at the hands of these madmen. After that last attack, he'd stopped fighting. Had even stopped moving.

As the two thugs began choosing the spot for their final video, she resigned herself to her looming fate. Though it was small comfort, at least, she thought, she would die alongside the man she loved.

While Frank Malloy did a careful preflight check of the Cessna, Grace loaded their supplies. Rifles, ammunition, high-powered binoculars. A duffel was stuffed with medical supplies and blankets.

To fill her restless, sleepless hours she had come to a decision. Though she knew the odds of finding the proverbial needle in a haystack, she would remain optimistic and make plans to take both her grandson and Vanessa to the clinic in Glacier Ridge as soon as they were located. She would hold to that thought throughout their ordeal, no matter how long it took.

When her husband climbed up and settled himself in the pilot's seat, she fought back tears.

Seeing her struggle, he closed a hand over hers. "A lot of chatter on our frequency overnight. It seems an hour or so ago Matthew saw something that could have been a light near the mouth of Glacier Creek. The others are headed that way. We'll join them."

He squeezed her hand before taking the controls. "All right, Gracie Girl. From the looks of that sky, the Lord is about to give us a bright, clear day. Let's put it to good use."

She nodded, not trusting her voice. The lump in her throat threatened to choke her.

They rolled along the asphalt strip behind the barn before lifting into the air. As they climbed, Grace felt the familiar lurch in her stomach that she always experienced when the plane became airborne. Though she'd been flying for more than fifty years, it was still a bit of a mystery to her that a craft the weight of a truck could soar like a bird.

As they left the barns and outbuildings behind, she picked up her binoculars and trained them on the ground below.

Luke parked his motorcycle beside Matt's empty truck. Tossing aside his helmet he grabbed up his rifle and started walking north.

He looked up, enjoying the way the dawn crept across the sky, switching on pale lights here and there in the darkness. Everything here in the hills looked and smelled clean and fresh.

He knew it was possible for bad things to happen even on deceptively peaceful days, but his heart kept denying what his mind calmly accepted.

From somewhere behind him a truck door opened and closed, and he sensed that Colin and Burke were just arriving on the scene. The low hum of Reed's ATV went suddenly silent, signaling that he'd joined them.

Luke didn't slow his pace, knowing they'd catch up eventually. He was grateful for the alone time. Since he had no idea what he would find up ahead, he needed to formulate a plan.

The problem was, he couldn't think beyond the fact that Matt had been here ahead of anybody, and the area was as silent as a tomb. Not a good omen. There should have been gunshots. Shouts. A scuffle. Anything.

There was nothing. No sound. No birds overhead. Not even the buzz of insects. A very bad omen.

He paused in a cluster of trees, watching and listening, and decided he would wait here for the others. They would make a much more imposing threat to a couple of Chicago thugs if they marched in like the Marines.

"I want the morning light behind me." Homer turned this way and that while holding his cell phone, trying for the clearest shot. He pointed to a flat stretch of earth. "Take her over there."

Jasper grabbed Vanessa's arm and dragged her roughly across the clearing. "Here?"

Homer took aim and motioned. "That's good. Now I want her kneeling, with her hands in front of her, so I can film the blood."

"Why not tie her up again? That'll look better in the video."

After a moment's thought, Homer nodded. "Good idea."

He waited while Jasper threw Vanessa down in the dirt, securing her wrists and ankles before tying the rope around her neck and feet, causing her to cry out in pain.

"That's good. I want that scream. Step out of the picture and we'll have her do that again."

When Jasper stepped away, Vanessa worked furiously to blink back her tears. She thrust out her chin in a haughty pose, refusing to show pain or fear, despite the fact that the plastic restraints cut her already raw wrists to the bone.

"You want me to knock her around until she cries again?" Jasper seemed almost eager to inflict some pain.

"Never mind." Homer took a video of Vanessa, showing a close-up of her bound wrists and ankles, and lingering on the blood streaming from her raw flesh. "Now cut her loose and we'll get her on her feet."

Vanessa bit down hard on the cry that threatened to escape when Jasper cut through all the restraints and yanked her to her feet.

She staggered, unable to get her balance, and Homer chuckled while recording it. "That's it, honey. Look like a drunk for Daddy."

Immediately aware of how this would look on the video, she struggled to remain as still as possible, knowing that these brief scenes would be the last images her father would have left to carry in his memory for a lifetime.

"Do another choke hold and put your knife to her throat. If you have to, cut her. I want a close-up of her face showing real pain and fear."

Jasper was only too happy to do as he was told.

Matt was entombed in a deep, dark hole. He couldn't see through the darkness. Couldn't concentrate on why he was here. Couldn't rise above the pain that enveloped him in a web of agony.

He knew there was something he had to do. Some evil

he had to overcome. But his mind and body refused to do his bidding.

He heard a cry. A woman's cry.

Nessa.

That single name pierced the fog, and he struggled to sit up.

He tried to see past the darkness, but it was punctuated with painful stabs of light that had him blinking rapidly.

He saw twin figures. Two huge shadows. Then two more, tall and muscular and menacing. And then two women, both of them Vanessa Kettering.

Nessa.

He could vaguely recall the beating he'd taken at the hands of the towering thug. Too many blows to his head, and now he was seeing double. But none of that mattered. What did matter was the fact that Nessa was still alive.

And right now, this minute, all the kidnappers' attention was focused on her.

If he hoped to rescue her, it had to be now.

On hands and knees he crawled slowly, painfully, toward his rifle, which was lying in the dirt a few feet away.

Using it as a crutch, he got to his feet and struggled to remain upright. Any slip now, and those two would be on him before he could fire off a shot.

At the entrance to the cave he heard the beefy thug say, "Mr. D. ordered us to film her dead body. And he wants it all to make the evening news. That'll show Mr. Big Shot DA just who has the real power in his town. If Mr. D. has to do time, he'll be greeted by the other prisoners like a freaking rock star."

Laughing, Jasper said, "Why don't we film her would-be hero lying next to her, covered in blood? That ought to grab some headlines."

"Good idea. Go get the body."

As the tall man started toward the entrance to the cave, he stopped dead in his tracks at the sight of Matt covered in blood and holding a rifle aimed at Jasper's chest.

"Take a look at this cowboy, trying to be a hero when he can barely stand up. Look at him, swaying like a drunken—"

Before he could finish, a single shot rang out, echoing and reechoing across the hills.

CHAPTER TWENTY-NINE

Luke was just greeting Reed, Colin, and Burke, when they looked up at the sound of a plane's engines. Seeing the Cessna in the distance, Luke dialed his grandfather's number and put the call on speaker as the others gathered around to listen.

Grace answered. "Yes, Luke? Any news?"

"Matt thought he saw a flash of light, so we've come here to back him up, in case he's found the kidnappers. We're all here now, at the mouth of the Glacier."

"We're almost right above you. In fact, we can see your vehicles." She glanced at her husband before adding, "Captain McBride reported that Nessa's phone was engaged for a minute before going dark. Could that be what Matt saw?"

"We'll find out soon enough. We figure Matt's somewhere ahead of us, though to be honest, I haven't heard or seen any sign of life."

His grandfather's voice came on the phone. "I'm going to give your news to Sheriff Graystoke. He can send in backup while alerting the Chicago authorities."

"The sheriff knows. We talked to him earlier."

"Good." The old man's voice was rough with impatience. "I'm going to land wherever I can find a clear spot. Keep us in the loop, son."

"Will do, Grandpop."

The group looked grim as Luke replaced his cell phone.

"It's too quiet," Burke muttered.

"I'm thinking the same thing." Colin motioned to the others. "Let's keep to the trees as much as—"

The report of rifle fire had them stopping dead in their tracks before they started out at a run.

Matt watched as the scene before him unfolded.

For the space of several seconds Jasper stood perfectly still as the bullet ripped through his chest. Then, as if in slow motion, blood spurted from the wound, and he staggered before falling face-first in the dirt.

Even before he dropped, Matt was moving forward, taking aim at the big man towering over Vanessa.

He blinked several times. When his vision cleared, he realized that the thug was holding a gun aimed directly at him.

"No." With a shout, Vanessa kicked out with her foot, knocking the gunman off stride, and the shot went wide, spewing dirt several feet from Matt.

Before Homer could take aim for a second attempt, Vanessa grabbed up the rope that had been tied around her neck and whipped it at his eyes.

He cried out, half blind with pain as he reached out a hand to stop her.

Matt took that moment of distraction to charge the thug, taking him down and throwing several punches that had his already-broken nose streaming a fountain of blood.

The gun dropped from Homer's hand. Before he could snatch it back, Vanessa kicked it and sent it flying out of his reach.

Enraged, the thug pummeled Matt with several vicious blows that had his ears ringing and his vision blurring.

Unable to see, Matt struggled to protect himself while returning punches.

Once Homer realized that he had the upper hand, he moved in for the kill, pounding Matt's head against the ground, fists sending blow after blow to Matt's face and chest.

Vanessa could see the fight turning as Matt's strength began to drain away completely. She couldn't imagine how he was still moving. His wounds were too severe, his body too drained to continue. Yet she watched him fight on valiantly, presumably going on nothing but pure courage.

She picked up the gun and wondered what good it would do her. She'd never fired one and was terrified that she would hit Matt instead of the thug.

Desperate, she fired into the air, and at the sound of it Homer brought his head up sharply. As he knelt over Matt, he saw the way Vanessa's hand was shaking.

"Firing a gun is the easy part, Daddy's Little Girl. Firing it at someone you intend to kill is something altogether different. Especially if you hit the wrong target."

His evil smile spread across his lips and turned into a leer. "Now you give me that gun, and I'll show you how it's done."

When she merely stared at him, face pale, lips quivering, Homer laughed. "I get it. You thought I'd just put up my hands and surrender, didn't you? But you don't have the guts to actually shoot."

As he lifted a fist to Matt's face, Luke's voice broke the stillness. "Ask us if *we* have the guts to shoot."

Homer turned to see the entire Malloy family, even Frank and Grace, who had landed their plane nearby, forming a ring around the area, and all of them holding weapons aimed directly at him.

He had no sooner raised his hands when Luke grabbed him by the front of his parka and hauled him to his feet. Then, before anybody could stop him, Luke drove a fist into the gunman's middle and dropped him to his knees, where he wheezed out a breath.

Luke was about to throw another punch when the sheriff's voice sounded from nearby.

"I'll take that piece of garbage..." He glanced at Vanessa before adding, "I'll handle the prisoner from here, Luke."

Several police officers stepped forward to handcuff the prisoner and lead him away. And then the scene became one of complete chaos.

A team of state police sharpshooters, weapons still in place, surrounded the area. Another group of officials moved about. One checked Jasper's vitals and declared him dead, another bagged evidence, while others roped off areas of the ground darkened with blood to collect samples.

Vanessa raced to Matt's side and dropped to her knees. Feeling for a pulse she shouted, "He's alive."

Her tears, held back for so long, now began streaming down her face, as she gave vent to all the raw emotions churning inside. Her composure, so tightly controlled, now slipped away completely. "He needs help. Now. Please. Somebody help him. You can't let him die."

With the Malloy family standing anxiously by, a team of medics hurried over. When they attempted to move Vanessa, she clung to Matt's arm, her tears falling harder and faster.

"Please don't die, Matt. Please stay. You fought so bravely. You endured so much. Please…"

"You need medical attention, Miss." A stocky medic wrapped his arms around her waist, and, with the help of a second man, attempted to place her on a gurney.

"No!" She fought off both of them and raced back to kneel beside Matt. "He's the one who needs help. Please. You can't let him…"

Her tears fell harder and faster as she saw just how badly wounded he was.

Frank dropped to his knees beside Vanessa. "Hush now, Nessa girl. Everyone's doing the best they can."

The stocky medic hovered nearby, while the other took Matt's vitals and hooked up an intravenous tube to administer something for pain.

Grace looked at the man, who shook his head gravely. "I have orders from Chicago authorities to get Miss Kettering to the nearest hospital as soon as possible."

"All we have in Glacier Ridge is a clinic," Frank explained.

"Then we'll head there first." The medic reached for Vanessa's hand, but she shrank back.

"I won't go without Matt."

"He'll be on the next copter, ma'am. I promise you."

"But what if he . . . ?" She couldn't speak about her greatest fear. That he might not survive his terrible injuries. The words, once spoken, would be too final. "Please let me stay."

"They can't do that, Nessa." Frank studied the somber faces of the two medics. "They have their orders."

Vanessa watched as a member of the medical team assessed her wounds. When she saw the way he shook his head, she dug in her heels. "I'm not going without Matt." She turned, searching until she saw Grace kneeling nearby, fighting tears.

"Grace." She stretched out her bloody hands and the old woman hurried over to embrace her. "Make somebody understand that I'm not leaving Matt. If not for him, I wouldn't be here. He sacrificed so much for me."

"I know." Grace stroked her hair.

"He's my hero. Please tell them . . ." Nessa's voice broke. "Please, Grace, tell them I need to stay with Matt. Oh, I love him so."

The old woman sent a warning look to the medics, who nodded their agreement. "You'll fly to the clinic with Matthew. It's what you need. What you both need."

"Thank you. Oh, thank you."

Grace pressed a kiss to her tear-streaked cheek as the team lifted the gurney bearing Matt's unconscious form. "Go with them. And hold on to the thought that it's all in heaven's hands now."

Minutes later the Malloy family watched solemnly as

a medical helicopter lifted into the air with a flurry of blades that flattened the grass and had the trees bending in a furious dance.

While several police units remained to photograph the crime scene and scour the area for evidence, a convoy of planes and vehicles began making its way from the Montana wilderness, all of them bound for the distant town of Glacier Ridge.

The scene at the tiny clinic in town was even more chaotic than the crime scene. A team of medics kept getting in the way of the lone, aged doctor, Leonard Cross, who had single-handedly run the Glacier Clinic for more than fifty years. Dr. Cross delivered babies, set broken bones, treated infections, and helped his patients through terminal diseases, and all with the same optimistic good cheer. But today, that cheer was being sorely tested.

He'd just brought his niece, Anita, here from Boston's finest hospital, in the hope of persuading her to join his clinic. For the past few years he'd been thinking of a way of cutting back to take some time for himself without leaving the citizens of Glacier Ridge without a doctor.

Since Anita had arrived several days earlier, her uncle had been extolling the virtues of small-town medicine, boasting that she would find plenty of time to pursue her dream of practicing family medicine while also writing novels set in the Old West.

As he dashed from one examining room to the next, he muttered to her, "Sorry. This wasn't exactly what I had in mind for your first days on the job. This isn't the good impression I was hoping for."

She shot him a sweet smile. "Uncle Leonard, no matter what life throws at me here, it can't possibly compare to my hectic hospital days in the trauma unit in Boston."

"That's good to hear." He led the way into the room where the entire Malloy family had gathered around the examining table.

Seeing them he skidded to a halt. "Is this Matthew?" The old doctor couldn't tell with all the blood and dirt that masked the patient's face.

Colin assigned himself speaker for the family. "My nephew Matt's been shot, Doc."

"I can see that." Dr. Cross watched as his assistant, Agnes, cut away Matt's bloody parka and shirt to expose his chest.

"And he survived a fiery truck crash." Colin stared at his nephew lying so still on the table, and forced himself to swallow.

Anita Cross, noting his pallor, put a hand on his arm. "Sir, if you faint at the sight of blood, you may want to leave the room."

He shook off her hand before giving her a look of pure outrage. "I've never fainted in my life."

"There's always a first time."

His eyes narrowed on her. "Look Miss..."

"Doctor. I'm Dr. Anita Cross."

"My niece," the old doctor said as he began to probe Matt's chest.

"Dr. Cross, I'm not leaving this room until I know my nephew will live."

Colin's harsh tone would have been enough to frighten most people, but seeing the fierce look in his eyes had Dr. Anita Cross nodding. "I understand completely. If you could step back a pace, we'll share everything we can with you." She turned to include the others. "With all of you. But this could be difficult, even painful, to watch. It might be better if you wait in the lobby."

In answer, they crossed their arms over their chests and planted their feet.

It was answer enough for her.

When the young doctor turned to her uncle, she saw him vainly attempting to remove a young woman who was clinging to Matt as though to a lifeline.

Her voice lowered to a command. "Young lady, you have to give us room to do our job."

As Vanessa looked up, her movements were slow and measured, as though she'd turned into a robot. Her face had gone ghostly white, and her hands were trembling.

Dr. Anita Cross took a firm hold of Vanessa's arm. "This woman is in shock and needs a bed immediately."

Before she could press an emergency button, Colin stepped up and swept Vanessa into his arms. "Where do you want her, Doc?"

The doctor turned to Agnes. "Show them to examining room two, and I'll be there as soon as possible."

As Vanessa was carried from the room, the others went deathly silent as the two doctors bent to examine Matt.

Dr. Anita spoke in low tones to her uncle. "Looks like he's been through a war. How is his heart?"

"Strong. But then, I'm not surprised. Some men might be taken down by a bullet, or a fiery crash." Dr. Leonard Cross muttered, "Though he's been through both, I'm thinking it will take more than that to do in a Malloy."

He stepped away and turned to the family, while his niece left the room to examine her next patient.

"I know you want to stay close. But I have to take Matt into surgery right now. We'll get that bullet out, set any broken bones we find, and deal with his burns and other wounds. Since it'll take the better part of the day, I suggest you return to the ranch, and I'll phone you when surgery is over."

Frank said, "We're not leaving, Doc." He turned to the others. "While you go to the waiting room, Gracie and I will head on over to the other room and check on Vanessa. She'll want to know that Matthew is going into surgery."

The family made their way from Matt's room, and Frank and Grace walked down the hall.

Posted outside the door to Vanessa's room stood two uniformed officers from the Chicago PD.

One of the men held up a hand. "Sorry. No one is allowed inside without permission."

Frank shot them a look of authority. "We are Frank and Grace Malloy. Vanessa stayed at our ranch during the trial."

The officers held a whispered conversation before one of them pulled out his cell phone and spoke into it. Listening intently, he stepped aside and held the door for the elderly couple.

As they paused just inside the door, a tall, handsome man in a rumpled white shirt, his tie undone, his mussed hair gray at the temples, looked up from the side of the bed with a look of pure anguish.

"Mr. and Mrs. Malloy, I'm Elliott Kettering." He offered his hand.

"Frank and Grace," Frank said as he accepted the handshake.

"I was on a plane from Chicago as soon as the verdict

was returned. Captain McBride kept me aware of what was happening during the flight. How is your grandson?"

"Doc is taking him into surgery now." Grace studied the young figure in the bed. "And your daughter?"

"I've never seen her like this. She was highly agitated and making little sense, insisting that she wouldn't accept any medical help until she knows what happened to her hero. That's what she kept babbling about. Her hero. Her Superman. And saying she was in love with him and willing to give up her own life if it meant he could survive." He ran a hand through his hair in frustration. "Obviously she's too badly traumatized to know what she's saying. I demanded that the doctor give her something for pain. Dr. Anita said the wounds to her wrists and ankles are deep and need to be treated for possible infection. Apparently the plastic restraints those thugs used cut clear to the bone."

Grace caught the young woman's hand, noting the heavy dressings at her wrists, and the bag of intravenous fluid hanging from a pole beside the bed. "I'm glad she's no longer awake and suffering."

"I'm glad, too. I had a wildcat on my hands until she was sedated. This terrible ordeal has really scarred her . . ." His tone softened. "My daughter needs the best possible care, so I've made a decision. Since the doctor said it would be a matter of weeks before she can completely forgo pain medication, I'm taking her back to Chicago immediately." His tone turned businesslike. "I'm grateful for all they did here at the clinic. I hope you understand. After all we've been through, I don't want her out of my sight for a minute longer than necessary. Vanessa's all I have."

Grace managed a halting smile. "I understand completely."

Frank moved in to lay a big hand on Vanessa's arm. "I know you can't hear me, darlin', but I hope you'll let your father pamper you. He's earned that right. And so have you."

Grace kissed her cheek. When she straightened, she turned to Elliott Kettering. "When Matt's surgery is over, we'll call you."

"Of course. I appreciate that. And I want you to know that you have my heartfelt gratitude for everything your family did for my daughter. You'll never know what agony I went through these past weeks."

"No more than we did." Frank cleared his throat. "We're grateful for the outcome. There were some moments . . ." His voice trailed off.

After more handshakes, while Frank and Grace watched, Elliott Kettering was flanked by the police officers as he followed the gurney toward a waiting ambulance that pulled away from the clinic the minute they were settled inside.

It was their last glimpse of the young woman who had come to mean so much to all of them.

A young woman who had changed and been changed by their grandson forever.

CHAPTER THIRTY

Matt lay a moment, eyes closed, listening to the now-familiar beeps and pings of monitoring equipment and the sudden squeeze of an automated blood-pressure cuff. He would rather face stampeding cattle than another day in this sterile room at the clinic.

He'd been here nearly a week now. Seven long days of being numbed with pain medication, shutting down his mind. He'd been poked and prodded, and forced to listen to plans for physical therapy in the coming months.

Seven long days of waking to find his family keeping vigil, taking turns being with him day and night. When he'd asked them to go home, they'd agreed to cut back on their visits, and then promptly doubled up their time with him.

The one face he'd longed to see was missing.

He'd called and left dozens of messages on her phone.

At first her father had answered, saying she couldn't be disturbed. After a while, the calls had simply gone unanswered.

It had to be by design.

As soon as the family noted his agitation, Dr. Cross had ordered all phones removed from Matt's room, including his cell phone.

As the days stretched on, and his questions to his family were met with silence, he gave up asking.

Every time he closed his eyes, he could see her as she'd looked that last time, before he'd lost consciousness. Her wrists and ankles raw and bloody, the fierce look in her eyes as she'd knocked aside Homer's gun and then whipped him with her ropes, desperately fighting to keep him from ending Matt's life. She'd been fighting for both of them.

What an amazing woman.

And yet, because of his carelessness, she'd nearly lost her life in the Montana wilderness. It wasn't something he could ever forgive himself for, nor forget. He'd let her down. Badly.

No wonder her father had whisked her away to Chicago. To have his own doctors care for her. To keep her safe and to ensure that she could resume the life she was meant to live.

Time spent back in her own environment had surely given her a chance to clear her mind and make her realize all she'd been missing.

A woman like that didn't belong here, on thousands of uninhabited acres, chasing herds of mustangs, sleeping in rough cabins or, worse, under the stars. She might have rhapsodized about the wonder of it all, but that was simply because she was, for a brief time, living her childhood fairy tale. Now it was time for a reality check. She was an urban career woman, chasing what everyone wanted—success on her own terms.

Over time, when her wounds were completely healed, and she was back at work doing what she loved, the time spent on his ranch would fade into the background. He and his family would become a pleasant memory.

A feeling of desolation swept over him, dragging him down.

Colin and the pretty young doctor walked into his room talking quietly about something. When they realized he was awake, they hurried to his bedside.

"Hey, Matt." Colin started to punch his arm, then checked himself and squeezed his hand instead. "How're you feeling?"

"Fine." He hated being coddled. Hated being the object of so much concern.

He turned to the doctor. "When can I leave?"

She smiled at him. "Your uncle and I were just talking about it. I think, if you promise not to do too much, you can go home today."

Matt brows shot up. "You mean it?"

She nodded.

He turned to Colin. "Get my clothes."

"Right. Quick, before she changes her mind."

Colin and the doctor both chuckled before she left the room, giving Matt enough privacy to dress. With his uncle's help he managed to get into his jeans, but when he lifted his arm to slip on his shirt, the shaft of pain in his shoulder had him swearing.

By the time he was completely dressed, he was sweating and hating the fact that he felt as weak as a newborn calf.

Agnes arrived with a wheelchair, and he gave her no argument, grateful he didn't have to walk.

At the door to the clinic, Dr. Anita was waiting with a list of medications and physical-therapy sessions already scheduled.

"One thing before you go, Matt." Her tone went from sweet and sunny to one of authority. "From everything I've learned about you, you'll go home and expect to resume your ranch activities tomorrow. Please don't push your body. It was seriously damaged, and it's healing. But in order to avoid any setbacks, let it dictate when you're ready to do all the physical activities you once did."

"Sure thing." He would say whatever it took to get out of here.

She glanced over his head to where Colin stood watching and listening. "I hope you'll convey to your family what I said. When you see Matt pushing himself, remind him that he still has a lot of healing to do."

"I will." He stuck out his hand. "And thanks, Doc. For everything."

Burke stepped out of the ranch truck and hurried around to help Matt up to the passenger seat. Colin stayed back to say something more to the young doctor before climbing into the rear seat.

As they started toward home, Matt was unusually quiet, holding himself tensely.

Burke glanced over. "That niece of old Doc Cross's is one damned fine-looking woman. Quite an improvement over her uncle."

"I didn't notice." Matt gazed hungrily at the scenery outside the window, grateful to be free of the clinic.

Burke chuckled and gave his elbow a nudge. "I guess your injuries were worse than we thought if you never even noticed a beautiful woman. Now if this had been your uncle, he'd have probably insisted on staying another week, just to have an excuse to look at pretty little Dr. Anita Cross every day."

When Matt didn't even smile, Burke exchanged a look with Colin in the rearview mirror. They both knew it wasn't only Matt's physical injuries that were causing him such pain. The damage to his heart was another matter altogether.

It looked like that injury still had a heap of healing to do.

Despite the doctor's warning, Matt eased back into ranch life, mucking stalls, tending to the millions of chores required to keep a ranch of this size operating smoothly.

But when the chores were done, his family watched helplessly as he rode off alone to the range shack to brood. The same shack where Vanessa had been abducted. The same shack where they'd once loved.

There, alone in his beloved wilderness, he chopped wood until his shoulder throbbed. He sat in front of a roaring fire, remembering what his grandmother had conveyed to him when Elliott Kettering had taken his daughter home. That Nessa wanted him to know how grateful she was that he'd come to her rescue. And that she loved him.

He didn't want her gratitude. And she'd obviously had time to realize he wasn't worthy of her love.

Not one phone call. Not a word. Not that he blamed her.

Everything bad that had happened to her had been his fault. Hadn't he ordered Burke to keep the wranglers at a distance because he selfishly wanted time alone with Nessa?

Time alone. It had been everything he'd ever dreamed it would be. And then it had all gone wrong. And he'd had no one to blame but himself.

And now, judging by the silence from Chicago, Nessa blamed him, too.

Each time he returned from the hills, his family watched for any sign that he was ready to let go of the sadness they could read in his eyes. But it was always there. Like a bruise that told of a deep wound. The only problem was, a bruise around a broken heart was much harder to heal.

Burke stepped inside the barn and paused, allowing his eyes to adjust to the dim light. It was barely dawn, and already Matt was mucking stalls.

The foreman leaned against the stall door and watched for a moment before breaking the silence. "I'm worried about you, son."

"I'm not overdoing anything." Matt deposited a load of dung and straw into the honey wagon and bent to his work.

"It's not the chores that worry me. It's you."

Matt paused to lean on the handle of the pitchfork. "What's that supposed to mean?"

"You know exactly what I'm talking about. You tackling ranch chores before dawn. You riding up alone to the range shack as often as you can get away."

"That's nothing new. I've always taken my alone time there."

"In the past, that alone time renewed your spirit, son. Now it has the opposite effect. You come back sad and quiet."

"There's not much to laugh about these days."

"Things around here are the same as they've always been. Nothing's changed. Not the ranch chores or the family business. Not even the small-town gossip. The only thing that's changed is you."

As Matt opened his mouth to speak, Burke held up a hand. "And don't try to deny it."

Matt looked away before nodding. "Yeah. I know what you're saying, Burke. But I don't know what to do about it."

"You can call her."

"I tried that. She never answers. That tells me she doesn't want to hear from me. Besides, what can I say to her except that I'm sorry?"

"You've got to stop carrying that load of guilt. It's weighing you down, son, and all of us along with you."

"I can't let it go. Don't you think I try to stop playing that scenario over every day in my mind? I was the one who asked you to keep the wranglers away from the cabin so Nessa and I could have some time alone. It was foolish and selfish, and Nessa nearly paid with her life."

"Son, I think there's something you need to know. Everybody here knew what you and that pretty little lady were feeling long before the two of you did. So when you asked me to give you some space, I said I would, but that doesn't mean I called off the wranglers."

Matt's head came up. "You didn't?"

The old man grinned. "I knew what the two of you were planning on doing, and it didn't involve leaving that cabin. So I left the wranglers in place, right where they'd always been, guarding the lady."

"Then how . . . ?"

"What none of us had counted on was having those Chicago thugs discover that old abandoned cattle trail, which they used to sneak up on the cabin, and which they'd probably hoped to use as their getaway, once they realized it was deep in wilderness. While we were watching for them, they were already in place, watching us. They spotted the guards, and to draw them away, they slit the throats of a dozen or so head of cattle. They knew once their dirty deed was discovered, the wranglers would ride out in search of the perpetrators. And that's exactly what happened. Even though we were nearby, our attention was on the herd, and not on the two of you in that cabin, as it should have been. Even when they shot you, the sound was drowned out by the lowing of cattle. If they hadn't shoved you and your truck over the ravine and caused that explosion, we wouldn't have known about their attack until hours later."

The shock Matt was feeling was evident in his eyes. "You're not just saying this to ease my guilt?"

"It wasn't your fault, son. You and Nessa did what any couple in love would do." Burke clapped a hand on his shoulder. "If you want to blame it on something, blame it on fate or timing or just plain bad luck."

Without another word the old cowboy ambled out of the barn, leaving Matt alone to mull all that he'd learned.

As he continued mucking stalls, Matt felt a measure of relief as some of the guilt began to slip away. But though these facts eased his guilt, nothing would change the fact that Vanessa didn't want to speak to him.

He swore under his breath.

He hoped the worst of her wounds had healed.

He hoped she'd been able to put behind her all the fear and pain she'd been forced to endure.

He hoped, desperately, that now that she was back to her old life in Chicago, she would think of him from time to time, and remember the love they'd shared.

CHAPTER THIRTY-ONE

After a long weekend up in the hills, Matt could feel old Beau straining to make a run for the barn. Instead he held the horse to a slow walk. His gelding might have been eager to return to the comfort of home, but Matt's heart was still at the range shack. There was no longer anything to come home to.

He'd seen the way his family tiptoed around him. He was weary of being the object of so much sympathy. He wanted things back where they'd once been. A happy, carefree family, a successful ranch business, a sense that he was making a difference.

But he had no idea how to make it happen. Ever since Nessa's abduction, he'd been feeling the way he had when he was twelve, learning of his parents' death on that snow-covered road. Broken somehow, and wondering how to put the pieces of his life back together.

Once in the barn he took his time rubbing down his

mount, then filling the troughs with feed and water, before making his way to the back door of the house.

The day had grown uncomfortably warm, and Matt, his shirt plastered to his back, was glad for the coolness of the mudroom.

As he began washing at the big sink, he could hear voices raised in laughter somewhere in the house.

He stepped into the kitchen, where the wonderful aromas of bread baking and meat roasting had his mouth watering, though Yancy was nowhere to be seen. Instead of heading toward the voices, he made his way upstairs to shower.

Half an hour later, dressed in fresh jeans and a clean denim shirt, he helped himself to a longneck from a tray on the kitchen counter and followed the sound of laughter to the great room.

In the doorway, with the bottle halfway to his mouth, he stopped and simply stared.

It was a scene he'd been a part of all his life. His family, loudly trying to talk over one another, as they shared the events of their day.

Luke, with his hair in a ponytail and a rough beard from his week with the herd, was telling them about a mustang stallion he'd spotted in a highland meadow.

Reed, also bearded, hair past his shoulders, was tipping up a longneck and suggesting that their grandmother ought to investigate, since it sounded like the white stallion she'd been trailing for over a year.

Nelson, seated in a chair next to Frank, was telling him about his latest foray into town. Someone had actually asked for his autograph, and the old man had been flattered and delighted to comply.

Though they were all talking and laughing, Matt didn't hear a thing, except an odd buzzing in his brain.

Standing in the midst of them was a vision.

She was wearing something prim and businesslike. A silk jacket and trim skirt. Her hair was soft and loose and spilling down to her shoulders.

Vanessa.

He knew he was imagining her. She looked as she had that first time he'd met her. A young professional, looking a little too intense, but doing her best to be bright and cheerful while getting her interview concluded so she could return home.

He blinked, but the image didn't dissolve. Instead she turned and stared directly at him, and he felt the quick sizzle of recognition clear across the room.

"It took you long enough, sonny boy." Frank moved aside to reveal a tall man wearing a suit and tie. "Look who's come all the way from Chicago to see us."

"There was no car outside."

Reed chuckled. "I got a call to pick up some passengers from a private jet in town." He waved a hand. "And look who I found."

"Elliott Kettering," the man said, extending his hand.

"Mr. Kettering." Matt moved woodenly across the room to offer a handshake.

"Call me Elliott. I want to thank you for all you did for my daughter. Not to mention what you did for her terrified father. It's beyond measure."

"I did what I could."

"According to my daughter, you were superhuman. After surviving both a bullet and a fiery crash, instead of sending for a doctor, as any sane man would, you just kept pushing through your pain until you found where those animals were holding Vanessa. Then, she told me, you endured even more beatings."

"Vanessa was the one who saved the day. If not for her quick thinking, I'd be dead now."

Elliott cleared his throat. "I'm here because Nessa threatened murder and mayhem until I agreed to bring her here. I tried my best to put her in a bubble and keep her away from the big, bad world, but once she realized what I was up to, she was having none of it. She let me know, in very clear language, what she thought of my tactics." He paused before adding, "I believe she has some things she wants to say."

Matt looked over at Vanessa, standing so still and quiet. He had to swallow twice. "You look good. You're healed."

"And so are you, I see." She started across the room and halted in front of him. "I'm told you tried calling me. Several hundred times."

He was aware that the others had gone completely silent. "I understand why you ignored me."

She arched a brow. "You do?"

"You needed to make a clean break. You needed time to get back to your life. The real one, not the one you were forced to live here."

"Is that what you think? That all of this was forced on me, and I was just going along, making the best of things?"

"No need to deny it. I was a witness when you learned about the threat to your safety."

She clenched her hands at her sides. "That's how it all started. And yes, I admit that I had a few bad moments." She dragged in a breath. "But then, everything changed."

"I'm sorry." Matt set aside his beer to give himself a moment to look away. The pain of seeing her, and not being able to touch her, was almost more than he could bear. But if he touched her, he'd never be able to stop. He would simply devour her. He would have to fill himself with her until he was sated. And so he stood, ramrod straight, forcing himself to breathe in and out.

"Sorry for what, Matt?"

"The pain you suffered. The fear. The danger. I thought I could keep it from you. But it was my carelessness that allowed it to touch you. To hurt you."

"You make it sound as though you're the one who kidnapped me and forced me to be with you."

"I..."

She put a hand on his and he was rooted to the spot, though he thought about stepping back, away from the heat. Away from the current of pure electricity that sizzled through his veins. But he needed the heat more than he'd realized, and so he stayed, feeling the touch of her all the way to his shattered heart.

"I was with you because that was where I wanted to be." She looked into his eyes. "Where I needed to be. And everything that followed can't be allowed to erase what we have, Matt."

He chose his words carefully, aware they had an audience. "I know that when two people get caught up in...forces they can't control, they sometimes forget for a while that they come from very different worlds. Seeing you up in the hills, sharing that once-in-a-lifetime experience with Grace and a herd of wild horses, I forgot that you were only here for a little while, and that sooner or later you would need to return to the very satisfying life you've made for yourself in the city."

"I see." She nodded. "So when I didn't return your calls, you decided, in your infinite wisdom, that like my father, you know what's best for me."

His eyes narrowed slightly. "What's that supposed to mean?"

Elliott gave an exasperated sigh. "There was a time, right after I got Vanessa back home, that I said exactly what you just said, Matt. I figured in a few days she would put the danger, and all this foolishness about spending the rest of her life on a ranch in Montana, out of her mind, so she could get back to being my successful, well-adjusted daughter. And when she insisted that she loved you, I decided that she was confusing gratitude with love."

Matt's gaze was fixed on Vanessa. "You loved me? You've talked about spending the rest of your life on a ranch?"

"Isn't that what you led me to believe? Or was everything we shared up in that cabin a lie?"

His tone lowered. Softened. "It was real. At least for me. But what about you? What about your career?"

"I represent wildlife organizations. You can't get more wildlife than here."

"You represent them in Washington, DC."

She lifted her chin a fraction. "Matthew Malloy, I know you understand the function of airplanes. I believe you use them to fly all over the world. When I'm needed in DC, I'll go. And then I'll fly back *home*." She emphasized the word.

"Home? Here? You'd do that? You'd give up your life in the city—?"

She stopped him with a finger to his lips. "Stop talking about what I'd give up. Why don't you ask what I want in return?"

He caught her wrist and shook his head. "You've seen my life. What you'll get is hard, never-ending work. Long, frigid winters and hot, sticky summers. And more work than anyone should ever have to do."

"What I'll get in return is this big, loud, fun family." She looked at the faces, some smiling, some somber, staring back at her. "I'd have brothers. Grandparents. A great-grandfather." She grinned at Burke and Yancy. "My very own bodyguard and cook." She turned to him, and this time she touched a hand to his chest. Over his heart. "And best of all, I'd have my very own cowboy. A cowboy, I should add, who makes my heart go crazy every time he looks at me. Who fills my life with so much sizzle."

Matt had gone as still as a statue, afraid to speak, or breathe, or even blink.

Luke broke the silence. "You'd better grab the girl fast, bro, or Reed and I are going to draw straws to see which one of us gets to take your place."

The laughter that followed managed to penetrate the fog that seemed to have clouded Matt's brain. In an imitation of their grandfather he drawled, "Find your own girl, sonny boy."

He turned to Vanessa. "Is that why you're here? To declare your feelings?"

"Can't you see? I'm wearing them on my sleeve." Her voice grew soft. "Cowboy, in case you've forgotten, I learned my lesson when I was just a teen. I'm not going to be discouraged by a few setbacks. Whether you reject me or not, whether my father fights me every step of the way, I came to dance. I'm not leaving without it."

Hearing the hoots and catcalls from his rowdy brothers, he shoved open the door. "Would you mind if we took this to another room?"

Turning their backs on their audience, they walked stiffly, side by side, into the kitchen, trying not to touch.

Once they were safely inside the empty room Matt dragged her into the circle of his arms and poured himself into a kiss like a starving man. She returned his kisses with wild abandon, her arms around his neck, her body straining toward his.

They were so close they were nearly crawling inside each other's skin.

When they finally came up for air, hearts racing, breathing ragged, Nessa batted her lashes at him. "Now that's what I'm talking about. It was worth flying halfway across the country for just that."

"That's still not enough." Matt caught her hands in his. "There's still one thing missing."

Matt dropped to his knees. "I want you to know I'd crawl over hot coals for you." He stared into her eyes. "Nessa, I'm not a man who likes to beg, but please marry me. I give you my word, whenever my crazy family or the isolation of Montana gets too much for you, I'll take you away to any place in the world, as long as you promise to never leave me again."

She framed his face with her hands. "Oh Matt. This is the easiest promise I've ever made."

"Is that a yes?" He got to his feet and pressed his lips to the top of her head, breathing her in.

"Yes. Yes. Yes." As she stood on tiptoe and crushed her mouth over his, the door burst open and the entire family toppled against one another as they fell inside.

"Sorry." It was Nelson, trying to regain his dignity after being caught leaning on the door. He moved aside to make room for all the bodies spilling into the room. "We wanted to be sure we didn't miss a thing."

Matt was grinning. "You notice the rest of them didn't even bother to apologize. You're all shameless."

"Even you, Dad?"

At Nessa's words, her father managed a sheepish grin. "The Malloy family is a bad influence on me."

"They seem to have that effect on both of us." Vanessa held Matt's hand before turning to all of them. "Now it's my turn to apologize. I know I've behaved shamelessly. I should be sorry about it, but I was afraid that if I didn't bully my father into bringing me here to apologize for hiding Matt's phone calls from me, Matt would just slip further and further away."

Luke burst into laughter. "I'm just glad somebody knew how to get him out of that dark place he's been in." He turned to Matt. "Good to see you smile again, sonny boy."

Gracie hurried over to gather Vanessa into her arms for a warm embrace. "At last I get to welcome another woman into this family." She held the young woman a little away before saying, "I hope this doesn't sound too bold, but we'd be honored if you and Matthew would have your wedding here on our ranch."

Vanessa looked suddenly shy. "Nothing would make me happier."

"Here?" Elliott looked confused. "What about all our friends in Chicago?"

Vanessa crossed to him and touched a hand to his cheek. "I could say it's punishment for keeping Matt's calls a secret. But the truth is, Dad, that as much as I love you and our life together in Chicago, I've learned to love this place, too. It's become a second home to me.

"Besides, I'd really love to show off my new lifestyle to my friends. I know I can persuade my BFF Lauren to be my maid of honor on a real, honest-to-goodness Montana ranch." She looked pleadingly at her father. "Am I asking too much?"

Elliott gave a gentle shake of his head. "All I want is your happiness, Nessa."

Yancy was already rubbing his hands together. "I'd love to put together the finest banquet anyone's ever tasted."

Grace was elated. "This is more than I could ever hope for."

Frank joined her to whisper, "I'm so glad you're here, Nessa Girl."

While Luke and Reed pumped Matt's hand and hugged his bride-to-be, Burke waited until Nessa and the others gathered around her father before putting a gnarled hand on Matt's shoulder. "It does my heart good to see you two together. It's where you both belong."

"Thanks, Burke. Did you have anything to do with this?"

The old man shrugged and then grinned. "This was all on her. That little lady's got spunk, son. That one will never let you down."

Matt nodded. "You should have seen how she fought

her attackers, Burke. She was really something." He added softly, "It's not something I'll ever forget."

"Sounds like she had to fight her father, too." The foreman handed him his beer before touching the rim of his bottle to Matt's. "Every time I look at you and Nessa I see another young couple who were so crazy in love that nothing could ever come between them. Like your folks, I think the two of you are going to have one hell of a love story, son."

Matt beamed as he looked at his bride-to-be, surrounded by his family and wearing the most radiant smile as she blew him a kiss. "My love story is right there. In Nessa's heart. In Nessa's hands. And thanks to my bride-to-be, our story can have a happy ending."

EPILOGUE

Montana spring had been as brief as a wink. Cold nights and cool mornings gave way to sunshine and heat as summer followed close on its heels. The meadows, a glorious green, were blanketed with colorful wildflowers. The hillsides were dark with sleek cattle, feeding on the lush grass that grew in the highlands.

The Malloy Ranch had seen its share of parties and celebrations through the years, but the wedding of Matthew Malloy to Vanessa Kettering promised to be the biggest ever.

Almost everyone in the town of Glacier Ridge had received an invitation, and folks made it a point to arrive early so they wouldn't miss a thing.

The wranglers, sporting their best shirts and string ties, their boots polished to a high shine, were directing traffic, while two others stood on either side of the rarely used front door to show folks to the great room, where the ceremony would take place.

Because of the overflowing crowd, some chose to remain outside. There they were free to watch and listen through the open double doors as they nibbled appetizers and drank longnecks arranged on tables on the front porch, which stretched along the width of the big house.

Elliott Kettering proudly stood beside the Malloy family as they greeted the members of his staff, who had made the flight to Montana. By their smiles and looks of amazement, they were more than a little dazzled by the size of the Malloy Ranch and by the handsome, loving family she was joining.

Yancy and the wranglers, who were assisting him in the food preparation, had arranged chairs, draped in white and tied with big white bows, in a semicircle around the fireplace in the great room. Tall vases of white roses and hydrangea, with ivy trailing from each, stood majestically in front of the fireplace screen; they also flanked the banquet tables set up for the guests under a giant white tent in the front yard.

As the room began filling up, and others in the crowd ambled outside to enjoy the sunshine, Nelson whispered to Frank, who beckoned his son and grandsons, as well as Burke and Elliot, to follow.

They made their way along a gravel path to the plot of land situated on a windswept hill. Opening the wrought iron gate, they gathered around a single headstone bearing a heart, and the names PATRICK MALLOY and BERNADETTE DOYLE MALLOY. Seeing the dates of their births and deaths, Elliott lifted a brow in question.

"Some would say they died too young." Frank took in

a quiet breath. "But I've always believed their love was so great, it will continue to burn hot enough for eternity."

Luke produced a bottle of Irish whiskey and filled several tumblers, then passed them around.

"To Patrick and Bernie," Frank said softly. "For I know they're smiling down on all of us this fine day."

As one, they lifted their glasses and drank.

"To my beautiful Madeline." Nelson's voice was husky with emotion. "How she would have enjoyed this."

They drank again.

Elliott cleared his throat. "I'd like us to drink to Nessa's mother, who is right here with us, too. To Danielle O'Conner Kettering."

Solemnly they drank.

Luke and Reed shared a grin before Luke said, "To Nessa, the only one who could have ever bullied my big brother into getting hitched."

As they chuckled and drank, Matt handed his glass to Burke before turning away.

"Hey," Reed called to his retreating back. "Where are you going?"

"To face my bully," he called over his shoulder.

His words produced a roar of laughter from the others.

"I have a powerful need to see her." He quickened his pace. "Right this minute."

When he was gone, Luke said, "Matt might try, but Gram Gracie is never going to allow him to see the bride before the wedding."

Burke chuckled. "My money's on Matt. When he sets his mind to something, the whole world had better get out of his way."

* * *

Vanessa stood in the middle of the upstairs guest room, with her best friend Lauren trying to affix a veil on the bride-to-be's flowing hair.

Lauren studied Nessa's reflection in the mirror. "Maybe a couple of pins?"

"Why do I have to wear a veil?"

"It's traditional." Lauren draped it this way and that, trying for the best effect.

At a soft tap on the door, Lauren hurried over to admit Gracie, who paused in the doorway, her hand to her mouth.

"Oh, Nessa. You're a vision."

Vanessa looked suddenly shy. "It was my mother's wedding gown. I thought by wearing it, I'd feel her here with me."

"It's perfect." Grace held up a jewelry roll. "I wore this when I married my Frankie. If you don't think it's too much, I'd love for you to have it."

"You mean borrow it."

"I mean have it. In my privileged youth, my parents lavished me with jewelry, but since my life here, I have no use for such things. Since you and Matthew are planning your honeymoon in Italy, you'll enjoy wearing it."

She unrolled the satin to reveal three strands of platinum studded with diamonds woven into a stunningly simple necklace. Both Nessa and her friend gasped at the beauty of it.

Gracie fastened the necklace before stepping back to study the effect. "What do you think?"

Nessa touched a hand to it before turning from the mirror with a smile. "I think it's perfect."

"And so are you." Gracie caught her hand. "You've made Matthew so happy. If I didn't already love you, that would be reason enough. All of us are so thrilled to have you in our family."

The two women embraced just as the door opened. They both looked up as Matt stepped inside.

"Oh, Matthew, you musn't see your bride before the wedding."

Before Gracie could block his view, Vanessa stopped her with a hand to her arm.

"What's wrong, cowboy? Having second thoughts?"

For a moment he was unable to speak. He stood perfectly still, staring at her with a look of blinding love. Then, finding his voice, he gave a shake of his head. "I just needed to see you. Alone."

Lauren gave a soft laugh and turned to Gracie. "Come on. I'm so glad you still have two eligible grandsons left. Not to mention that bachelor son of yours. Can I have my pick?"

"Be my guest. The more women in my family, the happier I'll be."

The two women left on a trill of laughter.

When the door closed, Matt stepped closer. "I was afraid I'd dreamed all this. Afraid when I got here, the room would be empty."

"You're not getting rid of me that easily, cowboy. You promised me forever, and I'm holding you to it."

She stepped into his arms, and he pressed his lips to her temple, breathing her in.

She looked up with an impish grin. "Why does Gram Gracie think we're heading off to Italy?"

"Because ever since Vittorio and Maria arrived, they've

been insisting that we use their villa. Maybe this winter we can slip away for a visit." He feathered her mouth with his. "But tonight we'll head up to the cabin. Away from everyone and everything."

"Our very own simple shack in the woods."

He chuckled. "Not exactly simple. I had Burke haul up a case of Maria's wine, and Yancy threw in enough prime beef and lobster to feed an army of wranglers."

She smiled. "I hope they're both sworn to secrecy."

"They know better than to say a word to anyone. The last thing we want is the whole family barging in on our honeymoon."

Her eyes sparkled with mischief. "That might not be so bad."

"Don't even think it." His arms tightened around her. "After all the time you spent in Chicago getting ready for this, I've built up a powerful hunger for alone time with my best girl. There'll be plenty of time with the family. Just promise me that if you ever feel crowded, you'll let me know and we'll go anywhere you want."

Against his lips she whispered, "The only place I ever want to be is with you." She slipped an arm through his and started toward the door. "Now let's go make some memories, cowboy."

Memories.

As they started down the stairs toward the house overflowing with family and friends, Matt thought about how far they'd come. They'd survived the worst that life could throw at them. Had cheated death. Had begun as strangers and were now lovers, about to speak vows that would seal that love for all time.

He smiled at the memory of his mother and father, so wildly in love. As he caught sight of Frank and Gracie, hand in hand, looking so happy, his smile grew.

They already had enough memories to last a lifetime.

And they'd only just begun.

LUKE

For my second son, Patrick

And as always, for Tom
With love

PROLOGUE

Glacier Ridge, Montana—Thirteen Years Ago

Carter Prevost, owner-manager of the Glacier Ridge fairgrounds, stopped his pacing when rancher Frank Malloy and his foreman, Burke Cowley, walked into his office.

Though Frank was owner of one of the state's largest ranches—several thousand acres and growing—he was still just a neighbor and friend to the folks in Glacier Ridge. A man still struggling to pay the bills required to maintain such an operation.

"Okay, Carter. Now why the frantic phone call, and why couldn't you just tell me what you wanted over the phone?"

"It's about Luke."

The old man let out a slow breath. "It's always about my middle grandson. What did he do this time?"

"Luke signed up to compete in the motorcycle challenge during rodeo weekend."

"He did what?" Frank removed his wide-brimmed hat and slapped it against his leg, sending up a cloud of dust. "He's only fifteen, Carter."

"Don't you think I know that?" The thickset man ran a hand through the rusty hair that was now more gray than red. "But he paid the entrance fee and signed all the forms. Since there's no age limit, I didn't want to be the one to face Luke's temper, so I figured I'd call you and let you deal with it."

"Oh, I'll deal with it, all right." Frank swore and turned away. "No grandson of mine is going to risk his life jumping his Harley over a line of trucks."

"Everybody knows Luke's capable of a trick like that. If jumping vehicles was all there was to it, I wouldn't be so worried."

At Carter's words, Frank turned back. "What's that supposed to mean?"

"Jumping a line of trucks is just the preliminary. This year we're building a ramp higher than anything ever tried before. At the end of that ramp, the biker will see nothing but air. We've issued a challenge to all the professional bikers who want to enter the final. They'll have to land in one piece—and to prove they're still able to function, they'll be expected to circle the stadium. If more than one succeeds, the finalists will have to do it again, until only one is left standing. The first prize is ten thousand dollars."

"If it was a million dollars, it wouldn't be enough." Frank Malloy turned to the door and stalked toward his truck.

Burke Cowley followed more slowly.

As they started toward the ranch, Burke held his silence while Frank gave vent to every rich, ripe curse he knew.

"Damned hotheaded kid will be the death of me."

Burke cleared his throat. "I know Luke's a handful."

"A handful?" Frank was fuming. "There's a devil inside that boy. I think he sits up nights dreaming of ways to challenge his grandmother and me. I swear, he's the most ornery, fearless boy I've ever known."

"He is that." Burke smiled. "But he has a way of getting under the skin. Despite all the trouble he causes, you know we can't help but love him. He has the greatest heart in the world. And as Miss Gracie likes to say, he has an old soul. Like his daddy, God rest him, Luke's a sucker for a sad story."

The mention of Frank's son, Patrick, who had been killed five years ago along with his wife, Bernadette, on a snowy stretch of Montana road, had Frank Malloy sucking in a painful breath. Their death had left a void that would never be filled. Not for the Malloy family, and especially not for Pat and Bernie's three sons, Matt, Luke, and Reed, who were left to figure out a world rocked by the sudden, shocking loss of their parents.

Burke stared straight ahead, his tone thoughtful. "Luke's the kind who will always stand and fight beside anybody who's down and out. That boy would give you the shirt off his back."

"I know what I'm about to give him." Frank's eyes narrowed with flinty determination. "God knows, I don't like coming down too hard on the boy, after all he and his brothers have suffered. But this time he's gone too far. If I have to, I'll lock him in his room until rodeo days are over."

"Pretty hard to keep a fifteen-year-old locked away."

Frank's head swiveled. "Are you on his side?"

Burke shrugged. "The boy's wild and reckless. But he's not stupid. If you forbid it, he'll find a way around you. But if he knows he has your blessing, he might look at this challenge with a clear eye. He might even be willing to back down if he sees that it's too dangerous."

"And if he breaks his fool neck?"

Burke squinted into the sunlight. "It's his neck. Like you said, there's a devil inside him. Maybe in time he'll learn to tame it. Or maybe, whenever he feels it taking over, he'll just ride that devil into the eye of the storm and see where it takes him. Either way, he's the sort who's willing to play the hand dealt him."

After a few more miles, Frank muttered, "I guess we'll see."

"You're going to give him your blessing?"

Frank shrugged. "Like you said, it's going to be impossible to keep him locked away during rodeo week."

A week later, when Luke proudly handed his grandfather a check for ten thousand dollars, the old man's eyes narrowed. "What's this about, sonny boy? It's your money. You're the one who risked your neck for it."

Luke shrugged. "I heard you telling Gram Gracie the bills were piling up, and you were going to have to hold off on buying that bull you've been itching to import from Calgary."

"Are you telling me you risked your neck for a damned bull?"

"It's my neck, Grandpop. And honestly, it wasn't much of a risk."

"You weren't scared?"

The boy grinned. "Yeah. But it was really cool. I felt like I was flying."

"Here." Frank held out the check. "You earned this, boy. I won't take it."

"You know you need that bull." Smiling, Luke ambled away, leaving Frank staring after him.

It was then that he recalled Burke's words.

Despite all the worries and sleepless nights spent on his middle grandson, there was no denying that Luke Malloy had the biggest heart in the world. That breathtaking daredevil...that defiant rebel...had the heart of a champion. And the soul of a hero.

CHAPTER ONE

Glacier Ridge, Montana—Current Day

Luke Malloy sat easily in the saddle as his roan gelding, Turnip, moved leisurely up a hill. Luke had spent the last three weeks in the hills that surrounded his family ranch, tending the herds, sleeping under the stars. It was something he never tired of. Though some of the wranglers complained about the solitary lifestyle, it was the very thing that fed Luke's soul. He planned to build a home up here someday, far enough from his family to listen to the whistle of the wind in the trees, yet near enough to visit when he craved their company.

The time spent alone was a soothing balm to his soul, though he had to admit that after weeks of solitude, he wouldn't mind a night in town. A night of good whiskey, loud country music, and lusty women in the smoky atmosphere of Clay Olmstead's Pig Sty. That wasn't the name on the sign above the saloon. But Clay had been a pig farmer before opening his saloon in Glacier Ridge, and everyone there referred to it as Clay's Pig Sty. Just the thought of it had Luke grinning.

Luke's body was lean and muscled from hard, physical ranch work. He was heavily bearded, his long hair tied in a ponytail beneath his wide-brimmed hat. He was hot and sweaty, and now he was thinking about a swim in the welcoming waters of Glacier Creek.

As he and his mount crested a ridge, all thought disappeared at the sight of a herd of mustangs feasting on the rich vegetation of a meadow spread out below him, between two steep mountain peaks. Their leader, the elusive white mustang his grandmother had been trailing in vain for the past two years, stood a little apart from the herd, keeping an eye out for intruders. With five of the mares nursing foals, the herd was especially vulnerable to predators.

Urging his mount forward, Luke kept to the cover of the trees, hoping to get close enough for a clear photograph. With Gram Gracie's birthday approaching, he couldn't think of anything that would please her more than a framed picture of the mustang stallion she'd named Blizzard, since she'd first spotted the animal years ago during one of Montana's worst winters.

Luke lifted the expensive camera he carried with him. It was a gift from his grandmother, who was widely acclaimed for her photographs of the herds of mustangs that roamed their ranchland. He focused the viewfinder and started clicking off shots, all the while urging his mount into a run. The mustang stallion's head came up sharply, scenting danger. But instead of facing Luke, the mustang turned and reared, just as a shot rang out, missing the animal by mere inches. At the sound of the gunshot, the entire herd scattered.

Luke's mount, caught in the midst of it, reacted instinctively, rearing up before bucking furiously, tossing its rider from the saddle.

In a single instant Luke felt himself flying through the air. His last conscious thought before he landed on his head and saw the most amazing display of fireworks going off in his brain was that once again Blizzard had managed to slip away without a trace. Damned if he hadn't just missed his best chance ever for Gram Gracie's precious birthday gift.

Ingrid Larsen came up over a rise and heard the gunshot, followed by the herd of mustangs dissolving like ghosts into the surrounding forest. One minute they were grazing; the next there was only flattened bear grass left to suggest they'd been there at all.

As she looked around, she was surprised to see one horse remaining. As she drew near, she could see the reins dangling. Not a mustang. A saddle horse. But where was its rider?

When she got close enough to see the wide eyes and hear the labored breathing, she dismounted and approached the animal cautiously.

"Here, now. Steady." She took hold of the reins and spoke soothingly as she ran a hand over its muzzle.

Within minutes the big red gelding began to settle down.

"I know you didn't come all this way alone. So let's find out where your owner is."

Leading the horse, she peered over the edge of a steep cliff and caught her breath when she saw the still form of a cowboy on a narrow shelf of rock below.

"Hello." She cupped her hands to her mouth. "Are you okay?"

There was no response. The body didn't move.

With a sigh of resignation, she whistled her own horse over and removed the lariat. Tying it securely to the saddle horn, she stepped over the ravine and began inching her way to the rocks below.

Once there, she touched a hand to the man's throat. Finding a pulse, she breathed a sigh of relief. Not dead.

She lifted a canteen from her pocket and held it to the man's lips. He moaned and choked before instinctively swallowing. After a few sips, he pushed her hand away and opened his eyes.

"Think you can sit up?" With her hands around him, she eased him to a sitting position.

He swayed slightly, before fixing her with a look of fury. "What the hell...shooting at...herd? You damn near killed me."

"Save your energy, cowboy." She didn't bother saying more. Seeing the blood oozing from his head, she realized he was much more injured than he realized. From the spasms shuddering through him, he was going into shock. "I'm going to try to get you out of here. I'll need your help."

She looped the lariat under his arms, around his chest, and gave a hard, quick tug on the rope.

The rope went taut, signaling that her horse had taken a step back from the edge, jerking the barely conscious man to his feet. Satisfied, Ingrid wrapped her arms around his limp body and gave a whistle.

Both figures were lifted from the narrow rock shelf and eased, inch by painful inch, up the ravine until they were on solid ground. At once Ingrid scrambled to remove the rope. That done, she wrapped her blanket around the still form of the man and began cutting and lashing tree branches together, covering them with the blanket she found tied behind his saddle. Within the hour she'd managed to roll the heavily muscled body onto the makeshift travois, which she'd secured behind her horse. From the amount of blood he'd lost and the swelling on the back of his head, there was a good chance this cowboy was suffering a very serious head injury. And then there were the bones he might have broken in that fall.

Catching up his mount's reins, she pulled herself onto her horse's back and began the slow journey toward the ranch in the distance.

Black clouds scudded across the sky. Thunder rumbled, and lightning sparked jagged flashes overhead. The wind picked up, sending trees dipping and swaying. Minutes later the sky opened up, and a summer storm began lashing the hills. By the time Ingrid's mount crested the last peak and caught the scent of home, they were drenched.

It took all of her strength to hold her horse to a walk, when the animal's instinct to run to food and shelter was so strong.

When they reached the barn, an old man was standing in the doorway, watching her. "What you got there, girl?"

"Not what, Mick. Who." She slid gratefully from her mount and looked down at the still figure. "Some cowboy shot at a herd of mustangs and got himself tossed from his horse. Landed halfway down the mountain on a pile of rock. He's out cold."

"Injuries?"

She nodded. "Pretty bad head wound. Lost a lot of blood. Wasn't making any sense."

"Going to call for a medevac?"

"In this storm?" She bent down and felt the pulse. "I guess, at least for tonight, we'll just get him inside, keep him quiet, and hope for the best."

The old man unsaddled the stranger's horse and settled it into a stall with fresh feed and water. Then he moved along beside her as she led her horse to the back door. The two of them struggled under the man's weight as they removed him from the makeshift travois and half dragged, half carried him up the back steps and into the house.

"This cowboy's all muscle." Mick pulled a handkerchief from his back pocket and wiped his face, damp from the workout. "We'll never get him upstairs to a bed."

"You're right." Breathing heavily, Ingrid shed her parka before once more taking hold of her burden. "Let's get him to the parlor."

They dragged him past the kitchen and managed to roll him onto a lumpy sofa in the big room.

Mick glanced around the cold, dark parlor. "I'll get Strawberry back to the barn and bring in an armload of logs. You'll want to get this guy out of those wet clothes and wrap him in dry blankets."

She shot him a sharp look. "I'm no good at playing nurse. I'll take care of my own horse, thank you. And I can handle the logs. You can get him out of his clothes."

The old cowboy was already halfway across the room. With a chuckle, he called over his shoulder, "Your stranger, your problem."

His laughter grew as her curses followed him out the door.

Left alone, Ingrid gathered whatever supplies she could. Several thick bath towels. A basin of warm water and soap. Then she set to work washing the blood from the back of his head. That done, she folded a dry towel and placed it under his head before moving on to his clothes. Her attempt at unbuttoning his flannel shirt, which was completely soaked, was a huge effort. Next, she turned to his boots, but because they were so wet, she could barely budge them. It took long minutes of pulling and tugging, while muttering curses through gritted teeth, before she got them off. Then, with much tugging, she finally managed to get him out of the last of his clothes.

By the time old Mick returned with an armload of firewood, the stranger was wrapped in a blanket, and his clothes lay in a heap on the floor.

Once the fire was blazing, Mick walked to the sofa to stand beside Ingrid. "I brought his saddlebags inside." He hooked a thumb toward the doorway. "Tossed 'em over a chair in the kitchen. They might give you a clue to just what kind of cowboy you dragged in from the storm."

"Good idea." She huffed out a breath. "I just hope the idiot who was shooting at mustangs isn't also an ax murderer."

"I doubt he'd carry that kind of information in his saddlebags."

She turned away and headed toward the kitchen. "You never know."

"He wasn't your shooter."

She paused. Turned. "And you know that because...?"

"His rifle was still in its boot. If he was trying to take down a mustang, the rifle would have been in his hands." Mick poked and prodded the flames, adding another log to the fire before ambling back to the other room, where Ingrid had spread out the contents of the saddlebags across the kitchen table.

"Find anything interesting?"

She looked up. "Where'd you get this?" She held up the camera.

"It was hooked to the saddle horn."

"German. Expensive. Not what I'd expect from a wandering cowboy."

The old man shrugged. "Maybe he's a professional photographer."

She opened a worn leather wallet and began sorting through the cards stored inside. She picked up one. "Lucas Malloy. Twenty-eight. Height six feet two inches. Weight one hundred eighty-five pounds. Hair black. Eyes blue. Doesn't need glasses." She looked over. "Ring a bell?"

Mick shook his head. "The only Malloy I know is Frank. Owns one of the biggest spreads in Montana. Frank Malloy's my age. Got a famous wife. Some kind of photographer."

"Now this makes sense." She pointed to the camera. "Maybe he's their son?"

"What makes sense is he's probably a grandson. Unless she made medical history."

They grinned at each other.

"Okay. He's a long way from home. With a head injury, you never know what might happen. If I could find his cell phone, I'd notify his family."

"It could be back there on the mountain."

She nodded. "And trampled by a herd of mustangs."

"I'm sure you can find a number for the Malloy

Ranch." Mick filled two mugs with steaming coffee. Handing one to her, he said, "Lily and Nadine have been asleep for hours. You going up to your room, or are you planning on keeping an eye on your guest?"

"He's not my guest, Mick." She picked up her mug and headed toward the parlor. "But since I was the one who brought him here, I guess it's my job to see him through the night."

"You got that right, girl." With a grin the old man shuffled off to his room next to the kitchen. "If you need me—"

"Yeah." She didn't wait for him to finish.

It took her several minutes to move an overstuffed chair beside the sofa. She draped an afghan over her lap and cradled the mug in both hands as she watched the steady rise and fall of the stranger's chest.

Her head nodded, and she felt the hot sting of coffee on her skin before setting aside the mug and snuggling deeper into the warmth of the cover.

After the day she'd put in, she was asleep before she could form a single thought.

CHAPTER TWO

N ow that's what I call a hunk of burning love." The female voice was rough, fog shrouded, like someone who had consumed an entire pack of cigarettes in an hour while downing half a dozen whiskeys.

"Why am I not surprised?" A softer voice. One Luke had heard before, though he couldn't recall where or when. "He's more dead than alive, but all you can see is your next conquest."

"I'm seeing a killer body and the face of a devil. Honey, he can park his boots under my bed anytime. But for now, I'll wait 'til he has more fire in his chimney. I'm off to Wayside. Don't wait up."

"I never do."

As the door closed, a strobe light shot bursts of color across Luke's closed eyelids. A strange bell rang nearby. And his head ached with the worst hangover ever.

Had he been in Clay's Pig Sty in Glacier Ridge? He

couldn't recall. But since it was on his mind, he must have made it there. But where was he now?

He'd been in enough saloon brawls to know how the next day felt. He touched his face. No tender eye, no swollen cheek.

There was something sharp poking him in his back. He reached a hand around and located a metal coil of some sort, covered in cloth. He opened his eyes, as gritty as sandpaper, and saw the odd-colored lights flickering across the ceiling of a room, coming from a fire on the grate. And there was a terrible ringing in his ears. When he moved his head, he became aware of the pain throbbing in his temples.

He sucked in a breath and tried to remember what had happened. The herd of mustangs, the shot...

He'd been shot?

He felt around his body for fresh dressings. None. He touched a hand to the back of his head and felt the swollen mass. Not a bullet, he realized. He must have taken quite a fall. He could almost recall flying through the air and landing hard. Rocks. Yes, a solid rock ledge. Had he actually fallen off the edge of the cliff? But he wasn't there now. He was in a room, naked under a soft blanket.

How did he get here?

The shooter?

He struggled to sit up and felt the room spin at the same instant that a shaft of pain sliced through his head. Strong hands pressed him back against a springy cushion. The woman with the rusty voice? Or the one with the soft voice?

He tried to fight back but lost the battle. In his mind he was uttering a string of fierce oaths as the intense pain dragged him under.

* * *

"Good. You're awake. Try to drink this." It was the soft voice.

He struggled to focus. At first there were several blurred images swimming into his line of vision. Gradually they merged into a single woman perched beside him. She put a hand beneath the back of his head and gently lifted it high enough that he could drink from the cup she held in her other hand.

He liked her touch. Gentle. And he knew he wasn't dying when his body reacted instinctively.

At his first sip the mood was shattered. He gagged and pushed her hand aside. "You trying to poison me?"

She chuckled. A low, warm sound like the purr of a kitten. He would have taken the time to enjoy the sound, if it weren't for the fire sliding down his throat.

"Some crazy witch's brew Mick concocted. He swears it'll kill pain anywhere in the body."

"If it doesn't kill me first."

"You're angry. Good." She stood. "Sounds to me like you're feeling better than you did yesterday."

"Yester...?" His voice trailed off as he struggled with the implication of that. Had he been here overnight? "When...? How...?"

She held up a hand. "According to Mick, you'll be out in a matter of minutes. But you should wake next time in a lot less pain. When you're feeling up to it, we'll talk. For now"—she turned away—"sleep tight."

Luke tried to summon the energy to be angry at her patronizing tone. But in truth, he was already fading.

The world went soft and gray as he drifted off.

* * *

The room was in shadow. The only light came from the fireplace, where a log burned, giving off the comforting fragrance of wood smoke.

Luke had heard voices on and off during the day between his bouts of waking and sleeping. An old man's growl. A child's whisper. The two females, one soft, one rough as sandpaper, engaged in a slap-down of sorts, though he couldn't figure out what it was about. He only recognized the anger in their tones.

He was thirsty, but the thought of that vile drink he'd been given hours ago put him off. He could probably eat something, though at the moment nothing appealed to him. He felt vaguely restless, and he knew it was time to saddle up and head for home. But since he didn't know where he was or how badly he'd been injured in that fall, he figured he would just lie here a while longer.

"Mick said you'd be waking up soon."

The woman was little more than a shadow in the doorway, but he knew the soft voice now. As his memory cleared, he knew, too, that she was the one who'd offered him something to drink after his fall. The one who'd managed to get him to safety. The one who'd brought him here.

The shooter.

She switched on a light and he muttered an oath before lifting his hand to shade his eyes.

"Sorry. But I need to check your head wound." She eased down beside him on the sofa and gently lifted his head. "I'm Ingrid Larsen."

"Luke Malloy."

"Yes. I checked your saddlebags for ID and notified your family that you're recovering from a fall at my place." She seemed distracted as she poked and prodded. "Good. As Mick said, the bleeding stopped on its own, and the swelling's gone down by half. I guess we won't need a medevac after all."

"Is Mick a doctor?"

"Of sorts. He doctors the herd and for years kept all our wranglers in good condition."

She pulled a chair beside the sofa and sat facing him.

It was his first real look at her, and he couldn't look away.

Despite the faded denims and a plaid baggy shirt with the sleeves rolled to her elbows, she was stunning. Pale corn silk hair cropped close to her head. Eyes the color of a summer sky. A dimple in each cheek whenever she smiled, which he suspected she did rarely. There was something stiff and unyielding in her demeanor, as though his very presence here annoyed her.

Maybe it did. But this was all her fault. She was the one to shoot at the mustangs, sending them into a frenzied stampede.

She was studying him as closely as he was studying her.

"So. Why did you shoot at the mustangs?"

Her question caught him completely by surprise. "Me? *You're* the one who shot at them."

She shook her head, sending a lock of pale blond hair dipping over one eye. She brushed it back absently with her hand. "I heard the shot and came running. When the herd vanished, I saw your horse, reins dangling, and realized its rider was nearby. You're lucky I took the time to search or you'd still be out there. I doubt you'd have survived in that storm."

He remembered the rain falling on his face as he'd been transported across the meadow and, later, the sound of a furious storm howling in the night. The storm was still ongoing, though now there was just the steady tattoo of rain on the roof and the occasional flash of lightning, followed by a rumble of thunder that shook the house.

"If you didn't shoot, who did?"

She shrugged. "All this time, I thought it had been you, even though Mick disagreed. Now I haven't a clue."

He studied her slender frame, which she tried to camouflage beneath the baggy clothes. "How did you manage to get me here? Did you have help?"

"I made a travois out of tree limbs and tied it to my horse."

He thought about the effort it must have cost her to rescue him, bring him down from the mountain, and then get him to this place. "Sorry I caused you so much time and muscle."

She smiled, showing those dimples. "See that you don't try that again."

"This Mick. Is he your husband?"

"No."

"Is this Mick's ranch?"

She arched a brow. "It was my father's. I hope soon it will be mine."

"Oh. I thought…"

Her smile faded. "Yeah. I get it. What woman in her right mind would want to take on all the work of running a ranch without a man by her side?"

"I didn't mean that. It's just…you mentioned Mick a lot." Luke shrugged.

"When my dad was alive, Mick was in charge of the wranglers. I'm grateful he stayed on, even though he's doing triple duty for half the pay. He tends the herds, keeps all the buildings and equipment in repair, feeds me, and keeps me from ripping Nadine's head off."

"Nadine?"

"My mother. She's in town tonight. If you're lucky, maybe she'll stay there until you're well enough to leave. If not, you'd better be prepared…" She didn't finish her sentence as a girl of about six or seven rushed into the room.

"Mick says supper's ready. Oh." The girl skidded to a halt when she realized Luke was awake.

"This is my sister, Lily."

"Hi, Lily. I'm Luke." Luke managed a smile at the girl, who looked nothing like her older sister. Her hair, a wild tangle of thick, dark curls, fell nearly to her waist. Her eyes were the color of chocolate. She wore faded, patched denims and a shirt that was missing a sleeve.

"Hi, Luke. Are you going to eat with us?"

Ingrid got to her feet. "I think tonight I'll bring a plate for Luke in here. Maybe by tomorrow he'll feel strong enough to join us in the kitchen."

When her older sister walked away, the little girl remained, staring intently. "Are you a bad man?"

"Do I look like a bad man?"

She shrugged. "You look funny with all that hair."

He touched a hand to his heavily bearded face. "I guess I look more like a big old hairy bear."

"You do. Or a bad man. But if you say you're not…" She smiled, displaying the same dimples as her sister. "Do you like roast beef and potatoes?"

At the little girl's question, he winked at her. "It's my favorite."

"I'll tell Mick." As she started to scramble away, she paused and turned. "I believe you. I don't think you're a bad man."

"Any reason in particular?"

She shrugged. "I don't know. Maybe it's your smile."

"Thanks. I like yours, too."

He lay listening to the sounds of voices in the kitchen and found himself reliving the scene on the mountain, when the herd of mustangs had scattered at the sound of a gunshot. He was pretty sure he'd suffered a concussion. It was the only explanation for this feeling of malaise. It wasn't like him to willingly lie around doing nothing.

"Here's your supper." Ingrid shoved a scarred old coffee table close to the sofa and placed a plate on it before turning away.

"Thanks. And, Ingrid…"

She turned back.

"Thanks for saving my hide and for contacting my family."

She shot him a look of surprise mingled with pleasure. "You're welcome. That's not what you said when Mick and I dragged you in here."

"What did I say?"

"You condemned us both to…" Her smile was quick and brilliant. "I'd better not repeat it while Lily is apt to overhear. I believe there were a few amazingly inventive curses even I hadn't heard before."

"Yeah. That's me. Creative." Luke tried to remember. Bits and pieces of being half dragged, half carried across the room, leaving him feeling more dead than alive, played through his mind. His entire body had been on fire by the time they got him to this sofa. He could only imagine how many curses he'd lashed out with. Probably as many as he'd been able to think of before passing out cold.

Ingrid returned a little later with a cup of steaming coffee. She glanced at the plate and then at Luke. His eyes were half closed, the remains of most of his dinner still untouched.

Her sister, Lily, trailed behind her. "You didn't like Mick's roast beef?"

Luke struggled to rouse himself. "It was good. So were the mashed potatoes. But I didn't have the energy to finish."

Lily glanced at Ingrid. "That's how I felt when I fell off the hay wagon and hit my head. Remember?"

Her older sister's smile disappeared. "Yeah. You scared me half to death." She turned to Luke. "Mick wants to know if you want any more of his medicine."

"You mean his poison? Thanks, but I'll take my chances without it."

She bit the corner of her lip to keep from grinning. "I'll tell him not to bother mixing up another batch."

"Does he draw a skull and crossbones on it when he's through?"

Lily stepped closer. "What's a skull and crossbones?"

"A warning sign for dangerous, poisonous substances."

"Oh. Like paint thinner and stuff?"

"Yeah. In fact, my first taste of Mick's medicine reminded me of paint thinner."

She glanced at Ingrid. "He's making a joke, isn't he?"

"I'm glad you recognized that. Proof positive that he's

feeling much better." She shot a meaningful look at Luke. "Isn't that right?"

"Yeah. Feeling like a million dollars."

Ingrid stepped closer and picked up the plate. "Do you need anything?"

Enough energy to get off this lumpy sofa and head home.

Aloud he merely said, "No. I'm good. Thanks."

"All right. Good night, then."

"'Night."

Lily hung back, staring at him as though he had two heads.

He tried for a smile, though his energy was definitely at low ebb. "What's wrong, Lily?"

"Does your beard tickle?"

"Yeah."

"Why did you grow a beard?"

"I've been tending a herd in the hills for the past couple of weeks."

"I heard Nadine telling Ingrid that even with all that hair she could tell you were"—she struggled to think of the word—"hunkly...huntly. Hunky. What's *hunky*? Did she mean like the Incredible Hulk?"

He had to choke back the laughter that bubbled up. "Yeah. Something like that."

"Do you think Ingrid's pretty?"

Her question caught him off guard. "Yeah."

"Prettier than Nadine?"

"I don't know what Nadine looks like, but Ingrid's not as pretty as her little sister."

Lily giggled behind her hand. "I'm not pretty. I don't look at all like Ingrid. And she's pretty. I'm just..." She tried to think of a word. "Mick says I'm a tomboy. I guess he's right. I'd rather be with the horses or cows any time than with people."

"I bet Mick means that as a compliment. I happen to like tomboys."

As she started to leave, he asked, "Why do you call your mother Nadine?"

Her eyes rounded in thought. "'Cause that's her name."

"You don't call her Mom?"

She shrugged. "She said not to. She likes Nadine better. It makes her feel young." She danced out the doorway, closing the door behind her.

Whatever other questions Luke had dissolved in a fog of sleep.

CHAPTER THREE

Sunlight streamed through a crack in the curtains, shining a light in Luke's eyes. He awoke and lay still, listening to the morning sounds. A pair of doves cooed outside the window. Cattle lowed on a distant hill. Somewhere upstairs a door slammed.

The smell of bacon frying and bread toasting reminded him that he hadn't eaten anything substantial in days. His stomach was grumbling.

An old man ambled across the room and paused beside the sofa. "'Morning. I'm Mick Hinkley."

"Luke Malloy."

"You're looking more alive than dead today. Think you're up to taking a shower?"

Luke grinned. "That must mean I'm not smelling too good. You going to help me take that shower?"

The old man chuckled. "Not if I can help it. But Ingrid

asked me to follow you up the stairs to the bathroom, to see you don't keel over."

"You realize I'm naked?"

Mick's grin widened. "Nothing I haven't seen in my lifetime. But here." He handed Luke a bath towel. "This ought to cover your backside."

He offered a hand and Luke accepted, easing to his feet and waiting for a moment until the room stopped spinning. He used the time to fasten the bath towel around his hips.

With Mick leading the way, Luke followed him up the stairs and along a hallway to a bathroom. Inside, the old man pointed to an assortment of disposable pink razors and tubes of shaving cream.

"Yours?"

Mick shot him a foolish grin. "That's why I don't share this place with three females. I think they buy this stuff by the case. I've got my own bathroom downstairs."

He indicated Luke's clothes, freshly laundered and folded atop a basket of towels. He studied Luke, holding on to the edge of the sink. "You going to be okay by yourself?"

"I'll be fine."

The old cowboy turned away. "When you're done, come on down to breakfast."

"Thanks, Mick."

When he was alone, Luke began the tedious process of shaving a wild tangle of beard with several of the throwaway plastic razors he found in a beribboned basket of supplies. Using copious amounts of shaving cream and plenty of hot water, he managed to finish, cutting himself only four times.

When he stepped under the warm spray, he sighed with contentment as he shampooed his hair and soaped his body with some kind of girly body wash that smelled like a summer garden. And finally, when he was too weak to stand, he sat in the old-fashioned tub and allowed the water to run until it was nearly overflowing. With eyes closed, his head dropped back and he thought about just staying here all morning. The only thing that had him finally stepping out and toweling dry was the wonderful smell of food drifting up the stairs.

He dressed and tied his hair back, relieved to find a black ponytail elastic among the clutter of pink ones that littered the counter.

Gathering up his wet towels, he headed down the stairs, following the scent to the kitchen.

The chorus of voices stopped abruptly as he stepped into the room, but not before he caught the note of tension in the room.

He flashed Ingrid a smile and winked at Lily. "Thanks for the use of the bathroom." He held out the armload of towels. "I figured I'd save you a trip upstairs."

"Thanks."

As he handed over the towels, his fingers accidentally brushed the swell of her breast. Her head came up sharply as she took them from his hands, while her cheeks turned the most becoming shade of red. He couldn't stop the grin that spread across his face as she walked into a small alcove off the kitchen. When she returned, she avoided his eyes, while he studied her with a look of pure male appreciation.

Mick handed him a steaming mug of coffee. "You're looking better."

"Thanks." Luke took a sip. "I'm feeling like a new man."

"What a coincidence. So am I." The smoky voice behind him had him turning toward the doorway. A curvy woman with big hair dyed fire-engine red and enough makeup to start her own cosmetics company was looking him up and down. "I'm Nadine Larsen."

He extended his hand. "Luke—"

"Oh, I know. We met earlier, though you were out cold." She glanced at the others. "I see you've met my girls. I know it's hard to believe I'm old enough to have a twenty-three-year-old daughter, but like I tell everybody, I was a child bride."

She took his hand between both of hers, smiling up into his eyes. "While you were mending, you looked mighty tempting with all that facial hair, but now, with that naked face, I've got to say you're looking downright delicious."

The silence in the room was deafening.

"Hungry, Luke?" Mick held up a frying pan, where bacon sizzled.

"Yeah." Grateful to the old man, Luke extracted his hand and beat a hasty retreat to the table.

"Me too." Nadine settled herself beside him, nudging his knee with hers under the table. "A good-looking cowboy always makes me ravenous."

Mick circled the table, ladling scrambled eggs and crisp bacon onto each plate before returning to the stove.

While Ingrid and Lily ate in silence, Nadine kept up a running conversation.

"You know how to handle a rifle, Luke?"

"I grew up using one. Why?"

Nadine looked around at the others. "I always say you can't have too many men who know a thing or two about rifles willing to watch your back. Especially since we've become the Wild West way out here in the middle of nowhere."

Ingrid bristled. "This is none of Luke's business."

"What isn't?" Puzzled at the tone of the conversation, he looked from one to the other.

"Nothing." Ingrid clamped her jaw and shot her mother a warning look.

"Suit yourself. I think it's all in your twisted little minds anyway." Unfazed, Nadine went on as though she hadn't been interrupted. "You'll never believe who was in town yesterday."

When neither of her daughters responded, she continued on: "Alberta Crow. And believe me, she's looking more and more like an old crow. I can't believe she let her hair go gray. She was wearing one of her husband's cast-off shirts and the baggiest pair of jeans I ever saw."

"I heard they're losing their ranch," Mick muttered. "A crying shame. Three generations of blood, sweat, and tears going up for auction."

"That's no reason to look like something the cat dragged in." Nadine stared pointedly at her older daughter. "You know. The way you look when you're mucking stalls. Oh, I forgot." The sarcasm in her tone was thick enough to cut. "That's how you look all the time. You even wear the same tired clothes when you go to town."

"You spend enough on fancy duds for both of us." Ingrid pushed away from the table and set her empty dishes in the sink.

Nadine's eyes narrowed. "Where are you going?"

"To muck stalls. In my baggy work clothes. Unless you'd like to take a turn at ranch chores. Now, that would make headlines."

The two women stared at each other before Nadine picked up her mug and drank.

"Wait, Ingrid." Lily drained her glass of milk and carried her dishes, depositing them in the sink with a clatter. "I'll go with you."

The two sisters walked out, letting the back door slam behind them.

Mick stood up and began clearing the pots and pans from the stove before setting them in a sink filled with hot, soapy water.

Nadine turned to Luke with a satisfied smile. "Looks like it's just you and me now, cowboy." She strained toward him, showing plenty of cleavage in her low-necked tee as she put a hand over his. "Why don't you tell me all about yourself?"

"Some other time." He crossed the room and handed Mick his dishes. "Thanks for a great breakfast. I'm going to give the ladies a hand in the barn."

The old man's eyes went wide. "Think you're strong enough?"

He wasn't sure he could even walk to the barn, but he was willing to do whatever it took to get away from the shark at the table.

"I guess I'll find out." With a smile he ambled out of the room, pausing at the back door to retrieve his boots. He noted with surprise that they'd been polished. He removed his battered hat from a hook by the door before stepping outside.

As he made his way to the barn, he thought about the latest twist. So this was Mama Larsen. There was nothing subtle about her. She'd gone to a lot of trouble to try to look like a hot chick. The candy-apple-red hair, the heavy-handed makeup, and the skinny jeans and too-tight T-shirt were over the top. But nothing could hide the desperation in those eyes. She looked determined to hold on to her last vestiges of youth.

He thought of his grandmother, Gracie, at least twenty years older than Nadine but infinitely more beautiful. She had not only a physical beauty but also an inner light and peace that radiated from her, casting everyone around her in a golden glow.

Luke stepped into the barn and paused, allowing his eyes to adjust. In a far stall Ingrid forked straw and manure into a wagon. Lily worked beside her, spreading fresh straw.

Ingrid worked like the very devil himself was after her. It occurred to Luke that he always did the same, whenever he was working off a temper.

Though she'd remained mostly silent in the kitchen, Luke figured Ingrid had found a better way of expressing herself. He'd bet good money that she was not only angry but also embarrassed by her mother's behavior, and this was her way of getting past it.

He watched her for several silent minutes. Even the loose, faded work clothes couldn't hide a killer body like hers. And the unexpectedly short, tousled haircut that looked as though she'd taken scissors to it in a fit of anger only added to her cool, Nordic beauty.

She looked up in surprise when he helped himself to a pitchfork and walked to the adjoining stall.

Apparently she wasn't expecting a man to pass up the chance to be charmed by her mother.

Her tone expressed both surprise and anger. "What are you doing?"

"The same as you."

"You're not strong enough..."

He shrugged. "I'll quit when my body tells me to."

"Fine. It's your body." She bent to her work. "But don't ask me to pick you up if you fall on your face. Once was enough."

"I'll keep that in mind." He was chuckling as he turned away.

Lily climbed up to perch on the upper railing of a stall as Luke stepped into his horse's stall and was greeted by a friendly head-butt.

"Hello, Turnip." He ran a hand over the horse's fore-lock and was rewarded by a soft nickering. "How're you doing, old boy?"

"Why do you call your horse Turnip?"

"Because when he was just a foal, he wandered into Yancy's garden and started eating the turnip tops."

"Who's Yancy?"

"Yancy Martin is our ranch cook and all-around house-keeper."

"You have a cook and housekeeper?" The little girl turned to her sister with a look of amazement.

"The best cook in Montana. And when Yancy saw that animal chewing up his tender garden greens, he was ready to have him ground up into horsemeat. And ever since then, poor Turnip has had to endure that silly name."

"It is silly."

"But he likes it. Don't you, boy? Speaking of names..."

He studied her, perched on the top rail, looking like a tiny doll. "I think instead of Lily, I'm going to call you Li'l Bit."

The look on Lily's face was priceless. She couldn't hide her pleasure at having her very own nickname.

Luke began forking dung and straw into the wagon.

"Do you do this at home?"

"You bet."

"Do you own your own ranch?"

"I live on my family's ranch. My father and grandfather before him lived there, too."

"But if you can afford a cook and housekeeper, why not hire people to do your ranch chores?"

"I like doing my own, like my daddy."

"Is your daddy as big as you?"

He paused for a moment before saying, "My dad is dead. My mom, too. They died when I was little."

"My daddy's dead, too. But I've still got Nadine and Ingrid. Who do you live with now?"

"My two brothers. My uncle. My grandparents. And old Burke, who's tough as nails."

"He's...mean?"

Luke shook his head. "Never. Burke doesn't have a mean bone in his body. But he's tough. When he says he wants something done, it had better be done to his liking. And he's fair. He's as much a pa to me as my own. You'd like him. He's like Mick."

"Ingrid says Mick is like our grandfather. Except he isn't." She watched him for long, silent minutes before asking, "Do you and your brothers always look out for each other?"

"Yeah." He laughed. "That's what brothers do."

"Do you fight?"

He winked at her. "That's one of the first rules of being a guy. You have to know how to fight. Especially if you have brothers."

Her tone grew wistful. "I wish I had a brother."

"You have a sister."

"I know. But she's not big and strong like a man and sometimes I worry..."

"That's enough, Lily." Ingrid shot her sister a warning look.

Her head swiveled as a shadow fell over the doorway and a rough voice called, "Where is she?"

Ingrid stepped from a stall. "Nadine isn't here."

"I didn't ask if she's here." The man was well over six feet, with a thick midsection and the muscled shoulders of a rancher. His face was red with anger, or possibly sweat. "I asked where she is."

"You know Nadine." The soft voice was tinged with sarcasm. "She doesn't leave us her itinerary."

"Don't be funny with me, girl." The man's breathing was ragged, as though he'd been working up a fierce anger. His hands were fisted at his sides. "I told her I wanted an answer to my offer."

"And as you already know, I told her not to accept your offer until the cattle are sold at the end of summer."

"Yeah. She told me. What right do you—"

As he started toward Ingrid, Luke stepped out of the stall he'd been cleaning, the pitchfork resting casually over his shoulder. "If you have something to say to Ingrid, you'll stop where you are and say it. You take another step toward her and you'll answer to me."

The stranger gave a sneer. "Think you're big enough, cowboy?"

"Try me."

"You'd better bring an army if you decide to go up against me."

"I don't need anyone but myself." Luke kept the pitchfork resting lightly on his shoulder. Though he smiled, there was something about his voice that had the man blinking before reaching for the gun at his hip. As he withdrew it, he grinned. "I don't give your puny weapon much of a chance against mine."

Luke set aside the pitchfork and reached for the rifle in the boot of his saddle, which was hanging over the top rail of the stall. Taking aim, he drawled, "Now that the odds are even, how about it? Are you a gambling man?"

That had the stranger backing up a step. He turned to Ingrid with a scowl. "Tell your mother I'm not in the mood to wait until the cattle come down from the hills. She'd better give me an answer soon, or else."

Luke never raised his voice, but the thread of steel beneath his words was clear. "You've had your say. Now get off the lady's property."

The stranger shot him a killing look before stalking away. Minutes later they heard the sound of a horse's hooves pounding the earth. Lily scrambled down from the railing to stand beside her sister.

Luke studied the two of them. "Who was that?"

"A neighbor. He wants to buy our ranch."

"This neighbor have a name?"

"Bull Hammond." Ingrid spoke his name with contempt.

Luke saw the way Lily's small hand crept into Ingrid's, their fingers tangling.

He set aside the rifle and sank down on a bale of hay.

Ingrid studied him as she stripped off worn leather gloves. "I'll give you this, cowboy. You surprised me. There aren't too many people around here who would stand up to Bull Hammond."

"I'm just glad he couldn't see that I'm almost out on my feet."

Ingrid stepped closer. "Come on. You need to get inside."

She caught his arm, then, seeing the dark look in his eyes, released her hold on him and backed up a step.

"In a minute. Tell me what happened to your wranglers."

"They left after my dad died."

"How long ago was that?"

"Nine months. He died last October."

"So Lily was . . . ?"

"Six."

"And you were . . . ?"

"Twenty-two. I was away at college. Just starting my senior year. I came home to bury my father and never went back."

"That's tough. It had to be hard for all of you. How did he die?"

"Mick said it looked like a heart attack while they were driving the herds down from their summer range."

"You didn't have a medic examine him?"

She shook her head. "He fell from his horse. Mick said he was dead before he hit the ground. We buried him up on the hill."

"I'm sorry." He looked out over the fields, with its fences in need of mending and its outbuildings looking neglected. "Was there no way to keep some of the wranglers?"

"Not when we checked with the bank and found out there was barely enough to pay them their wages. The only one willing to stay was Mick."

"Then why not sell to Hammond?"

Her voice frosted over. "My dad loved this ranch, and he promised it would be mine someday. I'm going to do whatever it takes to hold on to it."

"Isn't that up to Nadine?"

"As Dad's widow, she inherited it, but she wants out. She's always hated the ranch. I've asked her to hold off making a decision until the end of summer, to see if I can get enough from the sale of the cattle to buy her out."

"Aren't the cattle hers, too?"

Ingrid shook her head. "My dad left them to me. Us," she corrected. "Lily and me. But I'm the executor."

"Since you're family, wouldn't Nadine be willing to take a down payment and let you pay it off slowly?"

"You met Nadine. What do you think?"

Luke chose his words carefully, knowing this was deeply personal and none of his business. "I guess, if she holds the title on this place, she gets to call the shots."

"Yeah. And Bull Hammond has offered her cash to walk away." Ingrid glanced at her little sister, who had walked over to feed a carrot to Luke's horse. "Come on." She leaned close. "While Lily's amusing herself, I'll help you get to the house."

He shot her a wicked grin. "Much as I'd like your hands on me, I can get there on my own."

Her eyes flashed fire as she jerked back. "Don't ever confuse me with my mother. You want to play sexy games, call Nadine."

"Sorry." His tone went from teasing to contrite in the

blink of an eye. "I can see that's a sore spot with you." He lifted a palm to her cheek and she flinched and backed away as though burned.

His voice was barely a whisper. "Believe me. I'd never confuse you with Nadine."

At the look in his eyes, she crossed her arms and stared hard at the floor before turning to her sister. "Come on, Lily. It's time for us to saddle up."

Lily hurried over with a nervous look. "Can't Luke come with us?"

"After the work he just did, he wouldn't make it halfway out of the barn on horseback. We'll just check on the herd and get back in a couple of hours."

Over her shoulder she called, "That was my only offer of help. If you don't head up to the house and settle on the sofa, you're apt to pass out in the barn."

"I'll be fine." He watched as she tossed a saddle over her horse and began tightening the cinch.

Beside her, Lily did the same.

As they mounted, Luke called, "You stay close to your sister, Li'l Bit."

That had her smiling nervously.

Minutes later the two were riding across a meadow, heading into high country. After that angry visit from Bull Hammond, Luke wished he could join them, just to calm their nerves, but he knew it would be futile to try.

He turned and made his way slowly to the house, feeling every part of his body protesting the work he'd done.

He knew he was going to pay a dear price for today. But it was the least he could do to repay Ingrid Larsen for saving his hide.

He couldn't help wondering what Bull Hammond

would have done if he hadn't been here. The man looked furious enough to get physical, but it wasn't clear whether his anger was directed at Nadine or Ingrid.

Luke paused and looked out across the hills. He hadn't expected Ingrid's reaction to his touch. He'd bet all his money that Nadine was the reason she chopped all her hair off and hid that lush body beneath layers of bulky clothes. She didn't want to be confused with Nadine. Not that it was even remotely possible. They were as different in looks and temperament as two women could be.

And one of them, working so hard to hold him at arm's length, was doing strange things to his heart.

CHAPTER FOUR

Luke walked into the kitchen to find Mick alone. "I saw a truck hightailing it out of here, spitting gravel."

The old cowboy looked up. "That was Nadine. She likes fast rides and faster cowboys."

"I guessed as much. Ingrid and Lily don't talk about her."

"They live by the rule that if you haven't got anything good to say, don't say anything."

Luke grinned. "As good a rule as any."

"Yeah." Mick ran a wet mop across the floor before rinsing it out in the bucket at his feet.

Luke eased himself weakly onto a wooden chair at the table. "Kitchen duties part of your routine?"

"Not by choice. But I do them better'n the others around here. Ingrid never stops from dawn to dark, and Lily pretty much imitates her."

"What does Nadine do?"

"As little as possible." The old man shook his head. "I've never known her to do a lick of work."

"Even when her husband was alive?"

"Especially then. She liked to call herself a"—he wiggled his fingers to make air quotes—"free spirit."

Luke merely grinned.

The old man moved the mop around. "I think Lars always knew he'd made a bad bargain, so he just looked the other way. And once Ingrid was born, nothing else mattered to him. Father and daughter were like two peas. If he was working in the barn, Ingrid was right there beside him. And when he rode up into the hills, she went along. She rode in his arms until she was old enough to handle a horse on her own. No more'n two or three years old, I'd say." The old man smiled, remembering. "Lars was so proud of that girl. He used to say she was a born rancher. There wasn't anything on this spread she couldn't do better than his wranglers. And that was the truth. She could work circles around all of us."

"What about Nadine?"

"She was happy to leave their daughter to Lars. That freed her to do whatever she pleased."

"I have a grandmother like that. She goes off on camera safaris for weeks at a time, photographing the herds of mustangs up in our hills. She gets amazing amounts of money for her photos. But it isn't the money that drives her. It's the thrill of capturing the beauty of those mustangs." He chuckled. "I swear she works harder than anyone I know when it comes to her photography." He looked over. "So, what pleases Nadine?"

Mick snorted. "You've seen her. Men. Lots of 'em. She craves their attention the way a drunk craves alcohol."

"That's it? That's all she does? Did her husband know?"

"How could he not? Especially when she started staying away for nights at a time. The first time she left Lars for over a month, Ingrid was probably five or six."

" 'The first time'?"

"There were too many times to count. Later, when Ingrid was just a teen, Nadine returned to the ranch with a surprise. She was expecting a baby. Lars took her back and loved that baby, even though Lily wasn't his. And because they'd never divorced in the eyes of the law, Lily is his legal heir as much as Ingrid."

"How did Ingrid feel about sharing her father with another child?"

"You've seen them. Ingrid purely loves that girl. And Lily considers Ingrid her mama as well as her big sister."

Luke fell silent, trying to imagine what this family had gone through.

His grandpop often said that everyone had a story. This one was like a fairy tale gone bad.

Mick mopped at a spot in the corner of the room. "Ever since Lars died, Nadine's gone off the deep end. She leaves the two girls for weeks at a time, until she runs out of money. Then she's back, blackmailing Ingrid into giving her whatever she wants, or she threatens to sell the ranch from under her. A couple of weeks ago she brought a cowboy home with her. Said she was going to marry him. His name was Lonny Wardell."

"Wardell?"

Seeing Luke's head come up, Mick peered at him. "You know him?"

Luke nodded. "He worked as a wrangler on our spread for a while, until we caught him stealing."

"It was the same here. He'd done some work for Lars, and Ingrid knew he was a drunk and a thief. When she saw how he was taking over her pa's things, she ordered him off the property at the end of a rifle. It got ugly. He vowed revenge on the 'bigmouthed female who thinks she can order me around.'"

Luke shook his head. "How did Nadine take that?"

"Just like you'd expect. She screamed and hollered at Ingrid, saying Wardell was the first man who'd seriously offered to marry her since Lars, and now her own daughter had spoiled everything. She accused Ingrid of being jealous because she had a life, and all Ingrid had was hard work stretching out in front of her. Then, after she'd said her piece, she headed out to find Wardell in Wayside, the little spit-and-you're-through-it town where she hangs out. When she finally came back, she refused to talk about Wardell. I don't know if that means he walked out on her for good, or if she's seeing him without letting Ingrid know. Either way, as you can imagine, she's been mad as a spitting cat and making everyone dance to her tune."

The old cowboy set aside the bucket and mop and took a chair across from Luke. "What worries me is right after that incident with Wardell, odd things began happening."

"Such as?"

Mick shrugged. "A fire in the hay field left us with no hay for next winter. The authorities said there was no proof it was anything more than a wildfire started by a lightning strike."

Luke nodded. "It would be tough to prove otherwise."

Mick sighed. "Then Ingrid's dog, Tippy, that she'd had since he was a pup, was found dead up in the hills where he'd been guarding the herd. Just a few nights before that, he'd set up a loud yapping out behind the barn, but I figured he'd spotted coyotes. The next morning he was dead. And since there was no blood, I'm inclined to believe he was poisoned. But again, it's just a feeling. I have no proof." He paused before saying, "And now that gunshot that scattered those mustangs. Though Ingrid didn't see anybody but you, who's to say it wasn't directed at her?"

Luke's eyes narrowed. "You think Wardell would go that far?"

The old man shrugged.

"Does Ingrid have any other enemies besides him?"

After a moment Mick nodded his head. "There's Bull Hammond. He's our neighbor to the north."

"I just met him out in the barn."

The old man's eyes widened. "Is that what set off Nadine? I bet she caught sight of him and figured she'd hightail it out of here before she had to deal with him."

"He had fire in his eyes. He threatened Ingrid."

"That bastard." Mick's lips thinned. "I'm glad you were out there, Luke."

"Ingrid said she asked her mother to wait until the cattle sale, to see if she can make enough to buy the ranch."

"That's so. When Hammond heard that Nadine was strapped for cash, he came here and offered to buy her out. She was about to make the deal when Ingrid reminded her their deal had to wait at least until the cattle were sold."

"So that gives Hammond a reason to want revenge, as well. You think Bull Hammond's capable of doing all the things that have been happening around here?"

"I wouldn't put it past him. There was bad blood between Bull and Lars, though I don't know what it was. Lars never confided in me. But if Bull wants to buy this place for a song, all he has to do is wait. With all that's going wrong, Ingrid may be forced to give up and let her mother sell to him. With that field of hay burned, I don't see how the girl has a chance of making it through the winter if she has to buy hay from the grain-and-feed place in town."

"That makes two men with a grudge against Ingrid. Are there more?"

Old Mick took a long look at the sweat pouring down Luke's face. "Son, if you don't lie down right now, I'll be hauling you across the room again, just like I did when you got here, and you'll be swearing a blue streak."

"Yeah. And I'm running out of creative curses." Luke shoved out of the chair and barely made it to the other room, where he flopped down on the sofa, while his mind worked overtime.

Now he understood why Lily was nervous about riding up to the hills with Ingrid. There were too many unexplained accidents.

Not accidents.

Wardell was a drunk and a thief, and Hammond was a known bully.

Leaving two girls and an old man defenseless in the face of danger no way to repay Ingrid for saving his hide. Not that he wanted to get into Ingrid Larsen's business. But hell, he thought, he was already in her business. And now that he knew, he wasn't certain he could walk away.

He fell asleep cursing this weakness and questioning whether he'd be a help or a hindrance if he joined them in standing up to danger, if these incidents turned out to be the work of someone bent on real harm.

Luke's sleep was disturbed by the sound of a plane flying low enough that it shook the roof and vibrated through the parlor.

He sat up, pressing his hands to his lower back, aching from the springs of the sofa. He'd have been more comfortable if he'd slept on the floor, but the truth was, he'd been so exhausted by his workout in the barn, he could have slept on a bed of nails.

Hearing the rumble of voices on the back porch, he made his way there and stopped short at the sight that greeted him.

His uncle Colin and old Burke were talking to Mick, Nadine, Ingrid, and Lily.

From the way Nadine was invading Colin's space, her hand on his arm, her rough voice laughing at something he'd said, it was obvious that she'd decided to make her move on him.

"Well." Spotting him, Colin eagerly stepped away. Crossing to Luke, he gave him a friendly punch to his shoulder, causing Luke to suck in a breath at the sudden, shocking pain.

"When we got the call that you'd fallen off a cliff, we weren't sure what to expect."

Luke glanced at Ingrid while he rubbed at his shoulder. "You hoping to get rid of me?"

She shrugged. "I figured you'd be ready to get back to your family as soon as possible."

"We're grateful to Miss Larsen. We told her we'd fly up as soon as the weather cleared. So here we are." Colin studied his nephew, noting the red-rimmed eyes and the way he favored his shoulder. "Good thing you were on your horse and not flying across the hills on your Harley. You'd have probably broken your neck."

Ingrid arched a brow. "You ride a motorcycle?"

"When I can."

She frowned. "Why am I not surprised?"

Ignoring her insult, Luke grinned at Burke, who was sporting a black eye. "You look worse than me. Did you fall off a cliff, too?"

The old cowboy chuckled before touching a finger to the tender skin. "I was priming a pump at the range shack up on the north ridge, and the handle hit me in the eye, darned near blinding me."

"See?" Luke turned to Colin. "It's like I always tell Grandpop. There are a lot of things more dangerous than riding a motorcycle. Those pump handles can be deadly. And you ought to see what damage a sneaky shed door can do."

Nadine sidled up beside Luke. "Want to see what I can do behind a shed door?"

Colin shared a look with Luke before turning to Ingrid. "Thanks for taking care of my nephew until we could get here. I'm obliged that we didn't have to listen to his lame jokes for a couple of days." He glanced skyward. "If we're going to get you home in time for Yancy's special supper, we'd better get started."

Without a word, Ingrid crossed her arms over her chest and looked away.

Lily tipped up her head to peer into Luke's eyes. "I guess you need to go back to your brothers and your grandparents."

Luke knelt down and caught her hand. "I see you were paying attention when I told you about them, Li'l Bit."

"Uh-huh." She touched a hand to his cheek. "You're lucky to have all those people."

"Yes, I am." At her touch, he wondered at how light his heart felt. Little girls weren't something he'd had any experience with in his life. Still, those brown eyes were filled with so much sadness, they nearly broke his heart. "But you're lucky, too. You've got your ma and Ingrid and Mick."

She looked away, but not before he saw the knowledge in her eyes. She might be only seven, but in that instant he recognized a depth of wisdom beyond her years.

Luke stood and turned to Colin. "You realize Turnip is out in the barn. I can't leave without him."

Colin held up a hand. "He can keep for a few more days. We debated driving here with a trailer to accommodate Turnip, but we figured your well-being was more important. We decided to use the plane, in case you were so badly injured we needed to get you to a hospital right away. When you're up to it, you can bring a horse trailer over and haul Turnip home."

"That's not going to work. I wish you'd called to tell me you were on your way. I could have saved you a trip."

Burke and Colin were both looking at him with matching expressions of puzzlement.

Colin spoke for both of them. "What's that supposed to mean?"

Luke shrugged, determined to keep things light. "This is the first time I've ever had a chance to use girly soaps and lotions." He winked at Lily. "I don't think I'm ready to give them up yet."

The little girl covered her mouth with her hand and giggled, while Ingrid stared at him with a look of astonishment.

Luke turned to her. "Any objections to having me here a while longer?"

She showed no expression as she gave a curt nod of her head. "No objection from me. It's your life."

"Now I know you fell on your head." Burke looked at him more closely. "What this about, Luke?"

He clamped a hand on his uncle's shoulder and another on Burke's. "Come on. I'll walk with you to the plane."

Colin and Burke said their good-byes to the others before turning toward the plane, parked on a strip of asphalt behind the barn.

Along the way, Luke filled them in on what he'd learned. When he was finished, he added, "I'd like to pay these good people back for saving my hide."

"By putting yourself in the line of fire?" Colin said soberly. "You're talking about taking on a load of trouble."

Luke nodded. "I know. But I'd like to even the odds a bit. Two girls and an old man shouldn't have to stand up to this kind of bullying alone."

Colin hooked a thumb in the direction of the house. "What about the mother?"

Luke shrugged. "As far as I can see, pretty useless."

"But she's got her eye on you, sonny boy."

Luke grinned. "Not going to happen. Besides, from what I could see, she had designs on you, too."

"Honky-tonk angels aren't my type."

As they laughed, Colin glanced back toward the ranch house. "As soon as we're airborne, I'm phoning Sheriff Graystoke."

Luke nodded. "I'm counting on it. Tell him I'd like him to look into this Lonny Wardell. See if anybody's seen him in the town of Wayside. I hear that's where he picked up Nadine. Or where she picked him up," he added. "And see what Eugene can dig up on Bull Hammond. Somebody's going to a lot of trouble to scare this family off their land."

"You always did enjoy a good brawl." Colin gave his nephew a bear hug before climbing into the plane.

Old Burke put a hand on Luke's shoulder. "You take care, son. But keep in mind, this isn't a game. Whoever is going to all this trouble is playing for keeps."

"I agree, Burke."

"You know how you get fired up when trouble comes. You can be more bullheaded than anyone I know. Keep that temper in check and keep a cool head, son."

"Yeah. Sure."

"And pigs'll fly," Colin muttered. The three of them laughed, breaking the tension, as the old cowboy climbed into the copilot's seat.

"One more thing." Colin beckoned Luke close. "I expect you to check with us on a regular basis. If we don't hear from you for several days, we're flying in to tan your hide. You hear me?"

"Yes, sir. Loud and clear." Luke paused before adding, "I'll remind you it's been years since any of you were able to tan my hide. I'd like to see you try it now."

"Nothing's changed," Colin muttered under his breath. "From the time he was just a pup, he was always trouble. He's still trouble, only older."

"I heard that."

"Figured you would." Colin exchanged a look with Burke.

Minutes later the little Cessna was moving down the rough patch of earth. Luke watched it until it was airborne.

When he turned, Ingrid and Lily were standing to one side of the barn. As he drew close, Lily reached up and put her hand in his. "I'm glad you're staying, Luke."

"Me, too, Li'l Bit."

He looked over her head at her big sister, who said nothing. From the fire in her eyes, he couldn't tell if she was glad or mad.

Not that it mattered, he thought. This wasn't about her, or about the fact that something about this stoic female touched something deep inside him.

He wasn't in this for hot sex. Or even for a quick fling.

She had saved him. He was just trying to return the favor.

He bit back a grin.

Yeah. That was his story and he was sticking to it.

CHAPTER FIVE

Lily bounded up the stairs ahead of Luke. "Come on. Ingrid said I could show you where you'll sleep."

He followed more slowly. He'd suggested the bunkhouse, but apparently they'd allowed it to fall into disrepair. *Like everything else around the ranch*, he thought. Now he would be upstairs, sharing space with three females. As he'd come from a male-dominated family, this was an alien experience to him. But now that he'd made his decision to stay, there was no turning back.

Lily opened a door and stepped inside. "Ingrid said this was Daddy's office."

It was a big room, with a desk and chair and shelves crammed with books and ledgers. The old brick fireplace in the downstairs parlor extended through this room as well, soaring to the ceiling. Judging by the soot on the hearth and the pile of dried logs in a basket, it had been well used.

Leaning against one wall was a wooden bed frame and mattress, apparently hauled down from attic storage by Mick.

Luke set to work putting the frame together before lifting the mattress into place.

Ingrid entered, carrying an armload of bed linens. Without a word she shook out a fitted sheet. Before she could start to fit it onto the mattress, Luke took it from her hands and stretched it into place, before reaching for a top sheet. He shook it out and tucked it around the three sides with an ease of efficiency.

She stood back, arms crossed over her chest. "You look like you've made up a bed or two."

He chuckled. "Yancy does our laundry. But he expects us to haul down the bedding and then make up our own beds. He likes to remind us he isn't our maid."

"I think I'd like Yancy."

"I know you would."

She watched as he smoothed a plaid blanket over the bed and added two pillows.

"Mick's got supper started. You can come down when you're ready."

"Thanks."

As she turned away, he put a hand on her arm. Ingrid reacted as though burned, stepping back just out of reach.

"Sorry." Luke lowered his hand to his side. "I was just going to say I don't want to be any trouble."

She gave him a long, slow look. "I wouldn't bet on that. I think you're nothing but trouble, Luke Malloy." She turned to her sister. "Come on, Lily. Let's give Luke some time to settle in."

The little girl was wriggling like a puppy. It was clear

that she was excited at the prospect of having a visitor staying with them. "I won't be any bother. Can I stay, Luke?"

"Sure, Li'l Bit. Since I don't have anything to unpack, I'm just going to open these windows and air out the room." He forced open the first window, sending the curtains billowing inward. As he started toward the second window, he added, "Then we'll go downstairs and see if we can give Mick a hand."

Ingrid paused in the doorway. "You're handy in the kitchen? Do you cook?"

He gave a nonchalant shrug. "Some. Not like Yancy. But then, nobody can cook like Yancy. I can do plain and simple things like burgers and chili."

Lily sighed. "I love burgers and chili. What else can you cook, Luke?"

"I make a mean grilled cheese sandwich. And one of the wranglers showed me how to grill a whole chicken on a can of beer." He winked. "Best chicken I ever tasted. Of course," he added with a grin, "it might have tasted that good because of all the beer I had to drink before that bird was done."

Lily looked at him with those big eyes. "Are you teasing again?"

"Maybe just a little. But I really do know how to grill a chicken on a beer can. Come on." He steered her toward the hallway. "Let's see if Mick needs a hand with supper."

"That was a great meat loaf, Mick." Luke sat back and sipped strong, hot coffee.

Lily drained her milk. "Do you know how to make meat loaf, Luke?"

He shook his head. "I missed that cooking lesson."

Mick set a platter in the middle of the table. "If anybody wants seconds, help yourself."

Luke didn't need any encouragement. He heaped more meat loaf and mashed potatoes on his plate before digging in.

The old man chuckled. "Looks like you're making up for lost time, son."

"Yeah. I figure I'd better build up these muscles if I'm going to lend a hand with ranch chores in the morning."

"Just don't overdo it. You took one heck of a fall."

"Like Colin said, as long as I landed on my head, no harm done."

While the others laughed, Ingrid sat, quietly watching and listening.

She sat at one end of the table, with Lily beside her. Nadine's chair was empty, and though no one mentioned her, Luke assumed she'd gone to the tiny town of Wayside looking for a little excitement.

"I liked Burke and your uncle Colin." Mick reached for the coffeepot bubbling on the stove. "Though he looked more like your brother than your uncle."

"Yeah." Luke sat back, feeling stronger than he had in days. "He was my dad's younger brother. He was just twenty when my dad and mom died."

"They passed away together?"

Luke nodded. "A car accident on a snowy road. I was ten. My brother Matt was twelve, and Reed was nine."

Mick glanced at Ingrid and Lily, whose eyes were downcast. "It's always tough when there's no time to say good-bye."

"My great-grandfather insists it wasn't an accident. But then, he's always had a flair for the dramatic."

"That so?" Mick held up the pot, and Luke passed over his cup.

When it was filled, Luke took a long, satisfying drink. "The Great One was a director in Hollywood before he came to live with us."

Ingrid's head came up. "The Great One?"

"That's what we've always called him. He loves it, since his ego is as big as his reputation was."

Mick was grinning. "Would I recognize his name?"

"You would if you followed old movies. He's Nelson LaRou."

The old cowboy's eyes widened. "Is that a fact? Nelson LaRou. Huh." He turned to the girls. "I bet I saw every one of the movies he directed. Back in the fifties, his name was as big on the movie screen as all those movie stars' names."

For the first time, Ingrid looked suitably impressed. "And he lives with your family?"

"Yeah." Luke stretched out his legs under the table. "He and Yancy spend their evenings sharing stories about old Hollywood mysteries. There are a lot of unsolved crimes from those days, and both Yancy and the Great One have theories about who did what. As for my parents, the Great One took a handheld movie camera to the scene of the accident, and he swears that before all the cars and trucks arrived, there were two distinct sets of tire tracks in the snow. By the time the sheriff got there, his deputy, a neighboring rancher, and a couple of wranglers passing by were all on the scene, and the sheriff, considering the amount of snow and ice on the road, declared it an accident. Case closed."

Ingrid frowned. "What about your great-grandfather's film?"

"He showed it to the authorities. They studied it, but it's shaky, because he'd gone to the scene in his pajamas and slippers. And the only light was from the moon and stars, so they said they couldn't be certain just what they were looking at." Luke drained his cup. "Water under the bridge. They're gone. And they left an entire family devastated."

Seeing the glitter of moisture in Ingrid's eyes, he added softly, "At first, I figured I'd never get past the pain. But Burke told me something I've never forgotten. He told me to hold on to the happy memories, and one day I'd find something to smile about."

To hide her emotions, Ingrid scraped back her chair and began gathering up the dishes.

When old Mick started to stand, Luke put a hand on his shoulder. "You did the cooking. We'll clean up." He crooked a finger at Lily. "Your sister can wash. You and I will dry."

They carried the dishes to the sink before taking fresh towels from a drawer.

While Mick enjoyed a second cup of coffee, he smiled at the easy banter between Luke and Lily.

"Not there, Luke. The big plates go in this cupboard." It was obvious that Lily was enjoying her new role of teacher.

"Okay, Li'l Bit. What about the knives and forks?"

The little girl opened a drawer. "In here."

"Thanks." Luke scooped up the entire handful of tableware and began drying each one and dropping them one on top of another.

"Not like that, Luke." Lily pointed to the dividers. "The knives in here. The forks here. The spoons"—she picked up the ones he'd already deposited, and rearranged them until they were neatly stored in their proper slots— "like that."

"I can see I'm going to need a lot more practice before I get it right."

"That's okay." The little girl patted his hand. "I'll help you until you learn to do it the way Ingrid likes."

"Thanks, Li'l Bit." He winked at Mick, and the old man bit back the laughter that threatened.

"Now where does this go?" Luke said as he dried the big platter.

"Up there." Lily pointed to the cupboard above her sister's head.

Luke reached up and easily set the dish inside. As he lowered his hand, it brushed Ingrid's hair. He was pleased to note it was as soft as it looked.

He felt her stiffen. He grinned as he met her sharp-eyed look.

"Need anything else put away that's too high for you, Li'l Bit?" If so, he intended to touch that hair again, and this time he'd linger over it.

"No. Everything's done." The little girl took the towel from his hand and placed it on a rack beside hers. "We hang these over here so they can dry."

"Okay. I'll remember." He watched as Ingrid drained the sink before drying her hands. "What do you do when the chores are done for the day?" he asked.

While Ingrid pointedly ignored him, Lily jumped right in. "Do you play cards?"

"Sure. What's your game? Gin rummy? Poker?"

The little girl shrugged. "I don't know those. Ingrid usually plays Fish with me."

"Fish." He thought a minute. "Yeah. I guess my brothers and I played Fish when we were kids."

"Oh boy." She raced to the parlor ahead of him in search of a deck of cards.

As he followed, he turned to Mick. "You in?"

"Not me." Mick got up slowly and turned toward his room off the kitchen. "Tonight's *Perry Mason*. I've seen every episode a dozen times or more, and I still get a kick out of solving the crime."

"Come on." Lily caught Luke's hand and led him to a game table in the corner of the parlor.

He glanced at Ingrid. "How about you?"

She pointed to a pile of papers on a desk across the room. "I need to sort through the bills and see what I can pay."

"Isn't that Nadine's job?"

"It should be. But if I waited for her to take care of it, the heat and lights would be turned off for lack of payment. So I do what I can to stay ahead of it."

He settled himself at the game table and accepted the deck of cards. After shuffling, he separated the cards into two piles and riffled them so quickly, Lily clapped her hands. "How'd you do that?"

"What? This?" He did it again, even faster, until the cards in his hands were a blur of color.

"Ingrid. Watch." Lily was captivated. "Do it again, Luke. Please."

With a twist of the wrist, Luke not only shuffled and riffled, but he also allowed the cards to spill from one hand to the other, then back again.

Ingrid frowned. "I can see that a certain cowboy spends way too much of his time with card sharks. Better watch your hand, Lily, or that shark will bite it off."

"Over a game of Fish?" He grinned at the little girl as he dealt the cards and dropped the rest in the center of the table.

"Give me all your queens." At Lily's singsong voice, he handed over a card.

"Now your kings."

He handed over another.

"Now your jacks."

He gave her a long look. "Are you able to read my cards?"

"No. Do you have any jacks?"

He handed one over.

"Now your tens."

"Finally. Got you. Go fish." Luke watched as she picked up a card. "Now, give me all your aces."

"Aw, Luke. I have two of them."

"Good." He wiggled his brows like a villain. "Now you have none and I have three."

As Ingrid sorted through the bills and wrote out checks for those that were almost overdue, she listened to the voices across the room. It seemed odd to hear that deep, masculine voice teasing her little sister. The more he teased, the more Lily responded. Laughing in delight when he said something outrageous. Giggling each time she requested a card that he had. He would pretend to grumble as he handed over two or even three cards, all the while challenging her to try to beat him. And when she did, her little voice was high with excitement. They would high-five and then begin yet another game of Fish.

By the way Luke handled the cards, it was obvious that he played often. Probably with his wranglers. Or maybe even in town, at one of the saloons. But, though he must find this childish game tedious, he never showed it. Instead, he continued in the same cheerful way, teasing, laughing, and acting as though he'd never had this much fun in his life.

Lily was clearly enchanted by Luke. And for that, Ingrid was willing to overlook whatever faults he would surely reveal as the days passed. After all, it was for Lily's sake that she'd allowed him to stay on, knowing her little sister deserved some peace of mind.

Across the room, the two dissolved into peals of laughter. Ingrid paused in her work and smiled. She couldn't remember the last time Lily had laughed so easily.

She had to admit it. Luke was being really sweet. And as long as she was being honest, she'd admit, too, that Lily wasn't the only reason she'd permitted Luke to stay on.

When Bull Hammond showed up at the barn, she'd felt a momentary flash of fear. Not that she'd have ever admitted it to him. Or to her little sister. But Luke had been calm, cool, steady, and absolutely fearless. With all that was going on around her ranch lately, she would take all the strong backup she could get.

There was an edge of danger about Luke Malloy that frightened her even while it appealed to her.

At another burst of laughter across the room, she turned to watch. At that moment Luke caught her eye and shot her a devilish wink. She felt her face grow hot.

Who was she kidding? It wasn't just his fearlessness that she was drawn to. It was the man himself. That tall, muscled, self-assured cowboy whose simple touch left her breathless.

But her reaction to him frightened her just a little. His mere touch got her feeling all hot and off stride. When his hand had brushed her hair, she'd felt a rush of pure sexual tension down her spine, all the way to her toes. And when she'd glowered at him, he'd merely grinned like he knew a secret.

This cowboy was dangerous. And not just because of the way he handled a rifle.

She had no doubt he knew exactly how to handle women, too. Didn't he already have Nadine and Lily eating out of his hand?

Well, there was one Larsen who wasn't buying what Luke Malloy was selling.

CHAPTER SIX

One more game, Luke. Please?"

Luke stifled a yawn. "Sorry, Li'l Bit. I can't keep my eyes open." He glanced at the clock on the mantel. "Besides, shouldn't you be in bed?"

Before she could protest, Ingrid set aside the papers she'd been working on and shoved away from the desk. "Come on, Lily. You're lucky I was too busy to notice the time. You and Luke can always play again tomorrow."

"Okay." The little girl started toward the stairs. On the first step she turned. "Promise me you won't leave after I fall asleep."

"I promise." He winked. "Besides, you beat me six times in a row. I'm looking forward to a rematch. I plan on winning tomorrow night."

Her smile was back as she turned away and climbed the stairs, calling over her shoulder, "Are you going to hear my prayers, Ingrid?"

"I'll be up in a few minutes. I'm going to turn out the lights in the kitchen."

Luke gathered up the cards and set the deck in the center of the table. "What's up with Lily's question? Why did she think I'd leave in the night?"

"I'm not sure, but I think I understand." Ingrid's look was both sad and pensive. "Nadine has a history of leaving. But my dad's sudden death, with no warning, may have her believing that nobody stays for very long. I guess I'll try to get her to open up to me about her feelings." She sighed. "But I intend to wait for the right opening before I do."

She paused in the doorway of the parlor. "Good night, Luke."

"'Night." Luke climbed the stairs and made his way to the office that was now his bedroom.

He was aware of Ingrid moving through the house before coming upstairs and letting herself into Lily's room.

He thought he heard the back door open and close.

Sitting on the edge of the bed, he shoved off his boots and set them aside before unbuttoning his shirt and tossing it over the back of a chair.

Unsnapping his jeans, he turned in surprise when his door was shoved inward.

Nadine's rusty voice was like the scrape of nails on a blackboard. "Hey, cowboy. There was nothing shaking in town, so I figured you might like some company, to keep you from feeling homesick."

He stayed where he was. "Thanks. But I can handle being alone. I'm a big boy now."

She looked him up and down. "Are you ever." She sauntered across the room, swaying slightly, and lifted her hands to his naked chest. Her breath reeked of whiskey and cigarettes. "I've always been partial to good-looking, muscled cowboys."

He caught both her wrists to stop their movement.

His voice was low. "I'm only going to say this once. I know this is your house, but my room is off-limits."

Her eyes went wide before narrowing to angry slits. She yanked her hands free and took a step back. "Just who do you think you are? Accepting my hospitality and treating me like an intruder in my own husband's room?"

"You called it straight. Your husband's room." He glanced around. "I don't see much of you reflected on these shelves. Are you sure you've ever been in here before?"

She frowned. "Lars liked his privacy."

"And you like your freedom."

She put her hands on her hips. "Has old Mick been spilling family secrets? I ought to send that old geezer packing—"

"Yeah. That's just what your daughters need. Get rid of the last man standing. See that they're completely alone, with nobody left to look out for them. How long do you think this ranch could function without the help of old Mick?"

"It doesn't matter. Whether it's now or a month from now, this place is already dead. Ingrid and Lily and Mick are just prolonging the agony." She gave him a hopeful look and stepped closer. "That's why you ought to consider my offer while you still can. I bet I could show you a few moves—"

"You heard me, Nadine. Now get out." He stepped around her and pulled open the door.

"Your loss. Too bad you don't know what you're missing, cowboy."

Seething, she shot him a last look before she stepped through the doorway and started down the hall, head high, hips swiveling.

His glance was drawn to Lily's room at the end of the hallway. Ingrid was standing in the doorway. Her mouth was a tight, grim line of anger. Her eyes were fierce enough to shoot daggers through his heart.

He knew what she was thinking. He'd be damned if he'd say a word in his own defense. Let her think the worst of him.

Without a word she crossed the hall to her bedroom and let herself in before slamming the door.

Luke swore as he retreated inside his room and closed the door.

He couldn't blame Ingrid. It was a natural enough mistake. She'd been too far away to hear the angry words spoken between him and Nadine. And then there was her mother's history. Not to mention his own reputation for hard living. Hadn't Burke and Colin made it clear on their visit? That reference to him riding his Harley over mountain ravines like some crazy drifter. He'd even looked the part of a bearded biker when he first arrived.

He finished undressing and turned out the lights before crawling naked under the blanket. With his hands beneath his head, he stared at the outline of the distant mountain peaks touched by moonlight, framed in the window.

What in the hell was he doing here, in the middle of nowhere, thinking he could do anything to help these people? From what he'd seen so far, they didn't stand a chance of saving this falling-down hulk from sinking under its own debt.

But then he thought about Ingrid Larsen, with that boyish cap of hair and that lush body she kept hidden under layers of bulky clothes, and he knew why he was staying against all odds.

In the beginning it might have been the allure of her rare beauty, which seemed at such odds with her determination to keep it hidden. But now, he had to admit to himself it was much more than Ingrid's good looks.

There was just something about her. The way she fought so hard for an impossible dream. The way she seemed determined to make it on her own. The way she protected her little sister, even from their own mother.

He'd always been a sucker for a hard-luck story.

Ingrid lay in her bed, wallowing in misery. Why was she not surprised? After all, Nadine could no more change her habits than a zebra its stripes. Her mother had a testosterone radar that never failed her. If there was a horny cowboy within miles, it was a certain bet that Nadine would not only find him, but also lure him into bed.

But she'd thought better of Luke.

Not at first, of course. He'd been a wounded stranger, whom she suspected of shooting at a herd of mustangs. And even after he'd convinced her that he wasn't the shooter, she'd been wary of him. There was something bold and dangerous about him. Something…tempting. Like a wild creature that, though badly wounded, would fight anyone who came too close. She admired the stoic way he'd accepted his pain. And he'd caught her completely by surprise when he'd decided to stay and help with the chores, to repay her for taking care of him.

And then tonight, watching him playing a dozen games of Fish with Lily, she'd seen a side to him she never would have expected. Though he must have been bored out of his mind, he'd made it such fun for her little sister.

It had been rare and wonderful to hear Lily's laughter. The giggles behind her hand. The way the little girl got caught up in the game, cheering right out loud whenever she beat Luke. Ingrid had caught that teasing light in his eyes when he'd turned to her and winked. Her heart had actually swelled with pleasure, knowing he was going to such pains to make it fun for her little sister.

For a minute or two, she'd actually thought he was someone rare and special. Now she'd been shot down to earth with a resounding thud. He was just another drifter on his way to someplace else. Someplace more pleasurable. More...adult.

At a knock on her door she sat up.

"Ingrid?" Lily's voice, soft and tentative, had her switching on a bedside light.

"What's wrong, honey?"

Lily hurried over. "Can I sleep with you tonight?"

"Sure." Ingrid pulled back the covers. "Climb in."

The little girl snuggled close while Ingrid pulled the covers over the two of them.

"I heard the back door open and close. I think Nadine's home."

Ingrid sighed, remembering the scene she'd been trying to block out of her mind. "She is."

"Why?" Lily lifted her head to stare at her sister. "She

never comes home this early. Do you think she's sick? Is she going to die like Daddy?"

"Of course not, honey." Ingrid looked away, switching off the light. As she moved lower into the blanket, she sighed. "Maybe she couldn't find anyone interesting to talk to."

"Oh." After a long silence, Lily whispered, "You still awake?"

"Uh-huh."

"I want to talk about Luke. I really like him. He's fun."

"It sounded like the two of you were having a grand time."

"He's so silly. He makes me laugh. Don't you like him, too?"

"I guess. Why do you ask?"

"You frown when you look at him. But I know he likes you."

"How would you know that?"

"I saw him looking at you a lot tonight. Sometimes, when I was dealing the cards, he'd forget to pick them up for a minute 'cause he was too busy staring at you."

Ingrid was grateful for the dark. She knew her cheeks felt hot. "I think you imagined that."

"Uh-uh." Lily snuggled closer. "Luke had a funny look on his face when he was looking at you. Like seeing you made his heart happy."

Her voice grew softer with each word. "I never had a nickname before. Well, Daddy used to call me Lily Lally Lolly sometimes. But only when he thought I needed cheering up. Anyway, I like when Luke calls me Li'l Bit. It makes me feel special, you know?"

"Honey, you shouldn't let yourself get too fond of

Luke. He's...he's a cowboy. They come and go, and they rarely stay in one place long enough for anybody to really get to know them. I don't mean you shouldn't enjoy his silly teasing and jokes, but you don't want to start trusting him to always be around. If you do that, you're bound to be disappointed. It would be better if you could just treat him like a neighbor or one of the wranglers that used to work for us, and not like a real friend. Do you understand?"

She listened to the soft, even breathing that told her Lily hadn't heard a word she'd said. With a sigh she realized the little girl was sound asleep.

She ought to do the same. But all the worrisome thoughts swirling around in her brain had her wide awake and replaying that last glimpse of Luke as he'd held the door for Nadine. Barefoot, shirtless, his jeans unsnapped. And his eyes, those always piercing eyes, looking heavy-lidded and sleepy. And when he'd caught her staring, he'd turned away without a word.

Guilt, no doubt.

She couldn't blame Nadine. The man was sexy as hell.

And at the moment, she hated Luke Malloy with every fiber of her being.

CHAPTER SEVEN

With bright morning sunlight streaming through the upstairs windows, Ingrid stared at the closed door to Luke's room as she made her way to the bathroom.

A short time later she stepped out, wearing a bulky robe. Before turning toward her room, she again stared at the closed door. Was he asleep this late? Or was there another reason there was no sound coming from his room at this time of the morning? Was Nadine in there with him?

She gritted her teeth and dressed quickly, eager to get started on her chores. Maybe then she could dispel all the disquieting thoughts taking over her mind.

As she started down the stairs, Lily trailed behind. "Thanks for letting me sleep with you, Ingrid."

"You're welcome, honey. You know you can always sleep with me when you're feeling worried about something."

As they moved through the parlor toward the kitchen,

she draped an arm around her little sister's shoulders. She realized she was doing it as much for herself as for Lily. She was preparing herself for the pain of having to watch Nadine and Luke coming down the stairs together whenever they managed to rouse themselves. No doubt they'd be laughing and sharing secrets.

In the kitchen, Mick looked up from the stove. "'Morning, ladies."

"'Morning, Mick." Lily glanced around. "Where's Luke?"

Ingrid was quick to intervene. "Honey, that's none of our bus—"

"He's out in the barn." Mick handed Ingrid a mug of coffee, which she immediately bobbled, spilling it across her fingers and onto the table.

She hissed in a breath as she wiped it up, keeping her face averted. "He's in the barn?"

"Been out there for a couple of hours, I'd say. He was heading out the door when I woke up. By now, I'm betting he's worked up a powerful appetite."

"I'll go and tell him breakfast is ready." Lily was already racing toward the back door.

Mick grinned at Ingrid. "We'd better watch out. That little girl's falling hard for our guest."

"She'll have to get in line behind Nadine."

At her flat tone, the old man's look sharpened. "You know something I don't?"

She shrugged. "What they do behind closed doors is none of my business."

"Of course it is. But I'd bet good money you're wrong about this, girl. I can't see Luke Malloy buying what Nadine is selling."

"You mean giving away, don't you?"

At that, the old cowboy chuckled.

Minutes later Luke followed Lily into the mudroom, scraping his boots, then rolled up his sleeves and washed at the sink before ambling into the kitchen.

His shirt, stretched tautly across his muscled chest, was damp from the hard work he'd done. His hair was tied back, but a few wet locks spilled over his forehead. He looked so appealing, Ingrid was forced to clench her hands into fists in her lap to keep from giving in to the temptation to brush it aside.

"'Morning." He accepted a mug of steaming coffee from Mick before taking a seat at the table.

"You're up early." Ingrid hated the accusing tone, but she was determined to steel herself against that devilish light in his eyes.

"I grew up keeping rancher's hours." He sighed when Mick placed an omelet on his plate. "And you, Mick, understand a rancher's appetite."

"That I do." Mick circled the table filling their plates.

"Was there some reason why you wanted to tackle the barn so early?" Ingrid studied him across the table. Even the way he savored his food was annoyingly sexy.

"I figured with that out of the way, we'd get an early start on riding up to the hills to see the herds."

"We only have one herd." Lily drained her milk and wiped her mouth on her sleeve.

"Even better. That'll give us a chance to make sure they're all healthy enough for the end-of-summer roundup. It'll be here before you know it."

"Do you plan on being here for that?" Again, Ingrid thought, there was that note of sarcasm in her tone. But she couldn't quite believe this rolling stone would actually stick around long enough for roundup.

"How would I know? My crystal ball broke." Luke winked.

Lily burst into giggles. "You're funny, Luke."

"It wasn't that funny, Lily." Shoving aside her plate, Ingrid pinned him with a look. "Even without your crystal ball, what do you think? Will you be here, or will you be off on some new adventure, riding your…Harley across some challenging mountain ravines?"

He shot her a lazy smile. "You really ought to try it sometime. It's a feeling like no other."

"Oh, I'm sure you're good at chasing feelings."

"Since I was no bigger than Li'l Bit here."

At her nickname, Lilly's smile lit up the room as she said to Mick, "Did you hear what Luke calls me?"

"Yeah." The old man grinned. "I have to say, it suits you, girl."

Ingrid scraped back her chair. "I'm heading to the barn to saddle up and head to the hills."

Luke picked up his mug. "I'll be along in a few minutes."

Ingrid turned to her little sister, who could be counted on to shadow her. "You coming?"

Lily shrugged. "I'd rather stay here with Luke."

Ingrid stalked to the mudroom to pick up her denim jacket and wide-brimmed hat before slamming out of the house.

"Looks like somebody didn't get enough sleep last night," Mick muttered.

"I slept in her bed," Lily said softly. "Maybe I shouldn't have. Maybe I kept her awake."

"Don't you worry about it, Li'l Bit." Luke winked at her, and her smile returned. "Your sister can catch up on her sleep tonight, while I have my revenge on a certain little card shark."

"You mean we can play more Fish tonight?"

"I'm looking forward to it." He picked up his dishes and Ingrid's and placed them in the sink. "Thanks for that great breakfast, Mick. I'm feeling fortified for the day."

Lily carried her dishes to the sink, and following Luke's example, turned to the old cowboy. "Thanks for breakfast, Mick."

"You're welcome. You're both welcome. Now get out of here and find a way to put a smile on Ingrid's face."

Ingrid's horse was already saddled and nibbling grass outside the corral. Inside the barn Ingrid was busy rubbing oil into an old harness. She looked up briefly when Luke and Lily entered, but held her silence.

Lily opened a stall door and led her mount out into the sunshine, where she proceeded to wrestle a saddle onto the horse's back.

"Need any help with that, Li'l Bit?"

She gave a quick shake of her head. "I can do it, Luke."

He led Turnip outside. "Okay then. But that saddle's bigger than you."

"Ingrid said I have to be able to take care of myself, especially when we're up in the hills. That way, if there's ever an accident, I can go for help."

Luke tightened the cinch. "Your sister's a smart woman." He waited until Lily pulled herself into the saddle before doing the same on his horse.

Ingrid stepped out of the barn and took a pair of worn leather gloves from her back pocket. Drawing her hat low on her head, she mounted and, without a word, took the lead. Lily followed, and Luke took up the rear.

They rode single file until they crossed into a high meadow carpeted with wildflowers. They rode side by side until, at the very top of the hill, Luke reined in his mount.

As he did, Lily opened a zippered pouch hanging around her neck and took out a battered old camera, aiming it at the land below as she snapped off several shots.

"I don't believe there's a prettier picture in all the world than Montana in summer." Luke winked at Lily. "Unless it's Montana wearing a blanket of snow in winter."

"I love winter. Do you like winter, too, Luke?"

He nodded. "And spring and fall. I like all the seasons, as long as I can spend them here in Montana."

"Did you ever go away from here?"

He shook his head. "My grandpop thought I should study veterinary medicine. When I heard how far away I'd have to travel, I decided I'd just learn all I could about doctoring cattle from Burke."

"Did you go to school when you were my age, or did you get homeschooled?"

"Mostly homeschooling. Our ranch was more than an hour away from the nearest town."

"Me too. Miss Sarah, the teacher who checks all my online assignments, says I'm really smart." Lily was beaming as she tucked away her camera. "What do you like better, Luke? Riding Turnip or riding your motorcycle?"

"Now that's a tough question, Li'l Bit. You're asking me to compare apples and oranges."

She looked perplexed. "I don't understand. What does that mean?"

"I love oranges. They're sweet and juicy. But I have to peel them before I get to the good stuff. I love apples, too. They crunch when I bite into them. And I can even eat the outer peel. But I couldn't say if I liked one better than the other."

"Oh." She thought about his words. "So you love riding Turnip, 'cause you've had him since he was a foal. And your...Harley?"

"I've been riding bikes since I was thirteen. My first motorcycle was one of Burke's rejects. It was old and rusted and lying in the barn, and I spent months fiddling with it until I got it working. Then I took it out to one of the pastures, where nobody could see me, and taught myself how to ride. Pretty soon I decided it would be fun to try doing some tricks with it. In no time I could jump it clear over a couple of bales of hay. Then over a tractor." He shrugged. "After that, there was no stopping me."

"Didn't your daddy worry?"

"My parents were dead. And poor Grandpop was in a panic over what to do with his ornery grandson."

"Did he punish you?"

Luke shook his head. "He tried. But no matter what, I'd just take my lumps and get right back on my bike. Finally Grandpop gave up. I'm sure he's amazed that I've lived this long."

"What about your brothers? Do they ride motorcycles, too?"

"Matt's too sensible." Luke chuckled. "And now that he has himself a bride, I'm sure he's not going to do anything too dangerous. He's got way too much to live for."

Ingrid's eyes flashed. "Your brother Matt sounds like a smart man."

Luke smiled. He'd caught her listening to their conversation and had known that sooner or later she wouldn't be able to bite her tongue any longer. And though he figured her anger was about what she'd seen the previous night, or thought she'd seen, he had no intention of enlightening her. "Oh, Matt's smart. But so is my brother Reed. We refer to him as our very own technonerd."

Lily's eyes widened. "What's a...what does that mean?"

"Reed's a guy who dearly loves the challenge of learning all kinds of new technology. Give him a complicated gadget with enough directions to fill a book, and he'll sort it out in a matter of hours and have the gadget up and running. He's been that way since we were just kids."

"So." Ingrid's tone was pure ice. "Both your brothers are smart and follow the rules. It seems you're the only misfit in the family."

"That's me." He winked at Lily. "A crazy rebel. I thrive on challenge. Or, as I like to call it, opportunity."

"Do you have any pets, Luke?" Lily guided her horse close to his.

"Just old Turnip here. There's a bunch of barn cats out back of our place, but they're not what I'd call pets. How about you?"

She nodded. "I've got Little."

"Sounds like a hamster or a bunny. Which is it?"

"A chicken. Right after she hatched, I picked her for my very own. And I named her Little 'cause it was the name of a chicken in my favorite story."

"Is she a good pet?"

Lily shrugged. "I used to spend hours dressing her in dolls' clothes and pushing her around in a stroller. But now she just wants to be with the rest of the chickens in the henhouse. But whenever I feed them, she comes right over and sits down so I can pet her."

As they came up over a ridge, the herd of cattle was spread out before them in a rolling meadow of lush grass.

"That's a fine-looking herd." Luke drew back on the reins, allowing Lily to ride ahead, while he remained beside Ingrid. "How many do you figure there are?"

"Nearly six hundred." She dismounted, and Luke did the same. "With the calves born this spring, there should be well over a thousand heading to market this year."

He studied the animals, fat and sleek from the lush grasses in these hills. "You found the perfect place for a summer range. Even without a team of wranglers, they're pretty much fenced in here by the steep hills around them."

Ingrid tossed back her hat to allow the breeze to take her hair. "My dad chose this spot years ago. He divided the herd into three equal parts, leaving some to graze on a higher mountainside, some on a lower plain, and some here. At the end of that season, he realized the herd grazing in this spot brought in the highest profits."

"Your dad was a smart man."

At Luke's praise, she beamed with pleasure and turned to him. "He couldn't hide the love he had for this ranch. All he wanted was to teach me everything he could about ranching, so when the day came for him to slow down, he'd take comfort in the fact that his land was in good hands."

"And it is." Luke lifted a hand to the corn silk strands dancing around her cheeks.

At once her smile fled and she jerked back. "Don't. I told you before. I'm not Nadine."

His eyes narrowed on her. "For the record, there's no way I'd ever confuse you with your mother."

"Then don't try playing those games with me."

"What games are we talking about?"

"You know exactly what I mean. All those sexy moves."

"Really? Sexy?" He was grinning as he reached a hand to her hair. "Like this?"

Her chin came up. "If you want lots of hair, reach for Nadine's."

"Is that why you chopped yours off?" He allowed a silken strand to sift through his fingers. "To prove a point?"

"Well, aren't you the brilliant observer. For the record, there are a lot of things Nadine does that I refuse to do. I don't bother with makeup. And—"

"—and you try to hide your gorgeous body under this bulky shirt." He fingered the rough collar. His smile was quick and charming. "I'll let you in on a secret. It's not working."

She slapped his hand away. "Stop trying to be clever. I know what I am. I'm a rancher who's struggling to stay on the land I love. A big sister working overtime to raise Lily to be the best she can."

"You forgot the most important thing. You're a woman." His voice lowered to a near growl. "Maybe you'd like to forget that, but it's impossible for me to overlook the fact that you're not just a woman, but a gorgeous, amazing, very independent woman."

She actually gasped as he leaned close.

"Just so you know, I'm going to kiss you, Ingrid." His arms came around her and he gathered her close.

He'd known her lips would be soft and inviting. Had known it from the first time he'd looked at them. But he wasn't prepared for the taste of her. Sweet, yet tart. So strong, and yet he could feel the way her breath hitched, alerting him to her unease.

All woman, and yet fighting it. She kept her hands at her sides, refusing to give him any encouragement.

"I won't do anything you don't want me to do. So don't be afraid." He spoke the words inside her mouth.

"I'm not—"

"Just for a moment, Ingrid, let yourself enjoy something."

She responded with a soft purr in the back of her throat. For the space of a heartbeat he could feel her relax in his arms as she gave herself up to the moment.

A burst of heat shot through Luke's veins. His heartbeat was thundering, keeping time with hers. He changed the angle of the kiss and took it deeper, until he could actually feel the fire.

The ground tilted beneath his feet, and he knew he was losing control. He hadn't meant to take it this far. None of this had been planned. He'd merely wanted to kiss her and tease her a little. But now, too late, he realized that one taste of these lips would never be enough.

He lifted his head and held her for another few moments, while he struggled to bring the world around them into focus.

As his breathing settled, he took a step back, keeping his hands at her shoulders to steady himself as well as her.

Before either of them could say a word, Lily's horse trotted over to where they were standing.

The little girl looked down at them, her smile as bright as the sunshine. "Are we heading home now?"

Luke managed to find his voice. "Yeah. I think it's time. Want to race?"

"Oh boy." She turned her mount before calling, "What does the winner get?"

"It's a surprise." Luke would think of something on the ride home. For now, he could barely make his muddled brain work.

He turned to Ingrid, pulling herself into the saddle. "Want to join the game?"

She managed a cool smile. "Sure. I guess I'd be wise to brush up on all my games while you're around."

He shot her a dangerous grin. "Just so you know which ones are games and which are the real thing."

"Are you sure *you* do?" She urged her horse into a run, leaving him in her dust.

CHAPTER EIGHT

Chili." Luke shot a quick grin at Mick as he ladled out their supper.

"I'd better warn you, son. I like it hot."

"Even better." Luke reached for a platter filled with smaller bowls in the middle of the table, holding chopped onion, grated cheese, oyster crackers, and hot sauce. He spooned some of each into his chili before taking a taste. Then he closed his eyes and gave a sigh of pure pleasure. "Now that's what I call ranch chili."

"Around here we call it Mick's fire." Ingrid followed Luke's lead and added the garnishes before digging in.

Lily and Mick were too busy eating to say a word.

As usual, Nadine's chair was empty. Nobody seemed to notice or care. After a day of ranch chores and the long ride into the hills and back, they were ready for the slower pace of evening.

As dusk settled over the land, they enjoyed a leisurely

supper, while the others filled Luke in on some of the family stories from years past.

Luke took a third helping of chili before turning to Ingrid. "So your ranch goes back several generations?"

She nodded. "My grandfather came here from Norway. Dad used to say his father was a happy loner, comfortable with his own company. He didn't marry until he was in his fifties. Then he met a traveling teacher, Winnie, who used to visit ranch families on horseback. He was so taken with her, he asked her to marry him the next day. When she agreed, they rode into Wayside, found a minister, and returned to the ranch that same day. A year later my dad was born. By the time Dad was fifteen, both his parents were dead, and he just continued caring for the ranch like his father before him."

Luke helped himself to coffee, then topped off Mick's cup and Ingrid's. "Where did your father meet your mother?"

"In town. He went in for supplies and came home with a bride. She was a waitress at Barney's. That's the only bar in town. Dad was forty-two. Nadine was just shy of her twentieth birthday. When she realized how isolated this place was, she took off after just two weeks."

"Where did she go?"

Ingrid shrugged. "Back to Wayside. And Barney's. It was all she knew."

"What did your dad do?"

"What he's always done. He tended to the ranch, and when all the chores were finished, he drove his truck to Wayside and found her back at Barney's, slinging drinks."

"How did he persuade her to come back with him?"

Ingrid glanced across the table at her little sister. "If

you'd like, Lily, you can go in the parlor and get the cards ready."

"Okay." The little girl carried her dishes to the sink. Before leaving the room, she said to Luke, "I'll see you when you're ready to play Fish. And remember, you promised me a prize for beating you in our race."

"I haven't forgotten. You'll get your prize, Li'l Bit."

When she was gone, Ingrid sipped her coffee. "In answer to your question...Dad once told me there was only one way to deal with someone like Nadine, and that was to give her time to figure out whether she needed the freedom she craved or the stability he offered."

"Which did she take?"

"Both. Even all these years later."

"How long did she take to come home that first time?"

"A month. Eight months later I was born. And my father said he knew then that he'd never be alone again. He didn't care if Nadine stayed or left, as long as she understood that he was never going to allow her to take me with her."

Mick, listening in silence, let out a chuckle. "I met Lars Larsen when he was running this place all alone. A man who never had time to be a boy. A loner who never felt lonely. And I can tell you that the minute he laid eyes on his baby girl, he lost his heart completely. It was the same with Lily. He just purely doted on his two daughters."

Ingrid smiled. "Dad always lived on the edge. The edge of having the family he'd craved, but never persuading Nadine to stay and make it complete. The edge of making this ranch a success, but never quite attaining it. There were just too many things getting in the way. Nadine's need to party. Debts that never got completely paid. He died still struggling to make it all work."

Seeing the look of sadness coming into her eyes, Luke pushed away from the table. "Okay. We've been lazy long enough. Since Mick made that great chili, it's up to you and me to clean up."

He crossed to the sink and turned on the faucet. While he washed the dishes, Ingrid picked up a towel and dried. As they worked together, Luke kept up a running commentary about his brothers and the silly fights they'd had over the years.

At the table, Mick stretched out his legs and watched the two of them. He could see right through Luke. He was doing his best to keep Ingrid from dwelling on the sad facts of her life. His jokes and funny stories were doing the trick. But if body language could be believed, even though they were both laughing, they were working overtime to keep from touching. Which meant to him that they were probably dealing with some kind of itch to do just the opposite.

His eyes crinkled as a big grin spread across his face. Damned if it didn't look like Luke took his words to heart this morning and found a way to put a smile on Ingrid's face. And wasn't it the warmest smile he'd seen on her in a long time.

It was the way of men and women from the beginning of time. Throw them together long enough, and they were bound to strike sparks off one another. And some of those sparks were just apt to light a fire.

"One more game, Luke. Please."

Luke gathered up the cards and shook his head.

"Thanks for letting me beat you a time or two. It was darned nice of you. But I'm done for tonight. And tomorrow, I think it's time I taught you something new. Gin rummy. Or poker."

She clapped her hands. "Poker?" She turned to Ingrid, seated at the desk across the room, her head bent over the ledgers. "Is it okay if Luke teaches me to play poker?"

Ingrid shot him a look. "Gambling? Why am I not surprised?" To her sister she said sternly, "You'll stick to Fish, young lady."

"We won't play for real money." Luke winked at Lily. "We'll play for something else. Maybe for chores?"

Lily picked up on that instantly. "You mean, if I beat you, you have to do my barn chores?"

"Or, if I beat you, you'll have to do mine."

Her face fell, but only for a moment. She brightened. "Okay. 'Cause I beat you at Fish more than you beat me."

"Yeah. I noticed that. I've been meaning to ask if you've been peeking at the cards."

The little girl put her hands on her hips. "I would never cheat."

Luke laughed at the outraged look on her face. "I know, Li'l Bit."

Her smile returned. "Oh. You were just teasing me again." She dug into the pocket of her jeans and pulled out the dollar bill. "Thanks for my prize, Luke."

"You earned it, Li'l Bit."

"Good night, Luke." Without thinking she threw her arms around his neck and kissed his cheek. "I'll see you in the morning."

"Yeah. See you."

To her big sister she called, "You coming up to hear my prayers?"

"I'll be there in a minute."

Luke sat perfectly still and waited until Lily danced up the stairs. Then he touched a finger to his cheek.

When he saw Ingrid staring, he started toward the kitchen. "I think I'll make a fresh pot of coffee. Want some?"

"Sure. I'll just be a few minutes." She shoved away from the desk and climbed the stairs.

A short time later she returned to the parlor to find Luke on his knees in front of the fireplace, coaxing a thin flame to some kindling. On the coffee table was a tray holding two mugs and a pot of coffee, along with cream and sugar.

Ingrid poured the coffee and crossed the room to hand Luke a steaming mug.

"Thanks."

She nodded toward the fire. "That feels good."

"Yeah. Getting chilly in here. The temperature must be dropping."

"Mick said rain's coming in."

"He watched the news?"

She shook her head and picked up a mug of coffee for herself. "He claims his bones let him know when rain's coming."

They shared a laugh as they settled into two over-stuffed rockers in front of the fire.

Luke stretched out his long legs to the heat. "This is nice."

"Yeah." Ingrid fell silent while she sipped her coffee.

"I saw you going over the bills." He indicated the desk across the room. "Everything okay?"

She shrugged. "I do the best I can. I pay the most important bills first. Taxes. Insurance. But I lost a field of hay, and that's going to cost me this winter."

"You could sell off the entire herd after roundup, and then you wouldn't need the feed."

"What's a cattle ranch without cattle?"

"You could keep a bare-bones herd. A bull. A couple of broodmares."

"And start over?"

"It's what ranchers do when they're up against hard times. You'd not only save the cost of feed all winter, but you could also start saving to pay the salaries of a couple of wranglers next spring."

"There's not much need of wranglers without a herd."

"There are fences to mend. Buildings to repair. By the time you've built up a new herd, your ranch would be in good shape and you could concentrate on being a cattle rancher."

She gave a long, deep sigh. "Oh, Luke, you make it sound so easy."

He set aside his coffee. "It's never easy. If people like us wanted easy, we'd sell everything and take up a trade. Nobody around here is ranching because we're looking for a slick life. But this is our heritage. It's what our fathers did. Our grandfathers. It's in our blood."

He saw a tear slide down her cheek. Alarmed, he dropped to his knees in front of her and caught her hands in his. "Hey. I'm sorry, Ingrid. I didn't mean to make you cry. I always say more than I—"

"Shhh." She touched a finger to his lips to stop his words. "I never knew anyone else felt this way. I've never been able to put it into words. But you said exactly what's in my heart. I love this ranch, Luke. I want, more than anything, to make it work so Lily and I can stay here. And I'm so afraid I'll fail."

When she started to withdraw her hand, he caught it between both of his and lifted it to his lips, pressing a kiss to the palm and closing her fingers around it.

Stunned, she merely stared at him, her eyes swimming with tears.

Maybe it was the tears. Maybe it was the moment. Whatever the reason, he leaned into her and framed her face with his big hands.

And then his mouth was on hers, and his fingers were in her hair, and they strained toward each other with a hunger that caught them both by surprise.

The old rocker creaked as Luke stood, his arms going around her, dragging her to her feet.

She clung to his waist, offering her mouth for another drugging kiss. He took what she offered with a fierceness that had her gasping before she allowed herself to sink into the pure pleasure.

There was such strength in him. In the arms that gathered her close. In the control she could feel in him as he kept his kiss gentle, even though his breathing was ragged.

When at last she pushed slightly away and dragged in a rough breath, she saw the fierce look in his eyes and knew he could easily take this further. But to his credit, he respected her enough to allow her to set the pace.

"Fear is always biting at a rancher's heels. Fear of bad weather. Fear of a failed herd or crop. But we fight back the fear and keep going. It's what we do."

"Thank you, Luke."

He shot her a rogue's grin. "For the kiss?"

She flushed. "For the words. I needed to hear them."

Seeing him watching her closely, her flush deepened. "Well, for the kiss, too. I guess I needed it more than I realized."

"Always happy to oblige, ma'am. You just let me know whenever I can be of help again."

"So noble." She couldn't help laughing. "Don't let it go to your head, cowboy."

She walked to the stairway and turned to him. "You'll bank the fire before coming up?"

"Looks like I have no choice."

At his double meaning she laughed again.

And continued laughing as she climbed the stairs to her room.

CHAPTER NINE

Luke's sleep was disturbed by the sound of a door slamming and voices raised in anger. One he identified as Nadine's. The other was a male voice he hadn't heard before. He pulled on his jeans before reaching for his rifle beside the bed. Shirtless and barefoot, he started down the hall.

Ingrid's door opened. Her hair was tousled, her eyes heavy lidded from sleep. She was barefoot and wearing a faded football jersey that fell below her knees.

They stared at each other in silence, before Ingrid led the way down the stairs.

She paused in the doorway of the kitchen, and Luke stepped up behind her to stare at Nadine, hands on hips, facing a heavyset, grizzled cowboy who was shaking a fist in her face.

Neither Nadine nor her cowboy took any notice of Ingrid and Luke as they lobbed a fierce volley of curses at each other.

"I told you." His voice was fierce. "The money first. Then we'll go to your bedroom."

"And I told you. You'll get your money in the morning." A rough, scratchy chuckle. "If I think you earned it."

"Why you—" The stranger caught a handful of Nadine's hair and tugged her head back so hard she cried out. At the same instant, his hand was around her throat.

Luke stepped in front of Ingrid and took aim with his rifle. "Step away from the woman."

Two heads came up sharply as Nadine and the stranger turned to the doorway.

Luke's voice was pure ice. "I said step away from her. Now."

At once the man released his hold on Nadine, before turning on her with a look of absolute fury. "Who the hell is this guy?"

"Some cowboy who thinks he has the right to butt in where he isn't wanted." Nadine glowered at Luke, and then at her daughter. "You've got no right to interfere in my business."

"Some business." Ingrid's tone revealed a depth of sadness. "Are you reduced to paying for his service now?"

"Since you drove him off the property at the end of your rifle, he said he wouldn't come back unless he was paid."

Luke realized this was Lon Wardell. He wouldn't have recognized this bloated, worn-out cowboy as the cocky, muscled wrangler who had once worked on his family's ranch over twenty years ago. That Lon Wardell had walked with a swagger and had bragged about owning his own ranch one day. A sprawling ranch that would rival the Malloy spread.

Ingrid turned to the cowboy. "What's the matter, Lon? Can't afford a room in Wayside?"

His voice was old. Weary. "She wanted to come here."

"Well, she's here." Ingrid pointed to the door. "And you're still not welcome. So get. Now."

He opened his mouth, then shut it quickly when Luke took careful aim, backing up Ingrid's order.

He directed his fury at Nadine. "I'm done, you hear? I'm sick and tired of your empty promises."

"They weren't empty." Nadine shot a hateful look at Ingrid. "This ranch is still mine. And I can give it to who-ever I please. You make the right choice, Lonny honey, you could still have that dream of owning your own place."

"Over my dead body."

At Ingrid's words, he shot her a chilling smile. "Care-ful what you say. It can be arranged"—he snapped his fingers—"like that."

Luke took a step toward him. "You've got to the count of five to be out of here and off the lady's property."

It was obvious the cowboy was giving some thought to testing him. Then, seeing the look in Luke's eyes, he turned and beat a retreat.

As the sound of his truck faded in the night, Nadine vented all her fury on Ingrid. "How dare you interfere in my life?"

"Interfere?" Ingrid hissed out a breath. "He was about to use you for a punching bag."

"He didn't mean it. It was just love play."

"Of course it was." Ingrid faced her mother, her voice trembling with emotion. "If you believe that, you've got a twisted sense of love."

"You'd better be very careful how you treat me, missy. I'm still legal owner of this place. And if I feel like it, I can give it to anybody I please. Even Lonny."

"Then you'd have to live here. And being a rancher's wife has never been your style."

Nadine brushed past Ingrid and Luke and headed for the stairs, swearing a blue streak as she did.

When Nadine was gone, Ingrid sank down on a kitchen chair. Her hands, Luke noted, were shaking.

He set the rifle in a corner of the room. "I'll make some coffee."

Within a few minutes the air was filled with the fragrance of coffee bubbling on the stove. Luke filled two cups and handed one to Ingrid.

"Thanks." She sipped, and some of the color began returning to her cheeks. "And thanks for backing me up. Judging by Lon's temper, and the fact that he was very drunk, I doubt he'd have given up if I'd faced him alone."

"You should never be alone with that guy." Luke sat across from her. "Neither should Nadine. I didn't like what I saw in his eyes." When she raised a brow, he added, "A look of desperation. That can make a man do dangerous things."

He took his time, giving her the chance to steady herself before asking, "Is this a pattern with Nadine? Violent men?"

She shook her head. "Except for Lon Wardell, I've never met any of the men in her life. And Lon's temperament is as far from my father's as possible. My dad was soft-spoken, hardworking, and, with all of us, as gentle and accepting as a lamb. Whenever she came home after one of her absences, he always welcomed her back as though it was the most normal thing in the world for his wife to be gone for long stretches of time."

Luke fiddled with his spoon. "She seems a bit... desperate."

Ingrid nodded. "I agree. But I don't know what to do about it. Dad used to call it her crazy side. He said there was a crazy lady hidden inside her that fought to get out. And whenever it succeeded, all he could do was stand back and watch her go. Sometimes it took weeks, sometimes months." She shook her head. "Or years. Then she'd come back, all happy and normal until the next time."

Ingrid ran a hand through her cap of hair. "I'm so tired of it all. The threats of giving away all that Dad worked so hard to own. The drunken trips to Wayside. The strangers she hangs with."

"It's a lot of drama."

"And I'm sick and tired of it."

Hearing the weariness in her tone, Luke topped off their cups.

"Thanks." Ingrid eyed him over the rim of her cup. "Why are you staying here, Luke?"

He gave a nonchalant shrug. "Why not? You saved my life. I'd like to do something in return to help you."

She eyed him squarely. "Most people would say thank you and move on. If that wasn't enough, maybe a note, or flowers, or..." She sighed. "Most people would be so eager to get away from all this, they'd run screaming into the night."

He gave her an unexpected wink. "I guess I'm not most people."

"You're not like anybody I've ever known."

"Good. That's part of my charm."

She laughed out loud. "You always have the perfect answer to everything."

"Just part of the package, ma'am." He gave an exaggerated drawl. "Not only charming, but smart as a whip, too."

Before she could think, she closed a hand over his. "Oh, I needed to have something to laugh about." Realizing what she'd done, she lifted her hand away.

Luke caged her hand between both of his. "It's nice to have someone to share the laughter with."

She looked at their joined hands. "Yeah. It is nice." She paused a beat, letting her gaze trail that muscled chest and torso before adding, "Just don't fool yourself into believing that I'm falling for all that muscle and charm."

He bit back a grin. "Not for a minute, ma'am."

Seeing that their cups were empty, Luke picked up his rifle and caught her hand. "Come on. You can still manage a couple of hours of sleep before you have to start your chores."

Upstairs, Ingrid paused outside her bedroom. "I know I already thanked you, but let me say it again. I'm really grateful you're here, Luke."

"So am I. Good night."

He waited until she stepped inside and closed her door before moving on to his own room. Once inside, he walked to the window and stared out at the midnight blackness.

He admired Ingrid for fighting to salvage her father's heritage. He knew, in her place, he'd do the same. But a clear-eyed look at the odds against her had him wondering how much longer one determined woman could hold

out for the proverbial happy ending. Maybe he should en-
courage her to cut her losses and go to a place where she
and Lily could be safe. At least then they could live to
fight another day.

He thought about the very different lifestyle he was accustomed to at the family ranch. Teasing. A lot of trash
talk between brothers. The occasional fight that ended in
raised fists. But more, there was concern and love and
laughter. So much laughter.

It had been good to hear Ingrid laugh. She deserved to
do it more often.

While he peered out the window, he saw a flash of light
as the rusted pickup chugged to life. He could see Nadine
clearly outlined in the interior light of the truck as she put
it in gear and took off with tires spinning.

Apparently she hadn't had her fill of Wayside or its
cowboys yet.

The crazy woman inside her had won another round
over common sense.

After breakfast, Mick joined Luke, Ingrid, and her little
sister in the barn, mucking stalls after turning out a string
of horses into a fenced corral. With four sets of hands, the
chores were quickly completed.

Mick looked over at Luke, hanging his pitchfork on a
hook along the wall. "How's the shoulder holding up, son?"

"Good." Luke massaged the muscle. "Hardly a twinge
now."

"You up to lending a hand with the shed?"

"Sure thing." Luke turned. "Lead the way."

The two crossed a pasture and headed toward a small
shed in the distance. Once there, they took down a sag-

ging door. While Mick replaced the rusty hinges, Luke removed his shirt in the hot sun before laying the door across a couple of sawhorses, and he began working a plane across the surface in smooth, even strokes.

While they worked, Luke brought the old man up to speed on what had happened the night before.

Ingrid and Lily came riding across the pasture and reined in their mounts.

Ingrid had to call on all her discipline to tear her gaze from Luke's muscled, sweaty body. He was, quite simply, beautiful.

"You two need our help?"

Mick shook his head. "We've got this, girl. You heading up to the herd?"

"Yeah." She decided to say no more, afraid to trust her voice over the knot of lust she couldn't seem to swallow.

Lily's voice was almost pleading. "I was hoping you'd be able to come with us, Luke."

He winked at her. "If you'll give me a few minutes, I'll go along." He lifted the door and held it in place while Mick tightened the hinges.

Luke opened and closed the door several times to be certain it was level. Then, snatching up his shirt, he grabbed Turnip's reins.

"If you have any more chores, Mick, I can get to them in a couple of hours."

"There's always tomorrow, son." The old cowboy lifted his Stetson and wiped a sleeve across his brow. "The chores will still be waiting."

"Can we race again, Luke?" Lily was already crouching in the saddle, determined to win.

"Sorry, Li'l Bit. I think this hot sun calls for a slow, easy ride so our horses don't get overheated." He pulled Turnip beside Ingrid's mount, and the two exchanged a look.

As the three horses started across the meadow toward the distant hills, Mick stood watching. Luke hadn't fooled him. That young man wasn't so much interested in the herd as he was in keeping Ingrid and Lily safe.

After hearing about their midnight encounter with Lon Wardell, he was grateful for Luke Malloy's presence on their ranch.

The old man squirted oil on the hinges and tested the door one more time before turning toward the house. He'd seen a hunk of beef in the freezer and figured it was time for some good old-fashioned pot roast. Comfort food. After the scene Ingrid had been forced to witness last night, it was just what the doctor ordered.

Of course, so was Luke Malloy. He was more than the doctor ordered.

His presence on the ranch gave the old cowboy a feeling of security he hadn't felt since Lars had passed away so suddenly.

CHAPTER TEN

Luke, Lily, and Ingrid enjoyed a leisurely ride across the meadows before pausing at the top of the ridge to study the herd below. As before, Lily urged her mount into a fast run down the hill, where horse and rider moved slowly among the grazing animals. These hills, and this herd, were part of the child's comfort zone. She was as easy with these cows as a city kid would be with a skateboard.

While Luke watched, something in the scene below looked out of place, but it took a minute for it to register in his mind. "That can't be right."

Ingrid saw the grim set of his jaw. "What?"

He shook his head slowly. "I hope I'm wrong. But from what I can see, there can't be more than a couple of hundred head of cattle down there."

After scanning the scene, she tried to cover the little cry that escaped her lips before she bit down hard. "That's impossible."

He drew his mount closer to hers. "With no wranglers, it wouldn't be hard for anyone to help themselves to your cattle."

"Rustlers?"

"With enough cattle haulers, they could truck away an entire herd in a couple of nights."

"But who . . . ?"

His eyes narrowed. "I can think of two men who would benefit from stealing your herd."

He saw her eyes fill before she turned away.

He left her alone while he slowly circled the herd, mentally tallying as he did. By his calculations, there were less than four hundred cattle in this meadow, when there had been more than six hundred earlier.

And for every cow missing, Ingrid's chances of buying the ranch from her mother narrowed considerably.

When he returned, she and Lily were standing together, talking quietly, while holding to their horses' reins.

"Maybe they wandered off." The little girl put her hand on her big sister's arm.

"A couple of hundred?" Ingrid wrapped her arms around the little girl and hugged her hard. Against the top of her head she muttered, "I don't want you to worry. It's only cows. At least we're safe, honey."

Luke managed a smile for Lily's benefit. "I checked my phone and there's no service up here. Why don't we head back down to the house and see if we can make a call?"

While Lily mounted and started ahead, Luke waited for Ingrid. As they rode slowly behind the little girl, he said quietly, "As soon as you get phone service, you need to phone the sheriff and report what you suspect. There may be other ranchers around here who've lost cattle, too. If so, he'll be aware of a pattern. But even if yours is the only ranch hit, someone may have spotted a convoy of cattle haulers in the area."

"If they came in the night, they could be across the border into Canada by now."

He heard the note of grim resignation in her voice and wished he could think of something to lift her spirits. But they both knew this was serious business.

Neither of them could pretend any longer. This was one more in a string of unexplained incidents. And they were all directed against Ingrid.

Several hours later, Sheriff Eugene Graystoke pulled up to the Larsen house. A beefy man with a booming gravel voice, he commanded respect from the ranchers in the area.

He climbed the back steps, but before he could knock on the door, Ingrid opened it.

"Miss Larsen?" He removed his hat and held it at his side while extending his other hand. "Sheriff Eugene Graystoke."

"Hello, Sheriff." She returned the handshake before indicating the girl behind her. "This is my sister, Lily."

The sheriff smiled at the little girl. "Hello, Lily."

"Hello. You look like those men on TV." Lily couldn't hide her fascination with his badge and uniform.

He chuckled. "Now if only I could be paid what they're paid, life would be good."

Ingrid stood aside. "Thank you for coming so quickly, Sheriff."

He walked into the mudroom and hung his hat on a peg by the door before scraping his boots.

She led the way into the kitchen, where Mick had a pot of coffee perking. "Sheriff Graystoke, I believe you met my foreman, Mick Hinkley."

"Yes. When your field caught fire. Hello again, Mick." The two shook hands. "Sorry I couldn't determine the cause of the fire, but with so many lightning strikes during summer storms, it was a good bet that it was purely nature and not anything sinister."

"I understand. Coffee, Sheriff?"

"I've never been known to refuse." He looked over when Luke walked into the room from the direction of the parlor.

"Luke Malloy. Didn't expect to see you. What are you doing way over here?"

"I took a nasty fall up in the hills and Ingrid brought me to her place and tended my wounds."

"You doing crazy tricks on that Harley again, Luke?"

Luke grinned and shook his head. "I was riding Turnip this time. Anyway, considering all the trouble it took getting me here, I figured I'd repay the favor by hanging around awhile and giving a hand with the ranch chores."

"That's nice of you. I'm sure your help is appreciated." The sheriff turned to Ingrid. "I knew your daddy. Lars was a good man. And an honest one. I never had a single complaint about him, and that's more than I can say about a lot of folks in this county."

He accepted a cup of coffee from Mick and then indicated the table. "Why don't we sit and you can tell me about this suspected rustling."

As quickly as she could, Ingrid explained about their late-morning ride and the number of cattle that were now missing from the herd. The sheriff listened intently and waited until she'd given him as many details as possible before he began asking a few questions.

"How many wranglers do you employ, Miss Larsen?"

"Just Mick. He can do just about anything around the ranch. He cooks, he does barn chores, and he often rides up to check on the herd."

"How about this spring? You say you had a record number of calves born this year. How many wranglers were here to lend a hand?"

"Just Mick and me. And my sister, Lily."

"Most calves need a lot of help being born. You and your little sister don't look strong enough to pull a calf from its ma."

"We were born on this ranch. We know how to do whatever's needed to survive."

The sheriff gave her an admiring look before flipping a page and making notations. "You say the herd numbered close to six hundred?"

She bit her lip and nodded.

"Did you comb the hills for your missing cattle?"

"No. There wasn't time."

"I see. Have you fired anybody lately?"

"Not since last year. After my father died, I had to let all the wranglers go. But I paid them their fair wages."

"I heard. I was sorry about your daddy. As I said, he was a good man." He looked up, meeting her direct gaze. "You have any known enemies, ma'am?"

She flushed. "There is a cowboy I ordered off my ranch at the end of my rifle."

"You threatened to shoot him?"

She nodded.

"Can you tell me why?"

She stared hard at the table. "I didn't like him. And I didn't trust him."

The sheriff set aside his empty cup. "Would you care to elaborate? What did he do to make you distrust him?"

"He..." She ran a finger around and around the rim of her cup before clenching her hands together in her lap. "My mother brought him home and said she was going to marry him. I couldn't stand to see him sleeping in my father's bed, sitting at my father's place at the table. He even started driving my father's truck."

Sheriff Graystoke's voice softened. "That's not a crime, ma'am."

"I know. But he was...I had a very bad feeling about him."

"You were about to say something more. He was what?"

She sighed. "Creepy."

"So you aimed your rifle at your mother's...friend and ordered him off the ranch. Could he be angry enough to want to retaliate?"

She nodded. "He said as much."

"Can you give me his name?"

"Lon Wardell."

He scribbled in his notes before looking up with a distinct frown. "Are there any more people you can think of who might want to do damage to you or your ranch?"

"My neighbor, Bull Hammond."

"He has a reason?"

"He offered to buy the ranch from my mother. I asked

her to wait until roundup, to see if there was enough profit from the herd to buy it myself."

The sheriff looked puzzled. "If your mother owns this ranch, doesn't the herd belong to her?"

Ingrid shook her head. "My father's will stated that my mother owns the ranch, with all its property and buildings, but the herd belongs to me."

"So the only one harmed by this theft is you. It doesn't affect your mother's interest in the ranch?"

"That's right."

"Would that be common knowledge to Wardell or Hammond?"

She shrugged. "Only if Nadine told them."

Within half an hour he had as many facts as she was able to give. When the sheriff got ready to leave, Luke offered to walk with him to his vehicle.

They paused outside the police car. Luke leaned close. "You heard what Ingrid had to say. What do you know about Wardell and Hammond?"

"Wardell's bad company. A loose cannon. I have a file of paperwork on him as long as my arm. Wardell has been drifting from ranch to ranch in these parts for as long as I've been sheriff here. He's never been able to hold a job for long."

"He worked our place when I was just a kid. I know he was fired for stealing. Is there more?"

Eugene Graystoke shrugged. "Larceny, mostly. If it isn't nailed down, Wardell will find a fence willing to buy just about anything. Then he spends the money on booze. Most bartenders know whether he stole something big or small by the amount of time he stays drunk."

"Bull Hammond? What do you know about him?"

"A bully. Likes to throw his weight around. I heard years ago there was bad blood between him and Lars Larsen. Never heard what the beef was about, but I wouldn't be surprised if he still carries a grudge, even though Lars is in the ground. But there's no official complaints on file. I'd say Larsen's daughter better watch her back with those two out to cause trouble."

"There's more." Luke proceeded to tell the sheriff about the shot fired at the mustangs, the suspicious fire in the hayfield, the mysterious death of Ingrid's dog, and the ugly incident between Nadine, Lon Wardell, Ingrid, and himself the night before.

With a muttered oath, Sheriff Graystoke tossed his notebook into the car before settling himself in the driver's seat. "I think I'll take a ride to Wayside and have a chat with the bartender at Barney's. See if he knows anything. Most bar owners are able to hear more in a single drunken night than a lawman can learn in weeks of investigating."

He gave Luke a long, level look. "It may be nothing more than cattle straying from their usual pasture. Or we may be dealing with cattle rustling. But if what you've told me turns out to be deliberate, and not accidental, we may have something much more serious going on here. That young woman's life could be in danger."

"Then I guess that means I'm staying on."

The sheriff raised a brow. "You in this for the excitement? Or is that pretty lady the reason you're staying?"

Luke gave the sheriff the famous Malloy smile. "I'm not sure myself. I guess a little of both."

CHAPTER ELEVEN

Roast beef and mashed potatoes?" Ingrid stepped into the kitchen and breathed deeply. "What's the occasion, Mick?"

Luke stepped in behind her, trailed by Lily, who'd worked alongside Ingrid and Luke in the barn, finishing up the last of the evening's chores.

Mick looked up from the oven, where a cloud of fragrant steam was drifting. "Are you saying there has to be something special to enjoy a good meal?"

"All your meals are great, Mick." Ingrid paused beside her place at the table and held up a tall glass filled with ice water. "But this is the first time I've ever seen you do this." She drained it in one long, parched swallow.

"I figured you'd be thirsty after all that work." Mick reached into the refrigerator and removed two frosty longnecks, handing one to Luke. When Ingrid shook her head in refusal, he twisted the top off the other and took a drink. "Figured you've earned a thirst quencher, too, son."

After a long pull, Luke shot the old man a wide smile. "Now that was worth working up a sweat. Thanks, Mick."

Lily spotted the glass of milk beside her plate and needed no coaxing to enjoy the surprise.

"You can all sit." Mick began setting out a platter of roast beef swimming in gravy. The meat was so tender it fell off the bone. There was also a big bowl of steaming mashed potatoes, dotted with butter. The green beans were from the little patch of garden Mick tended all summer on the far side of the house. There was even a plate of store-bought rolls from the freezer, thawed in the oven until they were all soft and doughy, to mop up the gravy.

For nearly ten minutes nobody said a word. The kitchen was peppered with sighs and murmurs of approval as they dug in.

Finally, after her plate was empty and she'd finished her second glass of milk, Lily looked across the table at Luke. "Does your cook make roast beef like Mick?"

"He makes a lot of beef dishes. We are, after all, a cattle ranch." Luke shot the old man a smile. "But right this minute, I doubt anybody could match what your cook just did."

Mick gave a loud laugh. "Looks like all that flattery means somebody's hoping for thirds."

Luke shook his head. "I've already had seconds, and I'm as stuffed as a sausage."

That had Lily giggling.

Luke was careful not to look at Ingrid, but instead kept his eyes downcast. "I've been thinking that you all deserve a break from ranch chores. What would you think about driving over to my family ranch?"

Lily clapped her hands and turned to her sister. "Oh boy. Can we, Ingrid? Can we? Please?"

"A break would be nice if we had wranglers." Ingrid looked away from the pleading look in her sister's eyes. "But I don't see how it's possible. The ranch depends on all of us working together. Who would muck the stalls? What if the rest of the herd should disappear?"

Luke drained his beer. "The horses could be put to pasture. As for the rustling, it happened when we were all here. If thieves have targeted your herd, nothing will stop them except the presence of wranglers keeping watch."

"Fine." Ingrid crossed her arms over her chest. "Then I'll keep watch tonight."

"You think men bent on stealing are going to be stopped by one woman?"

She narrowed her gaze on him. "A woman with a rifle holds the same firepower as a man."

"I'll grant you that. But if there are enough rustlers, their sheer numbers will overwhelm you before you can stop all of them."

"If my dog Tippy were still here"—she looked on the verge of sudden, unexpected tears—"this never could have happened. That herd was as much his as ours, and he'd have fought to the last breath to save them from strangers."

Luke arched a brow. "Did anyone else know he was attached to the herd?"

She shrugged. "I guess just about everyone around here knew. Tippy could do the work of half a dozen wranglers. And he didn't need a rifle. He had his teeth. He used them to nip at the stray cows, and he'd have used them on anyone trying to encroach on his territory."

"So his death was more than a personal loss. He was the herd's guardian." Luke considered before adding, "All right. If you insist on staying with the herd tonight, I'm going along."

"I don't need a babysitter."

He merely smiled. "I'm well aware of that. But you have to admit that a second gun would be comfort during a raid."

Lily spoke up in a sad voice. "What about me? If you both go, I'll be all alone upstairs."

"It's only for a night, honey." Ingrid glanced at Mick, hoping he might calm the girl's fears.

Instead, the old man sided with Lily. "I don't like the idea of us splitting up. Too much going on around here. There's safety in numbers. If you want my vote, I say we either all stay in the hills with the herd, or we all stay here and trust that the cattle rustling was a onetime incident."

Ingrid fell silent as she mulled their options. On the one hand, she needed to hold on to what was left of her herd. On the other hand, she had no right to deny the rest of them, who worked so hard all day, the chance for a little rest from the grind.

Tapping her finger against the table edge, she gave voice to her thoughts. "I'm trying to think like someone with a grudge to settle. I guess it doesn't much matter whether we stay here or spend a night up in the hills. If we're here, the rest of the cattle could be gone by morning. If we go, we're draining our energy for the day ahead."

Mick watched her for a minute longer. "So. What'll it be?"

Ingrid gave a curt shrug of her shoulders. "We'll stay here."

Luke shoved away from the table. "Well, now that that's settled, it's time to thank Mick by cleaning up this kitchen."

As Ingrid started to rise, he turned to Lily. "I'm thinking we'll give your big sister a break, and you and I will do the dishes."

"Okay." The little girl was up and reaching for a dish towel before Luke had time to fill the sink.

Grateful for the break, Ingrid headed to the parlor to work on her ledgers.

Mick, free for the evening, drifted off to his room to watch television.

"Tell me more about your grandparents, Luke." Lily picked up a plate and dried it carefully before setting it on a shelf.

Luke realized the little girl was fixated on the things she'd never had. "My grandfather is Francis Xavier Malloy."

"That's a funny name."

"You think so?" He considered. "I guess it is to some people, but it doesn't matter. I never call him that anyway. I call him Grandpop, but my grandmother calls him Frankie."

"What's your grandmother's name?"

"We all call her Gram Gracie. And Grandpop calls her his Gracie Girl."

"Is she real old?"

"She would probably seem that way to you. But she's not as old as her father, the Great One."

"Why do you call him that?"

"Because when I was a kid, it was easier to say that than to call him Great-Grandpop. Besides, when he first came to live with us, he was a stuffed shirt, and not at all like the grandfatherly type. So he became the Great One. He loves the name."

"What's a stuffed shirt?"

"A person who's so stiff and formal, he'd probably break in half if he ever tried to bend the rules a little."

"Is he still like that?"

Luke thought a minute. "He's about as far removed from being a stuffed shirt as he'll ever be. He still misses the good life he left behind in Hollywood, but he's learned to love the ranch, too."

"Do your grandpop Frank and gram Gracie sit by the fire with a blanket over their laps, like the grandparents in my books?"

That had Luke chuckling. "Don't ever suggest that if you're around them. Grandpop can still work as hard as any wrangler on our ranch. And my gram Gracie often rides up in the hills for weeks at a time on her safaris."

"What are safaris?"

"That's what people call travels in Africa to study wild animals. But here it just means a trip to the hills for a few days."

"Oh. I read about Africa in my geography book. Next time, I hope I read about safaris. How about your . . . Great One? Does he sit around with a blanket on his lap?"

"Never. He keeps everyone in the family on their toes with his outrageous demands."

"Like what?"

"Well, for one thing, he loves exotic food and drinks."

LUKE 453

"What's exotic?"

"Fancy-schmancy meals you'd find in the most expensive restaurants in the world."

That had Lily giggling behind her hand. "Does he ever get any?"

"Does he ever. Yancy is constantly surprising him by making them exactly as the Great One remembers from his younger Hollywood days."

"You keep saying that. What are Hollywood days?"

"That's where the Great One lived and worked."

"Oh." The little girl looked suitably impressed. "Does the Great One drink"—she had to think a moment before continuing—"fancy-schmancy drinks, too? Or does he drink longnecks like you and Mick?"

Luke gave a snort of laughter. "Li'l Bit, he considers beer lower than soda pop. He prefers martinis. He calls that a gentleman's drink."

"And does Yancy make what the Great One likes?"

"You bet." He bent down, as though telling her a grand secret. "You know what?"

"What?" The single word was a whisper while her eyes went wide.

"I'd rather have an ice-cold longneck and Mick's roast beef anytime, but I'd never admit that to Yancy or the Great One."

She giggled.

After finishing the dishes, they strolled into the parlor, where Ingrid was busy at the desk.

She looked up at the clock on the mantel. "You two took your time."

Lily's smile was radiant. "Luke was telling me all about his grandparents, Frankie and Grace, and his great-grandfather the Great One. His grandma goes on…" Forgetting the rest of it, she looked over at Luke.

"Safaris."

"That's right. Safaris. That's what they call adventures in Africa to see wild animals."

Ingrid arched a brow. "That's pretty impressive." She turned to Luke. "You sure you aren't a teacher posing as a rancher?"

He gave a mock bow. "Just one of my many talents, ma'am."

They shared a laugh.

Seeing Lily yawning behind her hand, Ingrid said, "You may want to skip playing Fish tonight and save it for another night when you're awake enough to beat Luke."

"Okay." Lily smiled up at him. "Can we play tomorrow instead?"

"Sure thing." He winked. "Since I intend to win, I'd rather beat you when you're in fighting form."

Laughing, she called, "'Night, Luke. I loved hearing about your family."

"'Night, Li'l Bit. I loved talking about them."

Ingrid sealed an envelope and returned a pile of bills to a file folder. "I'll be upstairs in a few minutes, honey."

A short time later, as she got to her feet and started up the stairs, she hugged her arms to her chest at the sound of thunder in the distance. "Getting colder outside. Storm's coming."

Ingrid descended the stairs to find Luke in the parlor, seated in front of a roaring fire.

Some of the sadness disappeared from her eyes. "Oh, that feels good."

Seeing the way she eyed the paperwork piled on her desk, he held up a longneck and indicated the rocker beside his. "Let it go. You've done enough for one day."

She settled herself in the rocker and gave a soft sigh. "No matter what I do, it's never enough." She glanced at the bottle in his hand. "Where did you find that?"

"Hidden behind the milk. I hope it's not part of Mick's stash." He took a long pull before passing it to her.

She took a grateful sip. Suddenly, her eyes danced with laughter. "That old sweetie. Do you think he was hiding this?"

"Could be. But at least he shared some over supper. If I find out this one is his last, I'll have to make a trip to town tomorrow and restock the larder."

Ingrid laughed and leaned her head back, letting the heat of the fire seep into her bones. "Do you want to know what Lily prayed for tonight?"

He looked over.

"You and your family." She turned her head slightly, meeting his gaze. "She's falling under your spell, you know."

"That's awesome."

"You mean an awesome responsibility."

"What's that supposed to mean?"

She took another drink of beer before passing the bottle back to him. "It means you're becoming important in her young life. She looks up to you, Luke. I hope you realize how serious that can be to a little girl."

He nodded. "She's become special to me, too. She's a really sweet kid. And that's a tribute to you. Mick told me you're more a mother to her than Nadine is. Seeing the two of you together, I agree. You're setting a fine example for Lily. She's smart and independent. She's got the whole world ahead of her."

"I hope you're right."

When he offered her another drink, she shook her head. "Thanks. I've had enough. You finish it."

He emptied the bottle and set it aside.

They sat in companionable silence for long minutes, enjoying the sizzle of flames, the soft patter of rain on the roof.

Ingrid roused herself enough to push out of the rocker and get to her feet. "If I stay here any longer, I'll be asleep. This was nice. Thanks for sharing. Good night, Luke."

"'Night."

At the stairway she paused. "Do you want the light on or off?"

"You can turn it off. I'll just wait until the fire burns low before I head up."

When she was gone, he sat staring into the flames. He couldn't remember the last time he'd spent an evening just sitting with a woman in front of the fire, without making a move. But with Ingrid, it seemed the most natural thing in the world.

Had it been his imagination, or was she beginning to soften toward him?

Not that it mattered, he thought. Neither of them had time to develop a relationship. He was just putting off the inevitable. Though he was reluctant to leave until the sheriff resolved this situation, he knew it was only a matter of time. Sooner or later they would be able to get on with their lives, and he would return to his own ranch. He knew his family was able to function without him, but there was a certain amount of guilt knowing he was neglecting his own herds to help Ingrid with hers.

He checked the grate and closed the fire screen before heading up the stairs.

In his room he didn't bother with the light as he nudged off his boots and tossed his shirt on a chair.

He'd just unsnapped his jeans when he heard a sound like a gunshot, and for a moment his hands paused in midair.

Thunder? It sounded close, too.

At the same instant, he heard the distinct splinter of glass.

In one quick motion he snatched up his rifle and made a frantic dash down the hall, kicking in the door to Ingrid's room.

She was standing in a pool of lamplight, staring at the shattered glass that littered her bedroom floor.

Luke snapped off the light and threw himself against her, using the weight of his body to press her into the shadows before rushing to the broken window.

Instead of gunshots, all he could hear was the sound of an engine. Instead of a shooter, all he could see was the glare of red taillights as a truck disappeared into the night.

CHAPTER TWELVE

Luke turned to Ingrid. She hadn't moved. Her eyes, wide and unblinking, mirrored the shock she was feeling. She looked absolutely thunderstruck.

He crossed the room and cupped his palm to her cheek. "You okay?"

"I...yes. I guess so. I didn't even know what I'd heard at first. Then the window shattered, and I..." A shudder passed through her.

Seeing her delayed reaction, he gathered her close and simply held her as tremor after tremor rocked her.

She stood still, absorbing his quiet strength and breathing deeply before pushing a little away. "I know I should have dropped to the floor, but I couldn't seem to move. I felt nailed to the spot. I know it was wrong. I was making myself even more of a target, but I..." She let the words trail off.

"It's a natural reaction when your life is threatened. You freeze."

"I've never…" She tried again. "I've never been in the line of fire before." Her hand went to her mouth. "Oh, Luke, what if that had been Lily?"

"Hey now. Don't go there." He closed his hands over her shoulders and simply held her.

Mick raced into the room, red-eyed and bewhiskered, wearing a ratty robe hastily tossed over his long johns. "I heard a gunshot."

He looked down at the glass littering the floor, before his eyes narrowed on Ingrid. "You hurt, girl?"

"No. But whoever fired that shot had time to fire again. If Luke hadn't come racing in to drag me out of the light, I could be dead by now."

The old man had to clear his throat several times before he managed to say, "I'm glad you were here, son."

"Me too." Luke kept his hand on Ingrid's shoulder, propelling her toward the doorway. "Let's go downstairs and call the sheriff."

Seeing the door to Lily's room still closed, Ingrid stepped inside quietly to assure herself that the little girl was safe and sleeping.

Luke took those few moments to return to his room for his shirt and boots.

When Ingrid emerged, she said softly, "I guess she slept right through it."

"Good." Luke took her hand as they descended the stairs, as much for himself as for her. He felt the need to hold on to her, to be assured that she was truly safe.

Once in the kitchen, Luke phoned Eugene Graystoke, while Mick started a fresh pot of coffee.

The three of them sat around the table, talking in low tones.

"Did you recognize the vehicle?" Mick eyed Luke over the rim of his cup.

"It was too dark. All I could see were the taillights."

"I wonder how long the shooter was standing out there in the night, waiting for a light to go on upstairs."

Luke nodded. "I was just wondering the same thing." He turned to Ingrid. "If you had a dog, a big, barking dog, this couldn't have happened. You would have had plenty of warning."

"Tippy was big. And loyal. And fierce." She pressed a fist to her mouth to stop her lips from trembling. "A lot of good it did."

He reached over to close a hand on hers.

By the time they heard the crunch of tires on the gravel driveway an hour later, the three of them had gone over every detail of those few moments, speculating on the shooter, without once mentioning the names of the two men they suspected of having done the deed.

Sheriff Graystoke's face was grim as he greeted them and sat at the table to hear the details.

Mick handed him a steaming cup of coffee, which he barely tasted. "I want to see your room, Miss Larsen."

When Ingrid started to stand, Luke saw the weariness in her eyes and gave a quick shake of his head. "I'll go up. You stay here with Mick." To the sheriff he explained, "Lily is still asleep up there. We'll need to keep things quiet."

Eugene nodded in understanding. "No need for words. I just need to see the crime scene."

Luke led the way up the stairs. Once in Ingrid's bedroom, Luke snapped on the light to allow the sheriff to study the shattered window and the shards of glass littering the floor.

After several minutes staring out the window, Eugene Graystoke turned toward the doorway. "Leave the light on while I head downstairs. I want to see what it looks like from outside."

In the kitchen, the sheriff asked Ingrid to go to her room and stand in the spot where she'd been standing when the gunshot occurred.

Seeing the look in her eyes, Mick got slowly to his feet. "I'm going with you, girl."

While Ingrid and Mick made their way to her room, Luke and Graystoke walked outside to stand in the yard below Ingrid's window.

As she came into view above them, the sheriff's eyes narrowed in concentration. "Look at her. As clear as if she's onstage in a spotlight." He hissed out an oath of frustration. "Nobody in these parts ever feels the need to draw down a shade or close a drape. We don't expect something like this in the middle of nowhere. At least"—he spat a curse—"not on my watch."

Luke's voice was rough with anger. "I know you take it personally, Eugene. So do I."

The sheriff turned to look at him. "What's eating at me is the fact that I don't have the manpower to keep Ingrid and her sister safe, Luke."

"I do." Luke's eyes were hard as flint. "Now I just have to find a way to persuade them to come home with me."

"That would solve the problem, at least in the short term." Eugene started toward the back porch. "Maybe I can help."

* * *

The sheriff sat at the kitchen table, completing his report. While he worked, he accepted a plate of scrambled eggs and bacon from Mick's hand. He watched as the old man worked off his frustration at the stove. But when Mick tried to get Ingrid to eat, she refused, choosing instead to drink coffee and pace the length of the kitchen and back.

Across the room, Luke watched in silence, knowing each of them had to deal with their fears in their own way.

Finally Eugene Graystoke tucked away his papers and drained his fourth cup of coffee.

Ingrid stopped her pacing and took a seat across from him at the table. "Well?"

He steepled his hands. "I'll send my deputy Archer Stone out here at first light to scour the area and see if he can find any shell casings. The rain will probably wash away the tire tracks. If there's even a trace, I'll have Archer make a mold for the state police to trace. I also intend to interview both Lon Wardell and Bull Hammond. But I have to confess, without hard evidence, this isn't something easily resolved. And while I'm in the mood for some honesty, I might as well tell you that this was no random act. You were clearly the intended victim of this shooting. From where I was standing outside, there was no mistaking you in the window."

He watched Ingrid's face grow pale and lowered his voice. "Miss Larsen, it's my duty as a lawman to advise you to seek a safe haven."

Her chin lifted in a gesture of defiance. "Are you saying I should leave my own home?"

"I'm not talking about forever. But I do believe you

should leave here for a while. At least until this shooter is identified."

She got to her feet. "I have a ranch to run. A ranch I could lose if I don't keep a tight rein on things."

"The ranch isn't nearly as important as the life you could lose." Before she could protest, he added, "If you're not worried about yourself, I urge you to think about that little girl asleep upstairs."

"Lily?" Visibly shaken, she sank back down to her chair. "You think someone would harm her?"

"What better way to hurt you than to hurt the ones you love?"

His words brought a stunned silence to the room. Ingrid turned to look at Mick, whose hand had paused in midair. His brow was creased in a frown.

"My family ranch can offer a safe haven, Sheriff." Luke's voice, calm and assured, had Ingrid looking up. "Our house is big enough to accommodate a dozen houseguests without even feeling crowded. And there are enough wranglers around that anyone foolish enough to try to invade our space and cause any trouble to a guest would be outnumbered ten to one."

The sheriff sat back with a look of satisfaction. "There you go, Miss Larsen."

She was already shaking her head. "We're strangers. We couldn't possibly just barge in and—"

"But you're not strangers. You're my friends." Luke's tone was calm and reasonable. "You've already met my uncle Colin and our foreman, Burke. The rest of my family will make you feel so welcome, you'll think you're part of the family in no time."

"Luke isn't exaggerating. The Malloy family is just

about the most accommodating in Montana." Eugene Graystoke got to his feet. "At least think about it, Miss Larsen. For the sake of your little sister."

He reached across the table to shake Ingrid's hand and then Mick's, before heading for the mudroom and motioning for Luke to follow. At the back door he took his hat from a hook on the wall before stepping outside.

Luke offered his hand. "Thanks, Eugene. I think using her fear for Lily's safety will be the deciding factor."

The sheriff gave a grim smile. "That may take care of the immediate danger. But think about this, Luke. This thing could go on for months. And I'm worried that our shooter will try again, whenever he gets an opportunity. Next time, he may not miss."

"You think I haven't already thought of that?" Luke was equally grim. "But for now, I just want them all safe and out of harm's way. After that, I'll have to take it day by day."

The sheriff started down the porch steps. "I intend to ask the state boys for help in this. In the beginning, it sounded more like an insult against the mother's boyfriend, or a feud between neighbors. Now it's become attempted murder. This is getting too complicated, and too dangerous, to stand by and wait for the next shoe to drop."

"I agree. Tonight has changed everything." Luke took in a breath. "Thanks for all your help, Eugene."

He turned and made his way back to the kitchen, where Ingrid and Mick were having a spirited conversation.

"What do I do about the herd up in the hills?" Ingrid was pacing, arms crossed over her chest. "Or what's left of them?"

"They're up there right now without any wranglers.

They can certainly make it a few more days without you, girl." Mick scrubbed the skillet until it gleamed, then continued scrubbing it viciously, taking out his frustration in any way he could.

"And this house?" Ingrid stabbed a finger in the old cowboy's chest. "What if Nadine comes home and finds it empty?"

"So what?" Mick caught her wrist and lowered her hand to her side.

"So, she could decide to move Lon in while we're away. What's to stop her?"

"Let him move in." The old man looked around. "What can he do to this old place to make things worse than they already are?"

Ingrid flinched. "I'm not worried about him trashing it. But he'll be free to go through my private things. The mail. The bills and receipts. The ledgers. I don't want him knowing my business."

"Neither do I, girl. But if it's a choice between staying here and being shot at like fish in a barrel or leaving the house open to prying eyes, I vote for hightailing it out of here and taking Luke up on his generous offer."

Ingrid's eyes flashed fire as she turned away and began more pacing.

Luke poured himself yet another cup of coffee and sat quietly, letting the two of them go at it.

It looked as though it would be a very long night, with no one but Lily getting any sleep at all. But at least, he thought with a clenched jaw, they'd make it through the night alive.

Things could have taken a very different, and very violent turn, if the shooter had been successful.

The thought of someone standing in the dark, taking aim at an unsuspecting woman, had Luke itching for a good knock-down, drag-out fight. It would be so much more satisfying than sitting around and watching Ingrid and Mick verbally sparring. But for now, since the coward had slunk away under cover of darkness, he was forced to make do with this.

And to hope that in the light of morning, Ingrid would relent.

CHAPTER THIRTEEN

Oh boy. Are we really going to stay at your ranch overnight?" Lily was too excited to sit still. She and Mick were in the backseat, where Lily continued to bounce as much as her seat belt would allow.

Ingrid drove her battered truck, with Luke in the passenger seat. Towed behind them was a horse trailer holding Turnip.

Before Lily woke, the three of them had agreed to say nothing to her about the shooting. The little girl was told only that Luke needed to see his family and had invited them along. After morning chores, the horses had been turned out into a fenced meadow.

"Yes, we are, Li'l Bit. Or maybe more than a night, if we can persuade your sister."

Ingrid shot Luke a dark look before returning her attention to the highway. She had agreed to one night. Beyond that, she'd refused to speculate.

Lily missed the look. She was too busy playing tutor to poor, patient Mick.

"Now remember their names, Mick." Lily held up her hand, counting off each name on a finger. "There's the Great One. He's Luke's great-grandfather. He likes to eat and drink fancy-schmancy stuff like he did in Hollywood. Isn't that right, Luke?"

Luke couldn't help chuckling at her dead-on repeating of his own words. "Right you are."

"And then there's Gram Gracie and Grandpop. That's Luke's grandpa, Frankie," she added in an aside. "Then there's Luke's uncle Colin and Burke, the ranch foreman. We already met them when they flew in to take Luke home. But you didn't go home with them, did you, Luke?"

"That's right."

"Next are Matt and Reed, Luke's brothers, and Matt's new bride, Vanessa. Luke says she's really pretty, and down-to-earth for a big-city lawyer. And there's Yancy, the cook and housekeeper."

"You might not want to call him our housekeeper," Luke said with a wink. "He prefers to think of himself as simply a cook."

"Okay." The little girl was beaming. "When will we be there?"

"Not long now. We've been on our land for the last half an hour."

Ingrid's eyes went wide. "This is all your land?"

Luke leaned an elbow out the window, enjoying the view. "Yeah. I didn't realize how much I've missed it."

"But"—she allowed her gaze to sweep the rolling hills, folding one into the other, and all of them dotted with cattle as far as the eye could see—"it goes on for miles."

"That's Montana for you. More cattle than people."

Her voice lowered. "Looks like half the state belongs to you."

"To my family," he corrected with a grin. "Just around this bend you'll see the house."

They came up over a rise, and as they followed the curving gravel road, they caught sight of the sprawling ranch house in the distance and, beyond it, several barns and outbuildings, and not a one of them in need of paint.

The house was an ageless structure, three stories of stone and wood, looking as though it had sprung fully built from the towering hills and mountains looming up behind it. The barns and outbuildings were the same dark wood, gleaming in the sunlight.

For the longest time everyone fell silent. Then, as they drew near, Ingrid couldn't contain herself. "Oh my." She pulled up behind several ranch trucks parked in a row, and all bearing the logo of the Malloy Ranch.

Luke's smile grew. "Looks like everyone's here." He held up his cell phone. "I called ahead."

"It's nice to know we're not just crashing." Ingrid turned off the ignition and sat very still, fighting nerves.

Seeing it, Luke stepped down and circled around to open the driver's-side door and take her hand. "Come on. They don't bite."

Lily and Mick were already out of the truck and stood waiting for Luke and Ingrid to lead the way. Before they could climb the steps, the back door was thrust open and the family spilled out onto the wide porch.

"About time you came home, sonny boy." Frank

slapped Luke on the shoulder hard enough to jar his teeth.

Gracie hurried forward to hug her grandson before turning to the others. "Welcome to our home. We're so happy to see all of you."

"Gram Gracie, this is Ingrid Larsen and her sister, Lily."

Instead of the expected handshake, Gracie surprised Ingrid with a warm embrace, before turning to Lily and gathering her close with a murmured, "Oh. Finally. Some girls to even the score against all these Malloy men."

The smile on the little girl's face put the sunshine to shame.

Grace indicated the immaculately groomed man standing in the doorway, his white hair flowing like an aged lion's mane; a blue silk ascot was tied rakishly at his throat. "This is my father, Nelson."

"I know you," Lily said with excitement.

The old man's eyes lit with pleasure. "A bit young to know about my reputation, don't you think?"

"You're the Great One. Luke's great-grandfather."

"Oh, that." He gave a shrug of his shoulders. "Yes, indeed, I am. And you may call me Great One."

Luke indicated the old man in faded denims and scuffed boots. "This is Mick Hinkley, Ingrid's foreman."

Frank and Grace shook the old cowboy's hand before turning to handle the rest of the introductions.

"You've already met Colin. And this is our oldest grandson, Matt, and his wife, Vanessa."

While the others shook hands, Lily couldn't hold back. "You're as pretty as Luke said."

Vanessa dimpled. "Thank you, Lily." She turned to Luke. "And thank you, brother-in-law. You think I'm pretty? I don't believe you've ever said that before."

Luke shot her a wicked grin. "Just a slip of the tongue. Don't let it go to your head."

Frank turned to the others. "This is my youngest grandson, Reed."

Lily stared up at the tall, handsome cowboy to say loudly, "Youngest? But you're as old as Luke."

"Wrong, Li'l Bit," Luke said above the laughter. "He may be taller, but he's a year younger. That makes him the baby of the family."

Reed knelt solemnly in front of the little girl and held out his hand. "Hi, Lily. I'm sorry you had to put up with my brother, but now that you're here, I'll show you how to avoid being stuck with him."

"Oh, I don't mind." She missed the joke entirely as she looked at Luke adoringly. "Luke said he likes tomboys. Luke's my friend."

Reed got to his feet. "Just so he's not your boyfriend."

She put her hands on her hips. "He's too old for that. Besides, I think he'd rather be Ingrid's boyfriend."

That had everyone laughing and punching Luke's shoulder, while Ingrid's face flamed.

Gracie turned to the man with the bowl haircut standing in the doorway. "This is Yancy Martin."

As the others shook Yancy's hand, Lily dashed forward, then stopped in her tracks, her eyes growing round. "You're not much bigger than me."

Grinning, Yancy held out an arm, as though measuring her against himself. "Oh, I know I'm short, but I think you need a couple of years to catch up to me."

"I like having someone almost my size. Luke said you're the best cook in Montana."

Yancy's smile went up several notches. "He did?"

Luke shrugged. "I must have said it in a moment of weakness."

"Or hunger," Reed said to the others' laughter.

Burke ambled up from one of the barns after turning Turnip into a stall and joined in the handshakes.

"Let's go inside." Gracie led the way through the mudroom and into the large kitchen, with everyone following.

While the others laughed and chatted, Ingrid paused in the doorway and simply stared around the big, sunny room, where an oversized harvest table was set for supper, with colorful, matching plates and napkins. Across the room in an alcove of tall windows stood several overstuffed chairs and a sofa, where the family now gravitated while Yancy set out several plates of fruit and cheese, assorted crackers and small, round slices of bread, and a bowl of cheese dip on the low coffee table. A tray on the kitchen counter held frosty longnecks and several glasses of different beverages.

Luke offered Lily a glass of lemonade before handing a longneck to Mick. The old man shot him a grateful smile.

Gracie crossed the room to loop her arm through Ingrid's. "Feeling a little overwhelmed?"

Ingrid nodded. "Yes. Does it show?"

"Not at all. Come on." The older woman handed her a glass of white wine and walked beside her, drawing her toward the others, who were all enchanted by Lily, who was chattering like a magpie.

"Luke and I play Fish every night before I go to bed, and he hardly ever beats me."

"Fish?" Reed shot his brother a look. "Just don't let him offer to teach you poker, Lily."

"He's trying to. Ingrid said she wants us to stick to Fish."

"Smart woman." Reed turned to include Ingrid in the conversation. "Luke may be a lousy Fish player, but nobody can beat him at poker. So if you play him, don't play for money."

Lily said proudly, "We play for chores. And Luke has to do my share of mucking stalls whenever I win."

Nelson looked up from his favorite overstuffed chair, where he was enjoying a martini. "You play for chores?" He looked from Lily to his great-grandson. "I guess that makes sense."

He turned to his daughter. "Grace Anne, watching and listening to this lovely child has made me realize she would have been perfect in the role of Megan in my movie *Divine*."

Grace studied Lily before nodding. "I believe you're right, Dad. It wouldn't have been a stretch for her to play a girl who talks to animals. And she'd have been so much better than that awful child star you hired."

"A horrid little diva. And her mother was even worse." He gave a mock shudder.

Ingrid went very still as the truth dawned. "Oh my goodness. You're that Nelson LaRou. The famous Hollywood director."

Nelson couldn't have been more pleased. He puffed up his chest. "Right you are, Ingrid. I thought perhaps Luke would have mentioned me."

"He did. But I must have missed the part where he said how famous you are."

"Yes, he did." Lily looked confused. "He said you're his great-grandpa. Aren't you?"

"Indeed I am. But long before Luke was born, I was a Hollywood director, handling all the rich and famous movie stars."

Lily's eyes went wide. "Do you know Justin Bieber?"

It was Nelson's turn to look confused. "I haven't a clue whom that might be. And I pride myself on knowing the name of every famous actor from the thirties to the sixties."

Ingrid sighed. "He sings. And happens to be Lily's current crush."

The little girl shot her sister an indignant look. "He is not. You take that back. You know I don't like boys."

Ingrid gave her a gentle smile. "Sorry. You're right. That's too personal. Justin isn't your current crush."

"I think Luke is," Reed said with a wink.

Instead of a denial, Lily's face colored.

Grace quickly changed the subject to spare the poor child's feelings. "Tell us about your ranch, Ingrid."

Ingrid took a sip of wine to cover her embarrassment at being singled out. "I'm afraid it's small and insignificant next to all this."

"Nonsense," Frank Malloy was quick to add. "Every rancher knows it isn't the size of the ranch that matters; it's the heart and soul the rancher pours into it that counts."

"If that's all it takes," old Mick said with a grin, "then Ingrid's spread is as big as the state of Montana. She pours everything she has into that place."

"Good for you, Ingrid." Frank glanced out the window at a clap of thunder. "It was sunny just a few minutes ago."

Old Mick rubbed his shoulder. "I could've told you

it was going to rain. These old bones know long before those TV weatherpeople do."

Burke nodded. "I know what you mean. I'm getting better at predicting the weather every year."

Lily looked from one to the other. "Can my bones tell me when it's going to rain?"

"I'm afraid you're just going to have to wait until you're as old as us," Mick said with a laugh.

Lily turned to Nelson. "Your bones are even older than theirs. Can you tell when it's going to rain, Great One?"

His laughter rang through the room. "When you get to be my age, every little ache and pain can predict rain, snow, and even a cloud in the sky."

"See." She looked around at the others. "And that's why he's the Great One."

Luke winked at Ingrid before turning to her sister. "You got that right. And don't you forget it, Li'l Bit."

Just then Lily caught sight of a framed photograph hanging across the room. She pointed. "Look, Ingrid. They have the same picture I have hanging in my bedroom. Only mine is smaller."

"You have this one?" Grace started across the room.

Lily trailed behind her. "Uh-huh." She pointed to the stallion watching over his herd of mustang mares. "I've seen him. I've seen all of them. They're my herd."

Grace's brows shot up. "Yours?"

"Well, not mine exactly. But I see them sometimes up in the hills. I even took some pictures of them, didn't I, Ingrid?"

Her big sister nodded. "Quite a few, as a matter of fact. I don't know which she loves more: her herd or her camera."

"You love taking pictures?" Grace looked excitedly at the little girl.

"Uh-huh. Ingrid gave me our daddy's camera. I take it with me everywhere."

"Remind me to show you some more pictures I've taken of...your herd as well as several other herds."

"This is yours?" Lily moved closer, and as she read the name in the lower right hand corner, her eyes went wide. "This says Grace Anne LaRou Malloy." She turned to Grace. "I've got your picture hanging in my bedroom. Are you famous?"

"Maybe. To some who love photographs of mustangs."

Frank ambled over to drop an arm around his wife's shoulders. "My Gracie Girl is being modest. She's spent a lifetime photographing mustangs here in Montana and has earned quite a fine reputation around the world for her work."

"Oh boy." Lily's eyes were shining with excitement.

Yancy announced that supper was ready. As they gravitated toward the table, Lily saw Nelson struggling to ease himself out of his overstuffed chair.

She raced over and caught his hand. "Come on, Great One."

As the rest of the family stared in surprise, Nelson kept the little girl's hand in his as he allowed himself to be led to the table. When he was seated, he patted the chair beside his. "You can sit here, Lily."

"Thank you." As she settled in, looks were exchanged.

The stern Hollywood director they all knew and loved had made no secret of his disdain for the children he'd been forced to work with through the years. He'd once remarked that he'd rather work with the devil himself than deal with a single heavenly cherub who always proved to be sugar and spice only on the outside, with vinegar and acid in his or her tiny, shriveled little heart.

Apparently the little tomboy with the wild tangle of hair and the wide, trusting eyes had just become the exception to Nelson's self-proclaimed rule. The family wasn't quite certain how this had happened.

Was it her admiration for his daughter, Grace Anne, that endeared her to him? Or was it her sweet, sunny nature and her concern for an old man's welfare?

Whatever the reason, he seemed genuinely charmed by her.

CHAPTER FOURTEEN

I knew your daddy." Frank held a big bowl of mashed potatoes so Ingrid could help herself.

She paused with the spoon hovering over her plate. "You did?"

Frank nodded. "A good man. And from what I heard from the wranglers who worked for him, a fair one."

Ingrid's tension eased and she let out a long, slow breath before passing the bowl Luke's way.

He winked. "I figured you probably knew Lars Larsen, Grandpop. I guess you've met just about every rancher in these parts."

"That I have." Frank took a bite of beef burgundy and paused a moment to savor the taste before turning to Yancy. "This may be your best recipe yet."

"I was just about to say the same." At the other end of the table, Nelson cut off a second piece before giving a nod to the cook. "Even Pierre, head chef at the Bistro, couldn't have done it better."

Lily looked up at the old man beside her with eyes wide. "Is this one of those fancy-schmancy foods you love, Great One?"

Luke nearly choked on his beef.

Nelson glared down at the little girl. "Where did you hear that?"

"Luke said you only drink fancy-schmancy drinks and eat fancy-schmancy food. Isn't that right, Luke?"

Nelson speared a glance at his grandson. "I figured an innocent like this couldn't have come up with such a phrase on her own."

"You have to admit it defines you, Great One."

Silence descended over the room.

Nelson slapped a hand on the table. "That it does, Luke. That it does."

He looked at Lily. "Fancy-schmancy, am I?" Then, without waiting for her response, he threw back his head and roared with laughter, and the others joined in.

With everyone relaxed, the conversation around the table turned, as always, to the weather, the herds, and the expectations of market prices for roundup at the end of summer.

During a lull in the conversation, Grace turned to Ingrid. "You haven't said anything about your mother, dear. Did she pass away, too?"

"She's...alive."

"You left her alone at the ranch?"

Ingrid turned to Luke, feeling her face flame.

"She isn't at the ranch." Without thinking, Luke placed a protective hand over Ingrid's. "She's spending some time in Wayside."

Grace shook her head. "I'm not familiar with Wayside. Is it far from Glacier Ridge?"

"About an hour or so. It's much smaller than Glacier Ridge, just a few shops and such. But it's closer to Ingrid's ranch than our town."

"I see. Well, as long as she's safe there. But if she'd care to join you and Lily here, please let her know she's welcome, Ingrid."

"Thank you. I will, Mrs.—"

"Gracie." Grace reached over and, like Luke, squeezed her hand. "We don't stand on formality here. Just call me Gracie, or if you'd rather, call me what the boys call me. Gram Gracie."

"Oh boy." Lily couldn't contain her excitement. "I never had a grandma." She turned to Frank. "Or a grandpa. But I've got Mick, and Ingrid says he's like a grandpa, aren't you, Mick?"

The old cowboy chuckled. "As long as I'm everything else around the ranch, I may as well be your grandpa, too, girl."

Grace smiled at the little girl. "And I feel lucky to have a little girl call me Grandma, since all I've ever had around here is boys."

"Oh boy. Gram Gracie." Lily was beaming as she finished her meal.

The family left the kitchen to take dessert and coffee in the great room. They were treated to Yancy's chocolate layer cake and chocolate-marshmallow ice cream as they sat around a roaring fire that managed to drown out the sound of a summer storm that had begun raging outside.

Afterward, as Nelson enjoyed a glass of bourbon,

and the others sipped coffee or longnecks, Luke found a deck of cards and challenged Lily to a game of Fish, with the loser having to tend to Turnip's stall in the morning. It was all Lily needed to forget the storm and her weariness, and she threw herself into the game with renewed energy.

Reed took a seat beside her, cheering her on each time she beat his brother, and commiserating with her each time she lost, until Luke insisted Reed join the game. Then it became a fever-pitched contest that had the winner boasting, and the losers loudly grumbling and calling for a rematch.

Late into the night, when Lily could barely keep her eyes open, Luke took pity on her and suggested they continue the game another night.

"But I need to beat you two more times, or I have to clean Turnip's stall in the morning."

Like shook his head. "I'll clean it. Just this one time. And then we'll play again to see who wins the match. But right now, you need to get to bed."

Grace looked up. "Would you like me to show you to your rooms?"

Luke was already on his feet. "I'll take them up, Gram."

"All right." Grace turned to Yancy. "Will you show Mick his room?"

Yancy nodded. "You've got the room beside mine off the kitchen. Best spot in the house, if you like late-night snacks."

Mick said his good nights and followed Yancy from the great room.

Grace walked over to hug the little girl and her sister.

"Good night. If you need anything at all, be sure to let Luke know."

Ingrid closed her eyes for a moment, inhaling the lavender scent of the older woman as they embraced. "Thank you. I'm sure we'll be fine."

"I know you will."

Grace indicated Lily, who was almost asleep on her feet. "I think Lily might enjoy a horseback ride up to her room, Luke."

"Good idea." He knelt down and caught Lily's hands. "Climb on my back, Li'l Bit."

Lily giggled and called good night to the others before wrapping her arms around Luke's neck as he started up the stairs.

Ingrid trailed behind them, and she couldn't help laughing until she felt her heart suddenly hitch at the sight of Lily snuggling against Luke's broad back.

Once upstairs, Luke galloped down a hallway before stopping at a closed door. He opened it and stepped inside, turning on a light before pausing beside a big bed. "Here's your stall, Li'l Bit."

He knelt down, allowing her to climb down from his back.

She looked around with eyes gone wide, studying the desk and chair, a long, low dresser on which rested a flatscreen TV, and floor-to-ceiling windows overlooking the hills in the distance. "You mean this is just for me?"

"It's all yours." He crossed the room and opened a door, revealing a gleaming bathroom with both tub and shower and a wide expanse of marble counters.

"Ingrid's room is next door, and it's exactly the same."

"So," Ingrid said softly, "if you feel a little lost or uncomfortable, you can come to my room and climb into bed with me."

Lily rubbed her eyes. "I think I'm too tired."

"Okay." Ingrid indicated the bathroom. "Why don't you wash up and settle into bed, and I'll come back in a few minutes to hear your prayers."

"Okay."

Ingrid followed Luke out of Lily's room and paused as he opened the door to the next room.

As she stepped inside, he followed and turned on the light.

She looked around with a shake of her head. "This is...all too much."

He winked. "Yeah. I know it's pretty humble, but hey, it's home."

She couldn't help laughing with him. "It's so beautiful. So big and cozy and..." She shrugged. "I'm rambling. This is all wonderful. Like your family."

"Yeah. They're great. And they like you and Lily."

"I like them, too." She looked up at him. "Thank you."

"You're welcome. You heard Gram Gracie. If you need anything, just let me know."

As he turned away, she lay a hand on his back. He froze, before turning slowly toward her.

"I know I've been...difficult, Luke."

"It doesn't—"

She touched a hand to his mouth to still his words. "You knew I didn't want to leave, even though we weren't safe at the ranch anymore. And you pushed as hard as I resisted."

Unable to stand the heat of her hand on his mouth, he caught it between both of his. "I'm sorry about that."

"Don't be. This isn't easy for me to say, but I need to thank you for insisting. Now that we're here, I feel such relief at being somewhere safe. Not just for my sake, but even more for Lily's. It's plain to see that in a matter of hours she's fallen in love with your entire family."

"And they love her, too. How could they help it?" He looked down at their joined hands, before meeting her steady gaze. "Ingrid..." Something flickered in his eyes. Even the tone of his voice changed slightly. Gentler. More intimate.

She started to pull away, but he cupped the back of her head before lowering his face to hers.

The kiss was soft. Tentative. Testing. Tasting.

When she didn't resist, he leaned into her, taking her fully into the heat that flared up between them. He gathered her close, sinking into the pleasure as she made a soft sound in her throat. Surprise? Delight?

There was no time to wonder as a wave of desire, hot and swift, nearly swamped him. One minute he was simply acting on a whim. The next he felt the pull of raw, sexual need taking over his mind, his will, his senses.

Without a thought to what he was doing, he drove her back against the wall, touching her at will. His hands roamed her back, then skimmed her sides until they encountered the swell of her breasts. His thumbs moved over them, feeling her body's reaction, and all the while he spun out the kiss until they were both struggling for breath.

"Luke."

The sound of his name torn from her lips had him lifting his head. His eyes narrowed on her, and he became aware of just how far he'd taken her. Had taken them both.

He lifted his hands from her, forcing them to his sides. "Sorry. I didn't mean...I was rough."

"I should..." She swallowed and tried again. "I need to hear Lily's prayers."

"Yeah." But he didn't step away.

Instead, he pressed both hands against the wall on either side of her and leaned in to brush his mouth ever so softly over hers. Hot desire sparked between them before she put a hand to his chest.

He shot her a knowing smile. There was no denying that she was as aroused as he. "If you need anything through the night, I'm one room away."

"How...convenient." Her words were a little too breathless. She couldn't quite meet his eyes. "Good night, Luke."

"'Night, Ingrid."

He watched as she stepped around him and into the hall before returning to Lily's room. As he made his way along the hallway to his own room, he was still vibrating with need. A need that was slowly driving him mad.

He stepped into his room and closed the door, leaning against it as he drank in the sight of the darkened hills outside his window. He'd always loved the sight of those hills. Right now, he couldn't focus on them. All he could think about was Ingrid and that kiss.

He fully understood her intention to prove herself stronger than Nadine. Her reaction to his kisses was natural enough, under the circumstances. But for every time she retreated, he wanted her more.

He'd hoped that having her here at his family ranch,

surrounded by so many people, would prove a distraction for him. Now he realized that it had only made things worse.

Seeing her being charmed by the people he loved made him more aware than ever just how special a woman she was.

He undressed, giving vent to his frustration by kicking his boots against the wall. Naked, he climbed under the covers and lay with his hands beneath his head, deep in thought.

Until Ingrid Larsen, he'd never met a woman who cost him sleep. Until Ingrid, he'd never wasted a minute of his time worrying about the next step in his life. He'd been wild and carefree and loving every minute of his freedom to ride his Harley, wrangle his herds, and live the life of a cowboy.

Now the only thing that mattered was Ingrid. Her safety. Her ranch.

Who was he kidding?

He lusted after her like a teenager with raging testosterone. But he did care about her ranch, her safety, her sister, and old Mick.

More than anything, though, he just wanted her. Wanted to do all the things he'd been thinking since that first time he'd seen her, with that cap of fine blond hair and those big, haunted eyes that touched something deep inside his soul.

He turned and punched his pillow before giving voice to a string of curses. Yeah. He wanted her right now, here in his bed.

And the wanting was like a drug, driving him half mad.

CHAPTER FIFTEEN

The following morning, Luke stepped out of his room and paused at Ingrid's closed door. Hearing no sounds from within, he moved on and found himself hoping she'd slept comfortably, knowing she was safe here.

When he entered the kitchen, he saw Ingrid sitting in the pretty alcove with Frank and Grace, talking quietly while enjoying coffee.

Yancy was removing freshly baked rolls from the oven. At the stove, old Mick was flipping flapjacks onto a platter. The two men were working side by side as though they'd done this all their lives.

"Good morning." Luke greeted the two men before snagging a mug of coffee and ambling over to where his grandparents were sitting with Ingrid.

"'Morning, Luke." Frank was grinning from ear to ear. "We've just been comparing stories about our families. Ingrid's grandfather came here just about the time I did.

Our paths crossed hundreds of times. But through the years, with family obligations and all, we lost touch. I only saw her father, Lars, a dozen times or so, and then usually when we were both in town for supplies." He looked over at Ingrid. "But I remember the pride in his voice whenever he spoke about his daughter. He thought the sun rose and set in you."

Her eyes were shiny at his words. "That means the world to me, Frankie."

Her easy use of Grace's term of endearment for her husband caught Luke by surprise. He glanced at his grandmother, who was beaming.

She touched a hand to Ingrid's shoulder. "It's been fun catching up on old times."

The back door slammed, and Lily trooped in with Burke, Colin, and Reed. The four shed their boots and paused to wash up at the big sink before stepping into the kitchen.

Lily's wild gypsy hair had been pulled back in a pony-tail. Her shirt and jeans were faded and patched, but her face was wreathed in smiles.

"Where've you been, Li'l Bit?"

"Mucking Turnip's stall."

"But I said I'd do it."

"I told Reed I wanted to pay up. And he said I'm a…" She turned to the tall cowboy who was smiling down at her. "What did you call me?"

"An independent woman."

"That's right." Lily looked at her sister. "Ingrid says a woman who can pay her own way gets through life with-out owing anybody."

"Well said." Vanessa, who had just descended the

stairs beside her husband, Matt, gave the little girl a high five. "I can see that you and Ingrid will have no trouble living in today's world." She indicated the tray of drinks. "Would you care for some orange juice, Lily?"

"Thank you." Lily sipped, then looked over at Mick. "This is good. What did you put in it?"

Mick pointed at Yancy. "He squeezed the OJ. Ask him."

Yancy shrugged. "There's nothing in it. Just orange juice."

"But there's this good stuff in it." She ran her tongue over her upper lip, leaving an orange mustache.

"Oh." The cook grinned. "That's orange pulp. It falls in when I squeeze the oranges."

"You squeeze real oranges?" The little girl was clearly intrigued. "Why?"

"So you can enjoy fresh-squeezed orange juice." Yancy paused a beat. "You like it?"

"Yes. Will you show me how to squeeze oranges, Yancy?"

He couldn't hide his delight. "Later today we'll have our first lesson."

"Yay." She pumped a fist in the air before polishing off the glass of juice.

Vanessa, who had watched and listened in silence, broke into laughter before explaining. "The first time I tasted Yancy's orange juice, I sounded just like you, Lily. The only juice I'd ever had came from a plastic jug from my grocery store. I couldn't believe there were people who actually squeezed their own juice."

"And now she does the same for me," Matt said with a wink.

Luke and Reed put their hands to their throats in a gesture of gagging.

"Hey," Matt added. "Don't knock it until you've tried it."

"Having your juice served by a gorgeous woman?" Reed asked.

"Marriage." Matt chuckled at the looks that passed between his two brothers.

"But thank you both for referring to me as gorgeous." Vanessa dimpled.

"No question, Nessa. You haven't changed." Reed pointed. "It's my brother I'm worried about. Who is this mellow, old, married man? And what have you done with my wild brother, Matt?"

Matt simply chuckled. "These days, I leave all the wild stuff for Luke."

"Which is just the way I like it," Luke muttered.

"Breakfast is ready," Yancy announced.

The family gathered around the table and began passing platters of scrambled eggs, thick slices of ham, biscuits warm from the oven, and stacks of pancakes with maple syrup.

"Going to be a good day for chores," Colin announced. "The rain blew over, and the sun's coming out."

"What did you have in mind?" Burke cupped his coffee mug in his hands before drinking.

"Heading up to the hills to check on the herds." Colin helped himself to several pancakes and smothered them in syrup. After his first taste, he looked over at Mick. "Hey. These are good."

"Thanks." The old cowboy grinned. "I told Yancy I'm not in his league, but the few things I can make never get complaints from my girls."

"Or from me." Colin dug in while the others began outlining plans for the day.

After breakfast, Burke and the men headed toward the barn, ready to pack up the trucks before heading to the highlands.

Luke paused beside Ingrid. "Would you and Lily want to ride with us?"

At her hesitation, Grace remarked casually, "I was hoping I might have the girls to myself." She glanced at Nessa, Ingrid, and Lily. "Most days I'm outnumbered around here, and I thought it might be fun to take a day off from ranch chores and just have a girls' day."

Luke grinned before dropping an arm around his grandmother's waist and pressing a kiss to her cheek. "I'd say a girls' day is long overdue, Gram Gracie. Enjoy."

He turned to Yancy and Mick. "Care to ride along? Maybe you could bring enough supplies to surprise the wranglers with a barbecue."

The two men grew animated as they decided what to pack for the hills. An hour later the men were heading out in a caravan of trucks.

Ingrid watched Luke go, feeling a moment's indecision. She wasn't sure she'd be comfortable spending a day with women she didn't know. But since she was accepting the hospitality of this family, she thought it would have been rude to refuse. She would simply get through this as best she could.

Nessa seemed delighted at Grace's words. "Does this mean we might get a chance to visit your studio?"

"Oh." Grace gave an embarrassed laugh. "I can't imagine anything more boring than a visit to my studio. It's so crowded with stuff, I can barely move in there half the time."

"Now you're being modest." Nessa turned to Ingrid and Lily. "I'll bet the two of you are as excited as I am about seeing where Gram Gracie works."

"I…" Ingrid tried not to show her ignorance. "I'd love to see it."

"Well then." Grace started toward the mudroom. "We'll need boots and jackets. We've a bit of a walk to the barn."

Intrigued, Ingrid trailed along, while Lily caught Gracie's hand and skipped beside her.

Once outside, they passed the first barn and walked toward the second, smaller barn. As Grace shoved open the doors and switched on the overhead lights, Ingrid simply stared in silence.

The back wall of the building had been replaced with floor-to-ceiling windows, where sunlight streamed in, allowing a spectacular view of the hills and meadows outside. The rest of the walls were lined with tall shelves holding an assortment of photographs of every size and shape. Some were wrapped for shipping. Some were framed. Most were simply loose, stacked in piles on the floor and on tables.

Ingrid took her time circling the cavernous room, studying the photos, before she turned to Grace with a look of awe. "Oh my goodness. I can't believe I'm really in your studio and able to actually see your work up close. I've seen your photographs of mustangs since I was Lily's age. They're my absolute favorites. But I never dreamed I'd ever get to meet the famous photographer."

Grace beamed with pleasure. "Thank you. I'm so glad

you enjoy my photos. The mustangs that live in our hills are the great loves of my life. After," she added with a smile, "my sweet Frankie, of course."

Nessa dropped an arm around Ingrid's shoulders and kept her voice low. "I felt the same way the first time I was in her presence. And now, even though I'm still in awe of her talent, I think of her more than ever as Luke's grandmother."

"Luke was so casual about her."

"It's such a guy thing." Nessa laughed. "And such a Malloy thing. They figure everybody in the world already knows about their famous grandmother and great-grand-father, so they don't need to say a word."

"I guess I should have known that the Great One's daughter would find a way to express herself as beauti-fully as he did."

Overhearing, Grace nodded. "My father wasn't happy when I switched my college major from film studies to photography. But even then he believed that in time I'd use my love of photography to enhance a career in film. It never occurred to the great Nelson LaRou that a child of his could be anything other than a clone of the famous father."

Ingrid was clearly intrigued. "Luke told us that your father didn't approve of you living on a ranch in Mon-tana."

"Oh, he was horrified. The thought of his beautiful, tal-ented daughter throwing her life away on some cowboy in the middle of nowhere had him fit to be tied. Then, when his grandsons were born, he thought he might grace us with a visit. But he still wasn't sold on the idea of actually living on a ranch, until the day he had to make the critical decision to leave all that he loved in Hollywood and Connecticut to come and live with us permanently."

Ingrid's eyes went wide. "How long did it take for him to fall in love with this lifestyle?"

"Ha." Gracie laughed aloud. "I guess someday he'll let us know. In the meantime, he makes do, thanks to Yancy's excellent martinis and"—she turned to Lily with a grin—"fancy-schmancy meals."

The little girl joined in the laughter.

Ingrid crossed the room to a row of photographs of mustangs. "Do you mind if I look at these?"

"That's why we're here," Grace said simply. "Look all you'd like."

"Oh." Ingrid moved slowly along the rows of shelves, sighing over the spectacular photos. "I swear I can see them moving and hear the thundering of their hooves. You and your camera make them so alive. So real."

"Thank you." Grace stepped up beside her. "That's the nicest compliment you can give me."

Lily pointed to a smoke-gray mare, forelegs in the air, ears flattened. "I think I've seen her in our hills, Gram Gracie."

Grace nodded. "I'm sure you have. They come down from the hills in search of grass when the highlands are covered with snow. But often, in the summer, they graze for miles on the lush grass around the lower meadows."

"Ingrid and I always stop to watch whenever a herd of mustangs crosses our path." Lily's eyes took on a dreamy look. "I always think it would be fun to climb on the back of one of them and just race across a meadow like the wind."

"It's fun to think about." Ingrid tousled her sister's hair. "But it wouldn't be any fun to be tossed off one of those skittish animals. If they decided to trample you, you wouldn't have a chance to defend yourself."

Grace nodded. "It's taken me years to earn their trust. And some of them simply refuse to allow me to get close. But those that do are worth the effort." She pointed to a photo of a pure white stallion standing still as a statue on a distant hill, with snow swirling about him. "I snapped this picture more than two years ago, and I've never spotted him since. How I yearn to get close enough to study him and his herd, and to photograph him in all his many moods. I think he would prove a spectacular model."

Ingrid was studying the photo with interest. "I can't be certain, but I think . . ."

She let the words die, but not before Grace looked over at her. "You think what?"

Ingrid shrugged. "Just thinking out loud. I may have seen him not far from my ranch."

Grace's smile was radiant. "I know where my next photographic safari will take me."

An hour later they stepped out of Gracie's studio.

Grace adjusted her sunglasses. "Since the men will be gone the better part of the day, I think we'd be smart to head to town. We can shop a bit if you'd like and then have some lunch." She drew an arm around Lily. "And afterward, maybe we'll stop at I's Cream."

"Oh boy." Lily's eyes went wide. "Does that mean ice cream?"

"It does. Ivy has every flavor known to mankind. And a few nobody has ever heard of."

They climbed into one of the ranch trucks. With Grace at the wheel, they took off in a cloud of dust and laughed and chatted all the way to Glacier Ridge.

CHAPTER SIXTEEN

As the ranch truck rolled along the main street, Grace kept up a running commentary on the shops and their owners.

"That's D & B's Diner. That stands for Dot and Barb Parker. Twin sisters, though Dot claims to be older by four minutes, which she says makes her the boss."

Ingrid and Lily stared with interest at the pretty little white building, sporting black shutters and white polka dots.

"Oh," Ingrid said as a fact dawned. "The dots are for Dot?"

"Exactly." Grace and Vanessa shared a laugh. "Folks around here can tell the sisters apart because Dot's favorite clothes have polka dots. That's all she wears. But nobody complains about her choice of wardrobe, as silly as it sometimes looks, because she and her sister serve cowboy-sized burgers big enough that they boast nobody can eat more than one and the hottest chili in town."

Vanessa pointed to a pair of buildings across the street. "Matt told me this was originally a barbershop, and then the owner's wife added a women's beauty shop when she couldn't find any in town. Then they got the idea to add a spa."

"A spa?" Ingrid's brows shot up. "Does anybody from around here actually go there?"

Vanessa shrugged. "Not much call for a spa around here, but folks are intrigued by the idea. I've heard business is picking up since they added therapeutic massages to their menu. A lot of ranchers come in with aching backs and shoulder muscles and such, from all the tough ranch chores, and Dr. Anita at the medical clinic has begun writing prescriptions for massages, so it's considered medical instead of just vanity."

"Sounds reasonable to me." Ingrid pointed to the clinic. "You have a doctor here in town?"

"We do." Gracie nodded toward the medical clinic. "Actually two doctors. Old Dr. Cross has been thinking of cutting back on his practice, so he invited his niece Anita from Boston to come and share the workload. I understand she worked in the ER of one of Boston's biggest hospitals, and she was considered one of their best."

Vanessa added softly, "Dr. Anita happens to be not only a very good doctor, but also very pretty. A fact that hasn't escaped Colin's notice."

Grace swiveled her head to study her grandson's wife. "Has he said so?"

"Not a word. But I've seen the way he lights up whenever he sees her."

Grace put a hand to her heart. "Oh, now wouldn't that be grand? With all Colin's responsibilities since his brother Patrick died, I'd just about given up hope that he would ever find someone to settle down with."

"Oh, I don't think they're anywhere near that point, Gram Gracie. I doubt they've even said more than a dozen words to one another. But"—Nessa shook her head—"there's just a look that comes into Colin's eyes when he's around her that I've never seen when he's with anybody else. I may be reading too much into it, but I just have a hunch about it."

Grace smiled and patted her hand. "That's enough to give me hope, Nessa. And for that, I thank you."

They drove slowly until Grace pulled up to the curb outside a pretty little shop sporting a red-and-white-striped awning. The sign announced ANYTHING GOES.

"If you girls don't mind waiting," Grace called, "I need a new shirt." She touched a hand to the shirt she was wearing with her ankle-skimming denim skirt as she stepped from the truck. "Something along these lines, practical but with a feminine touch to it. Want to browse while I shop?"

They all climbed out and entered the shop, setting off a bell. A pretty young woman walked out of a back room, her face wreathed in smiles.

"Hello, Miss Grace. How nice to see you."

"Hello, Trudy. You know Matt's wife, Vanessa."

"I do. Hello again, Nessa."

The two shook hands.

"Trudy Evans, these are friends visiting the ranch. Ingrid and Lily Larsen."

"Hello. Welcome to my shop. Is there anything special I can show you?"

They shook their heads. Grace said with a laugh,

"We're going to browse, Trudy. Which means we intend to see everything before we're finished here."

"Well then, please make yourselves at home and let me know if I can help."

Grace made her way to a line of hangers displaying women's shirts. Within minutes she'd chosen a pale blue long-sleeved shirt with a delicate rose embroidered on the pocket.

While Vanessa stood in front of a mirror trying on wide-brimmed hats, Ingrid stopped at a display of baggy sweatshirts, and Lily crossed the room to stare at the array of girls' denim pants and jackets and an assortment of fancy boots.

Grace walked up behind the little girl. "See anything you like?"

Lily looked away. "No. I was just looking."

Grace held up a pair of jeans. "These look to be about your size. Why don't you try them on?"

"Oh, I don't think..."

The older woman was already rummaging through a stack of T-shirts. "Oh, look. You really have to try this on, too." It was pink, with vivid purple letters that read IN-DEPENDENT WOMAN. "Reed will be impressed, since he's the one who called you that."

The two of them laughed before Grace caught Lily's arm and led her toward the rear of the shop where a curtain hid a dressing room.

Minutes later Lily emerged in the jeans and T-shirt.

"Oh, they fit you perfectly," Grace called.

Ingrid walked over to study her little sister. "I have to admit they look a whole lot better than those old things you were wearing." She dug into her pocket to count her money.

Grace touched a hand to her arm. "You're not allowed to pay for a thing, Ingrid. This is my treat. In fact," she added, lowering her voice, "this entire day is really Frankie's treat. He insisted. He even gave me his credit card, with firm orders to spend his money."

Nessa ambled over, modeling a wide-brimmed hat in charcoal felt that perfectly matched the fitted charcoal denim jacket she was wearing. She managed to look both city-chic and country-casual at the same time. "What do you think?"

The others nodded their approval.

"It's too pretty to pass up," Grace called, while sifting through denim jackets in girls' sizes. She held one up. "Why don't you see if this fits, Lily?"

With a look of pure happiness, the little girl took it into the fitting room.

"Look, Ingrid." Nessa held up a pretty tee in deep teal. "This would look so great with your fair skin and hair. Want to give it a try?"

"No, thank you." Ingrid was actually backing away.

"Why not?" Nessa gave her an encouraging smile. "At least try it on."

"I'm more comfortable in…slouchy things."

"I've noticed." Nessa's smile grew and she thrust it into Ingrid's hand. "It's just a T-shirt."

Ingrid reluctantly walked to the fitting room just as Lily walked out, ready to model her entire outfit.

"Oh, Lily." Ingrid stopped in her tracks. "That's just perfect. You're going to be the prettiest girl in town."

Lily's eyes rounded. "You mean I can keep them?"

Ingrid couldn't hold back her smile. "Those clothes were made for you, honey. And since Gram Gracie insisted…"

"Oh boy." Lily danced around the shop, modeling her outfit for Grace and Vanessa.

Minutes later Ingrid pulled open the curtain to show off the tee. She actually crossed her arms over her chest and stared pointedly at the floor.

Nessa exchanged a look with Grace. "Who knew there was such a fantastic body beneath that baggy shirt?" She turned to Ingrid. "You really have to have that."

Ingrid stepped past the curtain, looking completely flustered. "Don't you think it's too"—she huffed out a breath—"too tight and revealing?"

"The only thing it reveals is the fact that you're a lovely young woman." Grace touched a hand to her arm. "Please let me buy it for you. The color is fantastic on you."

Ingrid caught sight of her reflection in a mirror across the room and felt her heart do a little dance. "It is awfully pretty, but…"

"And you deserve to feel pretty in it." Grace turned to the shop's owner. "Trudy, I think we've found what we came for."

"Will I wrap them, or would you ladies care to wear them and I'll wrap the clothes you were wearing when you came in?"

Lily caught her sister's hand. "Can I wear mine, Ingrid?"

"Absolutely. But I'll get my old…"

Before she could finish, Grace gave a firm shake of her head. "You're wearing that." She turned to Trudy. "You can wrap my new shirt and the clothes left in the fitting room."

"And these," Nessa added.

While Ingrid was busy admiring her little sister, Vanessa handed Trudy several T-shirts in deep shades of red, and yellow, and lime green.

At Grace's arched brow, she said softly, "They're the same size as the one Ingrid tried on, so I know they'll fit her. And the colors are fantastic."

Grace chuckled. "I have a feeling Luke will approve."

"All part of my plan," Nessa replied with a wink.

The shop owner rang up the sale, handed Grace her credit card, and then crossed the room to fetch the clothes they'd shed in the fitting room.

Minutes later they tossed the bags in the truck and began walking along the sidewalk, taking in the sunshine, waving at friends and neighbors who were out and about and pausing before each shop to peer in the windows.

At last they found themselves in front of Clay's Saloon.

Grace turned to the others. "This is the famous Pig Sty. We can eat here, or we can walk back to D & B's. Anybody have a favorite?"

Nessa was grinning. "The first time Matt took me here, I heard the name Pig Sty and was ready to put up with awful food and disgusting surroundings. But I have to tell you, it's a really fun, clean place. And Clay's pork meals are as good as Yancy serves." She leaned in to whisper, "Just never tell Yancy I said that."

The others laughed before Grace pushed open the door. "I think you've sold Ingrid and Lily."

The two sisters nodded as they followed her inside.

It was a typical lunch-hour crowd. Cowboys, in town for supplies, crowded the bar or sat in groups of three and four at the scarred wooden tables. Workers from the nearby small businesses made up the rest of the crowd.

The familiar voice of Willie, crooning about being on the road again, filtered through the chorus of raucous conversation and laughter.

A white-haired man in jeans and suspenders, his rolled sleeves revealing muscled biceps, stood at the grill, methodically turning pork chops while carrying on a running conversation with several grizzled cowboys seated on bar stools. From the jokes flying back and forth, it was clear that they were longtime customers.

"Hello, Clay."

At the sound of Grace's voice, his hand paused in midair and he made a courtly bow.

"Ms. Grace. Good to see you in town. How are you?"

"I'm just fine, Clay. I believe you know Matt's wife, Vanessa."

"Yes'm." He nodded in her direction.

"And these are guests of mine. Ingrid and Lily."

He gave them each a smile.

"What's on the menu today, Clay?"

Clay continued flipping chops on the grill as he went through the items available. "I have grilled pork chops. Stuffed baked chops. Pulled pork sandwiches on homemade sourdough bread. Pork chili. And pure pork hot dogs, also on homemade sourdough rolls. All served with a side of deep-fried onion rings or my special pork chili fries."

Grace turned to wink at the others. "They all sound wonderful. What's your pleasure?"

Vanessa opted for the pulled pork sandwich. Ingrid decided on the chili. Lily pointed to the foot-long hot dog.

And Grace ordered the stuffed baked chops, with a side of both onion rings and chili fries to be sampled by all of them.

"Careful, Ms. Grace," one grizzled old cowboy shouted. "Clay won't reveal what's in his stuffed pork chops. He calls it his mystery stuffing. We call it stuffing à la salmonella."

Above the laughter Clay asked calmly, "And to drink, ladies?"

"I believe I'm ready for a longneck." Nessa turned to Ingrid. "Join me?"

When Ingrid nodded, Grace turned to Lily. "Clay has root beer and lemonade. Is that right, Clay?"

"Right you are, Ms. Grace."

"Root beer," Lily called.

"And I'll just have ice water, Clay."

He nodded. "Find a seat, ladies, and I'll get that right to you."

Grace led the way to the rear of the room, away from the loud chatter of voices and Willie's crooning. She chose a booth in the corner, and the four of them settled in.

Minutes later Clay Olmsted was there with their drinks, followed shortly after with plates, bowls, and platters heaped with their orders.

They took their time, savoring the amazing flavors and remarking over the onion rings and chili fries.

Ingrid nudged Vanessa. "You were right. This isn't at all what I expected from the name Pig Sty. And even though you said it was clean and the food was good, you didn't do it justice."

"You realize it isn't really called the Pig Sty," Grace

explained. "It's called Clay's Saloon, but folks around here started calling it the Pig Sty, because Clay owned a pig farm before starting this business. He sold it and then bought a piece of land just outside of town, where he and his wife still raise hogs, but not nearly as many as he once did."

"And that's why all his recipes call for pork. He has an endless supply," Vanessa added.

Ingrid sat back, finishing her longneck with a wide smile. "I don't think I'll be able to eat again for a week."

"Me too." Lily took the last bite of her hot dog. Then, for good measure, bit into another chili fry. And another.

Ingrid shared a look with Vanessa and Grace, and the three of them broke into gales of laughter.

Lily looked around. "What's so funny?"

"You, honey." Ingrid reached across the table and squeezed her little sister's hand. "Should we get you another plate of chili fries?"

Lily gave it a moment's thought before shaking her head. "Now I'm full. That was so good." She turned to Grace. "Thank you for lunch. I haven't had root beer in forever."

"To a seven-year old, forever means at least a month or so." Ingrid was still laughing.

"Yeah." Lily nodded. "And I've never had a hot dog that big before." She stretched out her hands to show just how long it had been.

"That's because Clay's wife makes them at their little farm. Clay wanted them big enough to fit the long, sourdough rolls he bakes daily."

"So he's really a cook rather than a farmer," Ingrid remarked.

"And his wife is a better farmer than a cook." Grace laughed. "That's why they make such a great team."

Ingrid turned to Vanessa. "Did you and Matt grow up around here?"

Vanessa shook her head. "I grew up in Chicago. I work for a group of wildlife animal activists based in Washington, DC. I came to Montana to meet with Gram Gracie, but she was out on one of her photographic safaris, and she asked Matt to meet with me instead. But there was a problem. Matt was up at one of the range shacks, and after our meeting, a storm blew in and I was forced to spend the night." She looked over at Grace. "And the rest, as they say, is history."

Grace put a hand on Ingrid's arm. "I'm afraid she's left out most of the good parts of the story, but our family is delighted that they have their happy ending."

"And we continue to live it every day." Nessa's eyes went soft before she said, "You and Luke seem to have had an equally stormy meeting."

Ingrid's eyes crinkled with humor. "You could say that."

Grace's voice lowered. "I know Luke has a wild streak in him. And has had since he was just a boy. But I'd trust him with my life."

Ingrid nodded. "When I first met him, I saw only that wild side. But after a while, I started to see other things, too. He's generous. With his time. With his patience. With his energy. While he was at my ranch, he seemed to sense when one of us was at the end of our rope, and he quietly stepped in to give us some room to breathe."

Grace heard the change in Ingrid's voice and looked into her eyes in time to see them mist, for just a moment, before she blinked and the look was gone.

She put a hand on Ingrid's arm. "I know I'm prejudiced, but I happen to know that Luke is a good man. A very good man."

Seeing that the crowd had thinned considerably, they walked to the front of the room, where Clay was still flipping chops while carrying on a running conversation with his regulars.

"Good-bye, Clay, and thank you for a grand lunch," Grace called.

He gave a courtly bow. "My pleasure, ladies. You all come back. I hope you had a chance to recharge your batteries for the rest of the day."

Grace smiled and looped her arm through Lily's. "I don't know about the others, but I'm definitely recharged and reenergized."

CHAPTER SEVENTEEN

Grace turned in the direction of the hardware store, and the others trailed slowly behind.

At the door she paused. "Frankie told me he'd ordered a few things here. Care to join me?"

They followed her inside. While she walked to the counter to pick up the supplies Frank had ordered, the other three walked slowly around the store.

Nessa stopped to study an assortment of glass door-knobs. "These look just like the ones in my grand-mother's old Victorian house in Illinois."

"Oh, how pretty." Ingrid picked one up. "It's heavy. It feels like leaded glass."

"It is," came a voice behind them.

They turned to see Grace beside an elderly man with a walker.

Grace smiled at the others. "This is Melvin Hopkins Sr. He built this store. His son, Melvin Jr., runs it now, but as you can see, Senior is still very much involved in the products they carry." She indicated the young women. "Melvin, this is Matt's wife, Vanessa."

"Matthew got himself a beautiful bride," he said as he shook her hand.

"And these are our houseguests. Ingrid and Lily Larsen."

He gave Ingrid a look. "Was your daddy Lars?"

Both sisters nodded.

"A good man, your daddy. He was a regular customer here." He extended a hand to Lily, and then to Ingrid, meeting her direct gaze. "I was sorry to hear about his passing."

"Thank you." Ingrid spoke for both of them, clearly touched by his kind words.

The old man returned his attention to the bin of knobs. "I started collecting those when I was just a boy. Now they've become the choice for a lot of young couples who want to bring back the glory of the old days."

Vanessa looked down at the light glinting off the glass knobs. "I know where I'm bringing Matt when we get around to building our house."

"I hope it won't be soon." Grace lay a hand on Nessa's arm. "Frankie and I so enjoy having you both with us."

"And we love being with you, too." Vanessa brushed Gracie's cheek with a kiss. "But Matt has always wanted to build a place on the North Ridge. It's really special to him, and to me."

"I know. And I completely understand. You deserve your own place, where you can start your family and make a home uniquely yours. But whenever you move, you know that Frankie and I will miss you both terribly."

"We'll be so close, you'll soon find yourself wishing we'd move far away."

"Never." Grace gave a vehement shake of her head.

Nessa glanced at Ingrid. "Maybe we'll hold off long enough for you to find some other permanent guests, so you won't be lonely."

Seeing where this was going, Ingrid smiled gently. "I have a ranch to run. I told Luke this was only for a night or two."

"Of course. But please don't blame us if we try to coax you to stay longer." Grace caught Lily's hand and began leading her back to the counter, where Frankie's order was bagged and waiting.

A short time later, after calling their good-byes to Melvin Sr. and Melvin Jr., they left the hardware store and started up the street.

"We can't leave town without having dessert." Grace pointed to the pretty little shop with a sign that read I'S CREAM.

Lily read the words out loud. "I's Cream."

Grace winked at the others. "Say it aloud again."

"I's Cream. I's Cream." The little girl's eyes went wide. "Ice cream." She looked at Grace. "We're going for ice cream?"

"You bet we are." Grace caught her hand. "Come on."

"Oh boy." Lily's words sang on the air as the two skipped down the sidewalk.

Behind them, Ingrid and Nessa shared a giggle as Ingrid said, "I don't know which of them is more excited."

"Two kids in a candy store," Nessa remarked.

"Or in an ice cream shop." At Ingrid's words, they caught hands and hurried to catch up.

* * *

"Now this alone would be worth the drive to town." Grace licked the edges of her cone.

Nessa's eyes lit. "What in the world did you order?"

"A double-dipped Monster Chocolate Marshmallow Honeycomb Delight." Grace laughed like a girl. "How about you?"

"Mud Pie and Cookie Dough, with hazelnut topping."

"Ingrid?" Grace looked at the two sisters as they sat side by side on a smooth log, which rested on two massive tree trunks and served as a bench.

"Mine's Strawberry Cotton Candy and Jolly Cherry Cherub."

"Lily?"

The girl had to take a moment to lick away a drop that was about to fall from her sugar cone. "Once in a Blue Moon and Purple People Eater."

"Who would have believed blue and purple ice cream?" Grace gave a mock shudder. "I'm sure it tastes lovely, but those colors…"

Lily held out her cone. "Want a taste, Gram Gracie?"

The older woman laughed. "No, thank you. If I manage to eat all this, I'll be amazed."

"My money's on you," Vanessa said between licks of her ice cream.

As they sat in the sunshine, enjoying their sweet treats, they looked up when Nessa called, "Dr. Anita. How nice to see you."

A pretty young woman stepped out of the shop holding a cone of chocolate ice cream.

"Nessa. What a lovely surprise." She looked over. "And Ms. Grace. How are you?"

"Just fine, dear." Grace moved over to make room. "Will you join us?"

"Thank you."

As Dr. Anita sat, Grace added, "Dr. Anita Cross, these are guests of ours. Ingrid and Lily Larsen."

They smiled and greeted one another while keeping careful hold of their cones.

"How are things at the clinic?"

Dr. Anita rolled her eyes. "Busy. This is the first break I've had all day, and I thought I'd treat myself before the next go-round begins." She kept her gaze averted as she asked casually, "How is Colin, Ms. Grace?"

"Just fine, dear. He's currently up in the highlands with our wranglers."

"This has to be a busy time for ranchers."

Grace gave a small laugh. "I can't think of a time when we aren't busy. Whether it's calving in spring, or roundup in fall, or all the times in between, there's just never a lull in the activities."

Anita nodded. "It's the same for doctors. There just never seems to be enough time in the day."

Grace gave a knowing smile. "And still, despite all the demands on our time, we manage to live our lives. Sometimes, when Frankie and I look back, we wonder at all we've experienced. Birth, death. Laughter and tears. Good times, and some not so good that we'd rather forget. But here we are, still filling every hour of every day, and grateful for every minute of it."

Anita Cross polished off the last of her small cone before getting to her feet. As she did, she lay a hand on Grace's arm. "Thank you for the reminder that I need to take time for life while rushing through my busy routine." She glanced around at the others. "It was so good meeting you, Ingrid and Lily. And, Nessa, good seeing you again." In an aside to Grace she added, "Give my best to Colin."

"I will, dear."

Grace turned to watch as the pretty doctor hurried along the sidewalk toward the medical clinic.

She turned back to Vanessa. "I do believe I caught a glimmer of something in her eyes when she mentioned Colin's name."

Nessa gave a little cat smile. "You see? There's always hope, Gram Gracie."

The older woman returned her attention to the cone with renewed enjoyment. But she kept glancing down the sidewalk until the young doctor disappeared inside the doors of the medical clinic.

Dr. Anita Cross was pretty and bright and had an endearing personality. She probably also had half a dozen men standing in line in the hope of winning her hand. But that didn't stop Grace from wishing and dreaming.

As the ranch truck drew up alongside the back door, Ingrid spoke for all of them.

"Gram Gracie, I can't thank you enough for this day." She looked down at her new shirt, then at Lily's entire outfit. "Thank you for these beautiful clothes. And lunch. And ice cream. I can't remember the last time I did nothing except indulge myself."

Grace turned off the ignition and glanced at Ingrid in the rearview mirror. "And now I'll thank all of you. It was such a treat for me to have a girls' day. I've never done this before. Usually, when I go to town, I go with Frankie, or with Burke or one of my grandsons. I have to tell you, it's much sweeter doing it with girls."

Vanessa caught her hand. "Then we should make a pact to do this on a regular basis. And maybe next time we'll try Snips and Dips."

Grace held up her hands. "These old fingernails haven't seen polish since I was a bride."

"Then it's settled." Nessa turned to glance at Ingrid and Lily. "I see it as our duty to force Gram Gracie into having a manicure, pedicure, and massage."

"Only if you three promise to do it right along with me."

"A manicure? To shovel manure?" Ingrid looked horrified.

"Not only a manicure, but a pedicure as well," Nessa declared. "Think what a beating our poor feet take. Trekking up and down pastures. Locked in heavy work boots for days and weeks. Wouldn't it be fun to have your feet massaged with oils and your toenails painted a pretty shade of pink?"

Lily and Ingrid turned to one another with matching looks of amazement, as though they'd never even thought of such a thing.

But it was Grace who said, "You may have something there, Nessa. I do believe I've been mistreating my poor body for a lifetime. I just hope, if we decide to take you up on your suggestion, this old body doesn't go into shock."

The four of them laughed as they climbed down from the truck and carried their parcels through the mudroom and into the kitchen.

When Vanessa handed Ingrid her bag of clothes, the young woman jiggled the bag. "This feels heavy."

She opened the bag, and for a moment was speechless. Finally she lifted out the colorful T-shirts. "Whose are these?"

"Yours." Grace shared a knowing smile with Vanessa. "Once we knew your size, and how great you looked in that pretty teal shirt, we agreed that you needed a few more."

"Gram Gracie, I can't—"

"Too late. They're already bought and paid for. Now why don't you take them upstairs and, after a shower, decide which of them to wear this evening for dinner."

Ingrid pressed a kiss to the older woman's cheek and then walked over to do the same for Vanessa. "You two are very good at keeping secrets."

"Yes, we are." Nessa caught her in a hug. "Now I'm heading upstairs to shower and change."

The young women ran upstairs, with Lily and Grace following at a more leisurely pace.

When the men returned from the hills, they trooped up the stairs to shower and dress for supper. By the time they came downstairs, Grace and the girls were gathered in the sitting area of the kitchen, sipping their drinks and talking quietly.

Luke snagged a longneck from a tray on the counter and ambled over, stepping up between Reed and Colin to listen to Grace give a rambling commentary to Frank about their day.

Then he spotted Ingrid, her cap of fair hair curling softly around her face, eyes bright with laughter, a smile curving her lips. Frank moved, settling himself next to his wife and giving Luke a clearer view of Ingrid.

For a moment Luke forgot to breathe. Instead of her baggy shirt, she was wearing a tee of bright red, with a softly scooped neckline that revealed a hint of darkened cleft between her breasts. The material clung to her like a second skin, revealing that amazing body she'd always taken such pains to hide.

She lifted the glass of pale wine to her mouth and took a sip. Luke swallowed when she did and could have sworn he could taste her wine and, more, her lips. Just thinking about it had his pulse racing. Sweating, he lifted the chilled bottle to his forehead.

When he caught his grandmother staring at him, he couldn't help giving her one of those rogue smiles. Her own smile bloomed.

"I believe I'll have some ice water, Luke." Grace continued watching him as he turned away, then returned with her drink.

As he handed it to her, she said, "Gorgeous view, isn't it?"

He leaned close. "Yeah. And you're one sly woman, you know that?"

She managed to look every inch the prim-and-proper lady. "I do indeed."

CHAPTER EIGHTEEN

While the others took turns describing their day, Ingrid's phone vibrated in her pocket. When she lifted it and caught sight of the caller's name, she stood and made her way to the far side of the room, speaking softly.

Nadine's voice was high and shrill. "I drive all the way from Wayside, thinking I ought to look in on my family, and what do I find? An empty ranch. Nobody here. Where the hell are you?"

"We're staying with...friends."

"And Mick?"

"He's here, too."

"Do these friends have a name?"

At the fury in her mother's tone, Ingrid felt her heart drop to her toes. She glanced across the distance that separated her from the others, talking and laughing with such ease, and realized that the chasm between herself and them had just widened considerably. How could she have ever believed she had the right to be here with these good people?

"Well? Who are these so-called friends?"

Ingrid stepped into the mudroom, fearful that her mother's voice would be overheard during a lull in the conversation. "Luke's family."

"You're at the high-and-mighty Malloy Ranch?"

"What's that supposed to mean?"

"I've been asking around. According to folks in Wayside, the Malloy family is the closest thing Montana has to royalty."

"Nadine, that's not…" Ingrid sighed. There was so way she could describe or defend the decent, loving people she'd met here. "We'll be home first thing in the morning."

"Don't hurry back on my account." The conversation ended with an abrupt disconnect, followed by silence.

When Ingrid returned to the others, Luke put a hand on her arm. "Everything all right?"

"Fine." She couldn't meet his eyes as she added, "That was Nadine. She's"—she shrugged—"her usual self."

Luke hated the way the smile had been wiped from Ingrid's eyes. Leaning close, he whispered, "I've been wanting a chance to tell you how great you look."

Her frown deepened. The brief conversation with her mother had her in a defensive mood. "Is that a code word for *sexy*?"

"Miss Larsen, I'm shocked and appalled." He said it so sternly it took her a moment to realize he was having fun with her.

She gave his shoulder a quick punch. "Very funny, Malloy."

"But I had you going there for a minute."

"Only for a few seconds."

Luke was relieved to see her smile return.

When Yancy announced that dinner was ready, they gathered around the big table. Luke held a chair out for Lily, and then another for Ingrid, before taking the seat beside her.

Yancy had carved up several roasted chickens before arranging them on two big platters. He handed one to Frank at the head of the table and a second platter to Nelson at the opposite end. They, in turn, began passing them around, along with bowls of buttered mashed potatoes, tender garden beans, and sourdough rolls warm from the oven.

Old Mick took a taste and looked at Yancy. "I hope you'll give me this recipe."

Lily turned to stare at him. "Just so you're not thinking about cooking Little."

"Little?" Reed paused in the act of passing the rolls.

Lily dimpled. "Little is my pet chicken. I raised her from when she first hatched."

"A pet chicken?" Reed gave a quick laugh. "Does she sleep at the foot of your bed like a dog?"

Mick winked at Lily before saying to the others, "When Lily was four, Ingrid used to read stories to her every night. One of them was about Chicken Little and the sky falling. The next time a brooding hen brought her parade of chicks from the henhouse, Lily adopted the smallest one and named her Little. For a year or more she used to dress that chicken in doll clothes and push her around the yard in a doll stroller."

Lily smiled, remembering. "Until Little got too big and wanted to be with the other hens."

Reed looked around the table. "So, Little turned into Big?"

They all laughed. Even Lily joined in.

"And now," Mick added, "Little is way too old and tough to worry about ending up on anyone's table. That old pet is queen of the henhouse." In an aside he said to Yancy, "But I'd still like your recipe. This is the best darned roast chicken I've ever tasted."

"I'll write it down for you. Promise."

Yancy picked up a basket of rolls. "Who wants the few that are left?"

"I wouldn't want them to go to waste." Burke helped himself to one and passed the basket to Reed, who took two, and then to Matt, who took the last one.

Luke tried to shame Reed. "You should have left one for our company."

Reed held up a roll. "How about it, Ingrid? Lily?"

When the two sisters shook their heads, he raised a brow at Luke. "You really wanted this for yourself, didn't you, bro?" Before Luke could reply, he popped it into his mouth. Then, with a grin, said, "Oh, sorry. But I was afraid the sky was about to fall, and I wanted to save you from choking."

Around the table everyone was chuckling when the back door was thrown open with such force, it banged against the wall.

Luke, Reed, and Matt had already shoved back their chairs, prepared to do battle with some unknown intruder, when a figure stepped into the kitchen. A figure in tight, skinny jeans, fringed boots, and an off-one-shoulder top that exposed most of a lacy bra. Her red hair was piled on top of her head and held in place with a giant plastic clasp. The smell of her sweet perfume preceded her, drifting around her like a cloud.

Nadine put a hand to the kitchen counter to steady herself as she took her time studying the faces of all those at the table, before her gaze finally settled on Ingrid. "Well, here you are. I bet you weren't expecting to see me, were you?"

Luke's family turned to Ingrid.

In a subdued voice she managed to say, "This is my mother, Nadine Larsen."

Grace was the first to recover her composure. Pushing away from the table, she crossed the room and caught Nadine's hand.

"How nice to meet you. I'm Grace Anne Malloy."

In short order she proceeded to introduce all those around the table. The rest of the men, having recovered from their surprise, got to their feet.

"Nice to meet you all." Nadine waved a hand. "No need to stand on ceremony. I can see you're in the middle of supper."

Grace led her closer. "You'll join us."

Yancy had already brought a chair to the table, placing it beside Grace's.

"Don't mind if I do." Nadine settled herself at the table. "Something smells good."

"Roast chicken." Grace took her seat and held a platter, allowing Nadine to help herself. "And Yancy's mashed potatoes. Always a favorite around here."

Nadine took a spoonful before holding up her hands. "That's enough. I need to keep my girlish figure." She looked around the table. "I'll say this, Grace. You sure do have a bunch of handsome men in your family."

Grace gave her a smile. "Thank you. I have to agree with you."

Frank, watching as Nadine buttered a roll, remarked, "Ingrid said you were out. I assume you were with friends."

"Yeah." She shot a sly look at her daughter. "Friends. Just a nice, sociable evening. Or three," she added with a giggle.

She pushed aside her plate after just a single taste of everything.

Grace seemed surprised. "You're not hungry?"

"I ate earlier. With my . . . friends."

"Well then." Grace glanced across the table at Yancy. "I think we'll take our desserts and coffee in the great room."

He nodded. "You folks go ahead and I'll just cut up those pies cooling over on the far counter."

"Pie?" Luke's eyebrows shot up. "Fresh apple?"

"They are." Yancy's grin was quick. "Just for you, Luke."

As the family began pushing away from the table, Frank took Gracie's arm, leading the way to the great room, leaving the others to follow.

When Luke offered his arm to Ingrid, Nadine grabbed his other arm. "I'm impressed. Are the men in your family always such gentlemen?"

"We do our best." He stepped back to allow Nadine and Ingrid to enter ahead of him. When he turned, he saw Reed escorting Lily, who was more subdued than he'd ever seen.

He tugged on a lock of her hair. "What's wrong, Li'l Bit?"

"Nothing." She paused, then stepped back, signaling for him to wait with her.

When the others left the kitchen, she tugged on his arm to stoop down. The minute he did, she put a hand to her mouth to whisper in his ear, "Now that Nadine's here, does this mean we can't play cards?"

He knelt down and looked her in the eye. "Her presence doesn't change a thing." He saw the doubt and knew the little girl's fear wasn't just about playing cards. Though she was just a kid, she knew that her mother's behavior was out of place. Especially now that she'd had a glimpse of a different sort of family than hers. "As soon as we've had our dessert, I want my chance to beat you at Fish. Okay?"

Her eyes widened. "Okay."

He stood and took her hand. "Come on. I'm betting there'll be ice cream to go with that apple pie."

"We had ice cream today in town," she said as they entered the great room. The others looked up as she took a seat by the fireplace.

Nelson said, "You went to I's?"

She nodded. "When I read the sign over her shop, I didn't understand, so Gram Gracie told me to say it out loud a couple of times. As soon as I did, I got it." Her smile was back, blooming at the memory. "I's Cream. Isn't that funny?"

"It is. Not to mention clever." Nelson, charmed by the little girl's story, found himself getting into the spirit of the moment. "Why hasn't a dairy started calling its product Moo Juice?"

"Or," Reed put in, "why didn't a certain gifted director we all know and love call himself Art Tistic?" When the rest of the family erupted with a series of boos, he shrugged. "Hey. At least I tried. Can any of you do better?"

At his dare, everyone was tossing out clever names and titles, such as the new tailor in town calling himself "Lord And Taylor" and the veterinarian calling himself Hannibal the Animal Doctor, and the clinic's Dr. Cross calling himself Happy Not Cross. That, in turn, had the others teasing Colin about Dr. Cross's niece, Anita.

Though Colin refused to answer their taunts, he was grinning like a teen.

Yancy entered the room, shoving a trolley loaded with a carafe of coffee and mugs, along with slices of apple pie and a container of vanilla ice cream.

He held up an ice cream scoop. "Who wants ice cream on their pie?"

Minutes later, he began passing pie and coffee around. The family was full of compliments as they dug into their desserts.

"None for me," Nadine said as he paused beside her. "But I'll have one of those longnecks on that tray over there."

Yancy returned to hand her a cold beer.

She looked over at Lily, who had taken a seat as close to Ingrid as possible. "You get any closer, you'll be sitting on her lap."

Ingrid drew an arm around her little sister, who kept her head down, making swirls in her ice cream with her spoon.

To break the tension she could feel between the two sisters and their mother, Grace smiled at Nadine. "Now that we've had a chance to get to know your daughters, we're thoroughly charmed by them."

"Oh yeah. They're real charming." Nadine tipped up the bottle and drained it.

"Having only sons, I feel especially lucky to have spent the day with them. We had such fun, as I'm sure you've had through the years."

Instead of a reply, Nadine held up the empty bottle as a signal to Yancy, the way she would at a saloon.

He heaved himself out of the chair and brought her another.

"Thanks." She looked around at the others. "This is like having your very own butler. I could get used to this. All I can drink and handsome men for company."

In the silence that followed, Luke motioned to Reed. "I think you and I should challenge Ingrid and Lily to a game of cutthroat Fish."

Lily looked up. "What's 'cutthroat'?"

Reed stood and towered over her with a mock leer. "Be warned, little lady. You're about to find out."

"Oh boy." She turned to Ingrid. "Come on. Even if it's cutthroat, we can beat them."

The four gathered around a card table in the corner of the room, where Reed proceeded to shuffle the cards and deal them out.

While some of the family continued to make small talk, the rest of them gathered around the table to watch the action.

Nelson turned to Yancy. "Another fine dessert. You just keep on outdoing yourself, Yancy."

"Thank you, Great One. Ready for a nightcap?"

Nelson nodded and smiled a thank-you. Minutes later Yancy handed him a glass of fine brandy.

Seeing it, Nadine sidled over and pulled a chair close

to Nelson. "Now that looks good." She turned to Yancy. "I'll have what he's having."

The cook walked away and returned minutes later to hand her a drink.

"Why did he call you Great One?" Nadine asked.

Nelson stretched out his legs toward the warmth of the fire. "That's the nickname my grandsons gave me years ago, and it stuck." He looked at her. "Why do your own daughters call you Nadine?"

She smiled. "It sounds so much younger than Mom, don't you think?"

His expression hardened. "I can't think of a more beautiful name than Mom, or Mama, or Mother. There is nothing more important in this world than being a mother."

"Easy to say when you've never been one." Nadine polished off her drink in one long swallow and leaned her head back.

"But I had one. My own mother was one of the finest women I've ever known. Though she was a perfect lady, she allowed me the room to develop my talents, even though she understood nothing whatsoever about film-making and no doubt thought it a foolish waste of my time and talent. In fact, she . . ." His words trailed off when he re-alized that the woman beside him was snoring. Her chest rose and fell with each breath. Her mouth had gone slack, presenting a picture that was not at all flattering.

Seeing that her glass was about to spill its contents down the front of her shirt, he took it from her hands and set it aside.

He looked at his daughter. "Grace Ann, I believe our . . . guest needs a bed."

Frank and Grace hurried to either side of Nadine and gently got her to her feet. She never even awoke.

When Frank motioned toward the stairs, Grace shook her head. "She might wake during the night and, in her condition, get disoriented and take a fall. I think, Frankie, we'll put her in that small guest room beside the mud-room, in case she wakes and needs some night air."

"Good idea, Gracie Girl."

The two of them walked Nadine into the small room. While Frank held her by the arm, Grace turned down the bed linens, and together they eased her into the bed. After removing the fringed boots, Grace drew the covers over her.

Nadine hadn't once moved.

When they turned out the light and closed the door, Grace turned to her husband. "Those poor girls."

He nodded and said not a thing.

No words were needed. They had both seen more than enough to let them know something of what Ingrid and Lily had been going through.

CHAPTER NINETEEN

The card game lasted another hour, with Lily winning nearly every hand.

At first, Reed was giving Lily every opportunity to win. He would refrain from asking for something she'd already asked for, so she would have the upper hand. But after several losses, he realized the little girl didn't need his help. She was smart enough to win on her own.

When she won for the fifth straight time, he narrowed his eyes on her. "I think you've figured out the meaning of *cutthroat*, haven't you?"

She glanced across the table at Luke before her smile bloomed. "Luke told me."

"He may have told you what it means, but I don't think you needed his help to win at this game. You're killing me. It's a good thing we're not playing for money. You'd be the richest one in the room."

After watching the game, Matt and Nessa called their good nights and went upstairs to their suite of rooms. Colin did the same.

Yancy, Mick, and the Great One, discussing the finer points of gourmet cooking and exotic food, kept breaking into smiles at the teasing and laughter that erupted from the card players across the room.

Burke, sprawled by the fire, nursing a longneck, said to Mick, "That's music to my ears."

The old cowboy nodded. "I was just thinking the same. I haven't seen my girls this relaxed in a long time. Probably not since their pa died."

The Great One studied him. "You've been with them a long time?"

"Since before they were born."

"I'd say that makes them your girls."

"They'll always feel like mine," Mick said with feeling. "They're the only family I've ever had."

The Great One stifled a yawn. "Since Frank and Gracie went up to bed, I believe I'll do the same."

Yancy nodded. "My day starts early. I'll say good night, too."

Gradually Mick and Burke drifted off, as well, leaving the four to finish their card challenge.

Reed tallied the wins and losses. "Want to play one more?"

"Even three more wouldn't get you even," Luke said with a laugh. "I think we should call it a night."

Lily was too weary to disagree. But as she started up the stairs, she turned to call, "Thanks, Reed. I really enjoyed beating you."

"You realize you owe me a rematch."

"I can't wait." The little girl scampered up the stairs, trailed more slowly by her big sister.

Luke waited before shoving back his chair. He turned to his brother, keeping his voice low enough that he wouldn't be overheard. "Thanks. I know you'd have rather been doing anything tonight than playing Fish. But it meant a lot to Lily."

"I didn't mind. Really. I know it kept her mind off other things." Reed paused before adding, "Is her mother always like that?"

Luke nodded.

"Poor kid." Reed placed the cards in a box before setting it on a shelf and heading up the stairs. "'Night, Luke."

"'Night."

A short time later, as Luke passed Lily's room on the way to his own, he could hear the two sisters talking quietly. Ingrid's voice was low, soothing.

Lily was lucky to have a big sister like that. But, he wondered, while Ingrid was busy easing her little sister's fears, who could she count on to soothe hers?

Ingrid heard Lily's prayers and tucked her into bed.

Lily caught her sister's hand. "Wasn't that fun tonight?"

"Yes, it was."

"For a while I even forgot Nadine was here."

"Me too." Ingrid smoothed a hand over Lily's hair. "'Night, honey."

"'Night."

"If you need anything at all, let me know."

The little girl's eyes were closing. "I will."

Ingrid waited a moment at the door, watching as Lily slid ever so gently into sleep.

If only she could do the same.

She made her way to her own room and stepped inside, closing the door behind her. When she turned, she caught sight of Luke standing across the room, his back to her, staring into the darkness.

"Luke." Her hand went to her throat before she let out a quick breath. "Sorry, I wasn't expecting you to be here."

"I just wanted to make sure you were all right."

"Of course I am. Why wouldn't I be?"

He shrugged and stepped closer. "I thought having Nadine here might upset you."

"I'm not happy about it. But she's a fact of my life. I've had plenty of time to get used to it. But I'm sure it was quite a jolt for your family. I wish they hadn't been forced to see her like that."

She pushed past Luke and walked to the window, lifting her head to the night sky. "They were all acting so polite. So nice."

"They weren't acting. They *are* nice."

"I know that." She turned to face him. "But that just makes it even more awkward. After spending time with your family and seeing how kind they are, I can't help comparing them with what I've grown up with." She crossed her arms over her chest and studied the toe of her boot. "I felt ashamed tonight. And Lily did, too. I could see it on her face. That's not something I'm proud of. But the truth is, we don't belong here, Luke."

He put his hands on her shoulders and rubbed gently. "You've seen the way Gram Gracie reacted to having two more girls around. The rest of my family feels the same way. They all love having you and Lily here."

She struggled to ignore the little thrill that raced down her spine at his touch. "And I love them for that. But—"

"Shh." He lowered his face and brushed his mouth over hers.

It was the softest of kisses, but it had her hands gripping his wrists. "You know I don't—"

"Yeah. Sorry to break one of your hard-and-fast rules." His grin was quick. "But there's always been this devil inside me that just has to see how many rules can be broken."

Before she could respond, he dragged her close and covered her mouth with his in a kiss that had her forgetting everything but the hot sizzle of need.

His kiss was easy. Practiced. Hers was quivering. Awkward. The difference between them made her all the more wary. But she had to admit that she liked the taste of him. A purely male taste that had all her senses heightened. And more than anything, she loved the way it felt being touched and kissed by him.

Luke's hands tightened at her shoulders before gliding down her back and drawing her firmly against him.

Her arms found their way around his waist. Her breasts were flattened against his chest. A chest that rose and fell with every ragged breath. She was aware of his arousal, and she wondered at the way her poor heart soared at the knowledge.

"Now, isn't this nicer than playing Fish?"

He ran nibbling kisses down her jaw, then lower, to the little hollow between her neck and shoulder, sending the most delicious tingles along her spine.

"Is this where your mind was during the game?"

Without a thought to what she was doing, she angled her head, allowing him easier access.

He nibbled her earlobe, her throat, and all the while his hands, those clever, work-worn hands, were kneading her back, her sides, until they encountered the swell of her breasts. His thumbs began a gentle exploration that had her breath shuddering, before coming out in a long, deep sigh.

She pushed a little away. "Wait. Luke—"

"You want me to stop?"

"No." The word came out so quickly, it caught her by surprise. She quickly recovered. "I mean yes. I need...I need time to think."

She looked up into his eyes and saw the smile. "What's so funny?"

He shook his head. "Just giving you time to think. So?" He dipped his face to brush his mouth over hers.

At once the rush of sexual tension was back, stronger than ever.

She wanted, so badly, to just go with her feelings. But it was so contrary to every rule she'd set for herself.

What was happening to her? She hated this weakness in herself. She had probably inherited it from Nadine. This yearning to just let herself give in and enjoy the luxury of being held in a man's arms. Of being loved. But Luke wasn't just any man. He was so good at this, he made her believe that she was special. Cherished. Like some rare and beautiful treasure that he'd just discovered.

She ought to know better. As Nadine was fond of saying, if a man wasn't with the one he loved, he could always love the one he was with.

The thought was like being splashed with ice water.

She put a hand to Luke's shoulder. "I think I need some time. I can't think when you're holding me, kissing me."

"That's good." He let his fingers play through the short, silky strands of her hair, watching the way they settled around her face. "Sometimes you can overthink things. Maybe you should just go with your feelings."

"Like Nadine?"

The words had the effect of a slap across the face. The minute she said them, she felt him withdrawing.

She did the same, taking a step back. "I'm sorry, Luke. I warned you. I'm no good at this. You'd better go."

"I could stay. We could talk, if you'd like. Or"—he gave her one of those rogue smiles that did such strange things to her heart—"I could prove to you that you're a hell of a lot better at this than you think."

"It's late. Your family is nearby, and I wouldn't want them to overhear us."

"Is that what this is about?"

"No." She gave a quick shake of her head. "This is about me. I want you to leave now."

"Okay." He framed her face with his hands and stared down into her eyes. "Take all the time you need. I want you to feel safe with me, Ingrid. And comfortable. I want you to trust me, and trust yourself."

"Maybe that's the problem. I'm not sure I'll ever be able to trust myself. At least where men are concerned."

"I'm not just any man."

"I know that." Her tone softened. "Thank you for understanding, Luke."

He smiled. "You're welcome." He kissed the tip of her

nose. "But just so you understand, this isn't over. I want you. And whether you're ready to admit it or not, you want me. Whenever you come to terms with that, we'll take this to the next step."

She pushed free, breaking contact. "You're so sure of yourself."

"I'm sure of what I'm feeling." He winked. "And I'm even more certain of what you're feeling, even if you're not."

"This doesn't change a thing, Luke. First thing in the morning, Mick and Lily and I are heading home."

His easy smile turned into a frown. "What about the gunman?"

She shook her head. "I'll just have to be more cautious. I'll carry a rifle with me everywhere, but I'll also carry on as I did before. I have a ranch to run or I'll lose it. I can't afford to let some mystery man dictate my life. And I can't just stay here, feeling pampered, and pretend I don't have any obligations."

He gave her a long, considering look before slowly nodding his head. "Okay. If that's your decision, I won't try to talk you out of it. But just so you know, I'll be going with you."

"This isn't your fight. And don't say you owe me for saving your life. You've already more than repaid me for that."

"Then let's just say I'm doing this for my own selfish reasons."

"Which are?"

"Ask my family. They'll tell you I just can't resist a good down-and-dirty fight." He added with a smile, "Or a pretty woman in trouble."

He opened the door and walked out without a backward glance.

Ingrid closed the door and leaned against it, crossing her arms over her chest, deep in thought.

On the one hand she was grateful that Luke was willing to stand beside her in her fight. There was no one she would rather have watching her back.

But now that she'd met his family and learned their history, she found herself caring as much about them as she did her own family.

What right did she have to allow him to risk his life for her?

Allow? The word had her suddenly smiling as she began undressing. That wasn't a word that could be used in the same breath with Luke. He didn't ask permission for anything. He lived life on his own terms.

How she envied him that freedom.

She lay in bed, eyes pressed firmly closed, her mind working overtime. Though she tried to concentrate on the things she needed to do when she returned to her ranch, the image of Luke holding her, kissing her, kept intruding on her thoughts.

She found herself wishing with all her heart that she could just let go of all the hard-and-fast rules she'd set for herself and simply indulge in the pleasure he offered.

She fell asleep dreaming of things that, if she were awake, would have had her blushing.

CHAPTER TWENTY

Ingrid could hear the hum of voices as she approached the kitchen. Now that she'd become familiar with Luke's family, she could make out the low tones of Luke's brother, Matt, and the more cultured voice of his bride, Vanessa. She heard Yancy and Mick on one side of the room, and Frank and Grace talking with Luke, and Reed joining in. What was most surprising to her was Lily's voice, high-pitched with excitement. She'd thought her sister was still asleep. She hadn't even heard Lily leave her room.

The minute Ingrid stepped into the room, Lily dashed over to catch her hands. "Guess what? Gram Gracie is taking me on one of her safaris."

"Now, Lily," Grace was quick to add, "our agreement was that you'd accompany me only if your sister says it's all right."

Ingrid glanced across the room, where Luke was

lounging against the counter, watching and listening with a look of amusement. "I don't know." She looked from Luke to his grandparents. "Do you think it's safe?"

Frank set aside his mug of coffee. "Darlin', I'm betting Lily will be safer with my Gracie Girl than in her own bed. The wranglers and I will see to it."

"Will you come with us, Ingrid? Please?" Lily danced up and down, still clinging to Ingrid's hands.

Ingrid drew her sister close. "I can't, honey. I'm planning on returning to the ranch today. I was hoping..." She saw the pleading look in Lily's eyes and gave a sigh of defeat. "But you don't need to come with me. I can't think of anything more exciting than spending time with someone who shares your love of both photography and wild horses. As long as you promise to do everything Gram Gracie asks you to, I...I guess I'm fine with it."

"Oh boy." Lily hugged her sister before racing across the room to do the same with Grace. "We're going on a safari." She looked up into the older woman's face. "When do we leave?"

"In about an hour. As soon as you pack your things, and we take time to enjoy Yancy's fine breakfast."

Lily started out of the room, then hurried back. "What should I pack?"

"Everything we bought in town. A pair of jeans and a T-shirt. A jacket, hat, and comfortable walking shoes. I'll take care of the bedrolls."

"Bedrolls. Will we sleep in a tent or outside?"

"Outside, unless it's raining. Then we'll sleep in the back of my truck." Grace started laughing. "It wouldn't be a good trip if we didn't get to sleep out of doors at least once."

"Oh boy." Lily's voice trilled on the air as she dashed from the room and raced up the stairs.

Frank was grinning from ear to ear. "Gracie Girl, doesn't this remind you of someone else?"

Nessa kissed his cheek before turning to Ingrid. "He's talking about me. The first time I went to the highlands with Gram Gracie, I was so excited, I thought I was in heaven."

"She's not kidding." Matt put his arms around his wife and drew her back against him. "I think that's what sealed the deal on our relationship. Nessa fell in love with those mustangs the minute she laid eyes on them. And the rest, as they say, is history." He brushed a kiss across his wife's neck. Such a simple thing, but to those watching, it felt deeply intimate.

Ingrid happened to glance at Luke at that moment and felt her cheeks color. She could almost feel his arms around her in that same way and knew, by the look in his eyes, he was feeling it, too.

"Well, then." She drew in a deep breath. "I guess I won't worry about Lily. I'll just let her go and see if she returns from the hills a changed little girl."

"From the things she's said about 'her' herd, I can almost guarantee it," Grace said as Yancy called them to breakfast. "She can't wait to photograph them, and she confided in me that she really wants to try my zoom lens so she can get up close the way I did"—Grace pointed to a framed photograph hanging in an alcove—"in that picture."

"I know what she'll be asking for when her birthday rolls around." Ingrid had a sudden thought. "Isn't Nadine up yet?"

"Up and gone." Yancy turned from the oven. "The others had just left to do some barn chores when she helped herself to some coffee and whiskey and said she was headed out."

"Did she say where?"

He shrugged. "If she did, I don't recall."

Minutes later Lily hurried into the kitchen with her backpack stuffed. She set it carefully in a corner of the mudroom before taking her place at the table beside her sister.

As she began to nibble scrambled eggs and steak, she suddenly looked over at Grace. "Oh. What will we do for food? Will we have to fish in a creek?"

"Don't you worry. We may plan on roughing it, but it's not all that primitive." Grace nodded toward their cook. "Yancy will see that we won't go hungry."

He pointed to the plastic pouches, all neatly labeled and stacked in a metal container. "If you decide to stay in the hills for a month, you won't run out of food."

Lily's eyes went wide. "Could we? Stay for a month?"

Frank started laughing. "Not on your life. I can't stand to be apart from my Gracie Girl as it is. If you're gone more than a week, I'll find you both and drag you home."

"Or you could stay up in the hills with us, Grandpop."

The old man's eyes watered just a bit at her easy use of his name before he leaned over to tousle her hair. "I could be easily persuaded to do just that, Lily darlin'. I might decide to stay with both of you."

Around the table, the others listened in silence and smiled.

Ingrid gave Lily a fierce hug, closing her eyes for a moment before letting her go.

Lily climbed up to the passenger side of the truck, where Grace sat at the wheel. She lowered the window and waved until they were out of sight.

While the others made their way to the house or the barns, Ingrid remained, staring at the cloud of dust.

Luke took her hand in his. "She'll be fine."

"I know." Ingrid managed a weak smile. "But I keep thinking about all the things that could go wrong. An angry mustang stallion. A lightning strike during a sudden storm. A fall, far from civilization. A—"

"Has she ever left you before?"

Ingrid lifted her chin. "This isn't about me, Luke."

"That's right. We were talking about Lily." He gave her a heart-stopping grin. "But I'm just asking."

"This is the first time she's ever gone anywhere without me."

"She's going to have the time of her life." He put an arm around her shoulders and drew her close. Against her ear he murmured, "And her big sister will survive."

She couldn't help laughing as she pushed away and punched him in the arm. "You're being mean."

"I'm being honest. This will do you both good. And if Lily is serious about photography, she couldn't have a better teacher than Gram Gracie."

Ingrid slowly nodded. "I know. I still can't believe that the photographer of Lily's favorite photo is your grandmother."

"Small world." He nodded toward her ranch truck parked near the porch. "Looks like Yancy wants to make sure you have enough provisions for a year."

Ingrid caught her breath at the boxes being loaded by Yancy and Mick into the back of the truck.

"Is that all food?"

Luke chuckled. "You saw what Yancy sent along on the safari. I'd say he and Mick conspired to double that amount before you head home."

As they walked closer, Mick turned to her. "You ready, girl?"

She nodded. "I'll just say my good-byes and get my things."

Mick held out the keys to Luke. "You want to drive?"

"You drive." Luke headed toward the barn. "I'll be right back."

Minutes later, with Mick behind the wheel, Ingrid walked down the back steps and tossed her overnight bag into the passenger side of the truck before turning to hug each member of Luke's family, including Yancy. "Thank you for all that food, Yancy. It will certainly save poor Mick from having to tolerate my cooking."

"That's what he said."

The two shared a laugh before she turned toward the truck.

Before she could climb inside, Luke roared up on his Harley. He tossed her a helmet and indicated the spot behind him. "Climb on."

She stood a moment, staring in disbelief. "You can't be serious."

"Oh, he's serious, all right." Reed slapped his grandfather on the back. "I wondered how long it would take before Luke got the itch."

"Well, I don't have an itch to ride on that thing with him." Ingrid turned to Luke's family, none of whom seemed surprised to see him waiting for her to make up her mind. "Aren't any of you going to tell him he's crazy?"

"Oh, we all know that." Matt winked at his wife, who was covering her laughter with a hand over her mouth. "What we want to know is whether you're as crazy as my brother."

Vanessa added, "Nobody can be that crazy, Matt."

Ingrid turned to Colin. "You strike me as the sensible one. Am I taking my life in my hands by riding with him?"

"I guess you'll never know unless you try." Colin leaned close to add, "It's true that Luke's always been wild and crazy. But I'm betting he won't be taking any chances with you onboard. I'm thinking he considers you precious cargo."

Precious cargo.

Ingrid drew in a breath before accepting the helmet from Luke's hand. To his family she explained, "I know. Just call me crazy."

Then, with a shake of her head at her own foolishness, she settled herself behind him on the Harley and wrapped her arms around his waist. With a wave, he revved the engine and they took off in a roar. Mick followed more slowly in the ranch truck.

"You okay back there?"

"I'm fine." And, she realized, she was.

After the first mile or so she learned to take the dips and curves of the road by following Luke's movements. When he leaned left, she did the same. When he straightened, she would relax her hands a bit. But she kept her arms firmly around his waist, feeling a sense of being anchored.

Anchored.

She could get used to this.

The press of her body to his. The fresh breeze cooling her face, despite the heat of the helmet. The amazing feeling of flying as they sped along a smooth track. The dizzying blur of movement when they crested a hill and, seeing no one for miles, opened up and soared.

Every once in a while he would point to something, and she would be alerted to a herd of deer or elk, heads lifted, watching in silence as they rolled past.

She'd driven these roads and trails for a lifetime, but suddenly she was seeing them in a brand-new way. Without the encumbrance of a truck, she felt small and insignificant amid the towering hills and buttes.

It was, she realized, an experience like no other. She felt part of the scenery. She felt free. And wildly exhilarated.

When the motorcycle started up a steep dirt trail, she tightened her grasp around Luke's waist and pressed her face to his shoulder.

He turned his head slightly. "You're going to love this." Each word seemed to vibrate inside her head as they reached the top.

For a moment they were on level ground. But without warning they began a sudden descent, racing headlong down a steep hill at breakneck speed. It was more thrilling than any roller-coaster ride.

There was no time to react as the road raced past them in a blur of movement. Minutes later they were once again on a level stretch of road, moving at a normal rate of speed.

"How're you doing?"

"I'm loving it."

And she was. Though she should have been terrified, there had been no time for fear. It dawned on her that the presence of this man had made all the difference.

Colin had said she was Luke's precious cargo. If that was true, he was equally precious to her. She had somehow learned over these past weeks to trust him. Completely. She had the sense that, without a doubt, no harm could come to her as long as she was with Luke Malloy.

Was that the same as love?

The question flashed into her mind with such clarity, she was forced to suck in a breath.

Could it be? Was it possible for someone like her, who had vowed to never trust a man with her heart? Was it possible to love a man she'd known for such a short time? A man who was everything she wasn't?

Where she'd always been cautious, straightforward, Luke was fearless, jumping in where even angels wouldn't tread.

Yet here she was, having the time of her life on a dangerous vehicle, without an ounce of fear.

Because of Luke.

A wide smile split her lips, and she raised her arms above her head while giving out a shout of pure joy.

As they rolled up to her ranch, he brought the Harley to a halt and stepped off before taking her hand and helping her.

They both removed their helmets and listened for a moment to the silence around them.

He took the helmet from her hands. "Was that a victory shout-out?"

She couldn't stop the laughter that bubbled up. "Yeah. My version of the happy dance."

"I guess that means you're not sorry you gave up the truck in favor of this?"

"Not sorry at all. Oh, Luke, I loved every minute of it."

He was looking at her with such intensity, she knew he was going to kiss her. She actually lifted herself on tiptoe, barely able to contain herself as she placed a hand on his shoulder.

At that moment the old truck wheezed up behind them and came to a stop.

Luke leaned close to whisper, "Hold that thought. Sooner or later we're bound to find some time alone."

"You two crazy bikers going to stand there all day, or give me a hand with this food?"

At Mick's challenge, they turned and made their way to the back of the truck. But as they hauled the parcels inside, they kept exchanging knowing smiles.

Ingrid found herself tingling with a wild sense of anticipation at the thought of what was to come.

CHAPTER TWENTY-ONE

As Ingrid carried in a box filled with food packets, she began reading the labels aloud. "Roast beef. Fried chicken. Stuffed pork chops. Garlic mashed potatoes." She glanced at Mick. "We'll be eating like guests in a five-star hotel."

He chuckled. "Without paying a five-star price."

Ingrid unpacked the boxes and handed the packets to Mick, while he loaded them into the freezer.

Luke walked in with another box and set it on the table.

Ingrid was beaming. "This was so sweet of Yancy."

"He's a sweet guy."

"So is your family. All of them. I still can't believe your grandmother invited Lily to go on one of her photographic safaris."

He began unpacking the second box. "You should have heard Nessa when she returned from her first time up in the hills. She couldn't stop raving about the experience. The herds of mustangs. The chance to sleep under the stars. The fact that she was so far from civilization. For a city girl, it was pure heaven."

"Lily may be pure country, but I think she'll feel the same way. Just being in the presence of a woman she admires is such a treat. And then there's the chance to learn all about the techniques of photography that none of us could ever help her with. I'm betting she'll be in little-girl heaven."

Luke tugged on a lock of Ingrid's hair. "Yes, but will her big sister survive?"

Ingrid blushed. "I'm trying to stay positive."

"And doing a damned fine job, girl. You're not used to sharing Lily with anyone." Mick closed the freezer and wiped his hands on a kitchen towel. "Now the biggest decision we have to make today is which packet I should open for our dinner." He looked at the two of them. "Anything in particular you craving?"

"Nothing I can say out loud." Luke covered his words with a cough.

Ingrid colored. "Your choice, Mick."

"Okay. I'll surprise you."

Luke looked out the window. "I don't see Nadine's truck."

Ingrid's smile faded. "I guess, after the show she put on for your family last night, she isn't ready for the quiet ranch life yet. She's probably gone back to Wayside." She turned toward the door. "I need to get busy with chores. First I'll tackle the barn, and then I'm going to ride to the hills and check on the herd."

Luke kept his tone casual. "We'll both tackle the barn

chores, and then we can check on the herd together and still get back in time for supper."

"Thanks, Luke." Ingrid's smile returned. "Okay. I'll see you in the barn."

When the door closed behind her, Mick put the kettle on before turning from the stove. "That was smooth, son. I'm guessing you intend to see she's never alone."

Luke's tone hardened. "You got that right."

"Then you believe that shooter didn't make a mad dash out of town?"

"Who knows? He could be lying low. He could even be gone. But what I do know is this: He's a coward, who used the cover of darkness to shoot at an innocent woman. That sort of lowlife doesn't usually give up."

"Then how do you plan on keeping her safe? You can't be everywhere."

Luke managed a lazy smile. "Neither can he. But if I'm at the right place at the right time, he won't get a second chance."

"It's such a relief to see my herd still standing."

Ingrid and Luke kept their horses to a steady pace as they moved among the cattle.

They'd tackled the hard, never-ending barn chores before riding across the hills. In the heat of the late afternoon their shirts were plastered to their skin, their hair damp beneath their hats.

Spotting a calf that seemed to be favoring one leg, Ingrid slid from the saddle. Kneeling in the grass, she began to probe the animal's leg.

Luke studied her, wishing he had his grandmother's skill with a camera. Whether wielding a pitchfork or tending one of her herd, she moved with all the grace and poise of a dancer.

He sat back, enjoying the way her faded denims molded every line and curve of her backside. The fitted tee she'd bought in town provided him with a clear view of the body she'd always kept hidden inside those baggy tops. Her hair, cut in a haphazard manner, fell in damp wisps around her face.

As she worked, Luke couldn't keep his eyes off her. She did everything with quiet competence. From mucking stalls to hosing down the barn floors, from spending hours in the blistering heat to checking out her herd, she moved with both authority and competence, two traits he admired.

Of course, if he were being honest, it wasn't admiration he was feeling. It was lust, pure and simple.

He watched the darkened trail of sweat along the back of her shirt and had a vision of his hands following that trail. With every movement she made, he felt his throat go dry and his temperature climb.

If he thought she was beautiful in those trademark baggy shirts, she was dazzling in these new, skin-hugging tees.

"Ready to head back?" He remained in the saddle, watching as she finally pulled herself up on her horse's back.

"I guess so. There doesn't seem to be any discomfort in the leg. I think he was just feeling frisky and missed a step."

He couldn't keep the grin from his lips. "Yeah. Feeling frisky can do that to a guy."

With a last look at the herd, she turned her mount

toward home with a smile. Their horses moved easily across a meadow alive with wildflowers.

As they splashed through Glacier Creek, Luke shot her a sideways glance. "That water looks mighty tempting. Care to go skinny-dipping with me?"

"Oh, you don't know how tempted I am."

At her words, his hopes soared.

She lowered her voice. "But Mick will have supper ready, and it wouldn't be fair to keep him waiting on his first day home with all that fancy food to choose from."

"Oh, I don't know about that." Luke slid from the saddle to drink, allowing his horse to do the same. "We wouldn't be that late."

Ingrid stared longingly at the cool water.

To add to her temptation, he caught a handful of water and tossed it at her. "Can't you forget your schedule for a little while and just play?"

"Oh. You want to play?" Without warning, she was out of the saddle and into the stream, kicking a spray of water in his face.

A sexy smile curved his mouth as he wiped water from his eyes. "Lady, you just sealed your fate."

He made a dive for her, but she evaded him and sent another spray of water his way. She almost managed to run away, but he caught her ankle and she dropped face-first into the water.

She came up sputtering, only to find him standing over her, wringing out his soaked shirt, dripping a steady stream of water on her head.

She wiped at her eyes before making a grab for Luke. His reflexes were quick, but his foot slipped on a submerged log and he fell backward. Ingrid was on him in a flash, ducking his head below water when he tried to surface.

With a shout, he wrapped both arms around her and dragged her under with him.

They came up laughing. But as they continued wrestling, each fighting to topple the other, their laughter suddenly died in their throats when Luke lowered his head and captured her mouth.

For a moment Ingrid pushed back, eyes wide with surprise. Then, without a word, she wrapped her arms around his neck and kissed him with a hunger that caught them both by surprise.

They lingered over the kiss, taking it deeper, then deeper still, until they were both struggling for breath.

With his chest heaving, Luke nibbled the corner of her jaw. "Lucky thing we have all this nice, cold water. Otherwise, at least one of us would have gone up in flames." He stared into her eyes. "For a woman who doesn't like to be kissed, you really seem to have mastered the art."

"Thanks." Her voice was a purr of pleasure. "I thought I'd give it a try."

"Let's try it again." He lowered his face, his lips moving ever so slowly over hers, tasting, teasing, until, on a sigh, she wrapped her arms around his waist. When her hands came in contact with his naked flesh, she paused for a heartbeat before sighing and giving herself up to the purely sensuous feelings that curled along her spine.

When she came up for air, she touched a hand to his cheek. "That's nice. I do like kissing you, Luke."

"That's good to know. Because I intend to do a whole lot more of it."

He dipped his head and took her mouth. The kiss spun on and on until their breathing grew strained and their hearts were pumping.

He reached for the ends of her damp shirt. When his fingers fumbled, she surprised him by slipping her hands beneath his and quickly tugging it over her head.

He stared down at her with a look of pure male appreciation. "Oh, lady. Now you've done it. If a kiss is an invitation, getting half naked is a royal command."

He gathered her close and kissed her with a depth of passion that had them both struggling for every breath. "You know I want you, Ingrid," he said with a raw voice. "But you need to tell me if I'm misreading..."

She pressed a finger to his lips. "Yes."

He went very still.

She smiled then. A sly, woman's smile. "Yes, Luke. I want the same thing you want."

"Oh, God." On a moan he scooped her up and strode to the shore, laying her down in the grass and stretching out beside her.

There were no words between them as he dragged her close and nearly devoured her in a kiss so hot, so hungry, it rocked them both.

She responded, pouring herself into every kiss, every touch, with a passion that had them rolling in the cool grass together, hands clutching, mouths seeking as they kicked off their boots and shed their jeans.

Seeing her reaching for the fasteners of her bra, he whispered, "Let me help you out of—" In his haste he tore it from her. "Sorry. I didn't mean to..." He shook his head. "I want to be gentle, but..."

"I'm not some delicate flower, Luke." She framed his face with her hands and smiled. "I'm just a woman."

"Never call yourself *just* a woman. You're the most beautiful"—he closed his hands over hers and leaned in to kiss her—"most dazzling woman I've ever known. And you've got me so tied up in knots..."

Against his lips she murmured, "I think we should untie those knots."

His look was fierce. "Oh, the things I want to do with you."

She touched a finger to his lips. "Stop talking and show me, cowboy."

It was all the invitation he needed.

His big hands moved over her, touching her with a reverence he hadn't even known was possible. He moved calloused palms along the smooth trail of her back, the flare of her hips, and then up her sides until his thumbs found the swell of her breasts.

When she sighed with pleasure, he lowered his mouth to nibble and tease until she writhed and nearly sobbed from the exquisite pleasure.

On a growl, he showered her with deep, wet kisses and frantic touches. He explored every inch of her body with lips and tongue and fingertips, hungry to show her all that he was feeling.

No longer hesitant, Ingrid followed his lead, moving her hands over his muscled torso, pausing to follow the line of corded muscles. Her fingertips trailed the flat planes of his stomach, causing him to tremble. But when she moved her hands lower, he sucked in a breath before stilling her movements. "Oh, baby. I thought I could wait. But I'm so hot..."

Aware that she'd gone still, he froze. "I didn't mean to scare you. I'll wait as long as you need me to. Just tell me you want this, too." For a moment he couldn't breathe. His heart forgot to beat. "I don't want to hurt—"

She stopped his words with a long kiss that had all his breath backing up in his throat. Against his mouth she whispered, "You're doing it again, Luke. Talking. Just show me."

They came together in an explosion of passion that staggered him.

Ingrid reared up, her aroused body taut as a bowstring, her arms circling his neck, as he felt himself sinking fully into her. He tried to slow the storm inside him, but he had no control left.

He began moving with her, climbing, his heart pumping, body slick with sheen.

The world around him had narrowed to this place, this moment, this all-consuming need. If the skies had opened up, if the herd had stampeded and threatened to crush them beneath their hooves, he couldn't have stopped.

A desperate need inside him, like a beast fighting for release, had been waging a terrible war, and now free, it took over his will. He was helpless to do more than ride the passion.

"Ingrid. God, Ingrid!"

The words were torn from Luke's throat as he began racing, climbing, frantic to reach the very pinnacle of the mountain. As the climax slammed into him, he could feel himself touching the very center of the sun before shattering into thousands of hot, blistering fragments.

* * *

They lay in the cool grass, waiting for the world to settle.

Luke's face was buried in the hollow of Ingrid's throat. His breathing was as ragged as her pulse beat.

"You okay?"

She responded by touching her palm to his cheek and a murmured, "Mmm."

"I was rough."

"Hmm."

He lifted his head to stare down at her. "I hurt you."

"No." She smiled.

"Ah. She speaks." That had him relaxing. He nibbled the corner of her lips. "You don't have to say a word. I'll do all the talking."

"Mmm."

"Do you know how long I've wanted this? Just this. With only you."

Her eyes snapped open and she focused on him. "Since you first saw me?"

"Wait. How could you know? Have I already told you?"

She moved her head languidly from side to side. "I just know. It was the same for me."

He looked thunderstruck. "Are you kidding? I thought you could barely tolerate me."

"Yeah. Barely. I spent a lot of time fighting it. But honestly? First glance, and I was gone."

She saw the look of pure male pleasure on his face before glancing skyward, where the sun was already beginning to dip behind the hills. "We'd better go. Mick will be waiting."

"Wait. I want to talk about this."

"We can do it later."

"Later? Like later tonight?"

She merely smiled, like a woman harboring secrets.

Luke got slowly to his feet before helping her to stand. He drew her into the circle of his arms and kissed her. "I hope you'll agree to round two tonight."

"You make it sound like fight night."

"More like wrestling. You're strong for a woman. I like that. Round two later?"

She tried for a cool look before breaking into a laugh. "How can I resist such a sexy request? I wouldn't miss it for the world."

"Oh, thank you, God." He kissed her again before handing her the soaked clothes that lay in a heap on the banks of the stream. "And maybe tomorrow we can try actually skinny-dipping instead of water war."

"We can try. But I think I know how it will end." She had to struggle into the wet clothes that now fit her like a second skin.

She sat in the grass to put on her boots before pulling herself into the saddle. Then, with Luke beside her, they headed down the hill and toward the barn.

Inside, as they unsaddled their horses and turned them into a corral, Luke gave her a long, knowing smile. "I hope Mick can have dinner ready as soon as we've showered. I can't wait to get you upstairs and see what other moves you know."

"I'm betting you have a lot more than I do."

In his best imitation of an old codger he muttered, "Just so you know. I'm more than happy to share whatever knowledge I have with you, little lady."

"And I'm more than happy to take you up on that, cowboy."

They were both laughing as they made their way inside, where the kitchen was perfumed with the most amazing fragrances. Then they hurried upstairs to shower and change, eager to get through the evening so they could continue their newly discovered love fest.

CHAPTER TWENTY-TWO

That was amazing, Mick." Luke sat back, sipping coffee, feeling on top of the world.

"Thanks to Yancy." The old man helped himself to a second slice of Yancy's chocolate layer cake and topped it with ice cream. He looked at Ingrid and Luke, who had spent the entire meal smiling and darting glances. "Want seconds?"

They both shook their heads.

"Then I may have to eat your share, too." With a satisfied grin, Mick began to eat slowly, savoring every bite. "Girl, your pa loved chocolate cake more than any man I've ever known."

Ingrid's smile grew. "Probably because nobody ever baked him one. The only chocolate cake he ever had came from that little grocery in Wayside."

Mick nodded. "And it never tasted like this."

Luke circled the table, topping off their cups. "That's because those things are full of preservatives."

Ingrid shot him a look. "Well, listen to you. How would you know about such things?"

He gave her a wicked smile. "Lady, there are so many things you don't know about me."

"I'll bet you can't wait to fill us in on the real Luke Malloy." She turned to Mick. "Get ready for the big reveal."

Luke replaced the coffeepot and sat down beside her, stretching out his long legs. "The fact is, most of what little I know about such things I learned from my brother Reed. Ever since he was a teen he's been obsessing about all the harmful foods we ingest. Right now he's raising a herd of cattle that's been, from birth, completely hormone and steroid free."

Mick paused, his fork halfway to his mouth. "How can he keep an entire herd healthy without drugs?"

"It's a lot of work. He has to be really vigilant. One virus could wipe out his herd in a single season. But he figures it's worth the effort. An Italian beef supplier has given him a limited contract, to test the market. If they like the numbers, it could become a huge success for our ranch."

Mick turned to Ingrid. "You remember when your pa thought about that very thing?"

She shook her head. "I don't remember. How long ago was that?"

He thought a minute. "I guess it was just about the time you were getting ready to leave for college. He was moping around, missing you even before you left. Then he sat me down one evening and started laying out his plans for a new breed of cattle."

Ingrid watched the old cowboy's eyes. "Was it a solid plan?"

Mick nodded. "It was a good idea, but like so many of Lars's plans, there was no follow-through. He got side-tracked by having to deal with Nadine's wild side, and the fact that without you, he'd have to be both ma and pa to Lily. After a while, it was like everything else he ever planned. Life got in the way, and his plans fell flat. And then, without warning, Lars was gone."

"Sounds like he was a man ahead of his time," Luke remarked.

Beside him, Ingrid had gone strangely silent at the mention of her father's passing.

"Reminds me of another time, when Lars and I were riding across the southern ridge of his land and he mentioned that a mining company had approached him about taking some soil samples." Mick grew thoughtful. "They were pretty sure there were valuable minerals on his land."

Luke smiled. "Lots of ranchers make more on mineral rights than they do on cattle. Did Lars pursue it?"

The old man shook his head, remembering. "Lars always figured he'd take care of things tomorrow."

"We all do." Ingrid's voice was subdued. "We think we'll live forever, and if we're good enough, and work hard enough, we'll see all our dreams come true."

Hearing the thread of pain in her words, Luke caught her hand. "There's nothing wrong with that."

She stared at their joined hands. "You don't strike me as being a fool, Luke."

"You think it's foolish to believe in happily-ever-after?"

"That's for Lily's storybooks." She tugged her hand free. "I'm a realist. If life has taught me anything, it's this. The selfish takers of this world walk all over the good and kind and decent people who believe in playing by the rules."

He leaned over and planted a kiss on the corner of her mouth. "You're a hard-hearted woman, Ms. Larsen. Someday Prince Charming will come along and force you to admit how wrong you've been." He stood and walked to the sink. "In the meantime, I'll let you use your amazing talent to dry the dishes I'm about to wash. It's the least we can do to thank Mick for this meal."

Mick grinned as he picked up his cup of coffee and started toward his room. "I'm hoping to watch another rerun of *Perry Mason*. Good night, you two. After all this food, I'll be lucky to stay awake past the first commercial."

When his door closed, Luke winked at Ingrid as she stepped up beside him, towel in hand. "I thought we'd never be alone. How fast can you dry?"

She shrugged. "I guess that depends on how fast you can wash."

He wiggled his brows. "Five minutes tops. Then I'm getting you upstairs, all to myself."

After turning out the lights, Luke followed Ingrid up the stairs. Once there he pressed her against the wall, kissing her like a man starved for the taste of her. She responded with a hunger of her own.

"I thought dinner would never end." He ran wet, nibbling kisses down her throat.

She sighed and angled her head, giving him easier access. "I thought you were fascinated by all Mick had to say."

"Honestly?" He fumbled with the buttons of her shirt. "I can't remember a thing he told us."

She started to laugh, but it turned into a little gasp as his mouth trailed the swell of her breast, covered by the merest wisp of silk.

When he tried to tug it free, she whispered, "Luke Malloy, if you rip another bra, I'll soon run out of underthings."

"That wouldn't be the worst thing."

"You're impossible." She put her hands to his chest, but instead of pushing him away she found herself tangling her fingers in the front of his shirt to drag him closer.

Against her throat he muttered, "I want you out of these clothes."

"You're also impatient."

"I am when it comes to you, woman." He picked her up and started down the hallway. "Your room or mine?"

Before she could say a word, he strolled past her door and continued to the room at the end of the hall. Instead of setting her down, he merely nudged the door open with his foot, then kicked it shut behind them.

He lowered her to her feet and slid her shirt from her shoulders before reaching a hand to the snaps at her waist. She did the same for him, tugging his shirt over his head before unsnapping his jeans. Then he unhooked her bra and dropped it to the floor with the rest of their clothes.

"That's better." He ran his hands across her shoulders, then down her arms, gathering her close enough to feel her flesh against his. A smile warmed his voice. "Oh yeah. Much better."

She moved one booted foot up his leg. "I need to get out of these."

"Yeah. Leave it to me." He eased her down on the edge of the bed and sat beside her, nudging off his own boots and slipping out of his denims. Then he surprised her by kneeling before her to slide off her boots and jeans.

In the darkened room, illuminated only by a spill of moonlight through the window, he ran his rough, calloused palm along her leg to her thigh before bending close to press a trail of kisses.

"Luke..."

When she put a hand to his shoulder, he stopped her. "Earlier today, I promised you I'd make up for being too hot and frantic. Now that we have all night, this is for you, Ingrid. For both of us. Long and slow and easy."

He took his time, exploring her body with lips and tongue and fingertips, until her body shuddered, and they were both mad with need. He lifted her to the center of the bed and lay down beside her. His rough hands moved over her, surprisingly gentle, like a whisper of silk. His kisses followed. Soft, gentle kisses that had her sighing with pure pleasure.

"You're so beautiful."

"I'm not." The words spilled from her lips before she could think.

"Why would you say that? If you've ever looked in a mirror, you have to know how you look."

"I don't bother much with a mirror. I've no use for one."

"Then you've never seen what I'm seeing."

"What do you see, Luke?"

"A beautiful woman who tries so hard to hide that beauty so she won't become like her mother. It's why you cut off all your hair. Why you try to hide your body." He kissed her mouth when she started to protest. "But you can never be like Nadine. She's a selfish child. And you're a woman. A beautiful, generous woman who puts her own needs aside to care for those who matter to her."

He ran a trail of kisses down her throat. "I want to be one of those who matter to you, Ingrid."

"You are." Her words were muffled against his temple.

He gathered her so close he could feel her heartbeat inside his own chest. And though his passion threatened to overtake him, he'd do anything to give her all the pleasure she deserved.

Once again, his caresses slowed. His kisses gentled as the never-ending chores were put aside. For this night, the danger that threatened was also forgotten.

Now there were only the long midnight hours of leisure that lay ahead. And the knowledge that they could uncover all the hidden pleasures they'd so long anticipated.

As their kisses deepened, and their touches grew more demanding, they lay steeped in glorious feelings that lifted them above anything they'd known. Not just pleasure, but need. A quiet, desperate need that had their bodies slick with sheen, their hearts pumping in anticipation.

"Luke. Please. Now."

At her soft plea, he moved over her with deliberate care, entering her and holding back as she welcomed him. Every movement, every thrust was slow, deep, measured.

"Luke. Oh, Luke, I can't stop. I can't…" Her words died as she was lost in the unbearable pleasure.

Even now, with his passion building, his heart pounding, Luke waited until he felt her reach the very top of the mountain and slip over to the other side before allowing himself to give in to his own shuddering climax.

For the longest time they lay, still joined, as their world slowly settled.

When at last he could move, he framed her face with his hands and looked down into her face.

She smiled up at him.

No words were needed as she wrapped her arms around his waist and clung to him.

He moved his weight off her, gathering her close.

"That was…" She sighed, letting the sound express what she was unable to put into words.

Against her temple he murmured, "Sleep awhile."

She had already gone limp in his arms, her breathing soft and steady.

He watched her, loving the way she looked in his arms. His woman.

The thought caught him by surprise before he smiled.

She was his. He didn't know quite how it had happened, or when she'd gone from just another rancher to this amazing, beautiful creature who'd captured his heart. Or how pure lust had morphed into something much more.

He'd always prided himself on his freedom. From rules. From doing all the ordinary things other men did.

Yet here he was, thinking about permanence, and settling down, and happily-ever-after.

Prince Charming he wasn't. The very thought had him

grinning again. But he did intend to let her know that there was such a thing as a happy ending. Her cynical little heart might not be ready to accept it quite yet, but he would just have to wear her down until he made a believer of her.

CHAPTER TWENTY-THREE

Ingrid felt the mattress shift and looked up to find Luke facing her on the edge of the bed, holding two mugs.

"Coffee?" She breathed deeply before sitting up. "Oh, Luke."

"Yeah. I thought we could both use some caffeine." He handed her a cup before settling in beside her.

She drank gratefully before glancing toward the window, to see clouds drifting past a full moon. Caught up in the heady excitement of their newly discovered freedom, they'd barely snatched any time to sleep. Instead, they'd loved in the dark with a passion that left them both breathless.

"Only a few hours left until morning."

"Is that disappointment in your voice?"

She chuckled. "Sorry. But if I'm going to be honest, I have to admit that I hate to see this night end."

"About that honesty of yours..." He looked at her. "Yesterday, by the creek, you said I had you at first glance."

She looked down. "I was hoping you'd forgotten."

"A guy doesn't forget an admission like that. Why did you act like you could barely stand me?"

She cupped her hands around the mug. "I guess it was a survival tactic."

"Survival?"

She drank, then set the mug on a nightstand beside the bed before looking at him. "I vowed I'd never be like Nadine."

He gave a snort of derision. "You couldn't be if you tried."

"You've said that before, but it isn't so. I saw the moves she made on you. And I was jealous. And that jealousy made me afraid that I'd do something stupid."

"You mean liking me would be stupid?"

"No. Yes." She blew out a breath. "It's complicated. When you started paying attention to me, I was afraid I'd find out that you pretended to like me so you could get close to Nadine."

"Has that happened before?"

She nodded. "I brought home a...friend from college to meet my family over spring break. The next day I caught him coming out of her room."

"What did your father have to say?"

"I didn't tell him. I ordered Roger to leave. He was gone within the hour, and I told my dad that he'd had a family emergency."

"And Nadine?"

"She left later that day with a smug, satisfied grin. Knowing Nadine, she probably arranged to meet him again in Wayside."

"Oh, baby." Luke set down his mug and gathered her into his arms. Against her temple he murmured, "Roger

Whatshisname was a damned fool. In fact, the biggest fool in the world."

Ingrid sighed, wrapping her arms around his waist. "I hope I'm not just as big a fool."

He drew a little away to look down into her face. "What's that supposed to mean?"

"I saw that same smug look on Nadine's face that night she came out of your room. I don't want to ask, but—"

"No."

At the harshness of his tone she blinked. "No? You mean don't ask?"

"That's exactly what I mean. Don't lower yourself to ask. Not now. Not ever." He put a finger beneath her chin and tipped up her face, forcing her to meet his steady gaze. "There may be a lot of fools in this world attracted to someone like Nadine, but I'm not one of them. The only woman I see is you, Ingrid. The only one I've seen since being in this house is you. Only you."

She took in a long, slow breath. And then, without a word, offered her trembling lips to him.

He took them with a hunger that caught them both by surprise.

"You brought more coffee?" Ingrid shoved wispy hair from her eyes before sitting up.

"Yeah. Along with some food." Luke climbed into bed and set a plate of toast and cold roast beef between them. "I've burned more energy during this night than I would in a week rounding up cattle."

A look out the window showed the first faint smudges of dawn coloring the horizon.

Ingrid touched a hand to Luke's arm. "I wish we could hold on to this night."

He held the beef and toast to her lips for a bite. "But think about the fun we can have by day. Or have you forgotten about skinny-dipping?"

That brought a smile to her eyes. "Oh, I haven't forgotten."

"Good. I hope this turns into one long, hot, sweltering day. We could make it last for hours."

"I think you're getting spoiled."

"If so, you're the one who spoiled me." He leaned over to indulge in a long, lazy kiss. "For any other woman."

"Am I supposed to feel guilty?"

He set aside the plate to drag her on top of him. Against her mouth he growled, "Not guilty. Just thoroughly satisfied, woman. Because that's how you've made me feel."

And then there were no words as they took each other on a slow, delicious ride of pure pleasure.

Luke and Ingrid were laughing together as they stepped into the mudroom to wash after their morning chores.

"'Morning, you two." Mick opened the oven and retrieved a tray of biscuits when they entered the kitchen. "Sounds like you were having fun out there."

"Luke boasted that he could clean more stalls."

Luke stood back grinning. "I guess you showed me."

Mick looked from one to the other. "So I guess you won that bet, girl."

"Of course I did."

"And Luke got to lean on his pitchfork and watch you do the bulk of the work."

"And it was a damned pretty sight to behold." Behind her, Luke winked.

Ingrid turned in time to see it. "You conned me."

"You can't blame a guy for being a guy."

At that, both Luke and Mick burst into laughter.

Instead of her usual irate response, Ingrid joined in while playfully punching Luke in the shoulder. "And here I thought I was being so smart."

Luke reached up and smoothed a lock of her hair from her eyes, and the two of them shared a smile.

Mick's look sharpened.

He set out a plate of scrambled eggs and another of crisp bacon and toast. "You two heading up to the herd again today?"

"Later." Luke held the plate toward Ingrid before helping himself to the food. "But first, we have a chore to see to here."

Ingrid shot him a questioning look. "A chore?"

He took his time tasting the eggs, the bacon, the toast. "I'm hoping you'll give me a haircut."

"A . . ." She lowered her fork to stare at his head. "A haircut? Why?"

"It's hot. I'm tired of dealing with it. It's time for a change."

Mick was grinning. "Amen to all of that."

Ingrid looked from Mick to Luke. "All right. But I'm wondering how you'll look without that ponytail."

"I guess you'll find out." Luke turned his attention to his breakfast, soon helping himself to seconds.

"You've got yourself a healthy appetite, son." Mick topped off their coffees.

"Yeah. I burned a lot of calories—" Luke stopped himself before adding, "out in the barn."

Ingrid shot him a sideways glance and covered the laughter that bubbled up by coughing behind her hand.

Mick placed the coffeepot on the stove and returned to his seat at the table. "Maybe I'll join you two up in the hills. Looks like a good day for a ride."

Luke swallowed back the groan that threatened before pushing away his half-filled plate. "Looks like I wasn't as hungry as I thought."

"That's all right, son." Mick dug into his food. "You'll have plenty of time to work up another hunger for some of Yancy's Fancy Chicken by tonight."

"Yeah. I will." Luke carried his dishes to the sink. "I'll get started on washing up here."

Ingrid joined him, picking up a towel. "Where do you want me to cut your hair? Upstairs in the bathroom?"

He shook his head. "I don't think you want all this hair on the floor up there. I think I'll just haul a chair outside and you can cut it in the yard."

"Good idea, son." Mick drained his coffee and sat back. "I think I'm going to enjoy watching this."

Luke took off his shirt and draped a bath towel around his shoulders before taking a seat in the yard.

Mick settled himself on the back stoop to watch as Ingrid stepped outside with a mirror, comb, and scissors.

Luke reached a hand to the elastic holding back his hair. Once free, his hair fell to his shoulders.

Ingrid ran a comb through it, and Luke gave a humming sound.

She paused. "Something wrong?"

"No. That feels good."

She leaned close, so Mick couldn't hear. "Why are you insisting on me doing this?"

"The truth?" He turned his head, keeping his voice low. "I don't like the idea of my hair being longer than my woman's."

My woman.

Her heart took a hard, quick bounce before the smile touched her lips, and then her eyes. "Really?"

"Yeah." He closed a hand over hers. "Now get on with it, woman."

She shoved the mirror into his hand. "Use that tone again and I just might shave your head."

He laughed and turned away.

She approached the job hesitantly, snipping a few strands of hair, pausing to watch as they drifted to the grass. With each snip she could feel Luke watching her in the mirror. Each time their gazes met and held, she felt a tiny shiver of heat along her spine. Despite all that they'd shared, it seemed strangely intimate to be cutting his hair.

Before long she got so caught up in the task, she found herself taking bigger clumps of hair and cutting, then cutting even more.

She indicated the mirror. "Well?"

"Shorter."

She cut more, then more. And finally, using an extension cord that snaked all the way from the mudroom, she used the electric trimmer to shave his sideburns and the back of his neck.

Mick ambled over. "Now that's a man's haircut, son. You look like you just stepped out of BillyBob's barbershop in Wayside."

Ingrid arched a brow. "I'll take that as a compliment, Mick. Luke? What do you think?"

He studied his reflection in the mirror before giving a nod of approval. "Perfect."

He stood and removed the towel, shaking the hair from it. Tossing it over the back of the chair, he leaned close to press a kiss to the top of her head. "You're hired."

She stepped back, feeling the heat on her cheeks. "Thanks. Did I do as good a job as Yancy?"

"Better. But I'd appreciate it if you keep that our little secret." He picked up the chair and carried it inside. When he did, Mick followed.

Luke set the chair by the table and picked up his shirt.

Mick cleared his throat. "There's something I'd like to talk to you about before you and Ingrid head back up to the hills."

Luke tucked his shirt into the waistband of his jeans before turning. "I thought you were coming with us."

"I thought so, too. But I'd like to ask you something first."

"I'm listening."

"You and Ingrid." Mick was staring intently. "Since she has no one else to care about her, I'm asking. I'm thinking something has changed between you. Is that so?"

Luke nodded. "I think you already know the answer. And for your information, you're not the only one who cares about her. She matters to me, Mick. She matters more than my own life."

Mick cleared his throat. "Thank you for your honesty, son. And you're right. I did know. I could tell just by looking at the two of you. But I wanted to hear it from you. I'm glad for you. And glad for her, too." He ducked his head before adding, "She's a loner. Doesn't let folks get close, 'cause of her ma."

"Yeah. That's why I intend to take great care of her feelings. They're special. She's special." Luke turned toward the door. "I think it's time we headed up to the herd." He turned to Mick. "You coming?"

The old man shook his head. "I think it's way too late for me to play chaperone. Since the day's half over, I'll just stay here. You two go ahead."

"We'll be home in time for supper." Luke strolled out.

Mick stood at the back door and watched as Luke conferred with Ingrid before she led two saddled horses from the barn. She and Luke pulled themselves into the saddle and started up across a meadow.

The sound of their easy laughter trailed on the summer breeze, warming the old man's heart.

CHAPTER TWENTY-FOUR

Luke walked to the corral, where Ingrid stood holding the reins of their horses.

She glanced behind him. "Where's Mick?"

"He decided to stay here." Luke took the reins from her and held them while she mounted.

"How did you talk him into that?"

Luke handed over her reins before pulling himself into the saddle. "He said he figured it was too late to insist on going along to chaperone."

She laughed, until she realized he wasn't kidding. "Chaperone? Why would he say that? Unless…" Her jaw dropped. "You told him about us?"

Luke met her wide-eyed stare. "No need. Mick's a smart guy. He figured it out by himself. But when he asked me to confirm or deny it, I figured he deserved the truth."

As she digested his words, she looked dismayed. Then,

slowly, her smile bloomed. "I bet Mick appreciated your honesty."

"Yeah. He feels responsible for you."

She flicked the reins and started off at an easy pace. "Through everything that's happened in my life, Mick's been my rock."

"He's a good guy. And you deserve some good guys in your life." Luke reached over and caught her hand. "I hope I'm one of them." The flare of heat was instantaneous. "I'll race you to the herd."

"You're just a glutton for punishment, aren't you?" With a quick laugh, she yanked her hand back and spurred her horse into a run.

For several moments Luke held his mount still as he drank in the sight of her. She poured herself into this simple challenge as she poured herself into everything. Full out. Nothing held back. She made love the same way.

She was simply magnificent.

She stirred his heart.

She owned his soul.

"The herd, at least what's left of it, is growing sleek and fat on this grass. I could look at them for hours." Ingrid slid from the saddle to examine yet another cow.

"I get it. But I'm growing impatient to go skinny-dipping. Come on, woman. This sun is hot."

She shielded the blinding sunlight from her eyes and looked up at him. "My, my, cowboy. I didn't realize you had an impatient streak."

"I didn't, either, until I met you. You should know that not all this sweat is from the sun. I get overheated just looking at you. I hope you're going to take pity on me soon."

She couldn't help laughing at his frown. "Okay. The herd's fine. Let's get to that stream." She pulled herself into the saddle and nudged her horse into a run.

Halfway down the hill, Luke passed her, and by the time she reached the banks of the creek, he was already slipping off his boots and tearing aside his damp shirt.

He tossed a bar of soap in the grass. "Last one in gets to wash my back."

"That's not fair..."

He shucked his jeans and waded into the water before turning and watching as she stripped down and made a mad dash into the water.

Luke's eyes narrowed as the water lapped at her hips, then her waist, and finally, as she reached his side, the water spilled over her breasts.

She held up the bar of soap. "Okay. You won. Turn around and I'll wash your back."

His grin was quick and dangerous. "Thanks. But all of a sudden winning or losing doesn't mean half as much as enjoying the view."

At her questioning look, he explained. "The most perfect woman in the world just stepped out of her clothes and into my arms. Baby, that's a view that will never get old."

He dragged her close and poured himself into a kiss.

Against his mouth she whispered, "If I'd known it meant so much to you, I'd have taken more time. Want to see my imitation of a model's walk?"

"Models can't hold a candle to you." He lowered his head, running hot kisses down her throat, then lower, as his mouth closed around one slick nipple.

She shivered and ran her hands over the corded muscles of his shoulders and down his back. Still holding the soap, she left a trail of suds everywhere she touched him.

He kissed her again, slower, softer. She returned his kisses with a hunger humming with need.

His gaze sharpened. "You in a hurry?"

"No. Yes."

At her admission his arm encircled her while his other hand moved between them until he found her. He kept his eyes steady on hers as he began to stroke.

She gasped and her eyes widened as wave after wave of pleasure rippled through her.

She was wonderful to watch as, lost in the moment, she reached a hand to his shoulder and clung as she rode the feeling until she reached a shuddering climax.

For a moment her eyes closed and she wrapped herself around him. With a smile of triumph he lifted her and started toward shore.

With her legs around his waist, arms around his neck, she buried her face in the little hollow between his neck and shoulder.

For the space of a heartbeat, he paused. "You know what you're doing to me, woman?"

"It's the least I can do after what you did for me."

"That was just the opening act." He continued walking to the shore, where he lay her down in the grass.

His eyes were hot and fierce as he lay beside her and gathered her close. "Now for the main event."

There were no words as they came together in a blaze of passion that put the sun to shame.

"I've never had a day that could compare with this." Ingrid lay in the circle of Luke's arms.

"You've never gone skinny-dipping?"

"Of course I have. Alone," she admitted. She leaned up on his chest to smile into his eyes. "I mean I've never taken a day to just...play."

He gave her a lazy smile. "Lady, you're the perfect playmate. Any time you want another day off, I'm your man."

"Yes, you are. My big, strong man." She played with the hair on his chest. Her tone grew thoughtful. "When I first met you, I thought you were"—she paused, searching for the right phrase—"too quick with a joke, and too good-looking, to be anything but a tumbleweed. I figured you'd be gone the minute you were strong enough to stand without falling over. I certainly never intended to trust you. And especially with my"—she looked up to find him watching her—"heart."

He reached up to frame her face with his hands. "Thank you." At her raised brow he added, "For trusting me enough to say the words. I know that isn't easy for you."

Their kiss was soft. Sweet. As though sealing a very special bond.

The sun burned hot overhead. The summer breeze whispered over their heated flesh. The sound of the stream rushing over rocks formed a background of music that seemed to match the rhythm of their sighs.

As their kiss deepened, it exploded into something much more. Heat. Hunger. And a yearning of the heart that needed to be answered.

This time, as they came together, they savored each kiss, each touch, like lovers who knew they had all the time in the world to explore this newly discovered passion. And intended to make every moment count.

* * *

Luke and Ingrid held hands as their horses ambled across the high meadow toward home.

"Still worried about Lily?" Luke asked.

A laugh escaped Ingrid's lips. "I can't believe I'm admitting this. I haven't given her a single thought today."

Luke grinned. "I guess you had other things on your mind."

"Naughty things."

He couldn't help laughing. "Sorry. That's not the way I see it. But then, your naughty is really nice."

"I think you're a bad influence, cowboy."

"Or a good one. It all depends on your point of view." He squeezed her hand. "I hope Mick has supper ready. It just dawned on me that I'm hungry." He shot her a sideways glance. "Probably all those calories I've been burning."

She studied his toned body. "I guess that's one way to stay in shape."

"The best way." He withdrew his hand. "Come on. One last race to see who gets home first."

As he nudged his horse into a run, Ingrid drew back on the reins for a moment. Did he realize he'd just called her place home?

She didn't want to take the time to mull it over. It might have been a slip of the tongue. Or it might be that her place had become as special to him as it was to her.

Either way, right now she needed to get there first. There was still time to beat Luke. It just wasn't in her nature to ignore a challenge.

* * *

Mick looked up as they stepped into the kitchen. "You two have been gone a long time. The herd all right, or have more of them gone missing?"

"The herd's fine." Luke rolled his sleeves. "It's so hot, we couldn't resist a dip in the creek."

Mick shot him a speculative look before turning to Ingrid. "That so?"

Her cheeks turned a becoming shade of pink before she inhaled the wonderful fragrance coming from the oven and tried to change the subject. "Are you baking bread?"

"Just heating up rolls." The old cowboy grinned. "To go with Yancy's Fancy Chicken."

At the sound of a truck's engine, they glanced out the window.

Seconds later they gathered around the back door as Lily bounded toward them, trailed more slowly by Grace and Frank.

"Oh, Lily." Ingrid hugged her little sister fiercely. "I've missed you. How was your very first safari?"

"It was so much fun. But first I have to tell you…" Her words were forgotten as she stared at Luke, eyes wide. "You cut off all your hair."

"Well, actually it was Ingrid who did the cutting."

"Why?"

He shrugged. "I asked her to."

"Why?"

Another shrug. And then a lazy smile. "I figured it was time."

"More than time, sonny boy." Frank was grinning from ear to ear. "Don't you agree, Gracie Girl?"

His grandmother was studying him with a critical eye.

She touched a hand to his face. "Oh, Luke. With your hair short, you're the image of your father."

"There's nothing you could have said that would make me happier than that." He bent to kiss her cheek. "I consider that the ultimate compliment, Gram Gracie."

Ingrid closed a hand over her little sister's shoulder. "What were you about to tell me?"

"Oh yeah." Lily turned to Frank and Grace, who were smiling broadly. Her voice was high-pitched with excitement. "It's the reason why we're home early. While we were up in the hills, we found our missing herd, Ingrid."

CHAPTER TWENTY-FIVE

Y ou found our herd?" Ingrid could barely contain her surprise. "Where? When? Are they injured? Are they safe? Are they all accounted for?"

Lily turned to Luke's grandmother. "You tell her, Gram Gracie."

The older woman took up the story. "On the trail of our herd of mustangs, we came up over a rise and spotted, far below in a valley, a large herd of cattle. As far as we could tell, there were no wranglers around to tend them. They appeared to be on their own and isolated from any other herds. It was then that we realized we were on Bull Hammond's property."

At the mention of Ingrid's neighbor, Luke swore.

His grandfather surprised him by saying, "Hold on, sonny boy. I was just as upset as you when we checked their brands and realized they were part of Ingrid's herd. I figured I'd report that thieving crook to the sheriff the minute we got phone service. We'd just started driving them back toward Ingrid's place when Bull himself rode out and demanded to know why we were crossing his land with cattle. When we explained what we'd found and showed him the brand, he was shocked."

"You mean, he pretended to be shocked? That lying—"

Luke started to speak, but his grandfather held up a hand. "Now maybe Hammond's a really good actor, but he has me convinced. He seemed genuinely surprised to see those cattle on his land. When I confronted him with what I suspected, Hammond said he had nothing to do with the herd's disappearance."

"Then how did they end up on his property?"

"He didn't have a clue. It's all pure speculation, of course, but he suggested they could have simply wandered off, each one following the leader, and then found themselves stranded in a deep ravine with lush grass and a meandering creek and no reason to leave."

Luke was staring at his grandfather as if he'd just grown a second head. "And you believe that?"

The old man shrugged. "Like I said, Hammond seemed as surprised by this as we were."

"What else could he say when he was caught red-handed?" Luke plucked his cell phone from his pocket and dialed the sheriff's number before repeating what he'd just learned.

A minute later he announced to the others, "Eugene said he and Archer will be out here first thing in the morning. But to add weight to what Hammond told you, the sheriff assured me that nobody else in the county has reported the loss of any cattle. Ingrid's herd is the only one affected. Not that it proves Hammond's innocence, since he still seems to be the one who would benefit the most from Ingrid's loss. But the sheriff will make that determination when he's had time to look into this further."

Ingrid turned to Frank. "Where are my cattle now?"

"Back on the hill with the rest of your herd."

She gave a deep sigh. "Oh, wouldn't it be wonderful if this nightmare is over?"

"That doesn't explain…" Seeing Lily's questioning look, Luke felt a wave of self-annoyance and bit back the rest of his words.

They'd taken such pains to keep the dangerous facts as far away from the little girl as possible, and now in his anger, he'd almost revealed that gunshot through Ingrid's window.

Lily turned to Frank. "Is Ingrid right, Grandpop Frank? Are all our troubles over?"

Frank gave her an encouraging smile. "I don't know, darlin', but this gives us some hope. And at this point we'll take all the hopeful signs we can get."

For all his upbeat words, the old man exchanged a silent admonition with his grandson.

Seeing it, Grace tried for a further distraction. "Oh my, Mick. Something smells amazing."

"That would be Yancy's fine food." Mick grinned. "Ever since our return from your ranch, we've been eating like kings." He motioned toward the table. "Supper's ready, and there's enough for everyone. I'd be proud to have you join us."

While Lily and Grace and Frank washed up in the mudroom, Mick added three more place settings at the table.

"Perfect timing," Luke muttered to his grandfather as he returned to the kitchen.

"When have you ever known me to miss a meal?" The old man winked.

They gathered around the table and began passing trays of chicken and potatoes au gratin, a salad of field greens, and dinner rolls warm from the oven.

While they ate, Lily regaled them with all she'd seen while in the wilderness.

"We found a herd of mustangs. And we took lots and lots of pictures." The little girl turned. "Didn't we, Gram Gracie?"

"We certainly did."

Luke offered the basket of rolls to his grandmother. "Did you find your long-absent white stallion?"

"Unfortunately we didn't."

Lily broke in. "But we found a spotted black-and-white one, and he didn't even run away when he saw us. Did he, Gram Gracie?"

"No, he didn't. I told Lily that sometimes he looked tame enough to be a saddle horse posing for our camera. But whenever I'd get too complacent, he would prove to us just how wild and free he really is."

Lily turned to her big sister. "Wait 'til you see my pictures, Ingrid. Gram Gracie let me use her telephoto lens and even her wide-angle lens, and I'm going to help her frame some of them for you." She put a hand to her mouth. "Oh, I wasn't supposed to say anything about that. It's our secret."

Ingrid gave her little sister a gentle smile. "Well, then, I guess I'll just have to forget you ever said that."

"Good. 'Cause I'm saving it for your birthday."

"When would that be?" Luke asked.

"Next month." Lily spooned more potatoes onto her plate before digging in. "And now that we found the missing herd and I've got a special present, it's going to be the best birthday ever." She turned to Ingrid. "Isn't it?"

"You bet."

Under the table, Luke caught Ingrid's hand and squeezed. The two shared a look.

Seeing it, Frank and Grace exchanged a look of their own.

"...and we slept in bedrolls under the stars." Long after Frank and Grace had taken their leave, and Ingrid led Lily upstairs to say her prayers and get ready for bed, Lily was still recounting every detail she could recall of her safari with Ingrid, while Luke lounged in the doorway. "And we hiked up one side of the mountain and down the other, and Gram Gracie said I'm the best safari partner she's ever had, next to Matt's Nessa. She said I never get tired and I never complain when it gets too hot or too cold. And I love the herds of mustangs as much as she does. And besides, I love taking pictures as much as she does. She said I'm a natural photographer. She called me gifted. And..." She paused a moment to catch her breath.

"It sounds as though this trip was even better than you'd hoped it would be." Ingrid turned down the blanket and waited until Lily climbed into bed.

"It was. And you know what was the best?"

"Let me guess. Either getting photography tips from an expert or coming across our herd on your way back." Ingrid bent down to kiss her good night. "Which was it?"

Lily wrapped her arms around her sister's neck and

hugged her fiercely. "It was pretending that Gram Gracie was my very own grandma, and that Grandpop Frank was my very own grandpa, and that I could go places with them my whole life."

Luke stepped back into the shadows, unwilling to let Ingrid and Lily see how deeply those words affected him while he wiped at a speck of dust that made his eyes water.

"I love you, Ingrid. And I missed you."

"I love you, too, Lily. And I missed you something awful."

"I'm glad you had Luke here while I was gone. 'Night, Luke," Lily called.

"'Night, Li'l Bit."

Her smile deepened. "That's something else I missed. I missed having you call me that."

Composed, he poked his head in the doorway. "Then I'll have to say it twice tomorrow."

The sound of her giggles had his smile returning.

When Ingrid walked out of the room, he caught her hand. For a moment she simply rested her head on his shoulder, sighing deeply, before stepping back.

He pressed a kiss to her cheek, which still bore the dampness of tears. "It's nice to have her back home."

"Yeah. I was thinking the same thing." As they made their way down the stairs, she added, "Now I can breathe."

Ingrid, Luke, and Mick were enjoying their longnecks in a rare moment of quiet in front of the fire.

Luke turned to the old foreman. "You think Bull Hammond hid the herd in that ravine?"

Mick shrugged and tipped up his bottle. "Don't know

what to make of it. But I'm thinking a man would be pretty foolish to steal a neighbor's cattle and think he could keep them hidden for long."

Luke frowned. "It's no secret I don't trust him. Still…" He took a drink before setting aside his beer. "The fact that he didn't have any wranglers keeping them in place has me second-guessing myself. If I stole someone's cattle and hid them somewhere, I'd make damned certain they'd stay hidden."

"That's the problem I have with this." Ingrid stood and began to pace. "Even during roundup, with plenty of wranglers to keep watch, there are always strays that manage to break free of the herd and wander off track. Up there in the hills, with no one around to chase after them, if one old cow made a break for it, who's to say the rest didn't just blindly follow?"

Luke watched her pace. "Are you thinking that the disappearance of your herd isn't connected to the gunshot through your window?"

She paused. Sighed. "I don't know what to think anymore. None of this makes sense."

Mick rubbed at a spot between his eyes. "Don't forget all those other incidents. The range fire. Tippy." He saw Ingrid blanch and softened his tone. "And then there's the other gunshot. The one that caused the mustangs to stampede. The gunshot that brought Luke here."

Luke caught Ingrid's hand, causing her to pause in her pacing. "At least that one ended up being a good thing."

She managed a smile. "Yes. But at the time, I was scared to death."

"You've got a funny way of showing fear, woman."

His words had Mick chuckling. "He's got you there,

girl. You dragged him in here in such a temper, it was like unleashing the wrath of God."

"I thought he'd been the one who fired that shot. I figured he wasn't going to survive the night. And then, when he did, I thought he was such a pain in the..."

"Go ahead. You can say the word."

"I was going to call you a pain in the neck."

"Sure you were."

That had them all forgetting their tensions and bursting into laughter.

Ingrid settled down on the sofa beside Luke and helped herself to a long pull on his beer before handing him back the bottle. As their fingers brushed, they shared a secret smile.

"I'm just glad Eugene Graystoke will be here tomorrow to sort it all out." Luke stretched out his legs toward the warmth of the fire. "I'm still not convinced that Hammond is innocent. I saw the fury in his eyes when he accosted you in the barn. He was a man on a mission. And after that scene, half your herd just up and disappeared. And now they're found on his land. If that doesn't point to guilt, I don't know what does."

Mick stared into the flames, his tone thoughtful. "There was bad blood between Lars and Bull, though I never knew what caused it. Lars always played his cards close to his vest." He eased himself up from his easy chair and picked up the empty bottle. "I'm turning in now. I'll say good night."

"'Night, Mick." Ingrid blew him a kiss.

"See you in the morning," Luke called.

When they were alone, Luke passed his beer to Ingrid, who took a sip before passing it back to him. He drained it before linking his fingers with hers. "Ready to head upstairs?"

She nodded.

At the door to her room she paused. "I think I'd better sleep in here tonight."

"Okay. I get it. Lily's back." Luke reached around her to turn the knob.

When he remained in the hallway, she wrapped her arms around his neck and drew him inside her room before kissing him.

He gave a shaky laugh. "It's a really mean thing, to kiss me like this and then send me on my way."

"Who says I'm sending you away?"

"I thought…" His smile grew. "You want me to stay?"

"Not the night. Lily has a way of slipping into my bed when something wakes her. But I'd love it if you'd stay awhile."

"Just to rub your back or something?"

She laughed. "It's the 'or something' I'm hoping for."

He gathered her close and kissed her until they were both breathless. Against her mouth he whispered, "Woman, that's the kind of invitation I just can't resist."

CHAPTER TWENTY-SIX

I'll dispose of this." After finishing morning chores, Luke reached for the handles of the honey wagon and easily pushed it out of the barn.

When he returned, Ingrid and Lily had already peeled off their work gloves and were hanging their pitchforks on hooks along the wall of the barn.

They looked up when the sheriff's car rolled up, trailed by a second car driven by his deputy.

The two men stepped out and approached the barn.

"'Morning, Ingrid." Sheriff Graystoke touched the brim of his hat. "Lily. Luke."

Behind him, his deputy, Archer Stone, merely nodded a silent greeting.

Where the sheriff was stocky, with broad shoulders and a slightly bulging middle, his deputy was trim and walked with a swagger. Eugene Graystoke's uniform was rumpled and well-worn. Archer Stone's was crisp, his badge polished to a high shine.

"Bull Hammond showed me where your cattle were found." The sheriff flipped a page in his dog-eared note-book. "Then we followed the route back to your property, where your herd is summering. It's a direct path from there to Hammond's ravine."

Luke's eyes narrowed.

Before he could say a word, Ingrid touched a hand to her sister's shoulder. "Why don't you go inside, honey, and let Mick know we'll be in for breakfast in a few minutes?"

"Okay." Lily skipped away.

When she was gone, Luke's voice was low with a growing anger. "Are you saying, after a simple interview, you believe Hammond when he denies having anything to do with this?"

Archer stepped up beside the sheriff, his eyes narrowed on Luke. "Watch your mouth, Malloy."

"I'll let you watch it for me." He directed his words toward the sheriff. "What are you saying?"

Eugene kept his tone level. "I understand your frustration, Luke. I'm saying it's not impossible to make the case that Ingrid's cattle wandered away and found themselves in that ravine on Hammond's land."

"They wandered away from the rest of the herd and then just stayed there?"

"With enough lush grass and an endless supply of water in that stream, why would a herd make an effort to leave? Especially since they were surrounded by steep hills. It would have been much easier for them to wander in than to wander out."

"And this is the end of it?" Luke's tone was pure ice. "You're just going to walk away and give Bull Hammond the benefit of the doubt?"

"That's enough." Archer reached out a closed fist toward Luke, and Eugene slapped it back, shooting his deputy a flinty look.

"I know tempers are flaring. Let's not add fuel to the fire."

He turned a resigned look toward Luke and Ingrid. "My hands are tied. Unless there's a way to prove this was a deliberate act, carried out to cause harm, I can't do anything more than watch and wait."

"You mean wait until the next incident? Like the range fire that destroyed Ingrid's entire wheat crop? Like the death of her herding dog that looked suspiciously like poison? Like the shot fired that caused a herd of mustangs to stampede and nearly kill me?"

"That's right, Luke. And all of them without a shred of evidence to back up any claim that they were done with malice."

"And the shot through her bedroom window? Was that an unexplained incident, as well?"

"That's an entirely different thing. It's clear that was no accident. That one was a deliberate act of violence. And I intend to continue to pursue any and all leads."

"How many leads do you have so far?"

"Just one. Hammond claims to have been at the diner in Wayside at the time of that shot. Four of his wranglers backed up his claim. But I haven't had a chance to interview Lon Wardell yet."

"Forget Wardell." Archer Stone glanced at Ingrid before asking loudly, "What about Nadine Larsen?"

Ingrid's eyes betrayed her pain before she looked away.

Eugene said, "I haven't interviewed her, either."

Luke drew an arm around Ingrid's shoulders. "Thanks, Sheriff."

Ingrid seemed to pull herself together. "Would you two like to come inside for coffee?"

"Sorry, no time." Eugene touched a hand to the brim of his hat. "Archer and I will be on our way, ma'am. You know to call me if anything at all happens."

"Yes, thank you."

Ingrid stood beside Luke as the two police officers settled into their vehicles and drove off in a cloud of dust.

When they were gone, Ingrid turned to Luke, eyes blazing. "How dare the deputy hint that Nadine could have fired that shot."

"I know it hurt you. And I admit that I wanted to put my fist in his face. But I guess we have to accept that everyone is a suspect."

She shook her head emphatically. "Not everyone. Not Nadine."

"And why not?"

Her mouth was a thin, tight line of denial. "She may be guilty of a lot of things, but she would never try to kill me."

Luke realized with horror that she was dangerously close to tears. But was it from anger at what Archer had suggested? Or fear that the deputy could be right in his suspicions? From the look in her eyes when the question had first been posed, it was clear it had never occurred to her that Nadine would be a suspect. In truth, it hadn't occurred to Luke, either.

Banking his own emotions, he caught her hand and experienced a deep well of tenderness as he drew her close.

Against her temple he muttered, "Come on. We both need food."

"Great breakfast, Mick." Luke polished off his third cup before getting up from the table. "Let's do the dishes, Li'l Bit. You wash, I'll dry."

"Okay." Lily deposited her dishes in the sink and turned on the taps.

When Ingrid started to push away from the table, Luke stopped her with a hand to her shoulder. "Relax. We've got this."

Her smile returned. "All right. Then I guess I'll head to the barn to saddle up. I want to see my herd."

"I'll go with you as soon as we finish here." Luke turned to Lily. "Want to ride along?"

She shook her head. "I promised Mick I'd show him some of my pictures from the safari."

Ingrid paused at the back door. "When do I get to see them?"

Lily gave a mysterious little smile. "You have to wait until your birthday."

"You mean I can't see any of them?"

The little girl shrugged. "Maybe. I guess I can show you some, but not all. That would spoil my surprise."

"I can't believe I have to wait a month to see what Mick will see today." Ingrid was muttering and shaking her head as she left the house.

In the kitchen, Luke turned to Lily. "You've really got her going, Li'l Bit. I hope those pictures are worth it."

"Wait 'til you see, Luke." Lily's smile was radiant. "She's going to love her birthday surprise."

* * *

Ingrid and Luke reined in their mounts at the top of the hill and stared around with matching looks of appreciation.

"Oh." Ingrid let out a long, slow breath. "It's so good to see my herd together again. I really thought they were gone for good."

"Yeah." Luke remained on the perimeter of the herd as she urged her horse into the very center of the milling cattle.

She dismounted and led her mount as she walked among them, the look on her face telling him more than any words just how relieved she was feeling.

Nearly an hour later she returned to his side, where he stood holding the reins of his horse.

He reached over and took her hand. "I can tell you're feeling much better."

"I am." She gave him a bright smile. "I'm still not quite ready to believe Bull was telling the truth." She looked up into his eyes to gauge his reaction. "But I have to admit there's a possibility they just wandered off."

"Okay." He squeezed her hand. "I'll take that into consideration, though I'm still suspicious. It's hard for me to declare that hothead Hammond innocent. What about the other incidents?"

She shook her head. "I don't know. A part of me wants to believe they were just a coincidence. But in my heart, I know better." She glanced at their joined hands. "I'm so glad you're here with me, Luke. But I know you're neglecting your own ranch. How much longer can you afford to stay?"

"As long as it takes." He gathered her close and pressed his mouth to her temple. "Until all of this is resolved, I'm not going anywhere." As they mounted, he indicated the stream in the distance. "Got time for a quick dip?"

She laughed. "Will we get any swimming in?"

"Probably not. But if nothing else, we'll get in some hot exercise."

"Hot? You just said the magic word." She urged her horse into a run. Over her shoulder she called, "Win, lose, or draw, it's definitely time for you to scrub my back, cowboy. And then we can both cool down."

As they drew near the house, Luke caught the reins of Ingrid's mount. "You go ahead inside and I'll unsaddle these two and turn them into the pasture."

"Thanks." She slid from the saddle and started toward the back door.

Inside, she washed up at the sink before stepping into the kitchen. "I'm back, guys…"

She stared around with a puzzled look. The kitchen was empty, the table clear. There was nothing on the stove or in the oven. The usual tantalizing scents were absent.

She poked her head in Mick's room off the kitchen. "Hey, sleepyhead, it's dinnertime. Wake—"

His bed was empty.

"Mick! Where are you?" She raced toward the parlor. Seeing it empty, she hurried up the stairs and stepped into Lily's room, which was also empty. Alarmed, she ran down the stairs and out to the barn.

Luke was just rounding the corner of the barn, carrying the saddles toward a stall. Seeing her in the doorway, he frowned. "I had to haul feed and water to the pasture. You need to remind Mick and Lily about their chores—"

He caught the look on her face and let the saddles drop. "What's wrong?"

"The house is empty."

"Maybe Mick and Lily needed something in town."

"The truck is still parked by the back door. Besides, if they were leaving, even on horseback, they would have left me a note."

"Maybe you missed it."

She was shaking her head. "Mick wouldn't leave without leaving me a message. Oh, Luke, I'm—" Her words died as she caught sight of a booted foot sticking out from one of the stalls.

Seeing the direction of her gaze, Luke raced to the spot.

"Oh, no. Mick." She dropped to her knees beside the still form of the old man, who lay in a pool of blood.

At the sound of her voice, Mick's lids flickered and he struggled to sit up. With a moan he fell back.

"Don't move, Mick. Thank heaven you're alive. You took a nasty fall. How did this happen?"

Luke dropped down beside her as Mick struggled to get the words out. "Hit. Shovel. Wardell…" Mick touched a hand to his bloody head. "Grabbed…Lily."

"Lily? Where? Why?" Terror had Ingrid by the throat. She could barely get the words out.

The old man moaned, before his eyes flickered, then closed.

"Mick." Ingrid clutched at the old man's shoulders. "Tell me where he's taken Lily. Please."

Luke touched a hand to Mick's throat. "His pulse is feeble. Probably shock. We can't move him. I need some blankets."

"But Lily—"

"You looking for the brat?" A whispered voice had both Luke and Lily frozen as a muzzle of a pistol was pressed against the back of Ingrid's head. "She's right over there."

When Luke made a move to get to his feet, he was hit so hard it sent him crashing into the side of the stall, causing the wood to splinter and fall, revealing Lily, bound and gagged, in the adjoining stall. As Luke struggled to get his bearings and stand, a shot rang out, and he felt a river of blood begin to spill from his arm as it dropped helplessly to his side.

Ingrid let out a bloodcurdling scream.

"That's just a taste of what I've got in store for you, Malloy."

While Luke shook his head, trying to clear his vision, Lon Wardell's voice echoed off the walls of the barn. "You move a muscle, cowboy, and your woman's dead."

CHAPTER TWENTY-SEVEN

Luke watched in amazement as Ingrid spun toward Wardell, landing a fist in his midsection.

"Why you…" Instead of disarming him, it made him even more furious. He brought the pistol across her temple, dropping her to her knees.

Before she could clear her vision, her arms were twisted painfully behind her back and her wrists bound with plastic restraints. Wardell forced her to her feet and shoved her toward her little sister.

Blood trickled from a cut on Lily's head. Tears flowed freely down her face, but no sound came from her mouth, because it had been taped shut.

Once there, Ingrid was knocked to the straw and her ankles tightly bound.

"Oh, honey…" Ingrid attempted to soothe Lily, but her words were halted by a second blow to the head that had her moaning in pain.

"Not one word. You hear me?" Wardell stood over them, his face twisted into a mask of fury. "The brat tried talking, and I taught her a lesson. You can learn from that, or you can learn the hard way." He gave a shrill laugh. "Your choice, girlie."

Ingrid bit down hard on the cry that threatened to escape her lips.

"Now that you understand the rules…" Wardell sat on a bale of straw, holding the pistol in one hand, while tilting a bottle of whiskey to his lips. "Isn't this cozy?"

As Luke struggled to tear off the sleeve of his shirt, he kept his gaze firmly on Wardell.

"Look at that. A Boy Scout." The gunman seemed to be enjoying Luke's clumsy attempt to stem the flow of blood.

Once Luke ripped the sleeve free, he wrapped it tightly around the gunshot wound, using his teeth to help tie a knot. As he fumbled with it, he managed to slip his cell phone from his shirt pocket. He knew he couldn't look at it, or it would draw Lon's attention. Instead, he blindly ran his finger down the list of favorites. Knowing many of his family could be in the hills, with no service available, the only ones he could count on were Yancy and the Great One. He pressed the speed dial, hoping he'd counted correctly. Hoping they were home, or at least in an area of phone service. As he buried the phone beneath a layer of straw, he prayed whoever answered would persist in listening long enough to realize the importance of what he was hearing.

Desperate to hide any sounds that might give away what he'd done, Luke decided to risk it all by shouting, "Why don't you tell us why you're doing this, Wardell?"

He knew breaking the code of silence would bring their attacker's wrath down on him, but it was the price he was willing to pay in order to keep Wardell's focus off Ingrid and Lily and to keep him talking to mask whatever sounds would be made by the phone.

"Weren't you paying attention, Malloy?" Lon got to his feet and looked over at Luke. Seeing the tourniquet he'd fashioned, he threw back his head and laughed. "Well now. You really are a Boy Scout, aren't you? A pity I'm not one of those do-gooders." He took aim with his pistol. "Let's see what the Boy Scout can do with this." With a swagger, he walked closer and shot point-blank into Luke's leg, sending up a fountain of blood.

Across the room, Ingrid let out a scream and struggled frantically against her restraints.

Wardell turned away and ambled back to the bale of straw as though he'd done nothing more than take a stroll.

Through a haze of blinding pain, Luke fought to remain conscious as he tore away the rest of his shirt and struggled to wrap the gaping wound.

"Now, where was I?" Lon downed another slug of whiskey before twirling the pistol like a professional gunslinger.

It was clear that he was enjoying his newly discovered sense of power. "All those good citizens who refer to me as some stupid down-and-out drunk ought to see the three of you. I guess we know who holds all the cards now.

"Oh yes. The reason I'm here." A slow, dangerous smile curved his mouth as he turned his attention to Ingrid. "You're going to sign over your rights to the cattle on this ranch. And if you do it nice and clean, I'll do the same to you. Give me any trouble, I'll shoot the brat just like I shot your lover boy. And I intend to shoot him a lot more times before I put him out of his misery. But if you're a good girl, I'll kill the two of you with the first shot, sparing you a whole lot of pain and misery."

Yancy was having a fine day. Earlier he'd picked fresh strawberries from his garden beside the house, and now he was baking Miss Grace a glorious torte, which he intended to layer with mounds of whipped cream and sweet strawberries. In his mind he could already see her smile blooming when she took her first bite.

"If you could spare a few of those berries, Yancy, my boy, I'd be grateful."

At Nelson's words, the cook looked over with a quick grin. "Says the man with the famous appetite. When's the last time you ate only a few of anything, Great One?"

"You've got me there, Yancy." The old man patted his stomach. "But I've discovered a yearning for fresh strawberries ever since I saw you washing them earlier."

"I figured as much." Yancy gave a warm laugh. "That's why I set aside a bowl just for—"

The ringing of his phone had him glancing toward the kitchen counter, where he'd set it earlier. "I'll just get this and then I'll fetch those strawberries."

"Or you could let it ring and get the strawberries first."

Yancy was still chuckling when he picked up the phone and glanced at the caller ID. "Hey. Hello, stranger." To Nelson he mouthed the word *Luke*.

Walking toward the refrigerator, he opened the door while asking, "When are you bringing those pretty little Larsen sisters back for another visit?"

He took out the covered bowl of berries he'd set aside for Nelson. When he straightened, he looked at the phone. "That's odd. No one's there…" And just as he was about to disconnect the call, thinking the wires were crossed, he heard a strange, muted sound coming from the phone. It sounded like a man's voice, distant, raspy. He couldn't place the voice, but it sounded angry. And then he heard a sound that had him going rigid with shock.

It was, without a doubt, a gunshot—followed by a woman's scream.

Sheriff Eugene Graystoke's day had gone from bad to worse. After that scene with Luke and Ingrid Larsen, he'd hoped for some good news. But now, as he did a follow-up on Lon Wardell, his mood darkened.

According to the bartender at Barney's in Wayside, Wardell had been on a weeklong bender, after his usual drinking companion, Nadine Larsen, had walked out on him following a bitter argument. By the time Lon left, after running out of money to pay his enormous bar tab, there was murder in his eyes. Even the toughest cowboys who frequented Barney's had backed off, knowing he was running on a very short fuse.

Eugene figured he'd warn Ingrid and then start looking for Nadine, just in case Wardell tried to hit her up for money. Though Ingrid had defended her mother, the sheriff had his doubts. In his years on the job, Nadine's name had appeared on too many drunk-and-disorderly complaints to count. But even a tough woman like Nadine, who could hold her own against most cowboys, deserved protection from a mean drunk like Wardell. There was no telling what he'd do when liquored up.

When his phone rang, Eugene pressed the speaker button on his dashboard. "Sheriff Graystoke here."

"Sheriff." Yancy's voice sounded breathless. "I got a call from Luke's phone, but he never said anything."

"Butt dialing." Eugene managed a quick laugh. "Happens all the time. My wife hates it when I do that."

"No. Listen. This was different. I heard a voice I didn't recognize. And then a really loud report like a gunshot and a woman screaming."

"You sure about that?" Eugene hit the brakes. "I know you and Nelson have a fondness for Hollywood drama, Yancy."

"That we do. I can't deny it. But I'm so convinced of what I heard, I'm calling the family as soon as I hang up with you."

"Now, Yancy—"

"There's trouble at the Larsen place, Sheriff. I feel it in my gut. Just as surely as I feel Luke was trying to get a message out. Okay. I've warned you. I'm hanging up now."

Eugene heard the click and then sudden silence.

He dialed the state police headquarters to report the gunshot and to request backup. Though he hesitated to call out the troops on what might be a false alarm, Yancy Martin wasn't the only one to trust his gut feeling. Eugene's told him this could be really serious.

As he turned his vehicle in the direction of the Larsen ranch and floored the accelerator, he punched the number for his deputy.

When he heard Archer's voice, he said, "Get hold of Nadine Larsen. Tell her to steer clear of Lon Wardell until he sobers up. Then get on out to the Larsen ranch.

It may be nothing, but I've got a report of a suspected gunshot."

Lon walked around the cavernous interior of the barn, obviously searching for something. While he walked, the others watched him with looks that ranged from terrified to thoughtful.

Poor Lily was trembling, probably as much from shock as fear. She'd been forced to witness Mick's assault, and then the attack on both her sister and Luke. The gunshots, the blood, the pain glazing Luke's eyes, had her traumatized.

Next to her, Ingrid leaned over to press a trembling kiss to her cheek, as if to offer a measure of comfort, but the painful bonds restricted movement.

Luke kept his gaze fixed on Wardell, watching for any opportunity to take him down. Though he knew the chances were slim, since he would no doubt fall on his face the moment he tried to stand on his badly injured leg, he was determined to try. He was troubled by the amount of blood he'd lost. If he didn't act soon, he could lose consciousness. But he was even more troubled by the fact that Mick seemed to slip in and out of consciousness. The old man had taken a powerful blow to the head. A blow that could cost him his life if he didn't get medical help soon.

Wardell picked up a flat piece of wood from the splintered stall and dropped it next to Ingrid. "Here's your desk, girlie."

At her blank look he snarled, "You're going to sign over your rights to your cattle. I call this my declaration of independence."

He withdrew a wrinkled paper from his pocket, along with a pen. He dropped it on the wood and gave an imitation of a smile. "But you can think of it as your last will and testament."

Sheriff Graystoke's vehicle pulled up in Ingrid's driveway and parked behind her battered truck. Minutes later Archer Stone's truck arrived. By the time he stepped down, Eugene was beside him.

"You get hold of Nadine Larsen?"

Archer nodded.

"Where'd you find her?"

"She didn't say. But from the static, I'm thinking she was driving. Maybe she's on her way here." Archer looked around. "Awfully quiet to be a crime scene."

"Yeah." Eugene looked up in annoyance at the sound of a plane's engine. While he and his deputy watched, the Malloy plane circled the area and came in for a quick landing behind the barn. Minutes later Frank, Grace, Yancy, and Nelson made their way toward the house.

"You didn't waste any time." Eugene's voice was accusing.

"Neither did you, Sheriff." Frank nodded toward the back door. "Anybody home?"

"I haven't checked. We just got here." Eugene waved a hand to his deputy. "Go ahead and knock."

While they stood watching, a parade of Malloy Ranch trucks pulled up. One after the other, the doors opened, revealing Matt and Nessa, Colin, Burke, and Reed. All of the men were armed.

Archer returned to the others. "No answer."

"I guess we'll start checking the buildings one by one."

Eugene pointed to the house. "A couple of you go inside. I want every room inspected. Archer and I will start on the barn..."

The sheriff's words died in his throat at the sight that snagged his attention.

Lon Wardell was framed in the barn doorway, his muscled arm wrapped around Lily's neck. In his hand was a pistol pressed to her temple.

Tears were streaming down her cheeks, mingling with the blood to form a river of red staining the pretty denim shirt Grace had bought her in town. She was so small and vulnerable, so completely at the mercy of this madman, the sight of her tore at all their hearts. Nessa clutched her husband's arm and stifled the cry that lodged in her throat.

Lon's voice broke the stunned silence. "One by one, you'll walk over here and drop your weapons before stepping into my office." He smiled at his little joke. "If anybody tries anything stupid, I'll blow the kid's head off. And you can all watch, knowing you were the reason for her death."

He dragged Lily backward, causing her to gag, and waved his pistol drunkenly. "Move it. Or the kid pays."

CHAPTER TWENTY-EIGHT

Hearing Grace's sob, Frank Malloy put an arm around his wife's shoulders as he dropped his rifle and walked with her into the barn.

"Sit against the wall." Lon waved his pistol, and the two slumped down.

Lon turned to Nelson, being assisted by Yancy. "Move it, old man. First, your weapons."

"We are unarmed." Nelson's imperious tones were an odd contrast to Lon's slurred words.

"If you're lying, I'll blow the brat's head off." To prove his point, he jammed the pistol against her temple.

Matt, his eyes as hard as flint, held Nessa's hand as he tossed his rifle to the ground and joined his grandparents along the wall.

Next came Colin, Reed, and Burke, all silent and scowling as they deposited their weapons before joining the others.

The sheriff and his deputy walked in last, their grim faces betraying their outrage at being ordered about by this drunken cowboy.

Lon studied the pile of weapons before breaking into a smirk. "Well, now. Looks like I could hold off an army with all this firepower. I thank you all kindly for adding to my arsenal."

He gave Lily a shove, sending her sprawling headfirst into the straw beside her sister.

"Oh, Frank." Grace squeezed her husband's hand as she took in the horrifying scene. Mick barely conscious. Luke bloody and glazed with pain. Ingrid and Lily bound hand and foot, their pretty young faces smeared with their own blood. "This is like some terrible nightmare."

"Hold on, Gracie Girl." Frank drew her close. "Where there's life, there's hope."

She closed her eyes, and her family knew she was silently praying.

"Why are we here, Wardell?" In an effort to keep this man talking as long as possible, Eugene Graystoke's voice bounced off the walls and ceiling of the barn.

"We're here to celebrate my inheritance." Lon lifted his whiskey bottle in a salute before taking a long pull.

"What is it you inherited?" Eugene glanced at the others, then at the pile of weapons, and they nodded their understanding of his unspoken signal to watch for any opportunity to retrieve their guns and stop this before it turned into a slaughter.

"Didn't you hear?" Lon chuckled to himself. "Old Lars Larsen loved me so much, he considered me like the son he always wanted. And since all he had were a couple of worthless daughters and a drunken whore for a wife, he wanted to make sure I was put in charge of his ranch."

At his harsh words, Lily started crying again, and because of her bonds, all Ingrid could do was lean close to whisper words meant to soothe.

Luke felt a wild rage burning inside at the pain. Not his own pain, but the pain this drunk was inflicting on all the people he loved.

The people he loved.

He stared around, filling himself with the images of his grandparents, his great-grandfather, his brothers and sister-in-law, his uncle Colin, the ranch foreman Burke, who was as much family as the others, and Yancy, a sweet man who had been reborn because of them. He studied old Mick, so still and lifeless. And finally a tearful Lily and Ingrid, stoic even in the face of such violence.

He knew, without a doubt, that he was about to risk his own life for theirs. But his life no longer mattered. What mattered was that he could create enough distraction to give the others a chance to act. And if he died, at least his death wouldn't be in vain.

He gathered himself, forcing aside the pain radiating from his arm and leg all the way to his head and throbbing with an almost unbearable ache that nearly blinded his vision.

He didn't need to stand for any length of time, he told himself. He just needed to summon enough strength to make a mad dash to that bale of hay and force Lon Wardell to shift his focus for an instant. It could create enough of a distraction to help the others retrieve their weapons and take down this monster.

He moved his body, testing his strength. Closing his fingers around the rail of the stall, he pulled himself to a kneeling position and then made a valiant effort to stand.

Outside the barn, a car's brakes screeched, sending gravel spitting.

All heads turned to the doorway as Nadine raced inside, screaming and swearing at the top of her lungs.

Seeing her, Wardell made a grab for Lily, holding her in front of him like a shield.

"You liar! You no-good, cheating, scumbag liar!"

She flew at Lon like some kind of whirling dervish, shoving Lily aside before pounding his chest with her fists, her long painted nails scratching at his eyes.

"You promised me you'd never hurt my girls. And look at them." She turned, tears in her eyes at the sight of Lily and Ingrid, bound and bloody. "Now you'll have to answer to me, you filthy, lying piece of—"

"Shut up, you slut. I'm doing this for you as much as for me."

"For me? You'd hurt my girls for me? You've always known they were off-limits. You knew that, and you came here anyway? You swore it wasn't you who caused that wildfire. You said you'd swear on your mother's grave that you didn't poison old Tippy or fire that gunshot at the mustangs. You're a liar. A cheat. But this is one thing you won't get away with, you disgusting piece of—"

A gunshot echoed and reechoed around the barn.

Nadine's body stiffened. The fist she'd been shaking in Lon's face dropped to her side. Without a word she began to slide to the floor in slow motion.

For a moment Lon seemed unable to process what he'd

done. He simply stood there, gun in hand, watching in a drunken fog as she fell.

It was all the distraction Luke needed. Though he wasn't certain his wounded leg would support his weight, he made a flying leap across the distance separating him from Wardell.

Seeing him, the others sprang into action, grabbing up weapons and circling Luke and Wardell.

The sound of another gunshot had Ingrid screaming as Luke fell back, blood streaming like a river from his chest. For a moment Luke lay as still as death, and his entire family seemed suspended in time and space, unable to move.

Then he got to his knees, shaking his head to clear it. Before Wardell could fire again, Luke was on him, trading punches, fighting desperately to take control of his pistol.

The others circled around the two, preparing to shoot if they could get a clear shot at Wardell.

Hearing the sound of helicopters landing, Eugene Graystoke turned to his deputy. "Let the state boys know where we are."

Archer Stone dashed out the door.

As an army of sharpshooters raced inside, taking up positions, Luke gave a blow to Wardell's jaw that had his head snapping back.

Still holding his pistol, Wardell looked around at the assault rifles aimed at him. All the fight seemed to have left him. He grasped Luke's shoulders. "I want to make a deal, Malloy."

"A deal?" Luke swore. "The only deal you'll get is prison. I hope you die there."

"But I know something you'll want to hear."

Luke shook his head. "There's nothing you could say that would matter in the least."

"I know something you don't. Something I was sworn to keep secret about the night your parents died."

At his words, Luke's head came up sharply.

Across the barn, his family members riveted all their attention on the man who had just offered them the most tantalizing words ever spoken.

With a fierce oath, Luke grabbed Wardell by the front of his shirt and twisted. "Tell me what you know. Tell me now."

"Not without the promise of a deal." Wardell lifted both hands and shoved him backward with all his strength.

In that instant, seizing their only opportunity for a clear shot, a deafening volley of gunshots rang through the air.

Wardell, pistol in hand, fell to the floor.

Through a blinding mist of fury, Luke looked around at the line of sharpshooters, including the sheriff and his deputy. "Why the hell did you shoot? He wanted to tell me something. Something important."

"He was threatening you with a gun, Luke." The sheriff holstered his weapon and started toward Luke.

Luke's arms shot out like a prizefighter, holding him at bay. "You heard him, Eugene. He said he knew something about the night my parents died."

"He was playing for time, Luke. That's what men do when they run out of options."

Luke was shaking his head, unable to hear anything except the loud buzzing in his brain. He'd been so close. So close . . .

He turned to his brothers. "You heard him. He knew something."

Matt and Reed caught him as he began to fall to the floor.

He knew he was losing consciousness, but he managed to say, "Get help for Mick and Nadine. They've been hurt badly. And see if Wardell is alive. We need to know what secret he's been keeping."

"We'll see to it." Colin directed a medic toward the old cowboy, who remained, silent and still, in a pool of blood in the hay.

The sheriff turned to his deputy. "You've known Wardell since your teens. What do you make of this?"

Archer Stone shrugged. "You can know a man for a lifetime and not really know what goes on in his head."

Grace hurried over to Lily and Ingrid, cutting their bonds, before trying to lead them outside to safety.

"No." Ingrid pushed away and hurried to kneel beside her mother. Finding a pulse, she shouted and Lily raced over, followed by Frank, Grace, Nelson, and Yancy.

"Hold on, Nadine." Ingrid caught her hand. "The police are here. They'll take you to the clinic."

"Not...going to make it." Nadine's eyes opened, and she stared at her two daughters. "Hurts too bad."

"Don't say that. You're going to live, Nadine." Lily was crying.

"Don't call me..." She paused and looked up at Nelson before trying again, marshalling all her energy to say what she needed to say. "A very smart man once said Mother was the most beautiful name in the world. Would you...would you mind calling me Mama just once?"

The two sisters looked at each other in amazement.

Lily started to speak. "But you said—"

Ingrid closed a hand over her little sister's to stop her. "All right. If that's what you want, Mama."

Nadine managed a weak smile as she turned to Lily. "Now you. Please."

"Mama." Lily's lips trembled. "I...love you, Mama."

"Oh, my sweet girls. I never thought I'd hear that. Look how many years I've wasted. I'm so sorry. Can you forgive me?"

"There's nothing to forgive." Ingrid touched a hand to Nadine's cheek. "You're home now, Mama."

A medic walked over and began to check her vital signs. She pushed his hand away. "Don't waste your time, sugar."

She reached out, grabbing hold of her daughters' hands, twining her fingers with theirs. "If I could do things over..." Ever so slowly her fingers relaxed their grip and her hands went slack.

The burly medic touched a finger to her neck before glancing at the two grieving sisters. "I'm sorry. She's gone."

Ingrid and Lily were joined in their grief by the others who gathered around, forming a circle of love as they continued holding their mother's hands.

Ingrid left Lily kneeling beside their mother, with Grace watching over her, while she went in search of Luke, who had already been placed on a gurney. One medic was inserting an intravenous tube while the other covered him with a blanket and prepared to take him to a helicopter.

Seeing him, so still and bloody, had tears springing to her eyes. She caught Luke's hand. "Please don't die, Luke."

His eyes opened. He gave her one of those dangerous smiles. "Didn't you know? Only the good die young."

"Oh, Luke." Sobbing, she buried her face in his neck.

"Hey now." He wrapped his good arm around her. "Are all those tears for me?"

"Some." She swallowed. "The rest...Nadine...my mother is dead."

"Oh, baby." He brushed a hand over her hair, seeking to offer comfort. "She was the one who saved us. You know that, don't you?"

"No. It was you. You were so brave. So..."

She sniffled against his neck before straightening as the medics made ready to lift his gurney.

"Wait." He motioned them to move back a pace.

"You need to get to the clinic," a medic called Luke.

Ingrid started to step back, but Luke caught her hand and held her fast.

"If your mother hadn't come rushing in like a crazed grizzly protecting its cubs, we'd all still be hostage to that madman. Whether she planned it or not, whether accidental or deliberate, she turned out to be a true hero. I want you and Lily to hold on to that thought."

Fresh tears started falling, and Ingrid didn't bother to stop them. "Thank you for that, Luke. And for...everything."

He gave her another smile before calling to the medics, "Okay. Let's get me out of here." He squeezed her hand. "I'll see you at Glacier Ridge. Last one there has to scrub my back."

Despite her tears, she found herself smiling as the medics carried his gurney to a waiting helicopter and loaded it aboard.

In a whirl of sand and gravel, the copter lifted off and disappeared across the sky.

CHAPTER TWENTY-NINE

The state police crime unit was methodical as its members swarmed over the barn and ranch, bagging evidence, photographing anything that could be useful for their files.

After giving video statements, the family was allowed to leave.

A convoy of ranch trucks and police vehicles left the chaotic scene at the Larsen ranch behind as it snaked along the highway and through the town of Glacier Ridge.

Grace and Nessa opted to ride with Ingrid and Lily, patiently encouraging them to open up about all that had happened and offering comfort as the reality of their situation began to sink in, and their grief bubbled to the surface.

"Is Nadine...Mama really dead?" Lily kept asking.

"Yes, honey." Ingrid had her arm around her little sister's shoulders, feeling the tremors that rocked her body.

"Is Luke going to die, too?"

Grace closed her eyes against the pain.

Seeing it, Nessa was quick to reassure all of them. "Luke said himself that he's too tough to die."

"Nadine...Mama was tough."

"Yes, she was." Ingrid gathered her closer.

"But she died."

The words were muffled against Ingrid's chest, and she was forced to absorb a sudden jolt at the realization of all that had happened. Even now, she couldn't quite take it all in.

"Here we are." Nessa was relieved when their truck pulled up to the emergency entrance of the Glacier Ridge Clinic.

The women climbed from their vehicle and walked into another scene of complete chaos.

The Malloy men were already there, milling about the waiting room, asking endless questions of Agnes, the assistant to the Cross doctors, and demanding admittance to the examining room.

"Gracie Girl." Frank Malloy hurried over to hug his wife. "She won't tell us a thing about Luke's condition, or Mick's."

A pretty, dark-haired young woman in a white lab coat said, "Because, until now, she didn't know."

"Dr. Cross."

As she stepped into the outer room, the entire mob of people gathered around her, shouting questions.

"How is Luke? Is he alert?"

"Does he require surgery?"

"What about Mick? Will he recover from that blow to the head?"

She held up a hand and gave a quick shake of the head,

sending dark curls dancing around her face. "Luke is being prepared for surgery to remove the bullets. Mick is now awake and alert, but we'll keep him overnight for observation. I would suggest that, since you've all been through a terrible ordeal, you return to your homes and you can have a visit with the patients later."

When nobody moved, she glanced over their heads until she spotted Colin on the perimeter of the crowd.

He was staring at her in that quiet, thoughtful way she'd come to know. Of the entire Malloy family, he was the only one who was quiet and reserved. Traits she found admirable, especially at a crazy time like this.

Seeing the question in her eyes, he shook his head, causing her lips to curve in the merest hint of a smile. "Or, if you insist on staying, I suppose you could take yourselves off to D & B's Diner or Clay's Pig Sty. By the time you've eaten, both Luke and Mick should be ready to receive visitors."

Instead of doing as she'd suggested, they seemed to dig in. Now silent, arms crossed over their chests, faces stern or thoughtful or determined, they stared past her toward the doors leading to the patient rooms.

"Or…" Resigned, she sighed. "Maybe I could have Agnes show you to the surgery waiting room, where I can meet with you postsurgery and fill you in on how Luke's operation went."

They moved like a giant swarm toward the doors, and Agnes, the clinic's receptionist, wisely pushed the button to admit them, then led them down the hall and into a comfortable room equipped with TV, Internet connection, and several vending machines, as well as freshly brewed coffee. But one Malloy stayed behind.

"Doctor. Anita."

Anita paused at the sound of Colin's voice. "Yes?"

He managed a smile. "Thanks for your kindness."

She gave a small laugh. "It wasn't kindness. It was wisdom. I'm not prepared to go to war with a family as intimidating as yours, so I decided to make an executive decision that would please everybody and free me to get on with my surgery."

He arched a brow. "You'll be doing the surgery?"

"Does that worry you?"

He shook his head. "I'm glad." Then he flushed. "I mean, I trust your uncle. Old Dr. Cross has been our doctor for a lifetime." Colin touched a hand to her shoulder. "But I'm glad you're taking care of Luke."

She smiled before stepping back. "I'll make a complete report to you and your family as soon as the surgery is over."

While Colin watched, she stepped through the open doors and disappeared along a corridor leading to the sterile inner sanctum of the small-town clinic.

Luke lay in bed, pleasantly sedated, as an IV tube dripped fluids into him and a machine monitored his vitals.

He looked around at the sea of faces staring at him. The Great One in an armchair, with Yancy standing beside him. His grandparents, holding hands. Matt standing directly behind Nessa, his arms around her waist. Reed and Colin and Burke at the foot of the bed, looking somber.

Closest to the bed were Ingrid and Lily. Both of them had stitches at their temples, covered with gauze. Both were gripping his hand, and it seemed to him that their breathing was in sync with his. Each time he breathed in, so did they. Each time he exhaled, they did the same. He struggled for a way to put them at ease.

"Does it hurt?" Lily seemed very worried about his level of pain.

"Not right now, Li'l Bit. They've got me on too much happy juice to feel a thing."

"What's happy juice?"

"Some kind of painkiller," Ingrid whispered.

"Oh."

The Great One glanced around at the others. "Dr. Cross said the bullet in your leg went clear through."

Luke smiled. "I guess that's a good thing."

"I'd say so. And she said the bullet didn't tear through anything vital, like bone or ligaments, so the healing should go smoothly."

"So I'll be able to dance?"

Ingrid seemed surprised by his question. "I don't see why not."

He shot her one of those wicked grins. "That's great. 'Cause I couldn't dance before this."

The others laughed. Ingrid continued clutching his hand like a lifeline, until he could no longer feel his fingers.

He glanced around until he caught his grandmother's eye. "I'm feeling a little sleepy. Must be all this happy juice. Would you mind if I just close my eyes for a while?"

Taking the hint, Grace began herding the others from the room. "We'll all go back to the ranch, now we know you're in good hands. But we'll be back first thing in the morning." She turned to Ingrid. "I'd feel better if you and

Lily would stay at our place. At least until Mick is strong enough to go home. You shouldn't be alone right now."

Very gently she eased the little girl away from Luke's side, took her hand, and led her toward the door.

Before Ingrid could respond, Luke said, "As long as Lily's in good hands, maybe you could stay in town for a while. I think I could persuade Dr. Anita to get you a tray. Maybe even a bed."

She was shaking her head. "I couldn't—"

Burke stepped up beside her. "I was thinking I'd hang out in town. Maybe grab a beer and a sandwich at the Pig Sty before heading back. If you'd like a visit, I could drive you back later."

Luke shot him a look of gratitude.

Ingrid nodded. "I guess...as long as you're staying, and I'm not making extra work for anybody..." She turned to Luke. "You're sure I won't be in the way? You have to be exhausted."

"I'll sleep better knowing you're here."

She turned to Burke. "All right. It looks like I'll be coming back with you later." She hurried to the door to kiss her little sister. "Will you be okay with Gram Gracie?"

Lily nodded and tightened her grip on Grace's hand.

As the room emptied out, Ingrid returned to Luke's bedside and took his hand in hers. "Are you sure you're feeling up to this?"

In answer, he drew her down for a slow, leisurely kiss. "That's all I needed." He kissed her again, lingering over her lips until her smile returned. "Now I know I'm going to be fine."

* * *

The lights in Luke's room had been dimmed. Agnes had wheeled a recliner into the room and positioned it beside Luke's bed so that Ingrid could lie beside him without disturbing the tubes and wires leading to the monitor.

Both of them had been covered with warming blankets, to fight any lingering shock to their systems.

Snug, warm, content, they lay holding hands.

Luke turned his head to study Ingrid's face. "Feel like talking about Nadine?"

"No. It's all too fresh."

"Yeah. I get it. But whenever you feel like talking, I'll be here to listen."

"Thanks. Luke?"

"Hmm?"

"Did we really live through this?"

"I guess we did. Although"—he chuckled—"the way I'm feeling right now, maybe I've died and gone to heaven." He pretended to pinch himself. "Let's see. There's not a sound in this place, except for that annoying monitor. No drunken gunman. No blood. And I'm lying beside the most beautiful woman in the world, who could very well be my angel." He lifted her hand to his lips and pressed a kiss to her palm before closing her fingers around it. "Let's sleep on it, and figure things out in the morning."

Long after he'd fallen asleep, Ingrid lay with her hand in his, watching the steady rise and fall of his chest and thinking it was the most glorious thing she'd ever seen.

If they weren't in heaven, this was the closest thing to it. Lily was safe and secure in the loving circle of the Malloy family.

Mick was awake and alert, and Dr. Anita had assured

her that he could be discharged in the morning, as long as he agreed to return in a week for another X-ray.

Nadine…Mama…had been the catalyst to saving all of them.

How could Nadine have been attracted to a monster like Lon Wardell?

Attracted?

A poor choice of words. Nadine hadn't been so much attracted as addicted. She hadn't been able to stay away from his type. Hard-drinking. Hard-living. A loser.

But she'd redeemed herself by one unselfish act of love.

Love.

An image of Luke, charming, laughing, ducking her head beneath the water of the creek as they swam naked together, played through her mind, easing her pain, soothing her spirit. That man had a way of making her forget every hardship she'd ever endured. He was fun, funny, irreverent, fearless.

And here she was, after surviving impossible terror, calmly lying beside the man she loved.

The man she loved.

Were there any sweeter words in the world?

At last, exhausted beyond belief, she gave in to the need to sleep.

Hours later, when Burke stopped by to see if Ingrid was ready to leave for the ranch, he found Ingrid and Luke sound asleep, each wearing matching smiles.

With a nod of approval, he silently let himself out.

CHAPTER THIRTY

A convoy of ranch trucks moved slowly along the ridge of the meadow, abloom with wildflowers.

When they came to the small gravesite, the Malloy family stepped out. Wearing somber black pants and string ties, the men lifted a simple pine box from the back of Ingrid's battered truck.

Sheriff Graystoke was there, offering an apology that his deputy wouldn't make it, since one of them had to handle the duties back in town.

Bull Hammond rode up on the back of his dappled mare, his face dripping with sweat, his cheeks red from the sun. He dismounted and yanked off his hat before mopping his face with a handkerchief.

The Reverend Townsend from Glacier Ridge Church stood beside the open grave, flanked by Mick, Ingrid, and Lily.

The men removed their best Sunday hats and bowed

their heads as the minister spoke the words over the casket.

"We will be judged, not only by the way we choose to live, but by how well we love. No greater love is there than this: that a man would lay down his life for another. This day we send our sister Nadine to her eternal rest. May she sleep in the knowledge that her generous action resulted in the safe return from certain death of those she loved."

As Mick and Burke lowered the casket into the ground, Ingrid picked up a handful of dirt and scattered it on the lid. Lily, clutching a handful of wildflowers she'd picked, dropped them and watched as they fluttered down to cover the top of the box.

The others stood back respectfully while sand was shoveled and the grave was mounded with fresh earth. Then, with a word to the minister, and hugs to Ingrid and Lily, they walked to their trucks, giving the two sisters a chance to say their private good-byes.

When they finally turned away from the grave, Luke caught their hands and walked between them to Ingrid's truck. He helped them settle inside before taking the wheel.

"That was a nice service."

Ingrid nodded. "I'm grateful that Rev. Townsend would come all this way. He suggested a funeral in town, but I knew that wasn't something Nadine...Mama would have wanted. Besides, the only ones who will grieve her loss are right here."

Luke squeezed her hand. "Yancy's preparing a lunch."

She looked over. "We're driving to your ranch?"

He shook his head. "Yancy and the Great One are at your place."

"Poor Yancy. I bet he can't find any of the utensils he needs."

"Don't worry about Yancy. That man travels with half the kitchen in the back of his truck."

As they pulled up to the house, the others were standing around the back porch, sipping longnecks.

Reed handed a bottle to Luke and another to Ingrid, while Grace walked up to Lily with a frosty glass of lemonade.

It was the Great One who lifted his martini in a toast. "Here's to Nadine, who learned the wisdom of motherhood and the power of true love."

Ingrid shot him a grateful smile before lifting her glass to say softly, "To Mama."

To save space, Yancy had set the food out in buffet style. Along the kitchen counter were platters holding thick slabs of roast beef, as well as mounds of whipped potatoes, hot rolls, and a salad of garden lettuce, tomatoes, cucumbers, and peppers, all dressed with Yancy's famous vinaigrette. For dessert there were slices of carrot cake with dollops of freshly whipped cream.

The Malloy family and the few guests took over the entire house. While some snagged chairs at the kitchen table, others ambled into the parlor to sit at the game table or even on the lumpy sofa, while the rest stepped outside to eat in the shade of the back porch, where Yancy had covered an old log picnic table with a cheery red-and-white-checked cloth.

Spotting Ingrid and Luke standing off to one side of the porch, Bull Hammond walked over.

"I hope I'm not intruding."

Ingrid smiled and shook her head. "I'm glad you came, Bull. I'm sorry for the things I'd been thinking when all this trouble was happening."

"Please don't apologize. I'm not proud of the way I behaved. I guess, after years of feuding with your father, I forgot how to be a neighbor."

Ingrid seized on a single word. "What was the feud about?"

Bull flushed. "It's hard to remember now. I guess it started over some cattle that wandered into my hayfield. And then it escalated over the years, until every little slight became a giant insult." He fidgeted and cleared his throat. "I'm really sorry about you losing both your ma and pa. Ranching's hard enough with the proper help, but it's almost impossible on your own. I admire what you've managed to do, and I want you to know that my offer to buy your land still stands. I've always wanted to enlarge my holdings, and this place would be perfect. I could rent out your house to a tenant farmer and get not only an income from him, but also have extra help during calving season and roundup." He paused before adding, "But I'll understand if you want to hold on to it. Whatever you decide to do, I want you to know I'll respect it."

"Thank you, Bull." She offered a handshake. "I need some time. Whenever I make a decision, I'll let you know."

"That's fair enough." He shook hands with Luke and made his way to where he'd tied his horse.

When Rev. Townsend took his leave, followed by the sheriff, Grace and Frank walked up, hand in hand with Lily.

"We're hoping you and Lily will spend the night."

Ingrid smiled at her little sister, who looked so comfortable with these two people. "What would you like to do, honey?"

"I'd like to go with Gram Gracie and Grandpop Frank. Yancy said he's going to teach me to make peanut butter drops tonight."

Luke put a hand over his heart. "I haven't had Yancy's peanut butter drops in months now. Wait until you taste them, Li'l Bit. They're the best."

"Better than his chocolate chips?"

Luke leaned close. "Don't tell the Great One. You know how he craves his chocolate chip cookies. But I swear Yancy's peanut butter drops are the best in the world."

The little girl's eyes went wide. "You hear that, Ingrid? Can I please go?"

"Of course."

"And you, Ingrid?" Grace put a hand on her arm. "I'm hoping you and Mick will agree to stay the night, too." She glanced toward the barn. "I don't like thinking of you staying here yet. It's all too soon. Too fresh."

Mick ambled over. "I've already told Burke I'd be happy to go, but only if you're going, too, girl. You can't be alone here tonight."

As she was shaking her head, Luke interrupted. "I think this is the perfect time to invite you to go riding with me. And when we're done, I'll take you back to my place, or if you want to be here, I'll stay." He shot a grin at his grandparents. "Just so she's not alone, you understand."

"You're being too noble, sonny boy." Frank chuckled. "And not at all subtle." He turned to Ingrid. "It's your call, honey."

She thought a moment before saying, "Why don't we

go for that ride, and then I'll decide whether to come back here or go to your place."

"Fair enough." Luke winked at Lily like a conspirator, and she winked back before he followed Ingrid into the house to lend a hand with the cleanup.

When everything was in order, and the long line of ranch trucks had rolled away, Luke took the dish towel from her hand.

"You've done enough for today. Time to go riding."

They walked out the door. When Ingrid started toward the barn, Luke stopped her with a hand on her arm. "You ready to walk on the wild side?"

He pointed to his Harley, parked near the back porch. When she nodded, he handed her a helmet before putting on his own and climbing aboard.

Ingrid climbed on the back and wrapped her arms around his waist. He revved the engine, and they took off across a sloping, flower-strewn meadow, up the side of a hill, and down into a valley lush with grass.

As they rode, Luke kept turning his head to make silly comments, until Ingrid was laughing so hard, she had tears in her eyes.

Happy tears, she thought. On such a day, it seemed impossible that she could be filled with so much joy.

"Playtime," he called, and Ingrid was yanked from her reverie at the banks of the creek.

"Today? Luke, are you serious?"

"Woman, today is the perfect one for skinny-dipping." He pointed to the sky. "Look at that broiling sun. Look at that blue sky, without a cloud around. The day begs for a dip in cool water."

And they did. Laughing and pouncing on one another,

swallowing half the creek with their antics. Chasing and catching, hugging, and loving on the banks of the stream, feeling like the only two people in the world.

Her heart as light as air, Ingrid lay in the cool grass, pressing soft, moist kisses to Luke's throat. "I could stay here like this all night."

"Mmm. Me too. Except it gets really cold when the sun goes down in these hills. We might want to get dressed and chase the sunlight."

"If you say so." She slipped into her clothes and climbed on the back of his motorcycle.

As they sailed across rolling hills, she leaned close. "Where are you taking me?"

"To my secret hideaway."

They came up over a ridge, and he pulled over to enjoy the view. Below them lay a series of gently sloping meadows that seemed to fold one over the other for as far as the eye could see.

"Where are we?"

"This is Malloy land. One of my favorite places. It's where I come when I want to get away from the whole world and refresh my soul. It's my sacred retreat."

She was looking at Luke with a dazed expression. With a smile, she touched a hand to his forehead. "Who are you, and what have you done with that irreverent, silly guy named Luke Malloy?"

He laughed with her. "I know. I don't get serious about too many things. But this is my own private heaven. Someday I plan on building my home here." He took her hand. "What do you think of it?"

"It's breathtaking. I can see why you love it."

"Can you?"

She nodded.

"Don't be polite. I'm being serious. Do you really love it?"

"I do. It's amazing."

He sighed. "Good. I want you to share it."

She looked slightly dazed. "What do you mean?"

"I want you to share all this with me. I love you, Ingrid. I want you to share my life with me."

Because she didn't speak, he felt the need to say more. "I don't want to scare you off, dumping this on you so soon. I know you've just been through a really traumatic event. The attack. Losing your mother."

"Luke..."

He shook his head. "Just so you know, you can sell your ranch or keep it. You can live here with me, or I'll put it all on hold until a time when you're ready. Whatever choice you make, I'll respect it, as long as you're willing to let me be part of your life." His tone lowered. "I realized, when I thought I might lose you, just how important you and Lily had become. I can't imagine life without you. Either of you."

Tears sprang to her eyes, and he was quick to lift his thumbs to wipe them before framing her face and staring down at her. "Sorry. It's too soon. I should have—"

She put a hand over his. "Don't say another word. Just kiss me so I'll know I'm not dreaming."

"You're definitely not—"

She stood on tiptoe to press her mouth to his. And as the kiss spun on and on, she wrapped her arms around his neck and whispered, "Yes. Yes. Oh, yes."

He let out a long sigh before kissing her with a fervor that had both their heads spinning.

Against her mouth he whispered, "You've just made me the happiest man in the world."

The ringing of his cell phone shattered the moment. He pulled it from his pocket and muttered, "This is a fine time for the service to work. It almost never works up here."

He looked at the caller ID and handed the phone to her.

She heard Lily's voice happily chirping, "Well? Did he ask you? Did you say yes? Is Luke going to be my big brother?"

At the startled question in Ingrid's eyes, Luke gave her one of his most charming grins. "Sorry, baby. I had to share it with her. After all, she's going to be part of this, too."

"Oh, Luke. I ought to be really annoyed with you for letting her in on a secret you were keeping from me, but including Lily is just so sweet." She handed him the phone. "She's waiting for my answer."

With his eyes steady on Ingrid's, he spoke into the phone. "Li'l Bit, she said yes. Yes. Yes."

To the sound of the entire family cheering in the background, he gathered Ingrid into his arms and kissed her again, while letting his cell phone drop to the grass.

And then there were no words as they came together in a dance of love as old as time.

EPILOGUE

The sticky heat of late summer had given way to fresh autumn breezes. Soon it would be time to bring the cattle down from their lush highland meadows to winter in the more protected fields of home.

Luke had finished mucking stalls before loading his Harley into the back of one of the trucks. With his chores completed, he headed into the house to shower and change.

He was tucking his shirt into his waistband when a knock sounded on his bedroom door.

Reed's voice called, "The Great One's getting restless. It's time to pay a visit to the gravesite before heading over to the Larsen ranch. You've got five minutes, and then Matt and I have orders to carry you if necessary."

Laughing, Luke opened the door. "I can still walk."

"Your bride will be glad to hear that. Now get a move on."

The two brothers descended the stairs and slammed out the back door.

They made their way up the sloping meadow, where Nelson, Frank, and Matt had already gathered. Luke looked around. "Where are Gram Gracie and Nessa?"

"The women left for Ingrid's hours ago."

Luke shook his head. "Women and weddings."

Matt grinned. "Yeah. Tell me about it."

Frank passed around tumblers of Irish whiskey and the four generations lifted them as he offered the first toast. "To Patrick and Bernie, who left us far too soon. But this day, I have no doubt they're watching with great joy."

They solemnly drank.

Nelson cleared his throat before saying, "To my beautiful Madeline, who is smiling down on us this day and loving every minute of it."

They drank again.

Reed lifted his glass. "I should be toasting myself, since I'm the only one here who's managed to avoid the marriage trap. But since it's Luke's day…" He turned to his brother. "To you, bro, for at least having enough sense to fall for a gorgeous woman who's your equal in all things." Shaking his head, he added, "Though what she sees in you is beyond comprehension."

Luke good-naturedly tousled Reed's hair before they drank.

"And finally," Matt said, "here's to us. Family always. And always room for one more."

They drank, then tipped their hats at the graves before heading down the hill to climb into their trucks for the drive to Ingrid's ranch.

* * *

A long table had been set up on the back porch of Ingrid's house. It was covered with a white linen cloth and lined with a dozen chairs, each tied with a giant white bow.

Yancy and Mick were busy putting the finishing touches on the wedding lunch, which consisted of prime rib of beef and twice-baked potatoes, along with a salad, fresh corn from the garden, and a wedding cake baked by hand and decorated with fluffy white frosting. In the place of honor in the center of the cake were two figures. Instead of the traditional bride and groom, these two sported simple Western attire and helmets, while seated on a motorcycle.

Mick studied the figures. "You've managed to capture them perfectly, Yancy."

The cook gave a nod of appreciation. "Thanks, Mick. I'm pretty proud of this creation."

"You should be. Luke and Ingrid are going to love it." The old man turned away. "Time to get myself ready to give away the bride. I'll be back in a few minutes."

As Mick disappeared into his room, Yancy strolled out the back door to check on last-minute items.

Mick looked up from the stool where he was polishing his boots. As Ingrid stepped into the kitchen, all he could do was stare. She was dressed in a white sundress that fell to her ankles in a swirl of cotton and lace. Cap sleeves fluttered at her shoulders. On her feet were simple strappy sandals.

"Well, don't you look…" He struggled to find the words.

"I know it's not the usual. Luke and I agreed to keep it casual."

"Girl, that may not be a wedding gown, but you look every inch the beautiful bride."

He glanced at her freshly cut hair, which fell in fine wisps around her cheeks. "Guess I figured now that the big day was here, you'd let your hair grow."

"It's easier like this. Besides, Luke loves my hair short."

His eyes crinkled with humor. "Girl, that man would love you with no hair at all."

She was surprised by the sudden urge to weep. Instead, she wrapped her arms around Mick's neck. "Isn't it wonderful that someone like Luke could love me so much?"

He patted her hand. "Luke's a smart man. He knows a good woman when he sees her, thank the Lord. He wasn't about to let you get away."

Ingrid sniffed, deeply affected by his words, and turned away.

He watched her as she walked to the window to peer at the parade of Malloy vehicles pulling up to the back porch. "Is Lily ready?"

Ingrid gave a dreamy smile. "I think she's been ready since dawn. Wait 'til you see her. She went to town yesterday with Gram Grace, who went all out on my little bridesmaid."

"Think she'll outshine the bride?"

Ingrid laughed. "I hope so. She's so excited about her first-ever wedding."

They both turned to the doorway when the object of their discussion stepped through.

"Well?" Lily twirled, showing off the pale pink dress with a full skirt gathered here and there with darker pink bows. On her feet she wore glittering pink ballerina slippers that sparkled in the sunlight. Her usual tangle of waist-length hair had been tamed into shiny dark waves that spilled down her back and were tied off her face with pink ribbons.

Behind her stood Grace and Nessa, who had spent the better part of an hour fussing over the little girl's hair and dress.

"You do good work," Ingrid called.

"Do you like it? I know you said I could wear denim, but Gram Gracie and I found this, and..." Lily twirled in front of her sister.

"I love everything. The dress, the shoes, and oh my, your hair."

Lily dimpled. "And you look prettier than ever."

"Thank you." The two sisters hugged.

Hearing voices outside, Lily danced toward the door before turning with a look of pure bliss. "Luke's here."

In an aside, Grace said to Ingrid and Nessa, "You'd think she was the one getting married."

They laughed before Ingrid said, "In a way she is. Luke's been so sweet about including her in all the plans. And she's so excited about gaining this big family."

"Not nearly as excited as we are." Grace pressed a kiss to Ingrid's cheek. "Now I have two more females to counter all that testosterone."

Lily's excited voice called from outside, "Hurry, Ingrid. Rev. Townsend is here."

Arm in arm, Grace and Nessa started toward the back door. Grace blew Ingrid a kiss. "That's our cue to leave you and Mick alone in here."

As they walked outside to join the rest of the family,

Mick turned to Ingrid and offered his arm. "Come on, girl. Time to get you hitched."

"Oh, Mick." As Ingrid tucked her arm through his, she leaned over to press a kiss to his leathery cheek. "I'm so glad you're going to be staying at the Malloy Ranch while Luke and I are gone. I feel better knowing you're there if Lily should feel homesick."

"Girl, in case you haven't noticed, Lily's already adopted all of them as family." He patted her hand. "She'll be fine. I'll be fine. As for you, I don't have a worry in the world. You're one strong woman. And you're about to marry the only man I know who's your equal."

As they walked into the sunlight, Lily picked up two nosegays and handed one to Ingrid.

"What's this?"

"Luke brought them."

Ingrid looked up to see him standing at the top of the hill, dressed in a white shirt and string tie, his freshly cut hair slightly mussed, his smile causing her heart to start those funny little flips.

"Now remember," Lily said, enjoying her role immensely. "I go in front of you. Just follow me, okay?"

Ingrid couldn't stop the smile that curved her lips. "Okay."

They walked slowly up the hill until they came to the spot where the minister stood in front of their mother's grave, where a pretty stone marker had been added.

Flanking the minister was the entire Malloy family.

As she'd been instructed, Lily took the flowers from her sister's hand and crossed over to stand next to the others. Mick kissed Ingrid's cheek and then placed her hand on Luke's arm before stepping aside.

Instead of turning toward the minister, Luke closed a hand over hers and stared down into her eyes. "The words we're about to say will make it legal. But I want you to know I've been yours since I woke up on that lumpy sofa and got my first look at you. If ever a woman grabbed my heart and owned it, it's you, babe."

Ingrid blinked back the tears that had welled up out of nowhere to embarrass her yet again. "I love you so much, Luke Malloy, it scares me."

He draped one strong arm around her shoulders and gave her that famous smile. "After what we've been through, nothing should ever scare you again, woman. Now let's do this together."

Together.

The very word had her lifting her head and turning with him to face the minister.

As Rev. Townsend led them through their vows, Ingrid and Luke couldn't stop smiling and staring into each other's eyes.

Afterward, as they accepted congratulations from the family and hugged and kissed each one, they floated on a cloud toward the house and the lovely lunch prepared by Mick and Yancy.

They were sipping champagne, after yet another toast, when Lily approached with a tissue-wrapped package.

"Want to open my gift?"

As Luke and Ingrid began tearing off the wrapping, Lily said, "It was going to be your birthday present. And now, since you got married on your birthday, I wanted it to be for both of you."

They studied the framed photograph of a herd of mustangs grazing in a mountain meadow. Several mares had their foals beside them. The stallion stood watch on a rocky promontory, like a king surveying his kingdom. The entire scene was perfectly captured.

"Now that's just about as professional as it gets, Li'l Bit."

At Luke's words of praise, the little girl beamed. "Gram Gracie showed me how to"—she hesitated, then repeated the lesson she'd learned from Grace—"frame a shot so that all the elements are in proportion."

"Spoken like an apt pupil." Luke dropped a kiss to her cheek.

Ingrid gathered her close and kissed the top of her head. "I love this. And when Luke and I build our house, this will have the place of honor. And someday, I'll brag to everyone about my little sister who became a world-famous photographer."

Lily was fairly bursting with pride. "Is it all right if I go on a safari with Gram Gracie and Grandpa Frank while you and Luke are away?"

Ingrid glanced at Grace before saying, "Honey, we'll only be gone for a few days. But I think a photographic safari would be just the thing."

With her fist pumping the air, Lily hurried inside. A short time later she emerged, wearing jeans and a T-shirt and carrying her backpack.

Luke shook his head before leaning toward Ingrid. "And you were worried she might miss you. You think she's just a tad impatient to get started?"

Ingrid gave him a blinding smile. "She's not the only one."

Inside, Yancy and Mick finished up the last of the cleanup before loading the serving dishes into boxes they stored in the back of a truck.

With hugs all around, the family began the drive back to the Malloy Ranch.

When they were alone, Luke and Ingrid stood awhile, sipping the last of the champagne and watching the sun dip below the hills.

Luke framed her face with his hands for a long, leisurely kiss. "Ready to change and start on our fancy honeymoon?"

With a laugh, she led him inside. A short time later, dressed in faded denims and T-shirts, they climbed aboard his motorcycle and headed toward the hills.

"First stop, the stream," he called over his shoulder. With a roar of engines, he shouted, "And I promise, no matter who reaches the water first, I'll scrub your back."

"And after that?"

"Probably wild sex."

"Promise?"

"You bet. And then we're going to wander like tumbleweeds. Stop whenever we want. Make love as late as we please. Babe, as long as we're together, it doesn't matter where life takes us."

Ingrid wrapped her arms around his waist and pressed her face to his shoulder. As the wind took her hair, Nadine's face appeared in her mind, and her tears mingled with her laughter.

Oh, Mama, she thought. *We all had such a rough road. But I'm leaving the past behind and starting the first day of the rest of my life.*

As they soared and dipped, her laughter grew. Who

would have ever believed that a bearded stranger, who'd looked more like a shaggy beast than a rancher, would turn into her Prince Charming?

With this wild, unpredictable rogue in her life, she was absolutely certain she would never again be sad or afraid or lonely. For with Luke Malloy, all of life would surely be the adventure of a lifetime.

ABOUT THE AUTHOR

New York Times bestselling author R.C. Ryan has written more than a hundred novels, both contemporary and historical. Quite an accomplishment for someone who, after her fifth child started school, gave herself the gift of an hour a day to follow her dream to become a writer.

In a career spanning more than thirty years, Ms. Ryan has given dozens of radio, television, and print interviews across the country and Canada, and has been quoted in such diverse publications as the *Wall Street Journal* and *Cosmopolitan*. She has also appeared on CNN and ABC-TV's *Good Morning America*.

You can learn more about R.C. Ryan—and her alter ego Ruth Ryan Langan—at:

RyanLangan.com
Twitter @RuthRyanLangan
Facebook.com/RuthRyanLangan